DIE VOLUME 4:
BLEED

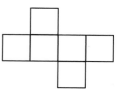

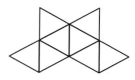

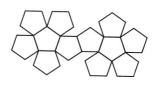

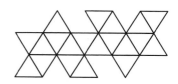

DIE VOLUME 4:
BLEED

KIERON GILLEN
Writer

STEPHANIE HANS
Artist

CLAYTON COWLES
Letterer

RIAN HUGHES
Designer

CHRISSY WILLIAMS
Editor

IMAGE COMICS, INC.
Todd McFarlane: President • **Jim Valentino**: Vice President
Marc Silvestri: Chief Executive Officer • **Erik Larsen**: Chief
Financial Officer • **Robert Kirkman**: Chief Operating Officer
Eric Stephenson: Publisher/Chief Creative Officer • **Nicole
Lapalme**: Controller • **Leanna Caunter**: Accounting Analyst
Sue Korpela: Accounting & HR Manager • **Maria Eizik**: Talent
Liaison • **Jeff Boison**: Director of Sales & Publishing Planning
Dirk Wood: Director of International Sales & Licensing
Alex Cox: Director of Direct Market Sales • **Chloe Ramos**:
Book Market & Library Sales Manager • **Emilio Bautista**:
Digital Sales Coordinator • **Jon Schlaffman**: Specialty Sales
Coordinator • **Kat Salazar**: Director of PR & Marketing • **Drew
Fitzgerald**: Marketing Content Associate • **Heather Doornink**:
Production Director • **Drew Gill**: Art Director • **Hilary
DiLoreto**: Print Manager • **Tricia Ramos**: Traffic Manager
Melissa Gifford: Content Manager • **Erika Schnatz**: Senior
Production Artist • **Ryan Brewer**: Production Artist
Deanna Phelps: Production Artist • **IMAGECOMICS.COM**

ISBN: 978-1-5343-1926-4

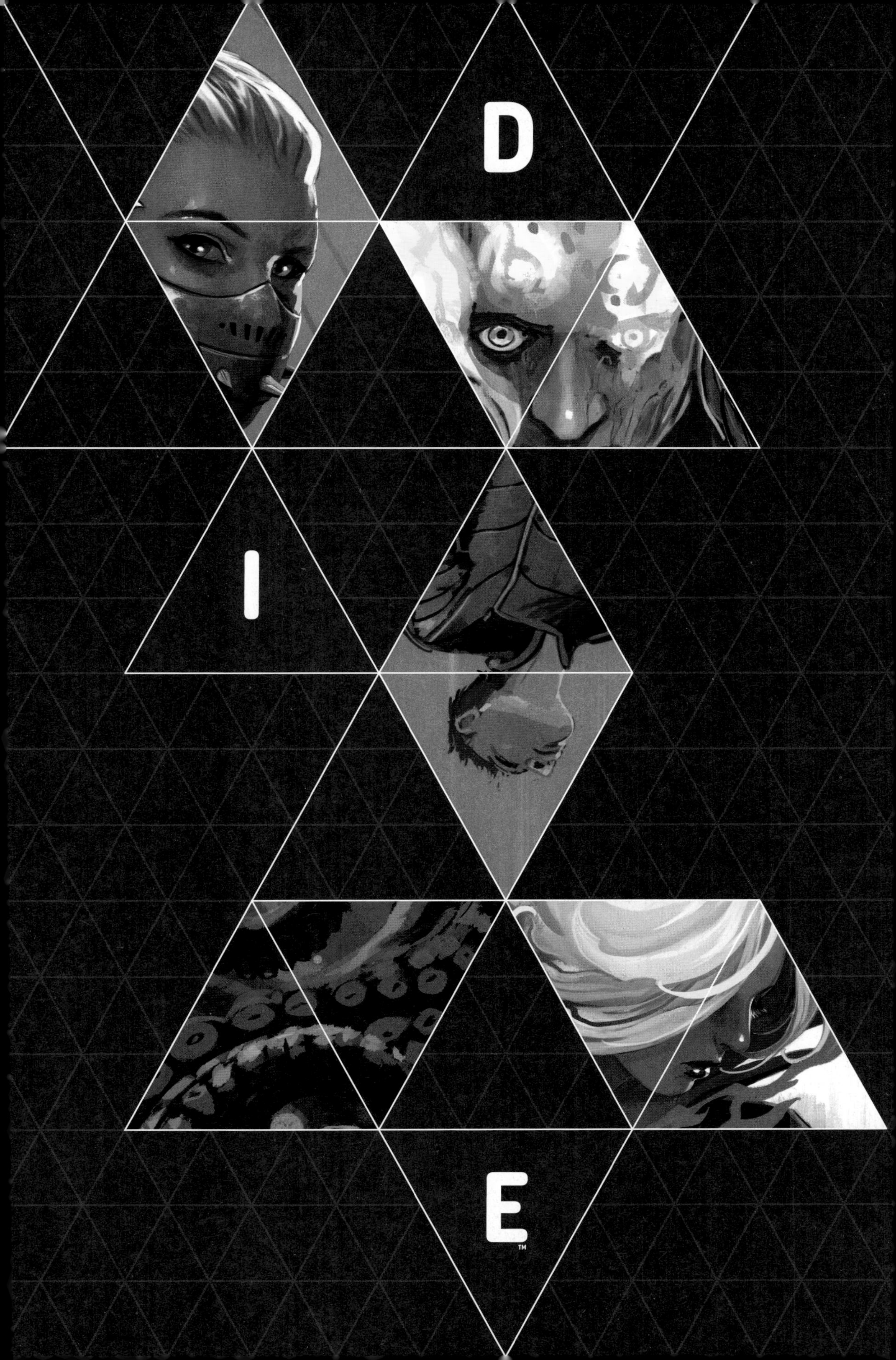
D
I
E™

In 1991, six teenagers disappeared into a fantasy role-playing game. Only five returned. In 2018, they're dragged back in.

As 2020 looms, they must travel to the centre of the planet to save Earth.

D4

ASH
Dictator

Dominic Ash in the real world, Ash in the world of Die. Married. Sol's best friend. Angela's sibling.

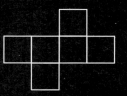

D6

CHUCK
Fool

Fantasy novelist with multiple ex-wives, no tact, and a film franchise. Has a fatal disease.

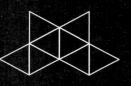

D8

MATT
Grief Knight

Parent and husband. Statistics professor at the local university.

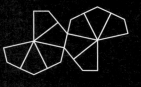

D10

ANGELA
Neo

Coder and parent on the outside, going through an ugly divorce. Her daughter Molly is here and is one of the Fallen.

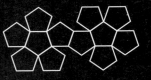

D12

ISABELLE
Godbinder

Divorced schoolteacher with aggressively bilingual intelligence.

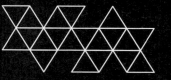

D20

SOL
Grandmaster

Solomon made the game but never made it out. Murdered by Ash and is now one of the Fallen.

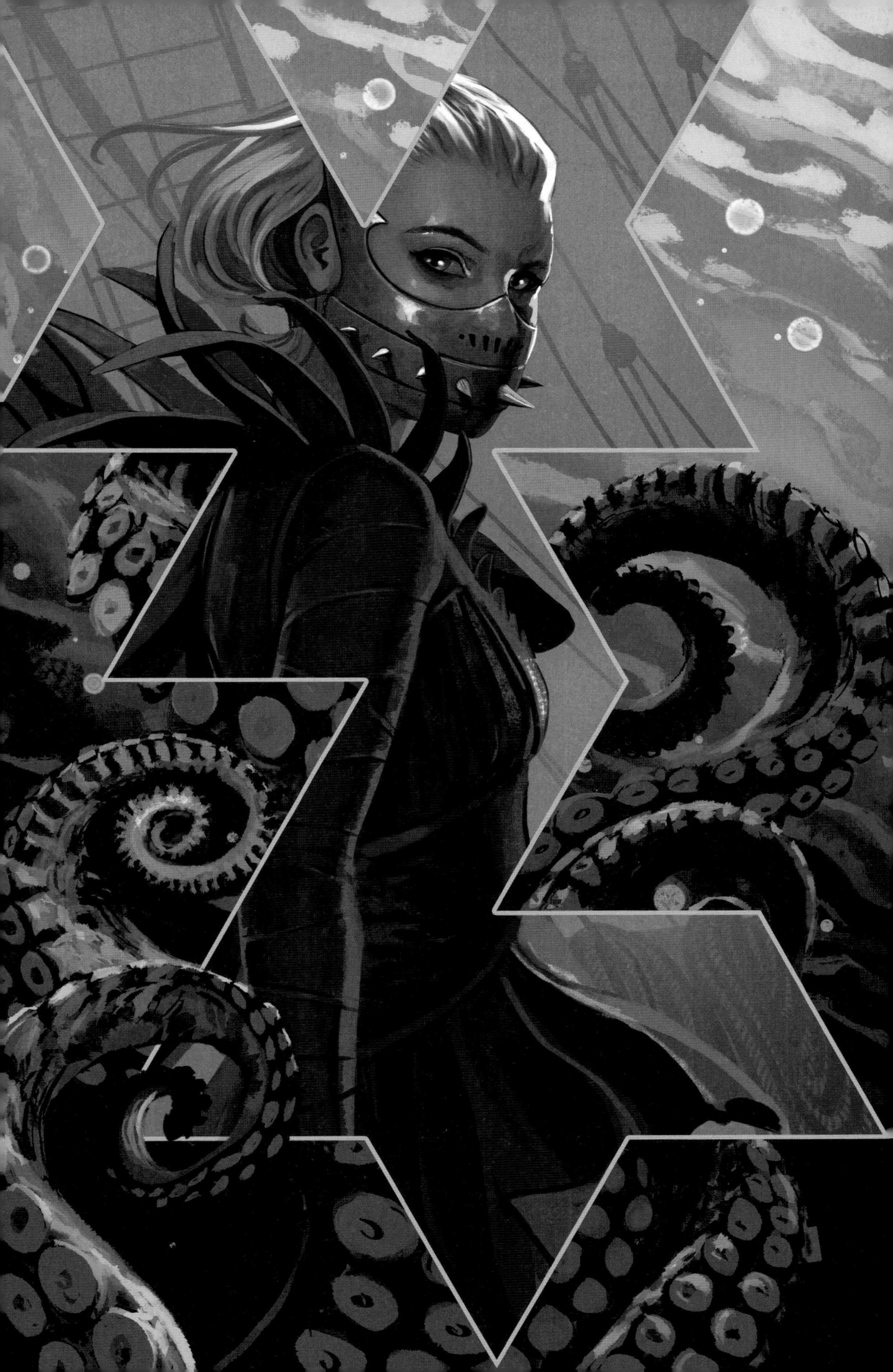

16:
THACO

"This is, fantasy is, almost a sea in which other genres swim."
– *Terry Pratchett*

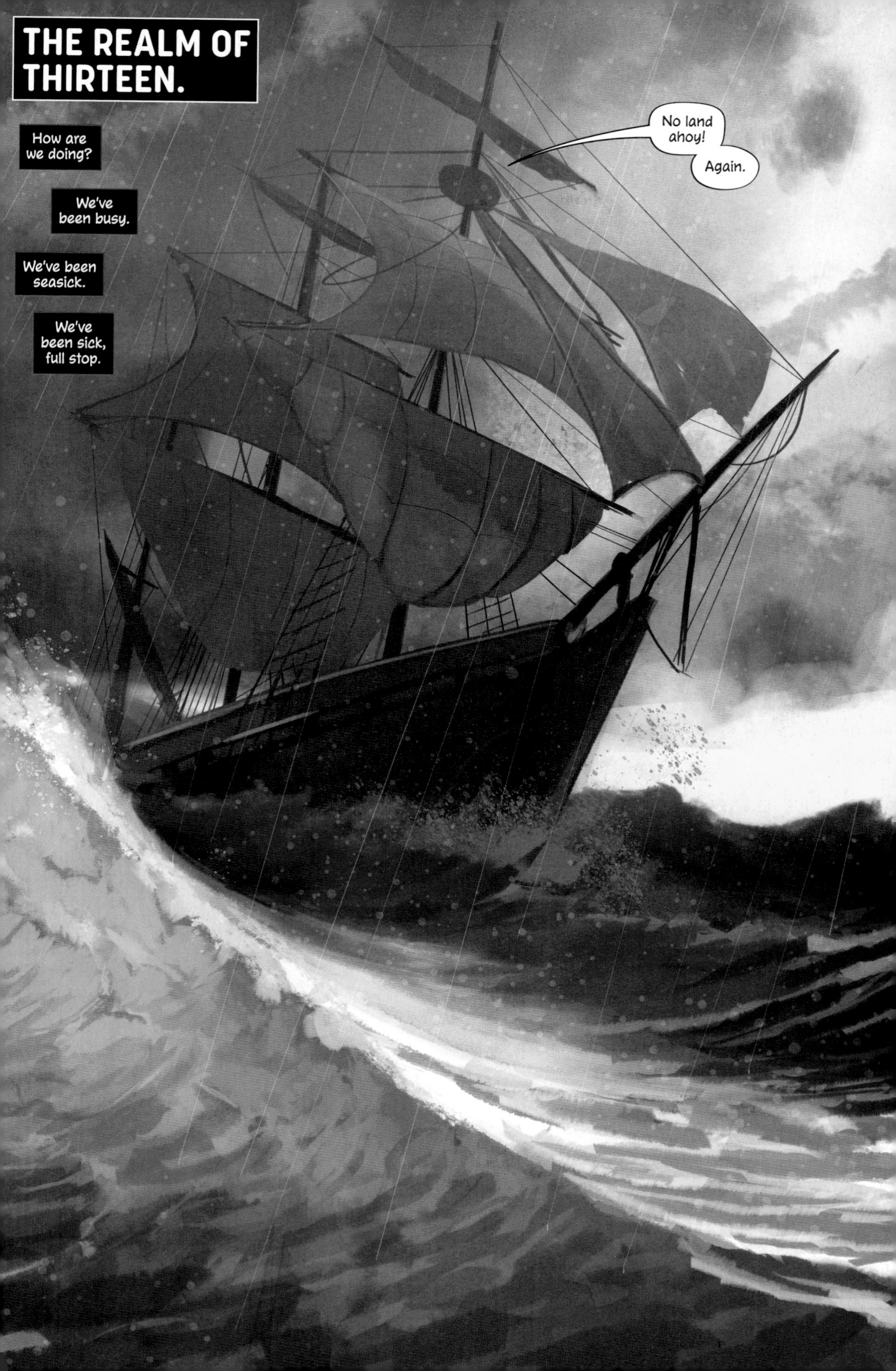
THE REALM OF THIRTEEN.
How are we doing?
We've been busy.
We've been seasick.
We've been sick, full stop.
No land ahoy!
Again.

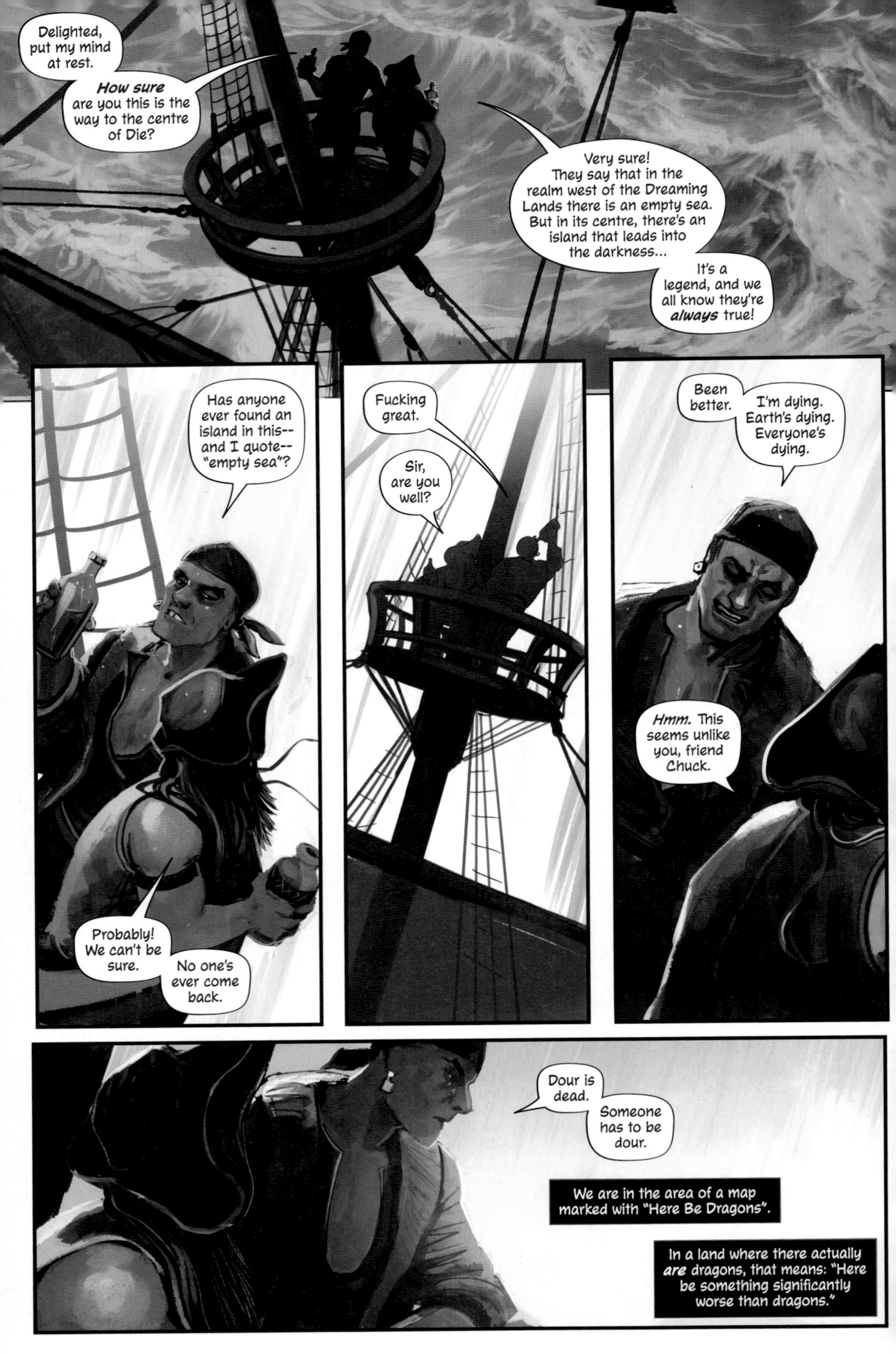

Delighted, put my mind at rest.
How sure are you this is the way to the centre of Die?
Very sure! They say that in the realm west of the Dreaming Lands there is an empty sea. But in its centre, there's an island that leads into the darkness...
It's a legend, and we all know they're *always* true!
Has anyone ever found an island in this-- and I quote-- "empty sea"?
Probably! We can't be sure.
No one's ever come back.
Fucking great.
Sir, are you well?
Been better.
I'm dying. Earth's dying. Everyone's dying.
Hmm. This seems unlike you, friend Chuck.
Dour is dead.
Someone has to be dour.
We are in the area of a map marked with "Here Be Dragons".
In a land where there actually *are* dragons, that means: "Here be something significantly worse than dragons."

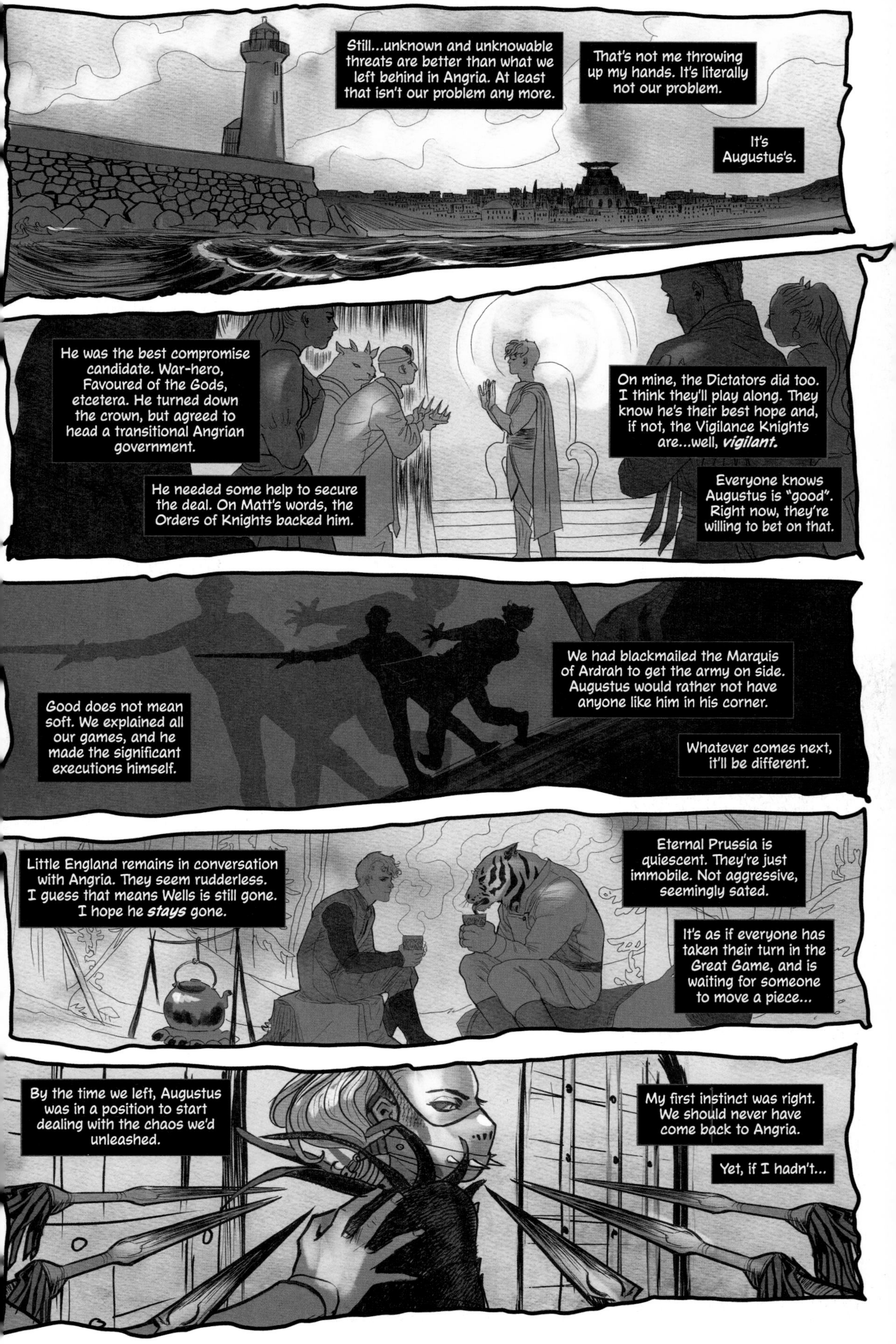
Still...unknown and unknowable threats are better than what we left behind in Angria. At least that isn't our problem any more.
That's not me throwing up my hands. It's literally not our problem.
It's Augustus's.
He was the best compromise candidate. War-hero, Favoured of the Gods, etcetera. He turned down the crown, but agreed to head a transitional Angrian government.
He needed some help to secure the deal. On Matt's words, the Orders of Knights backed him.
On mine, the Dictators did too. I think they'll play along. They know he's their best hope and, if not, the Vigilance Knights are...well, ***vigilant.***
Everyone knows Augustus is "good". Right now, they're willing to bet on that.
Good does not mean soft. We explained all our games, and he made the significant executions himself.
We had blackmailed the Marquis of Ardrah to get the army on side. Augustus would rather not have anyone like him in his corner.
Whatever comes next, it'll be different.
Little England remains in conversation with Angria. They seem rudderless. I guess that means Wells is still gone. I hope he ***stays*** gone.
Eternal Prussia is quiescent. They're just immobile. Not aggressive, seemingly sated.
It's as if everyone has taken their turn in the Great Game, and is waiting for someone to move a piece...
By the time we left, Augustus was in a position to start dealing with the chaos we'd unleashed.
My first instinct was right. We should never have come back to Angria.
Yet, if I hadn't...

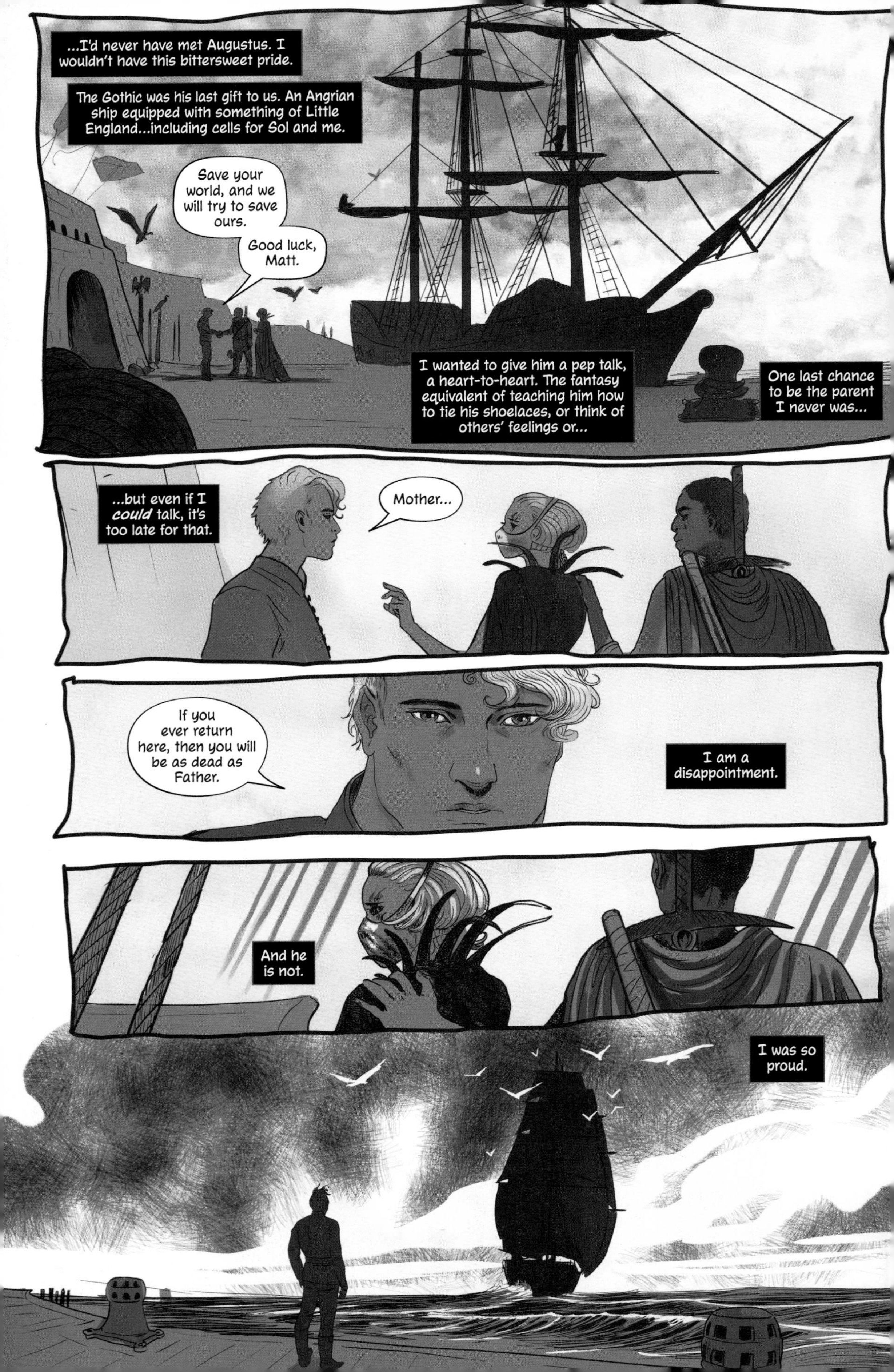
...I'd never have met Augustus. I wouldn't have this bittersweet pride.
The Gothic was his last gift to us. An Angrian ship equipped with something of Little England...including cells for Sol and me.
Save your world, and we will try to save ours.
Good luck, Matt.
I wanted to give him a pep talk, a heart-to-heart. The fantasy equivalent of teaching him how to tie his shoelaces, or think of others' feelings or...
One last chance to be the parent I never was...
...but even if I *could* talk, it's too late for that.
Mother...
If you ever return here, then you will be as dead as Father.
I am a disappointment.
And he is not.
I was so proud.

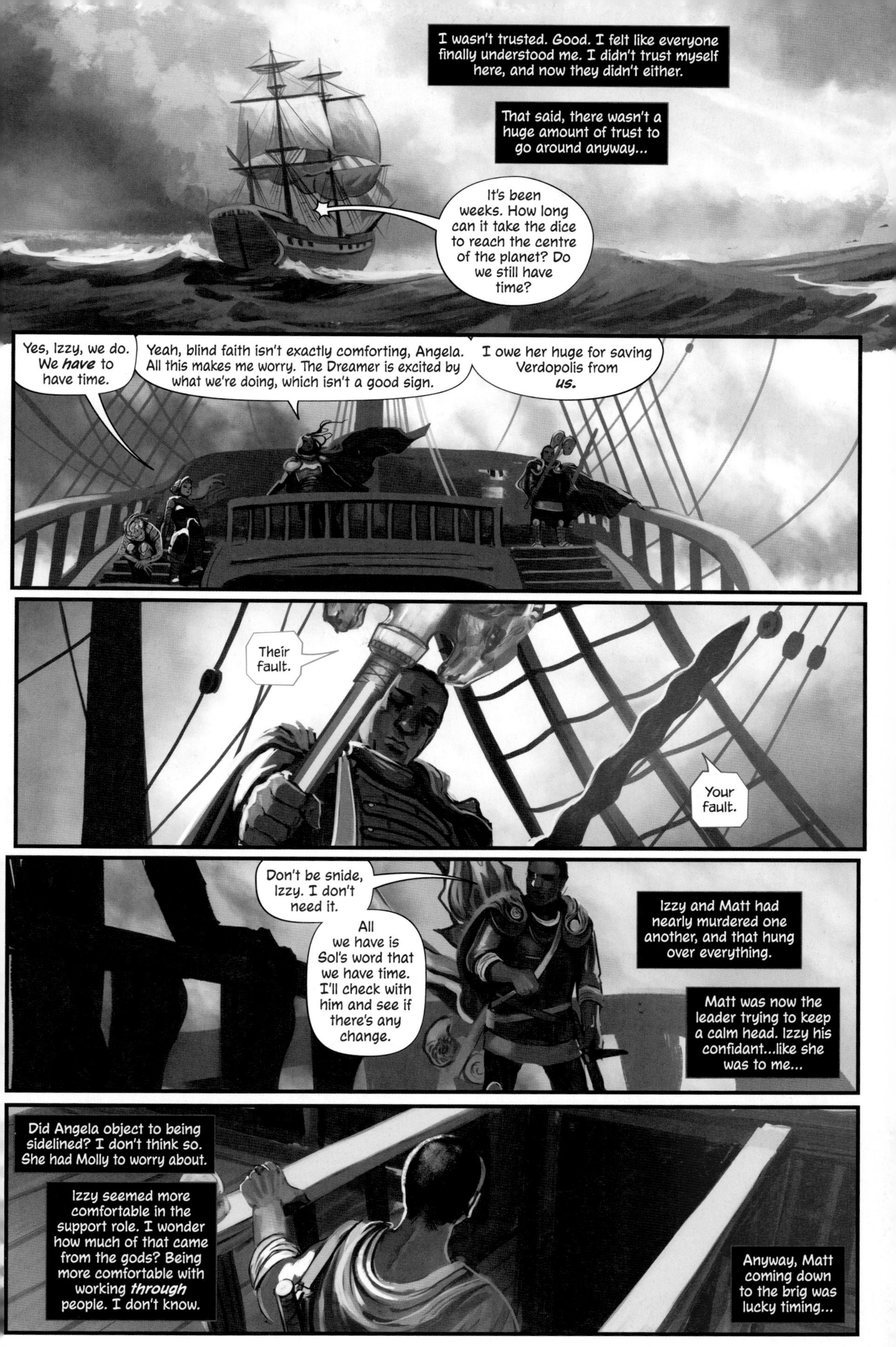
I wasn't trusted. Good. I felt like everyone finally understood me. I didn't trust myself here, and now they didn't either.
That said, there wasn't a huge amount of trust to go around anyway...
It's been weeks. How long can it take the dice to reach the centre of the planet? Do we still have time?
Yes, Izzy, we do. We *have* to have time.
Yeah, blind faith isn't exactly comforting, Angela. All this makes me worry. The Dreamer is excited by what we're doing, which isn't a good sign.
I owe her huge for saving Verdopolis from *us.*
Their fault.
Your fault.
Don't be snide, Izzy. I don't need it.
All we have is Sol's word that we have time. I'll check with him and see if there's any change.
Izzy and Matt had nearly murdered one another, and that hung over everything.
Matt was now the leader trying to keep a calm head. Izzy his confidant...like she was to me...
Did Angela object to being sidelined? I don't think so. She had Molly to worry about.
Izzy seemed more comfortable in the support role. I wonder how much of that came from the gods? Being more comfortable with working *through* people. I don't know.
Anyway, Matt coming down to the brig was lucky timing...

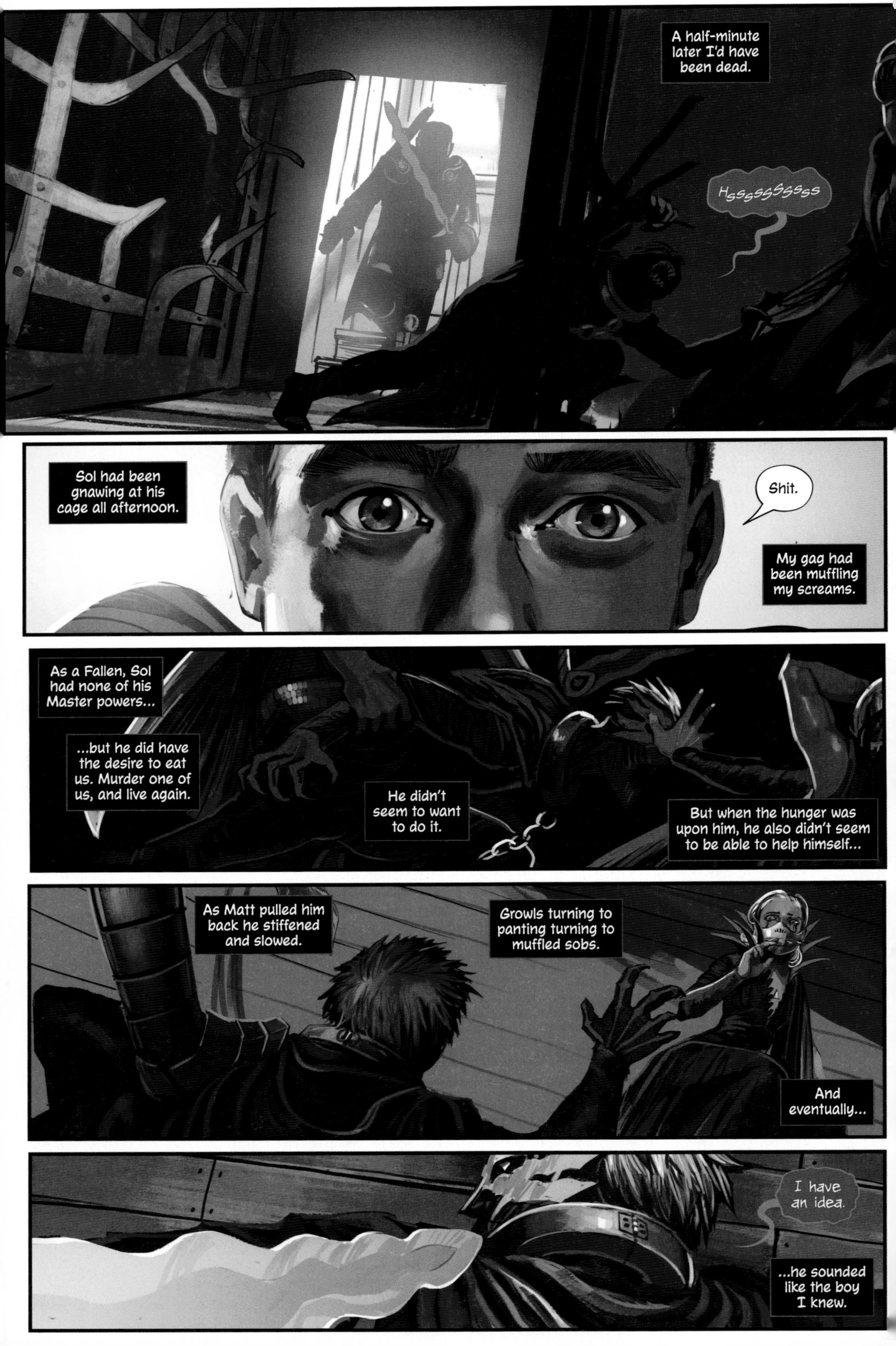
A half-minute later I'd have been dead.
Hssssssssss
Sol had been gnawing at his cage all afternoon.
Shit.
My gag had been muffling my screams.
As a Fallen, Sol had none of his Master powers...
...but he did have the desire to eat us. Murder one of us, and live again.
He didn't seem to want to do it.
But when the hunger was upon him, he also didn't seem to be able to help himself...
As Matt pulled him back he stiffened and slowed.
Growls turning to panting turning to muffled sobs.
And eventually...
I have an idea.
...he sounded like the boy I knew.

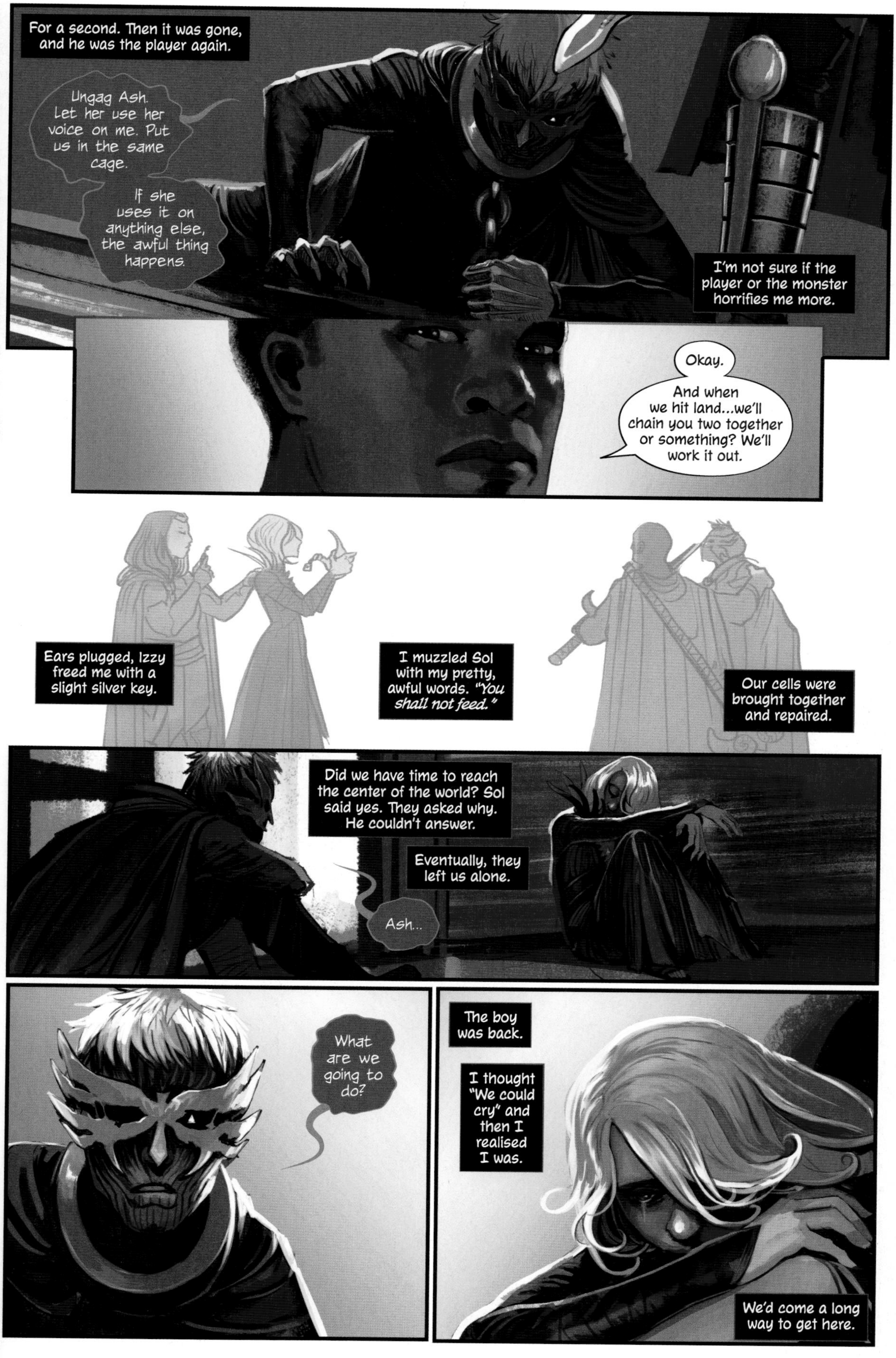
For a second. Then it was gone, and he was the player again.
Ungag Ash. Let her use her voice on me. Put us in the same cage.
If she uses it on anything else, the awful thing happens.
I'm not sure if the player or the monster horrifies me more.
Okay.
And when we hit land...we'll chain you two together or something? We'll work it out.
Ears plugged, Izzy freed me with a slight silver key.
I muzzled Sol with my pretty, awful words. *"You shall not feed."*
Our cells were brought together and repaired.
Did we have time to reach the center of the world? Sol said yes. They asked why. He couldn't answer.
Eventually, they left us alone.
Ash...
What are we going to do?
The boy was back.
I thought "We could cry" and then I realised I was.
We'd come a long way to get here.

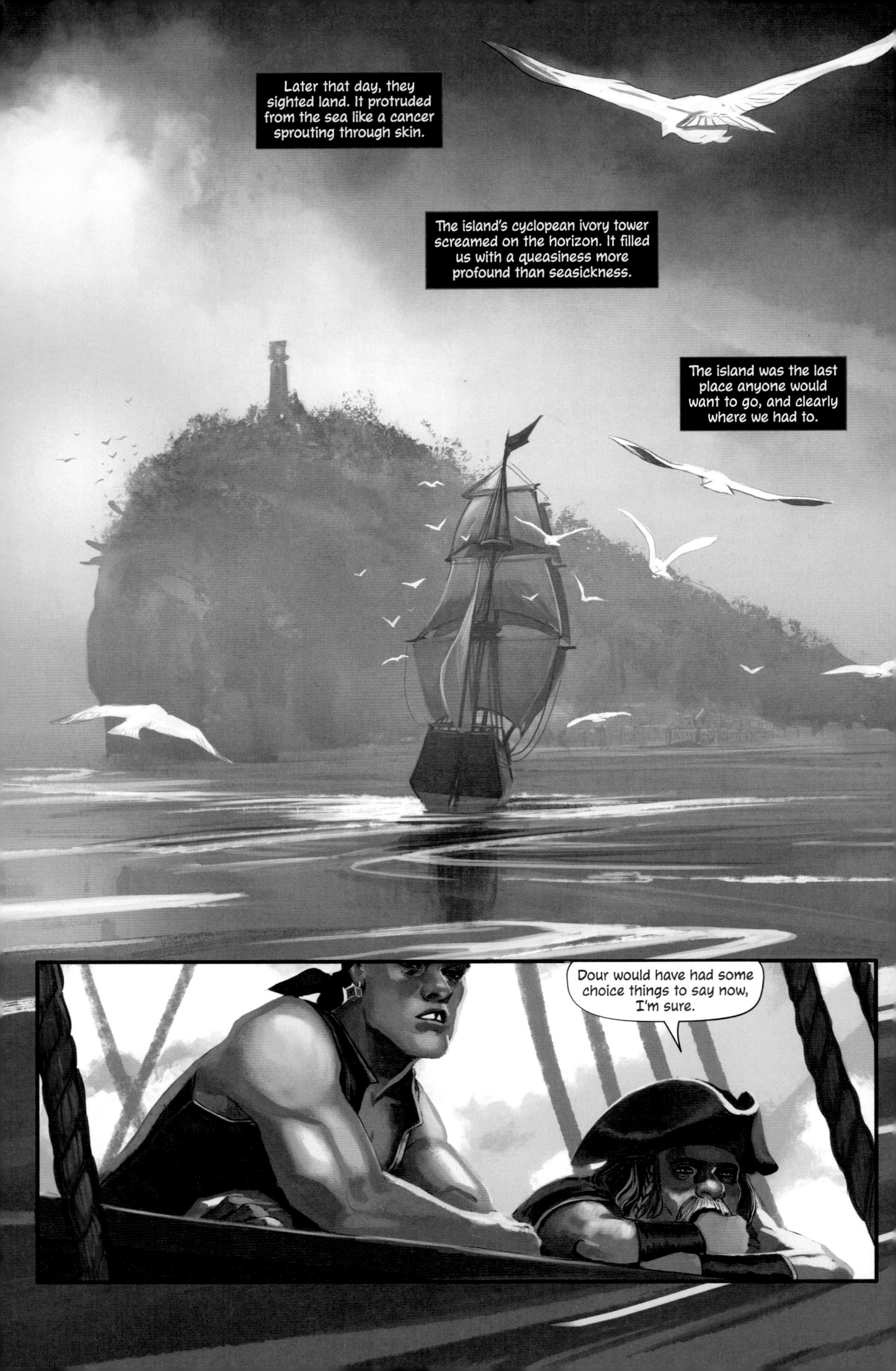
Later that day, they sighted land. It protruded from the sea like a cancer sprouting through skin.
The island's cyclopean ivory tower screamed on the horizon. It filled us with a queasiness more profound than seasickness.
The island was the last place anyone would want to go, and clearly where we had to.
Dour would have had some choice things to say now, I'm sure.

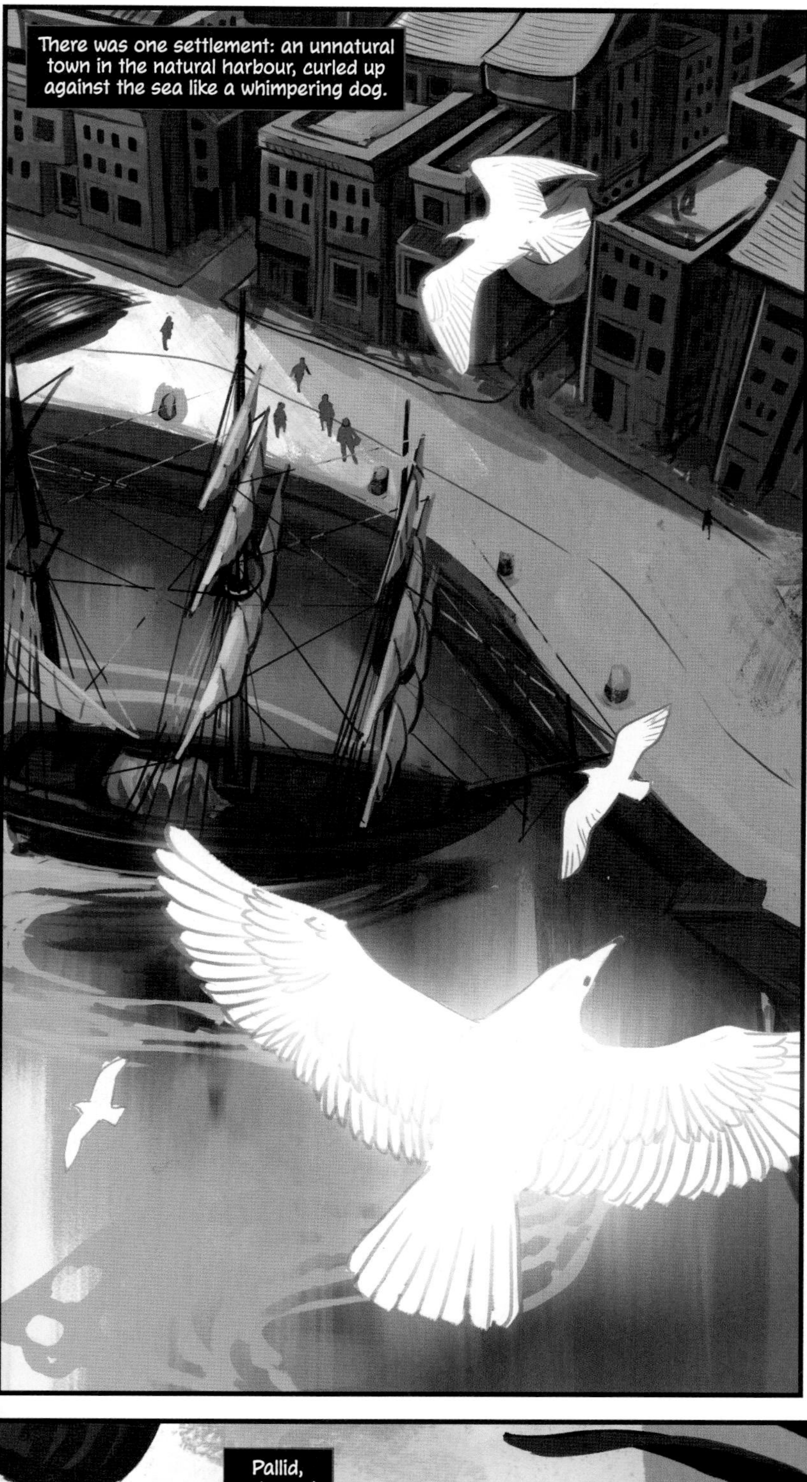
There was one settlement: an unnatural town in the natural harbour, curled up against the sea like a whimpering dog.

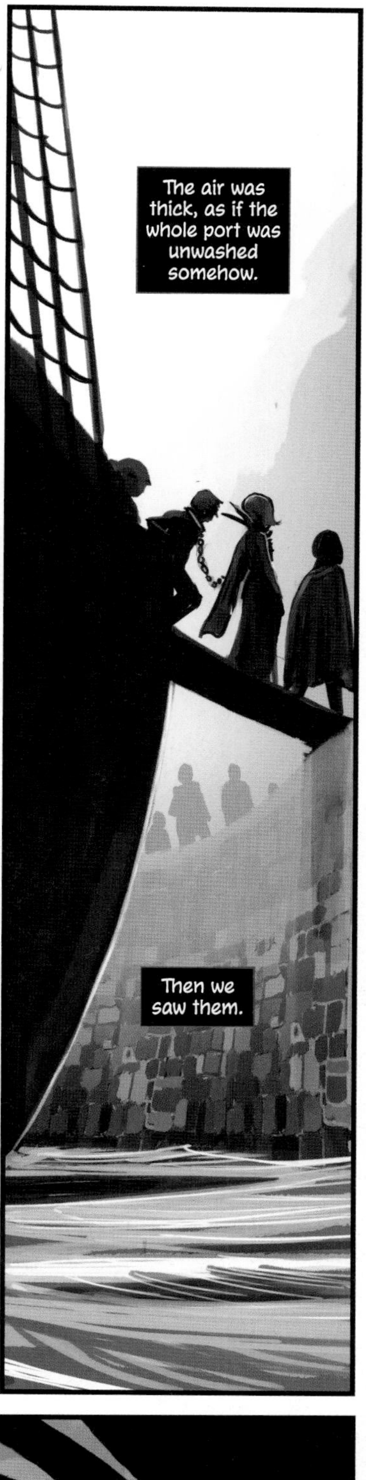
The air was thick, as if the whole port was unwashed somehow.
Then we saw them.

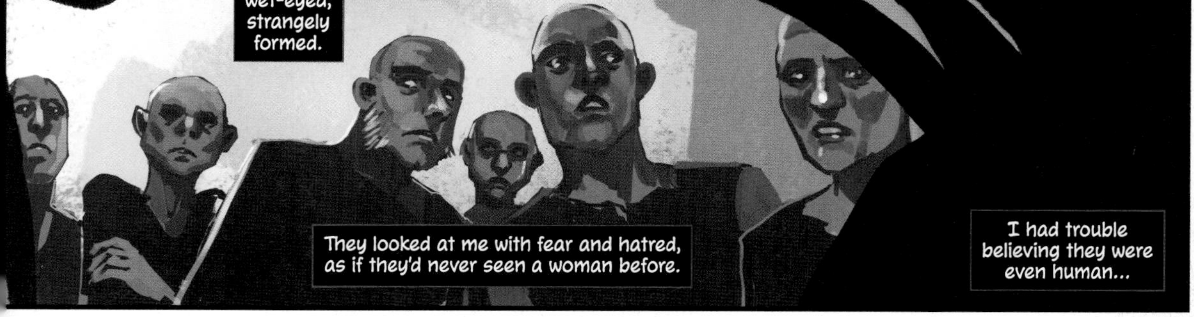
Pallid, wet-eyed, strangely formed.
They looked at me with fear and hatred, as if they'd never seen a woman before.
I had trouble believing they were even human...

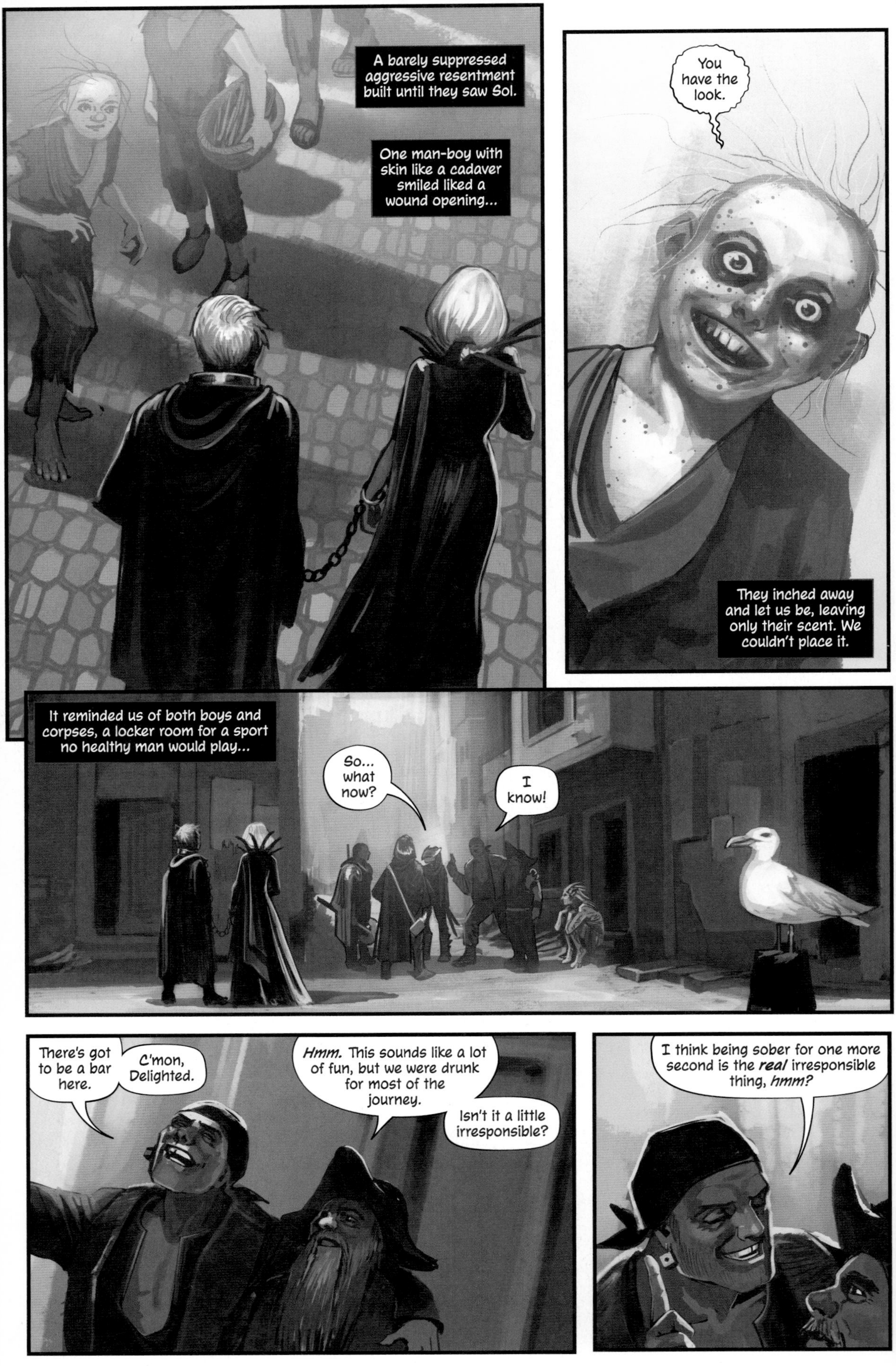
A barely suppressed aggressive resentment built until they saw Sol.
One man-boy with skin like a cadaver smiled liked a wound opening...
You have the look.
They inched away and let us be, leaving only their scent. We couldn't place it.
It reminded us of both boys and corpses, a locker room for a sport no healthy man would play...
So... what now?
I know!
There's got to be a bar here.
C'mon, Delighted.
Hmm. This sounds like a lot of fun, but we were drunk for most of the journey.
Isn't it a little irresponsible?
I think being sober for one more second is the ***real*** irresponsible thing, *hmm?*

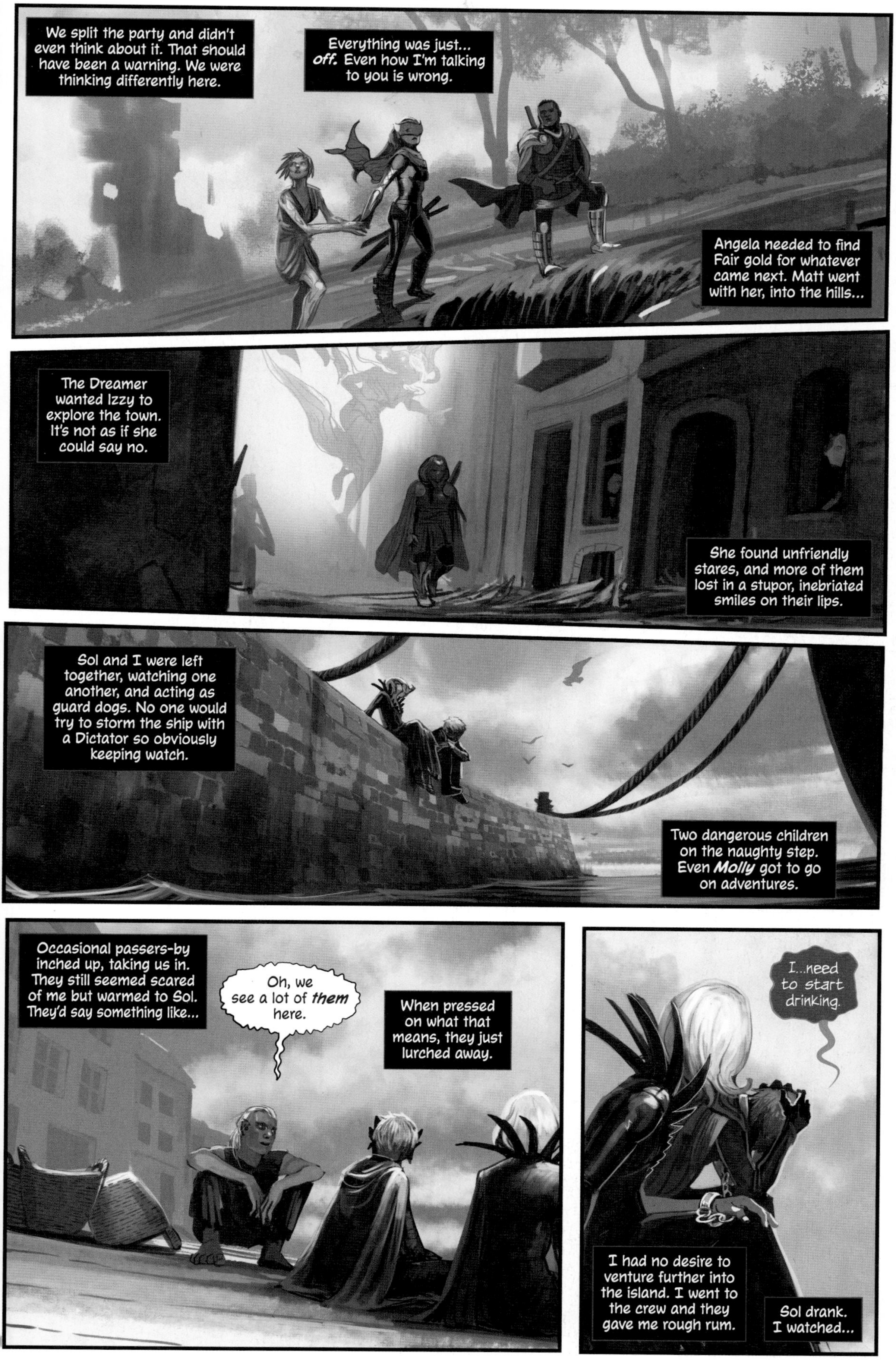

We split the party and didn't even think about it. That should have been a warning. We were thinking differently here.
Everything was just... *off.* Even how I'm talking to you is wrong.
Angela needed to find Fair gold for whatever came next. Matt went with her, into the hills...
The Dreamer wanted Izzy to explore the town. It's not as if she could say no.
She found unfriendly stares, and more of them lost in a stupor, inebriated smiles on their lips.
Sol and I were left together, watching one another, and acting as guard dogs. No one would try to storm the ship with a Dictator so obviously keeping watch.
Two dangerous children on the naughty step. Even *Molly* got to go on adventures.
Occasional passers-by inched up, taking us in. They still seemed scared of me but warmed to Sol. They'd say something like...
Oh, we see a lot of *them* here.
When pressed on what that means, they just lurched away.
I...need to start drinking.
I had no desire to venture further into the island. I went to the crew and they gave me rough rum.
Sol drank. I watched...

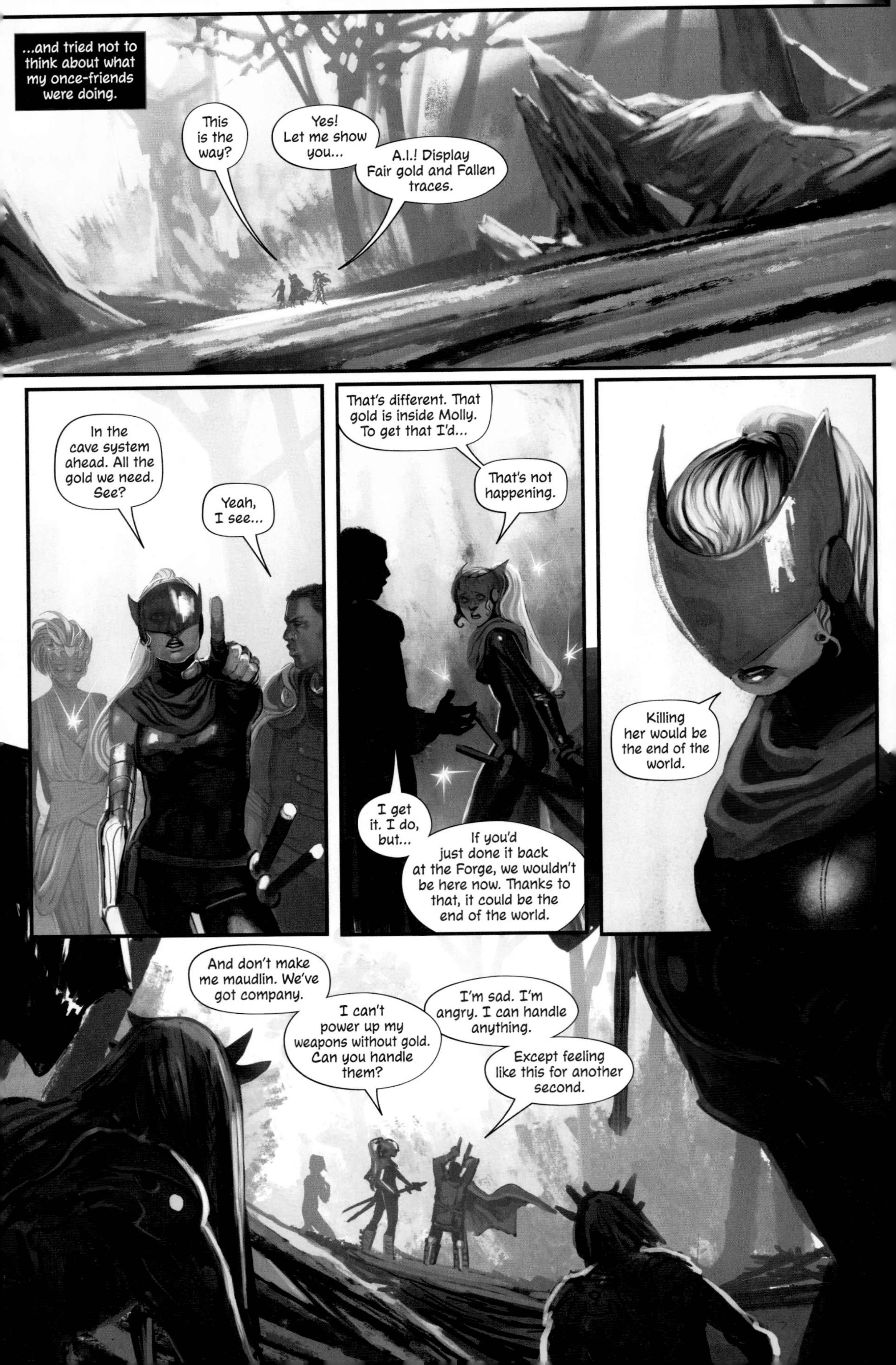
...and tried not to think about what my once-friends were doing.
This is the way?
Yes! Let me show you...
A.I.! Display Fair gold and Fallen traces.
In the cave system ahead. All the gold we need. See?
Yeah, I see...
That's different. That gold is inside Molly. To get that I'd...
That's not happening.
I get it. I do, but...
If you'd just done it back at the Forge, we wouldn't be here now. Thanks to that, it could be the end of the world.
Killing her would be the end of the world.
And don't make me maudlin. We've got company.
I can't power up my weapons without gold. Can you handle them?
I'm sad. I'm angry. I can handle anything.
Except feeling like this for another second.

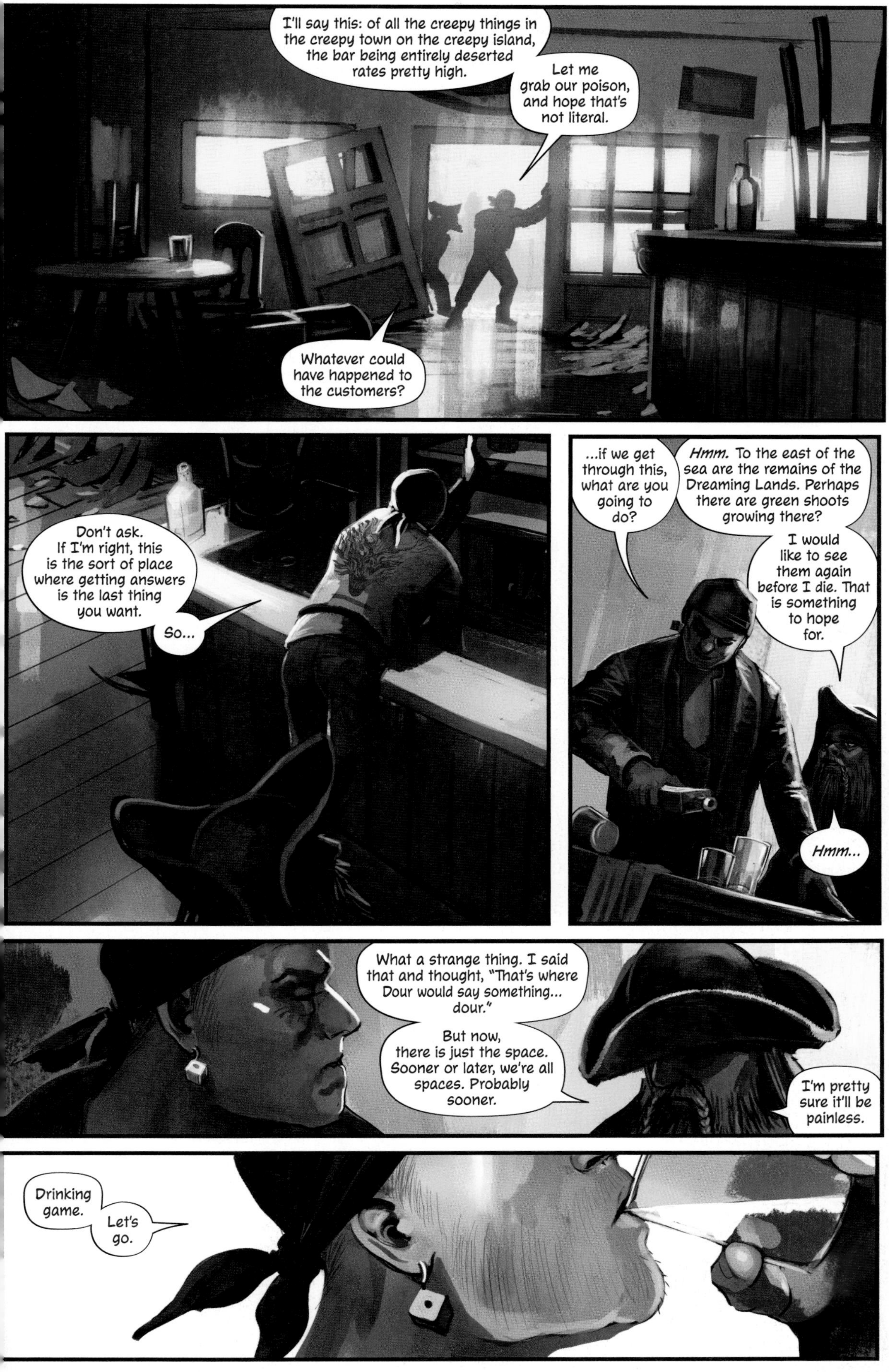
I'll say this: of all the creepy things in the creepy town on the creepy island, the bar being entirely deserted rates pretty high.
Let me grab our poison, and hope that's not literal.
Whatever could have happened to the customers?
Don't ask. If I'm right, this is the sort of place where getting answers is the last thing you want.
So...
...if we get through this, what are you going to do?
Hmm. To the east of the sea are the remains of the Dreaming Lands. Perhaps there are green shoots growing there?
I would like to see them again before I die. That is something to hope for.
Hmm...
What a strange thing. I said that and thought, "That's where Dour would say something... dour."
But now, there is just the space. Sooner or later, we're all spaces. Probably sooner.
I'm pretty sure it'll be painless.
Drinking game.
Let's go.

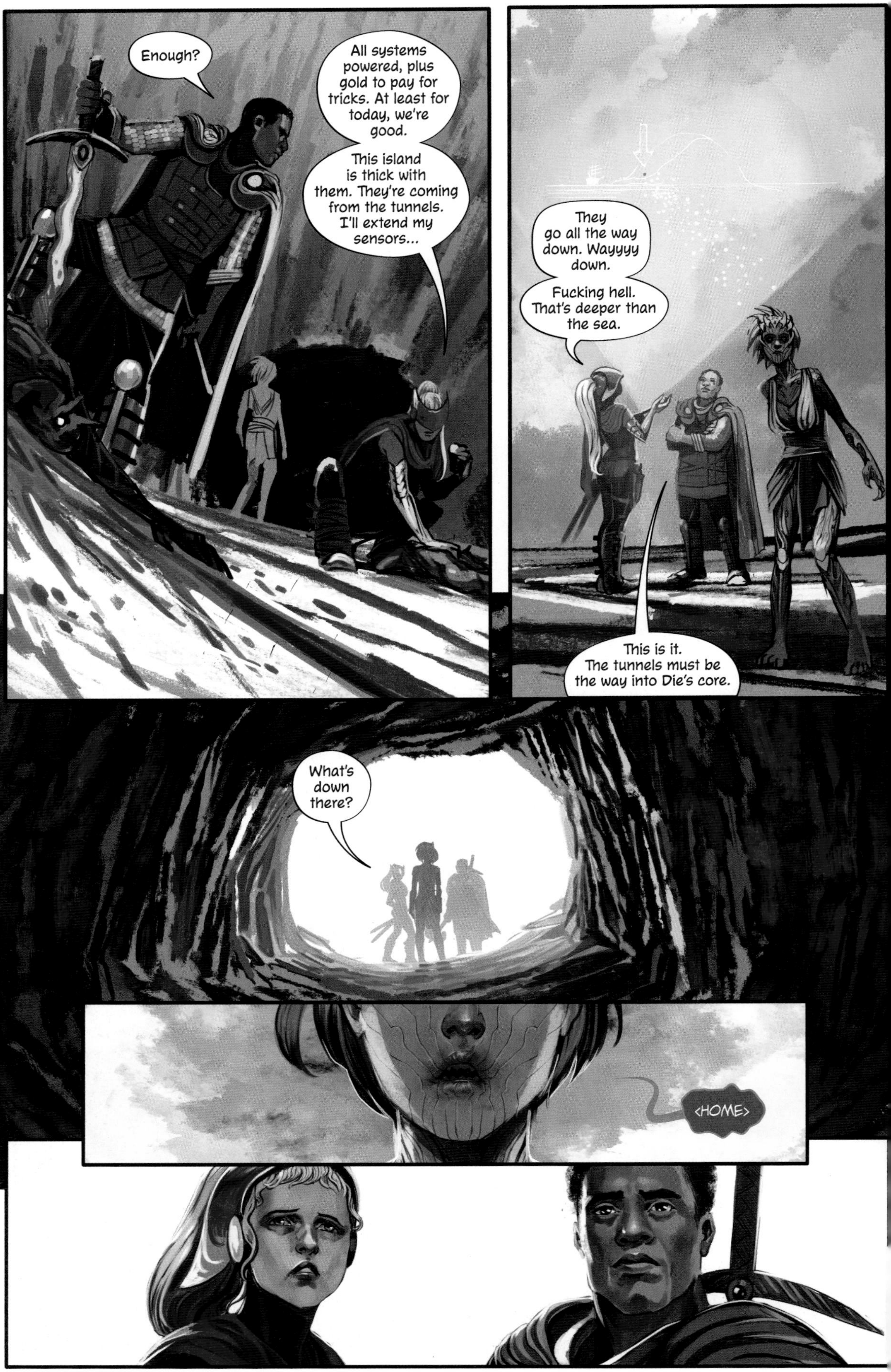
Enough?
All systems powered, plus gold to pay for tricks. At least for today, we're good.
This island is thick with them. They're coming from the tunnels. I'll extend my sensors...
They go all the way down. Wayyyy down.
Fucking hell. That's deeper than the sea.
This is it. The tunnels must be the way into Die's core.
What's down there?
<HOME>

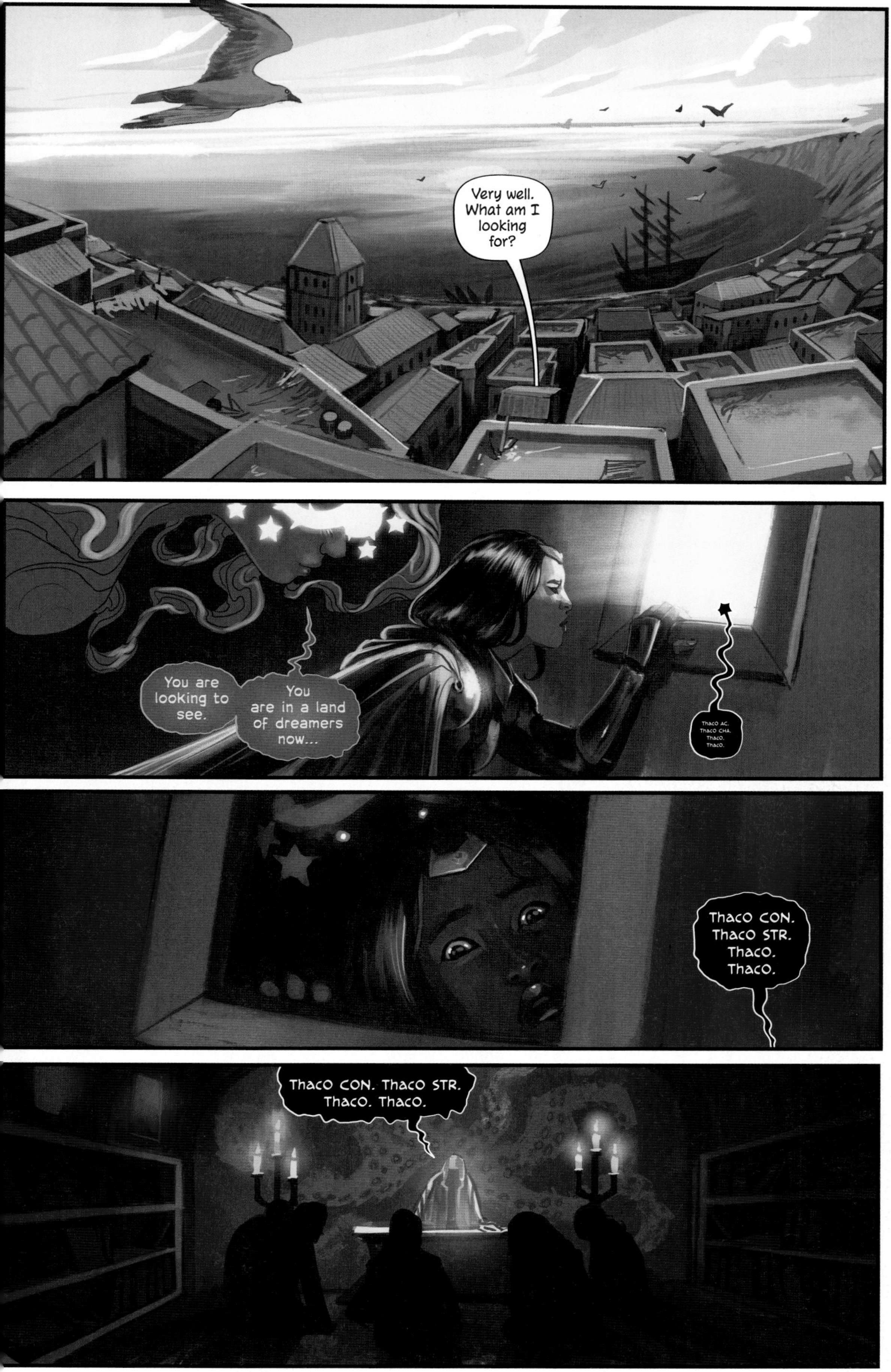
Very well. What am I looking for?
You are looking to see.
You are in a land of dreamers now...
Thaco AC. Thaco CHA. Thaco. Thaco.
Thaco CON. Thaco STR. Thaco. Thaco.
Thaco CON. Thaco STR. Thaco. Thaco.

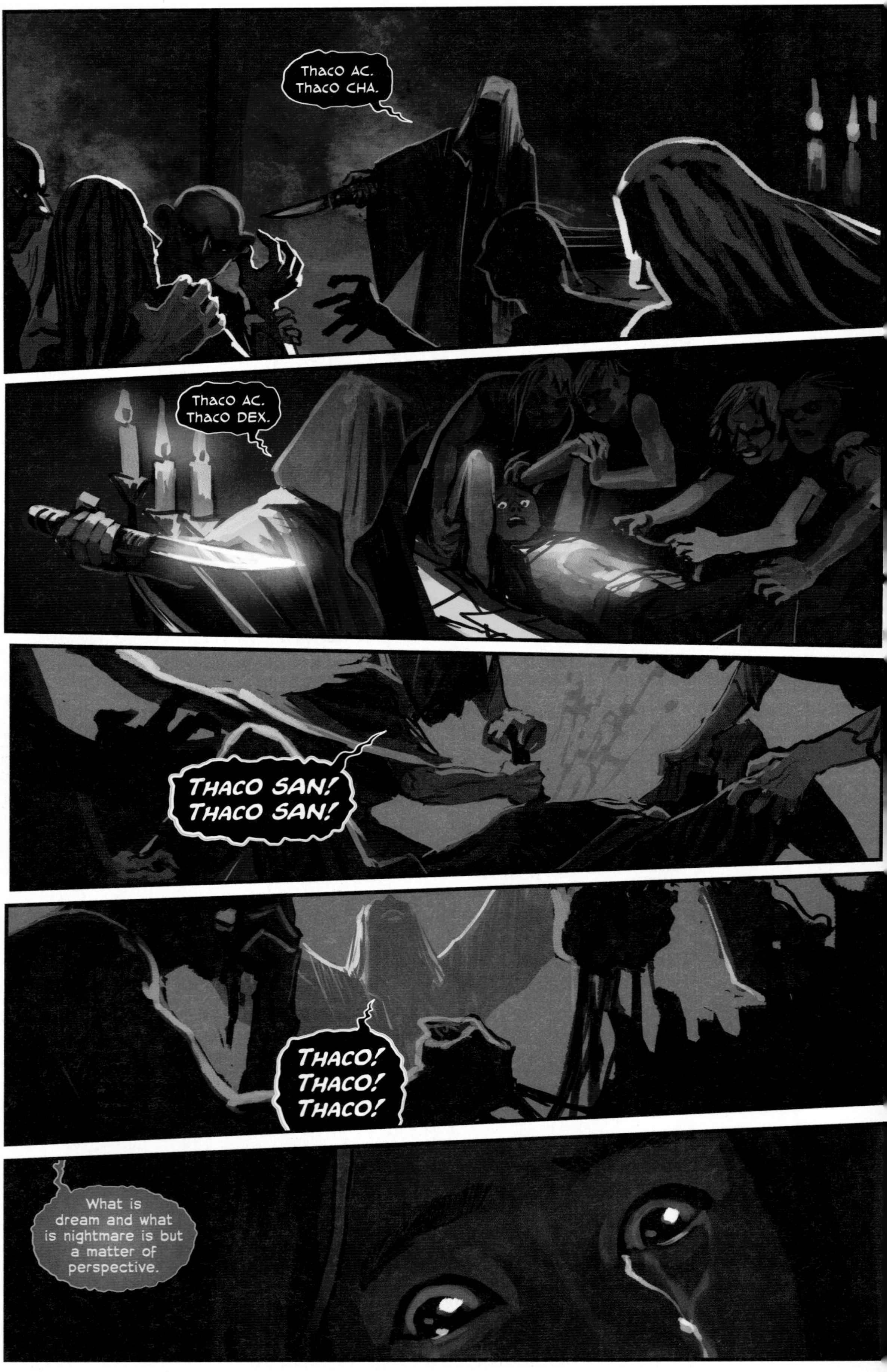
Thaco AC.
Thaco CHA.
Thaco AC.
Thaco DEX.
THACO SAN! THACO SAN!
THACO! THACO! THACO!
What is dream and what is nightmare is but a matter of perspective.

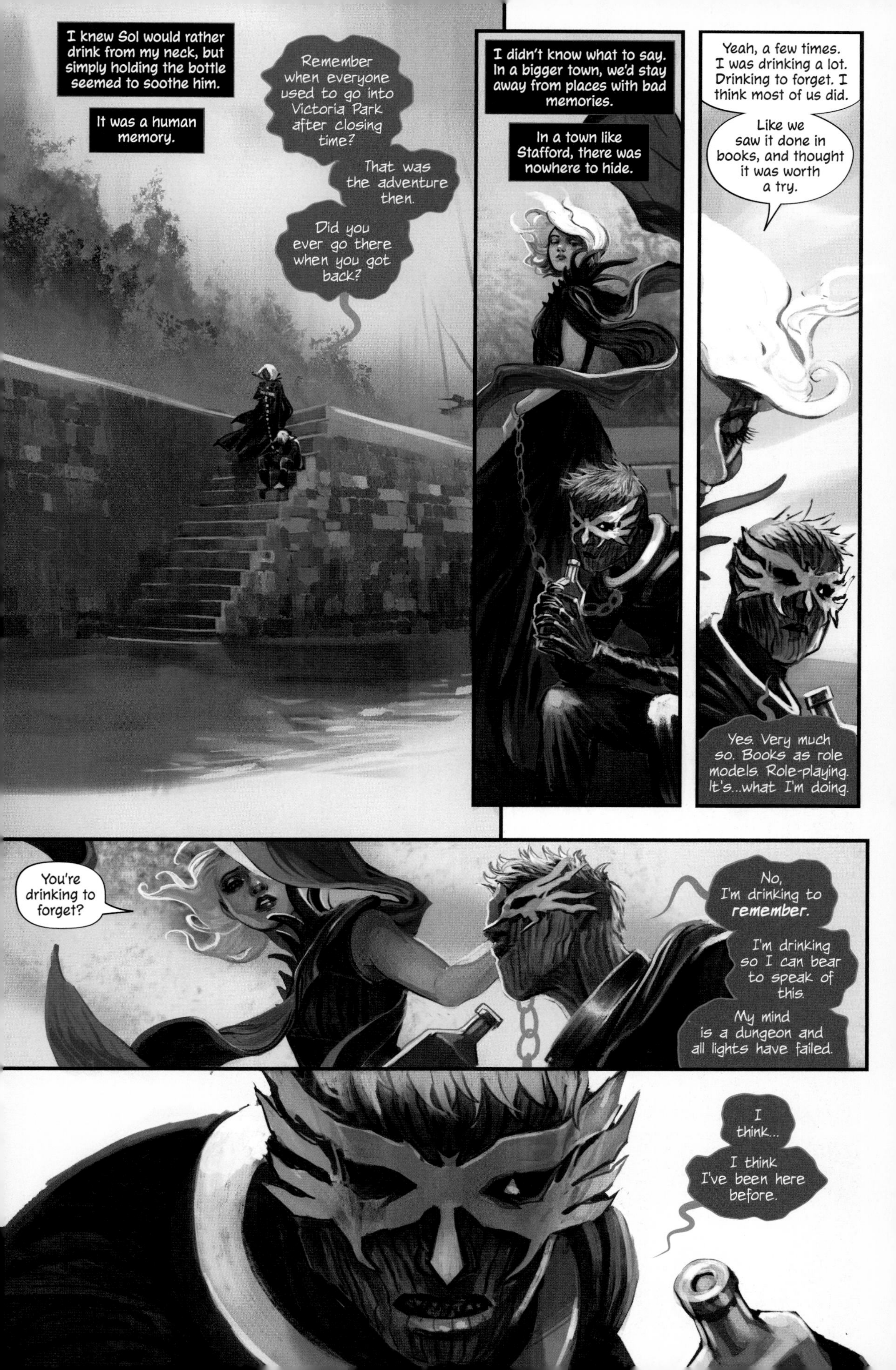

I knew Sol would rather drink from my neck, but simply holding the bottle seemed to soothe him.
It was a human memory.
Remember when everyone used to go into Victoria Park after closing time?
That was the adventure then.
Did you ever go there when you got back?
I didn't know what to say. In a bigger town, we'd stay away from places with bad memories.
In a town like Stafford, there was nowhere to hide.
Yeah, a few times. I was drinking a lot. Drinking to forget. I think most of us did.
Like we saw it done in books, and thought it was worth a try.
Yes. Very much so. Books as role models. Role-playing. It's...what I'm doing.
You're drinking to forget?
No, I'm drinking to *remember.*
I'm drinking so I can bear to speak of this.
My mind is a dungeon and all lights have failed.
I think...
I think I've been here before.

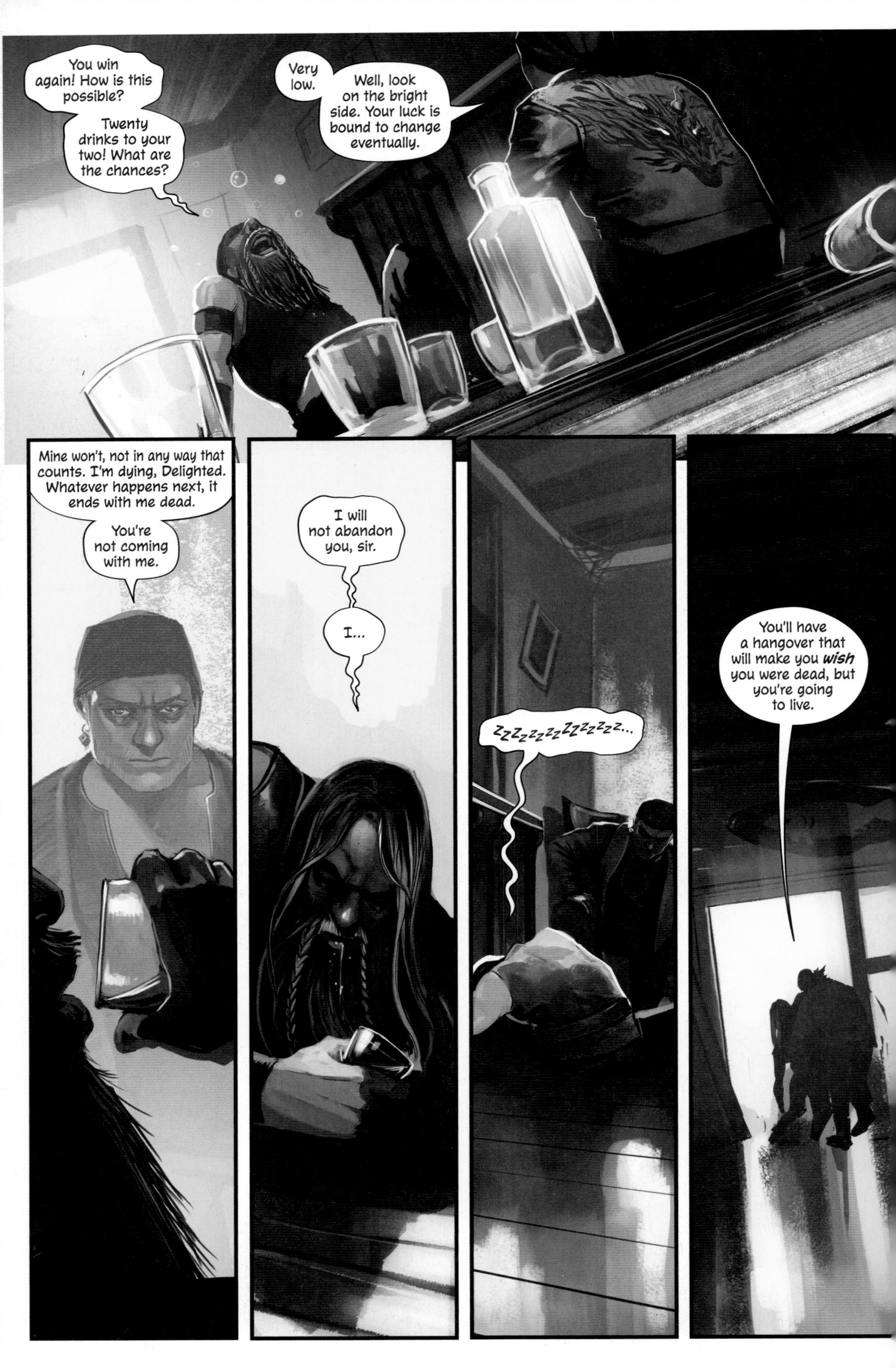
You win again! How is this possible?
Twenty drinks to your two! What are the chances?
Very low.
Well, look on the bright side. Your luck is bound to change eventually.
Mine won't, not in any way that counts. I'm dying, Delighted. Whatever happens next, it ends with me dead.
You're not coming with me.
I will not abandon you, sir.
I...
ZzZzZzZzZZZzZzZz...
You'll have a hangover that will make you *wish* you were dead, but you're going to live.

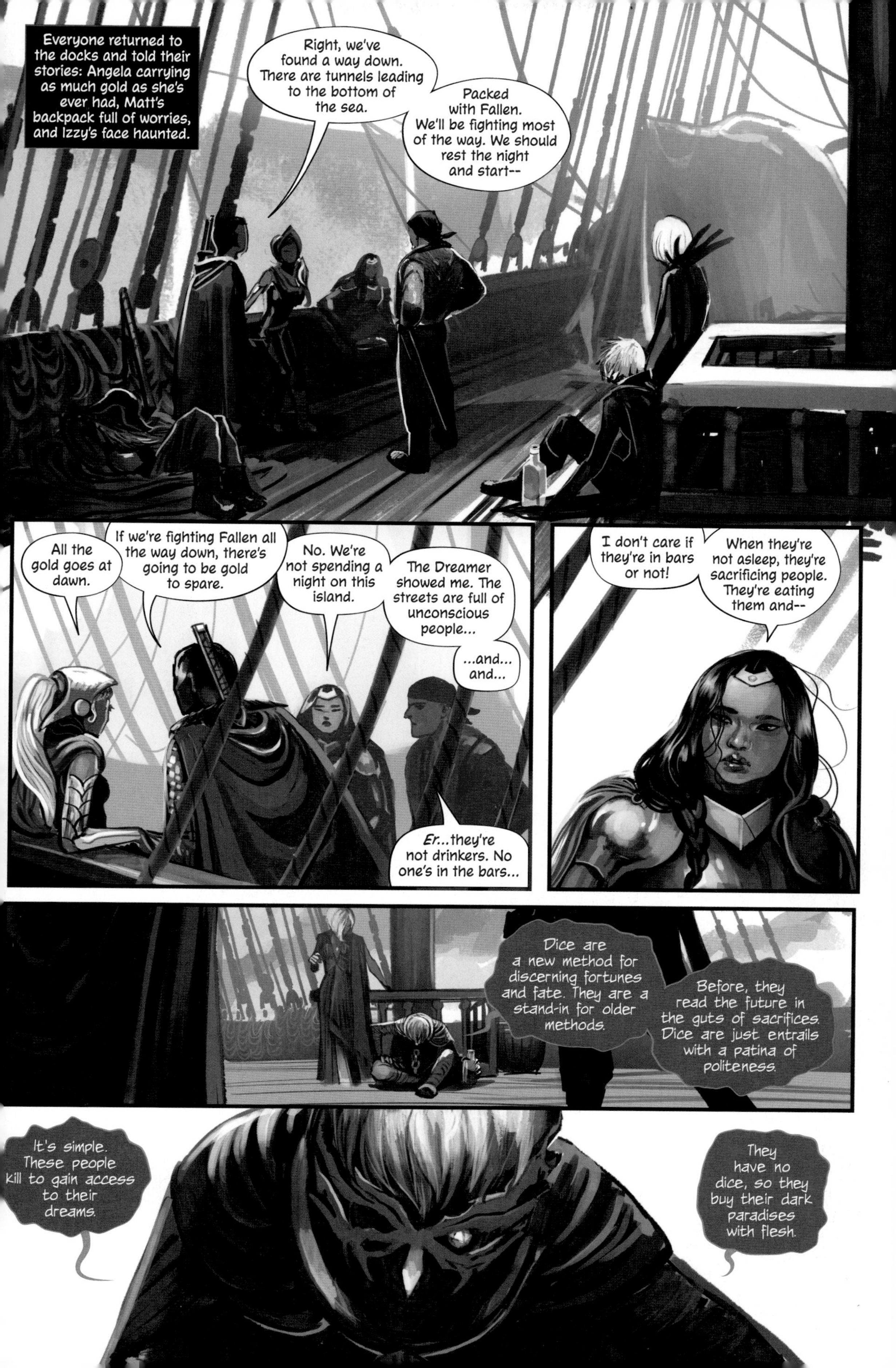
Everyone returned to the docks and told their stories: Angela carrying as much gold as she's ever had, Matt's backpack full of worries, and Izzy's face haunted.
Right, we've found a way down. There are tunnels leading to the bottom of the sea.
Packed with Fallen. We'll be fighting most of the way. We should rest the night and start--
All the gold goes at dawn.
If we're fighting Fallen all the way down, there's going to be gold to spare.
No. We're not spending a night on this island.
The Dreamer showed me. The streets are full of unconscious people...
...and... and...
Er...they're not drinkers. No one's in the bars...
I don't care if they're in bars or not!
When they're not asleep, they're sacrificing people. They're eating them and--
Dice are a new method for discerning fortunes and fate. They are a stand-in for older methods.
Before, they read the future in the guts of sacrifices. Dice are just entrails with a patina of politeness.
It's simple. These people kill to gain access to their dreams.
They have no dice, so they buy their dark paradises with flesh.

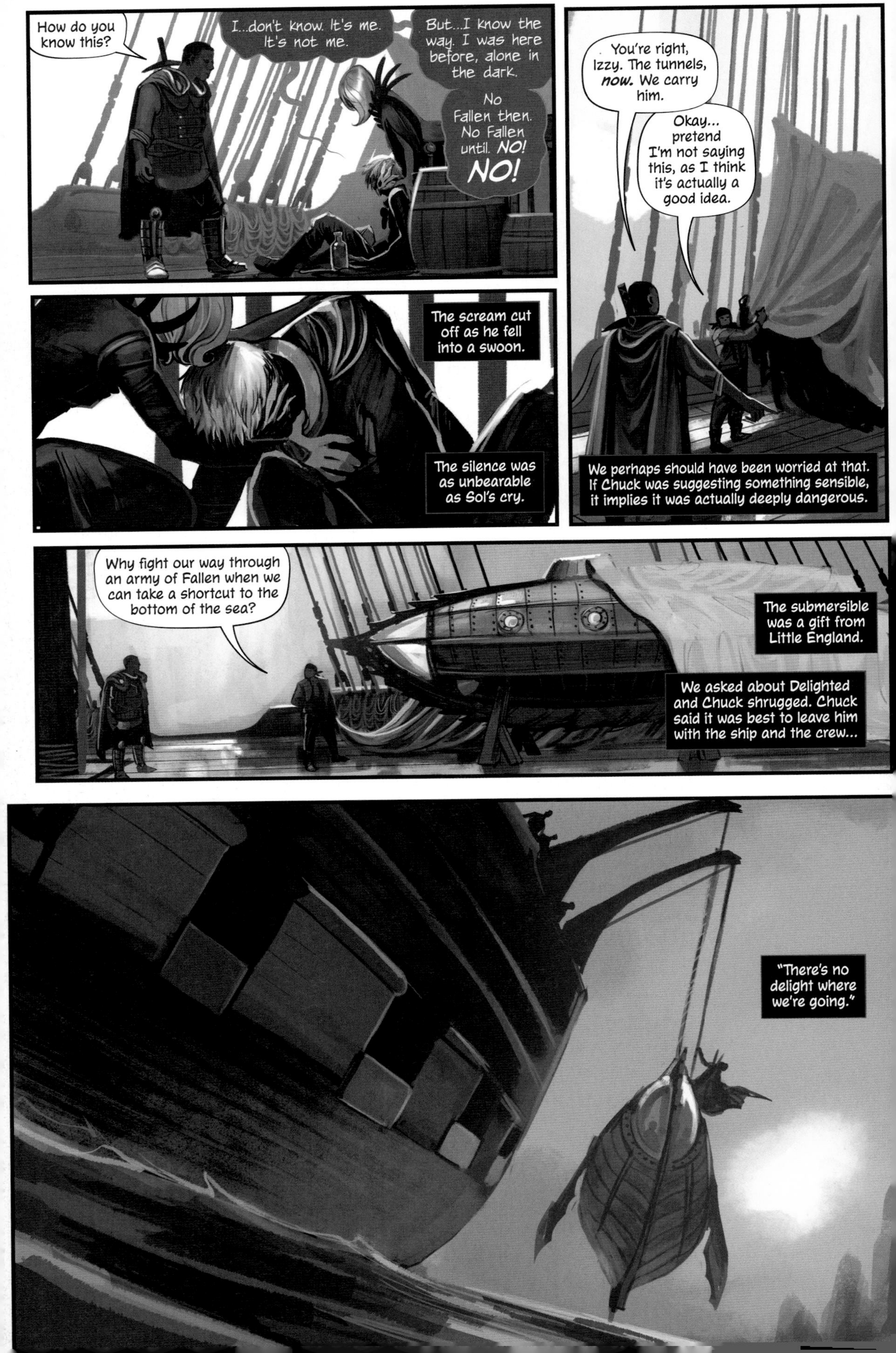
How do you know this?
I...don't know. It's me. It's not me.
But...I know the way. I was here before, alone in the dark.
No Fallen then. No Fallen until. NO! NO!
You're right, Izzy. The tunnels, now. We carry him.
Okay... pretend I'm not saying this, as I think it's actually a good idea.
The scream cut off as he fell into a swoon.
The silence was as unbearable as Sol's cry.
We perhaps should have been worried at that. If Chuck was suggesting something sensible, it implies it was actually deeply dangerous.
Why fight our way through an army of Fallen when we can take a shortcut to the bottom of the sea?
The submersible was a gift from Little England.
We asked about Delighted and Chuck shrugged. Chuck said it was best to leave him with the ship and the crew...
"There's no delight where we're going."

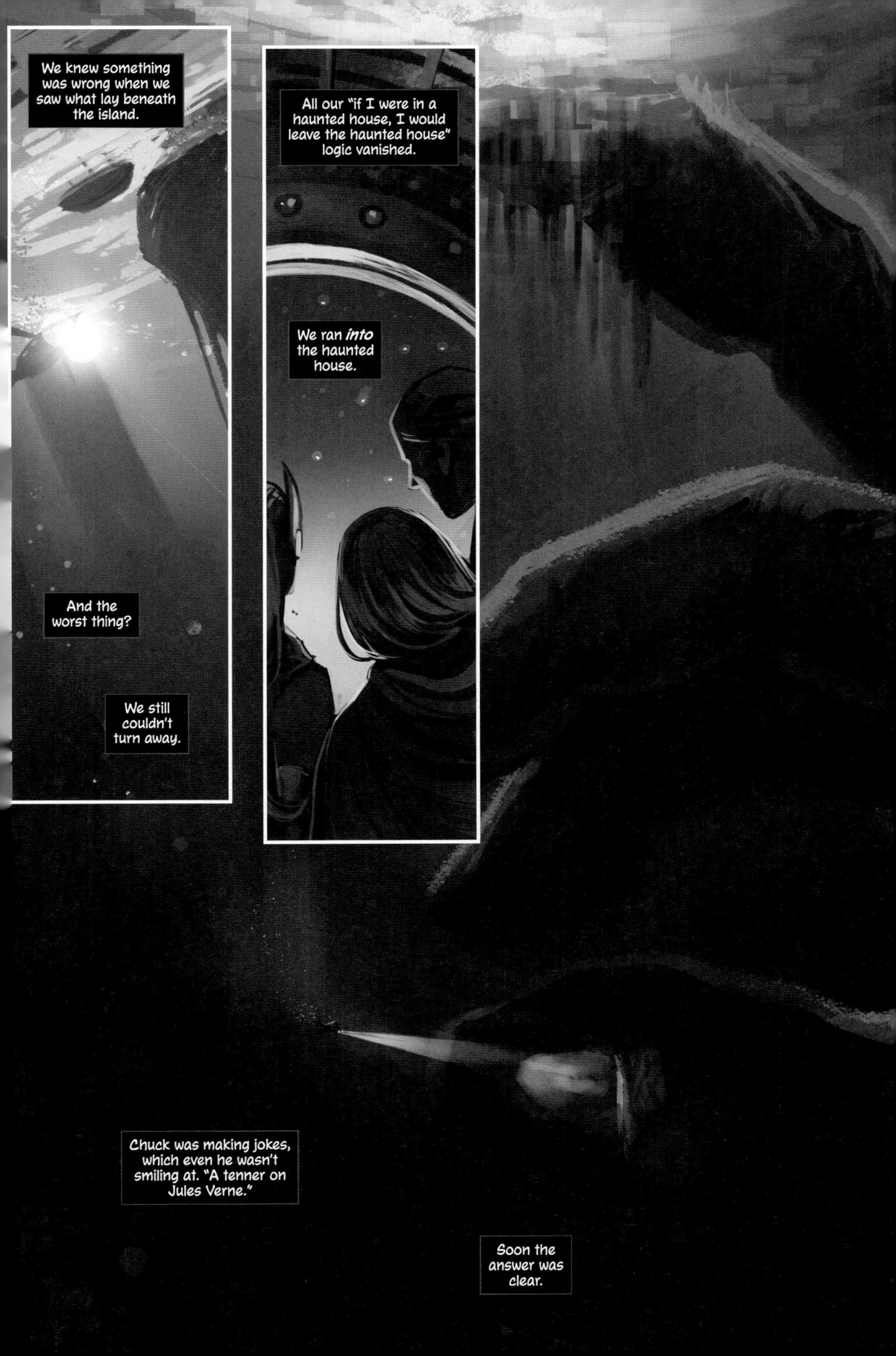
We knew something was wrong when we saw what lay beneath the island.
And the worst thing?
We still couldn't turn away.
All our "if I were in a haunted house, I would leave the haunted house" logic vanished.
We ran *into* the haunted house.
Chuck was making jokes, which even he wasn't smiling at. "A tenner on Jules Verne."
Soon the answer was clear.

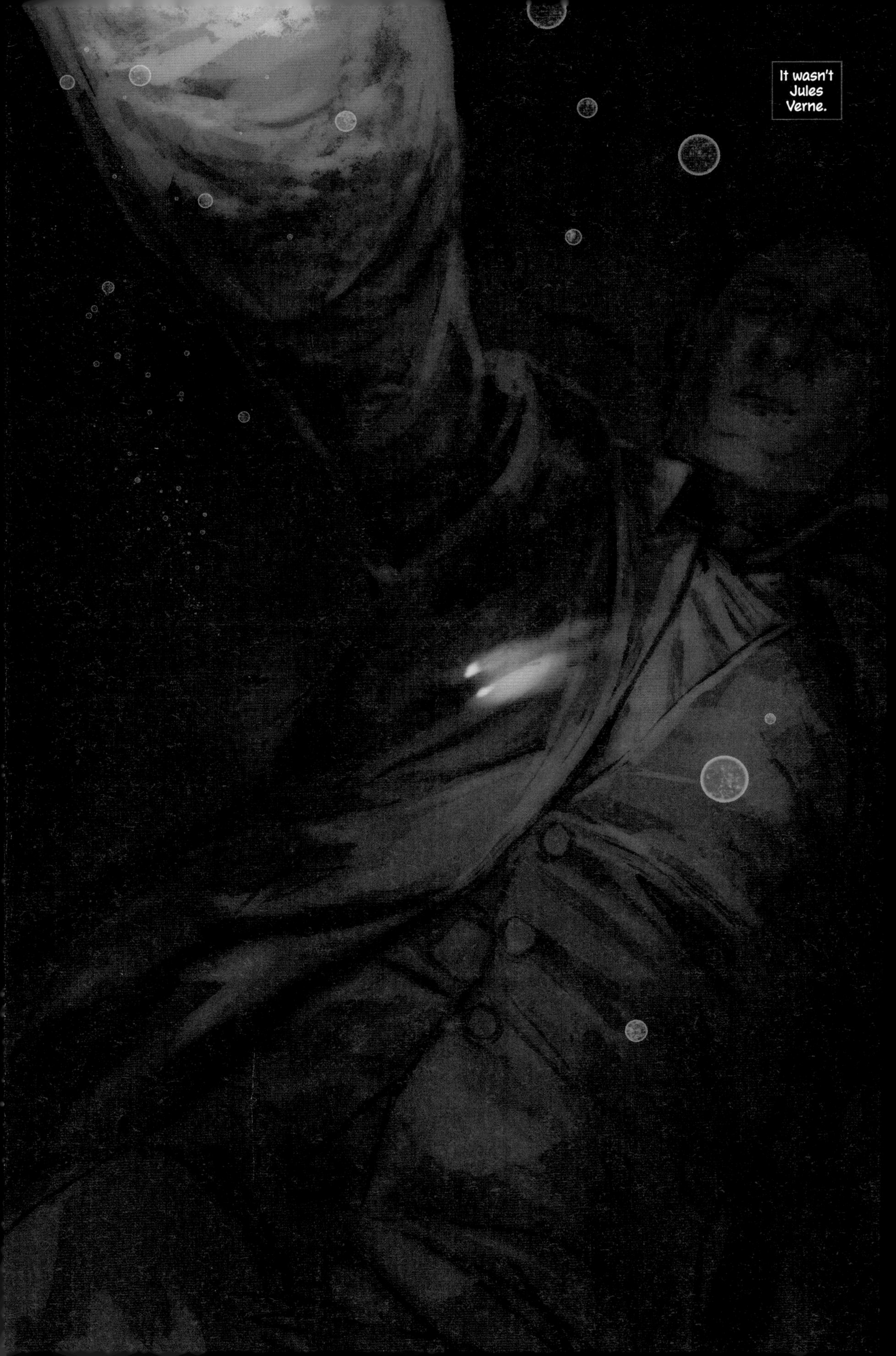
It wasn't Jules Verne.

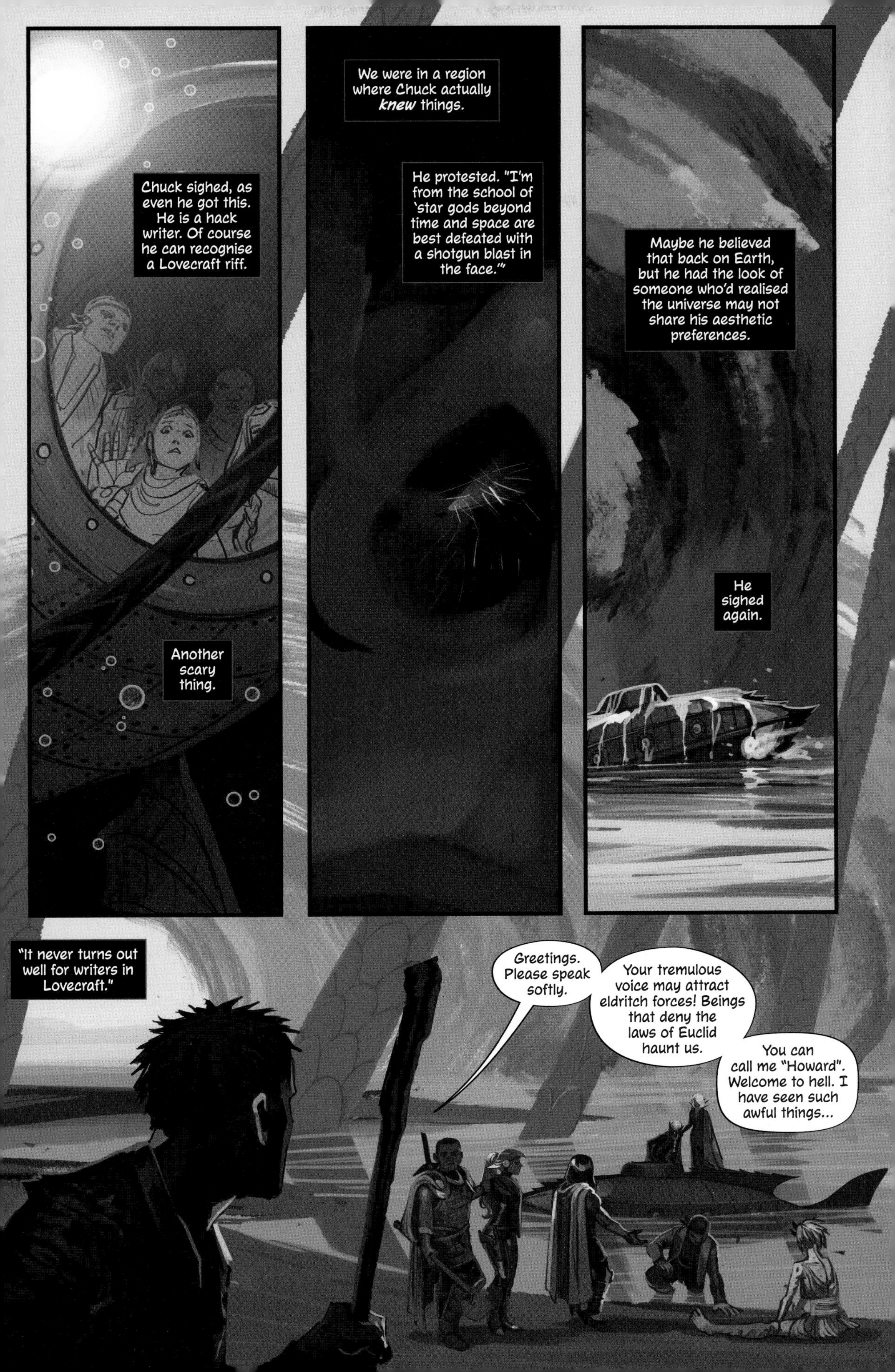
Chuck sighed, as even he got this. He is a hack writer. Of course he can recognise a Lovecraft riff.
Another scary thing.
We were in a region where Chuck actually *knew* things.
He protested. "I'm from the school of 'star gods beyond time and space are best defeated with a shotgun blast in the face.'"
Maybe he believed that back on Earth, but he had the look of someone who'd realised the universe may not share his aesthetic preferences.
He sighed again.
"It never turns out well for writers in Lovecraft."
Greetings. Please speak softly.
Your tremulous voice may attract eldritch forces! Beings that deny the laws of Euclid haunt us.
You can call me "Howard". Welcome to hell. I have seen such awful things...

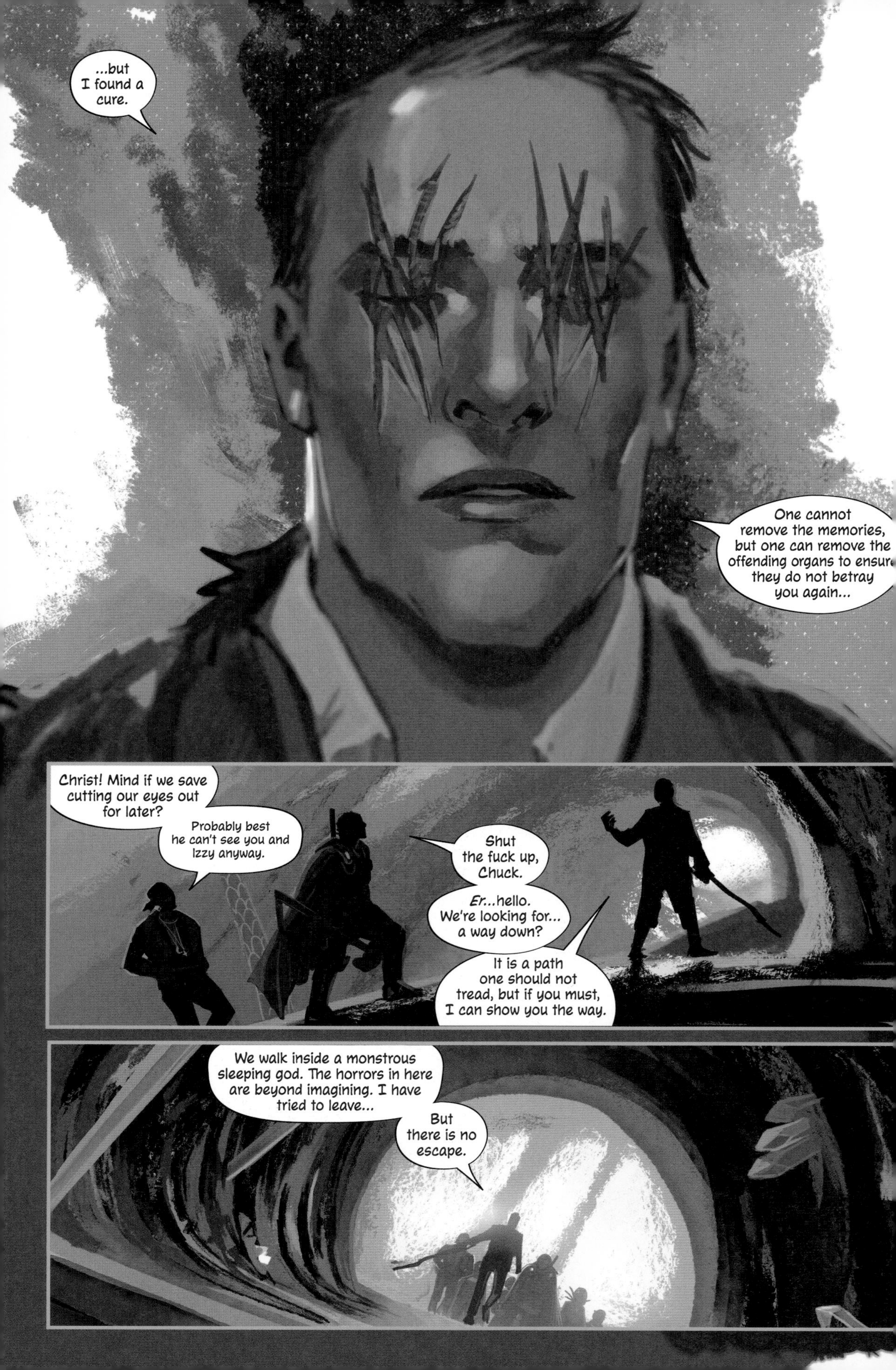
...but I found a cure.
One cannot remove the memories, but one can remove the offending organs to ensure they do not betray you again...
Christ! Mind if we save cutting our eyes out for later?
Probably best he can't see you and Izzy anyway.
Shut the fuck up, Chuck.
Er...hello. We're looking for... a way down?
It is a path one should not tread, but if you must, I can show you the way.
We walk inside a monstrous sleeping god. The horrors in here are beyond imagining. I have tried to leave...
But there is no escape.

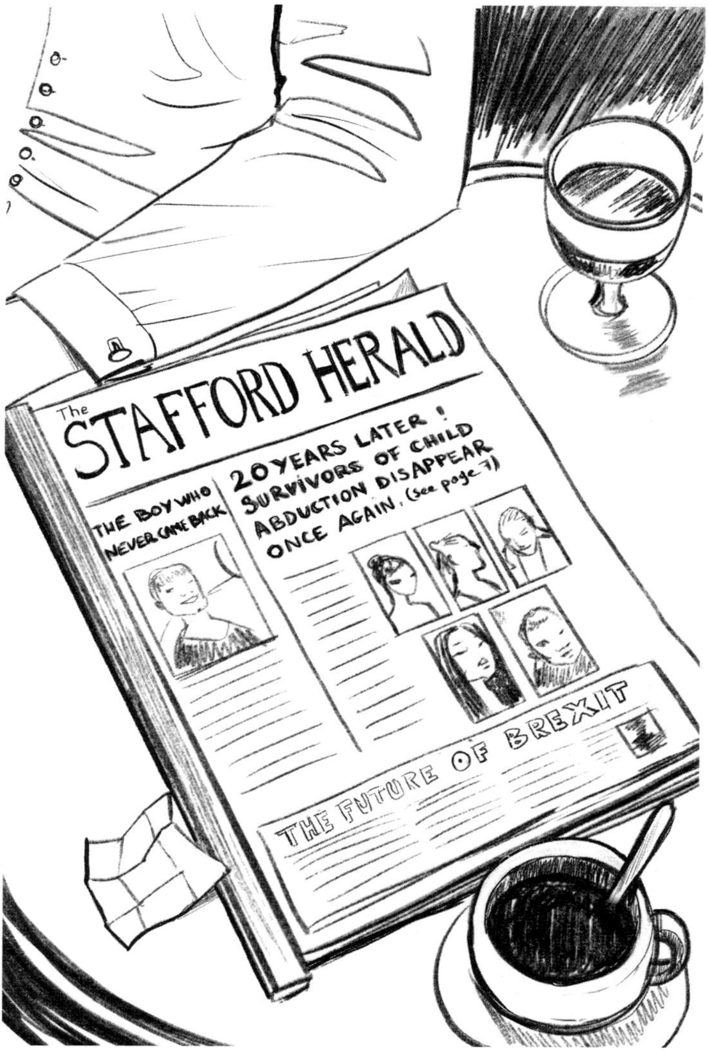
The STAFFORD HERALD
20 YEARS LATER! SURVIVORS OF CHILD ABDUCTION DISAPPEAR ONCE AGAIN. (See page 7)
THE BOY WHO NEVER CAME BACK
THE FUTURE OF BREXIT

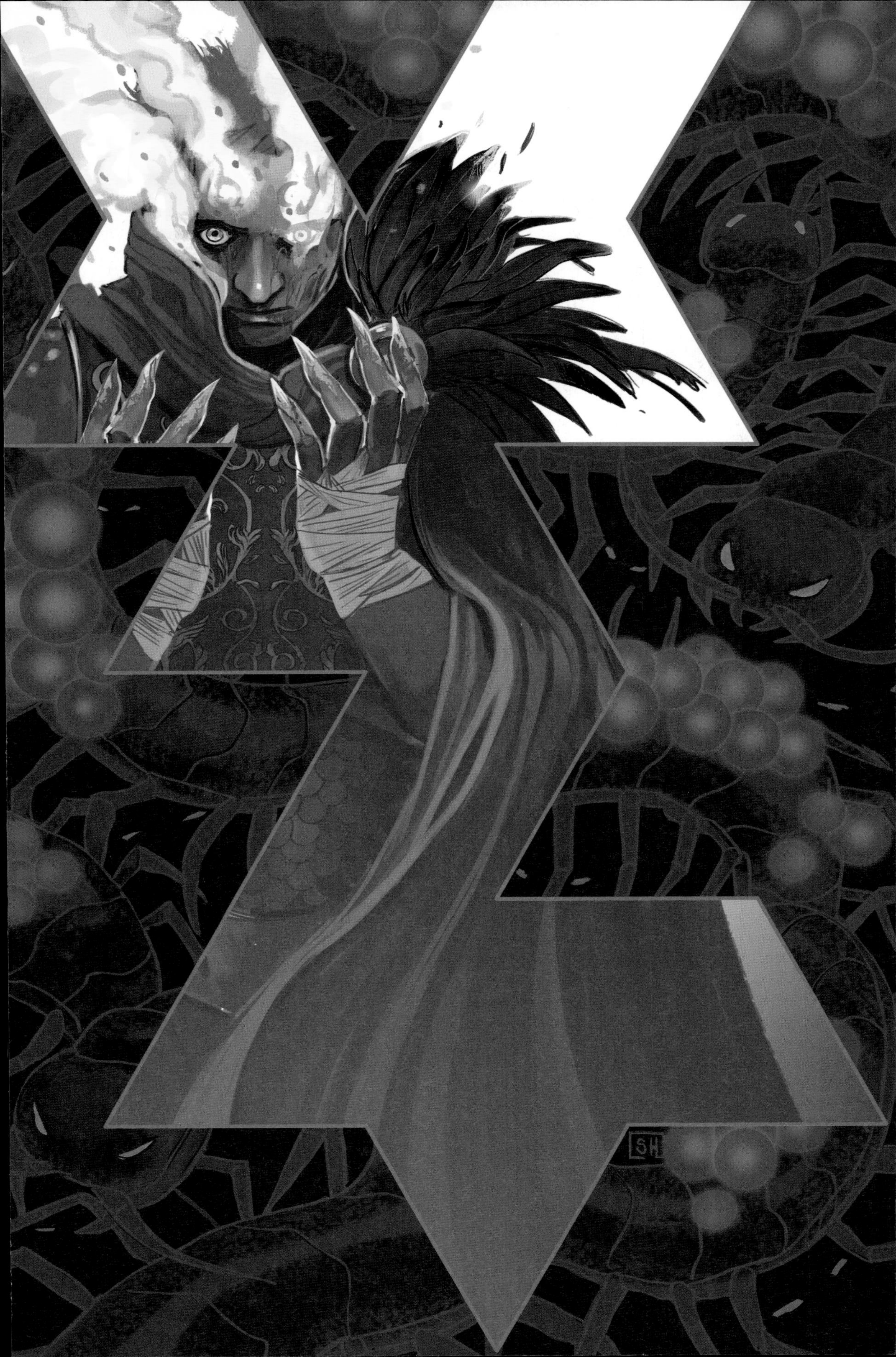

17:
TOTAL
PARTY KILL

"I wonder, though, if I have a right to claim authorship of things I dream? I hate to take credit, when I did not really think out the picture with my own conscious wits. Yet if I do not take credit, who'n Heaven will I give credit tuh?"
– *HP Lovecraft*

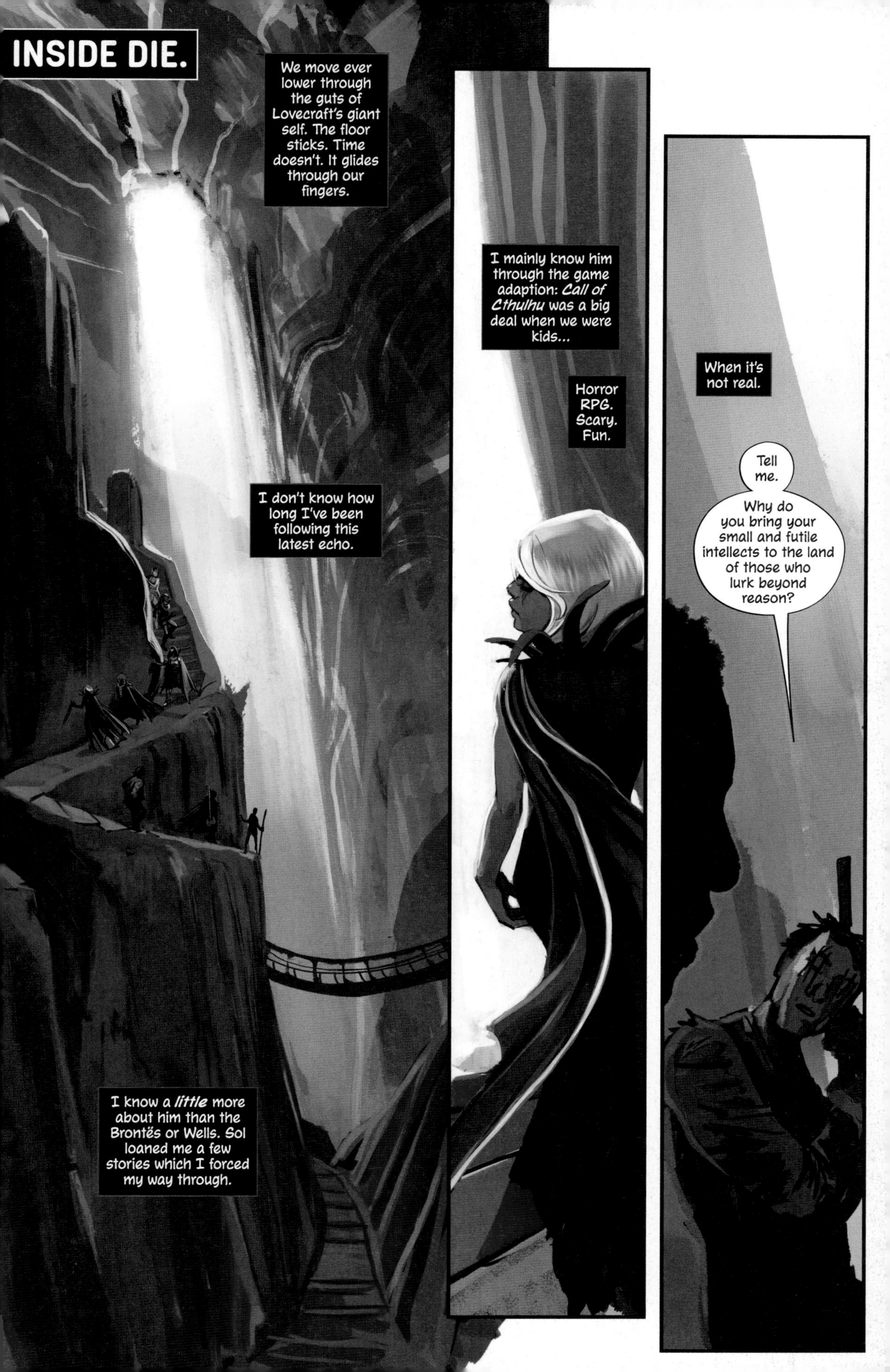

INSIDE DIE.
We move ever lower through the guts of Lovecraft's giant self. The floor sticks. Time doesn't. It glides through our fingers.
I don't know how long I've been following this latest echo.
I know a *little* more about him than the Brontës or Wells. Sol loaned me a few stories which I forced my way through.
I mainly know him through the game adaption: *Call of Cthulhu* was a big deal when we were kids...
Horror RPG. Scary. Fun.
When it's not real.
Tell me.
Why do you bring your small and futile intellects to the land of those who lurk beyond reason?

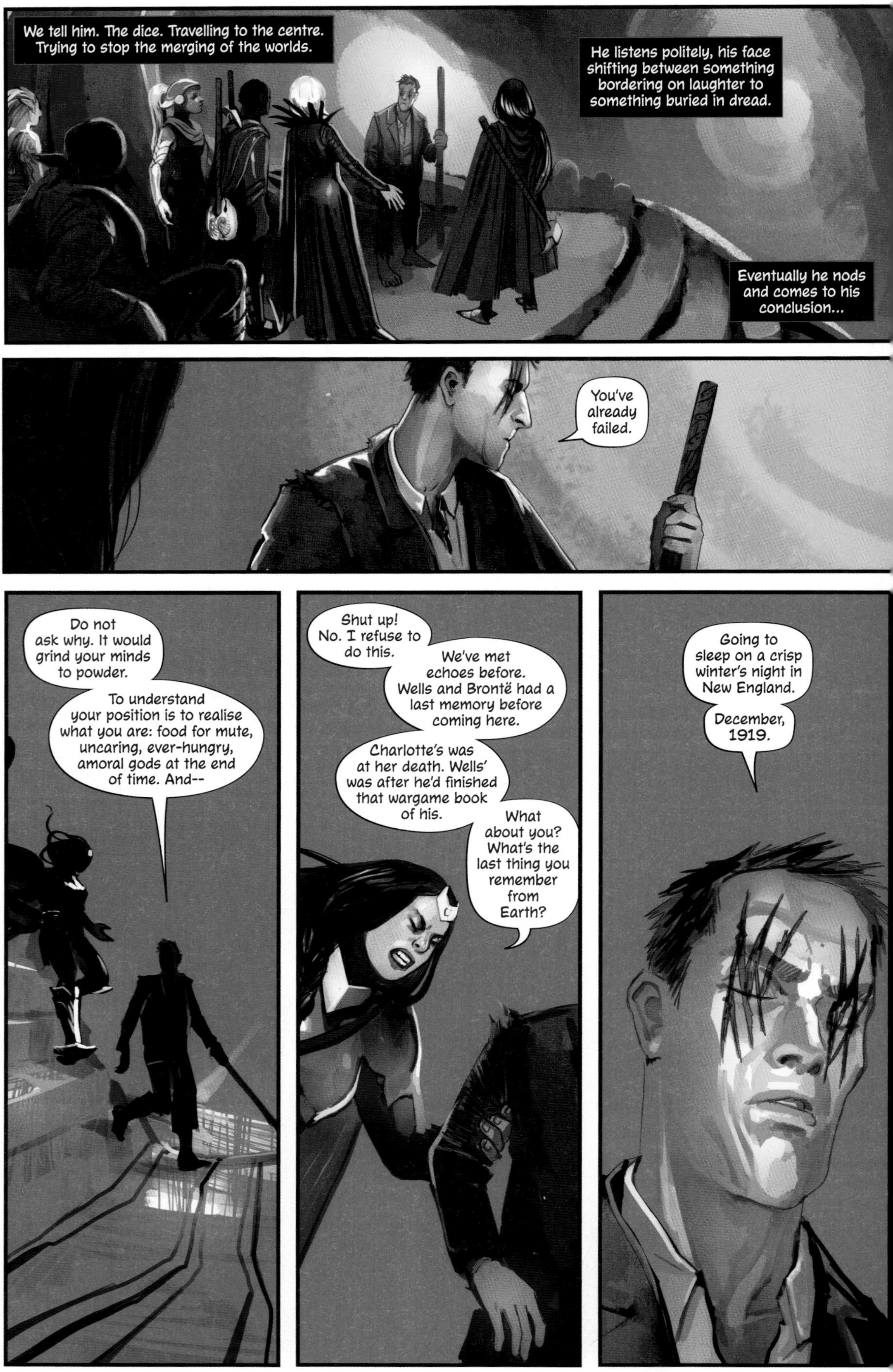
We tell him. The dice. Travelling to the centre. Trying to stop the merging of the worlds.
He listens politely, his face shifting between something bordering on laughter to something buried in dread.
Eventually he nods and comes to his conclusion...
You've already failed.
Do not ask why. It would grind your minds to powder.
To understand your position is to realise what you are: food for mute, uncaring, ever-hungry, amoral gods at the end of time. And--
Shut up! No. I refuse to do this.
We've met echoes before. Wells and Brontë had a last memory before coming here.
Charlotte's was at her death. Wells' was after he'd finished that wargame book of his.
What about you? What's the last thing you remember from Earth?
Going to sleep on a crisp winter's night in New England.
December, 1919.

Young. Before he had any real credits. Certainly well before anything in *Weird Tales*.

Some of the early short stories though? Maybe one of the Randolph Carter stories? That was his self-insert, right? Went to sleep and then went to a...land...of...dreams.

Oh.

The fear intensifies.

Chuck knows at least as much as Sol.

You read Lovecraft enough to know that?

Hell, forget "read enough Lovecraft". You *read*?

I always saw you as more of a Garth Marenghi *"I'm one of the few writers who've written more books than he's read"* sorts.

Hey, as I like to say, we're all one bad day away from being Garth Marenghi.

Don't get distracted, everyone.

So these dreams...they seem important to you...?

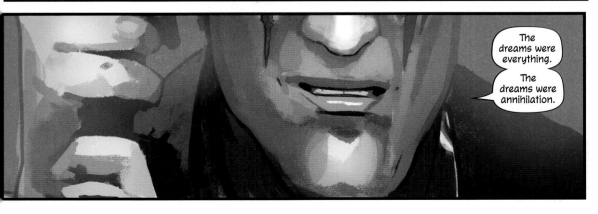

The dreams were everything.

The dreams were annihilation.

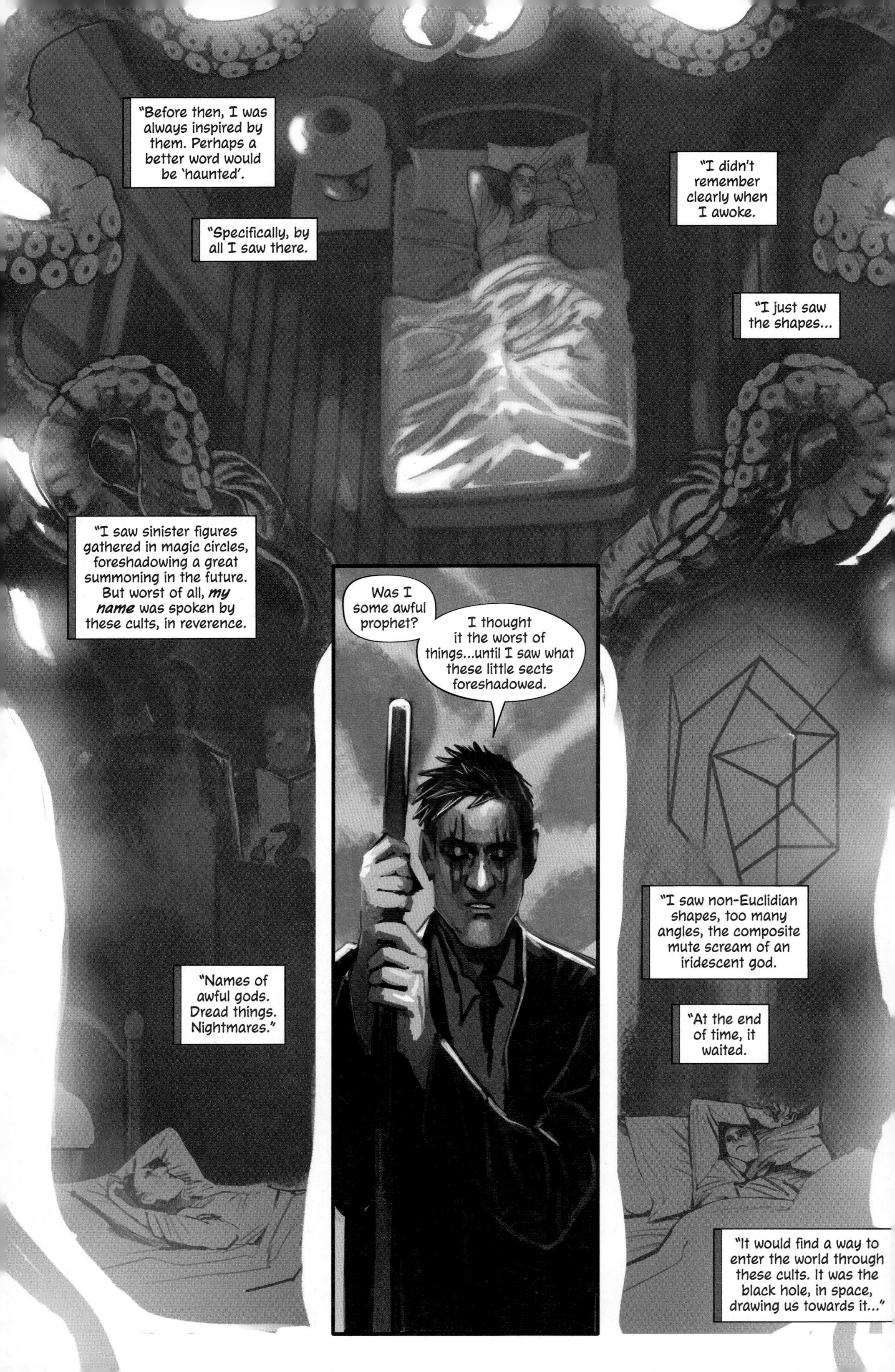

"Before then, I was always inspired by them. Perhaps a better word would be 'haunted'.
"Specifically, by all I saw there.
"I didn't remember clearly when I awoke.
"I just saw the shapes...
"I saw sinister figures gathered in magic circles, foreshadowing a great summoning in the future. But worst of all, *my name* was spoken by these cults, in reverence.
Was I some awful prophet?
I thought it the worst of things...until I saw what these little sects foreshadowed.
"I saw non-Euclidian shapes, too many angles, the composite mute scream of an iridescent god.
"Names of awful gods. Dread things. Nightmares."
"At the end of time, it waited.
"It would find a way to enter the world through these cults. It was the black hole, in space, drawing us towards it..."

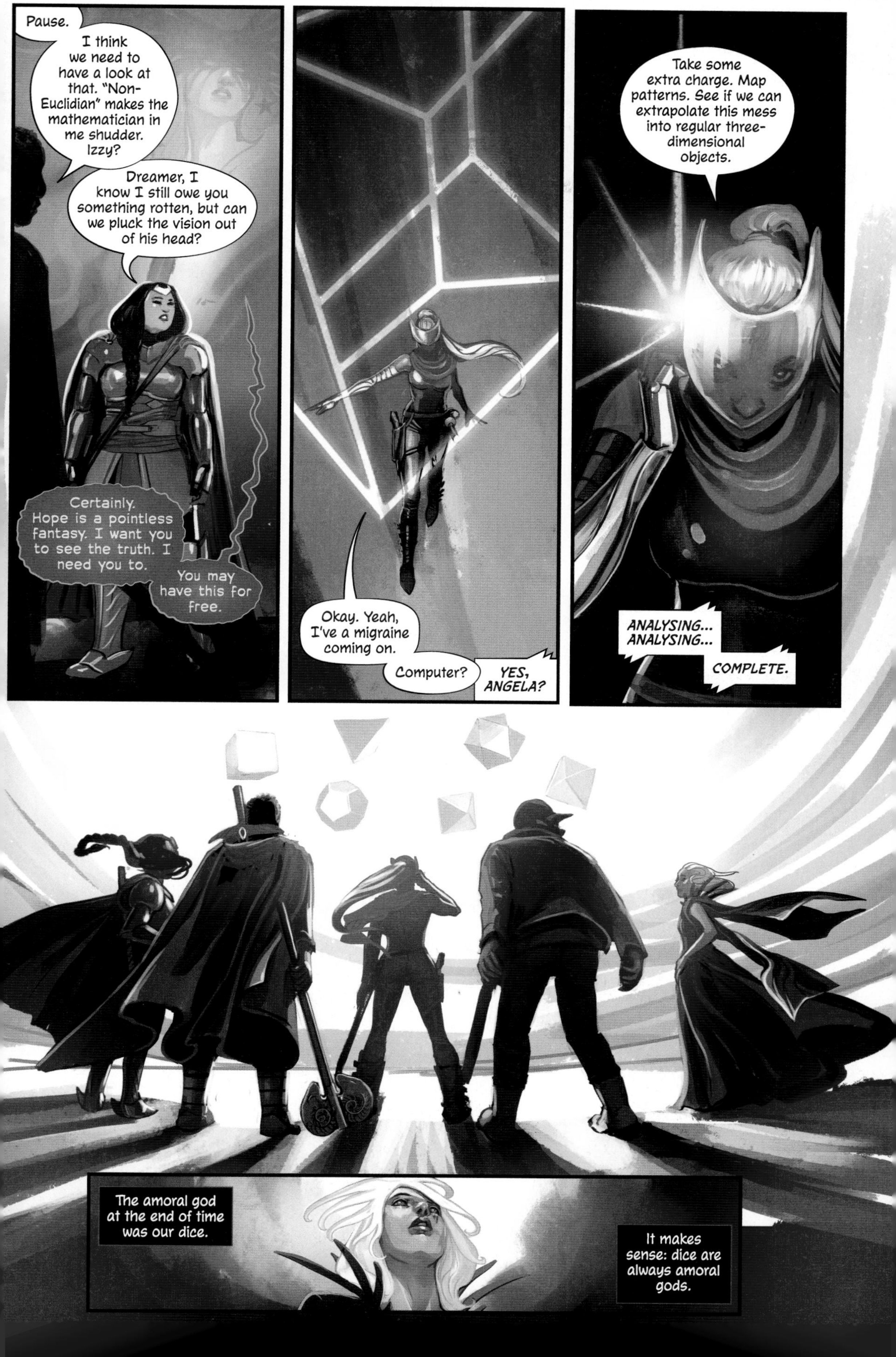
Pause.
I think we need to have a look at that. "Non-Euclidian" makes the mathematician in me shudder. Izzy?
Dreamer, I know I still owe you something rotten, but can we pluck the vision out of his head?
Certainly. Hope is a pointless fantasy. I want you to see the truth. I need you to.
You may have this for free.
Okay. Yeah, I've a migraine coming on.
Computer?
YES, ANGELA?
Take some extra charge. Map patterns. See if we can extrapolate this mess into regular three-dimensional objects.
ANALYSING... ANALYSING...
COMPLETE.
The amoral god at the end of time was our dice.
It makes sense: dice are always amoral gods.

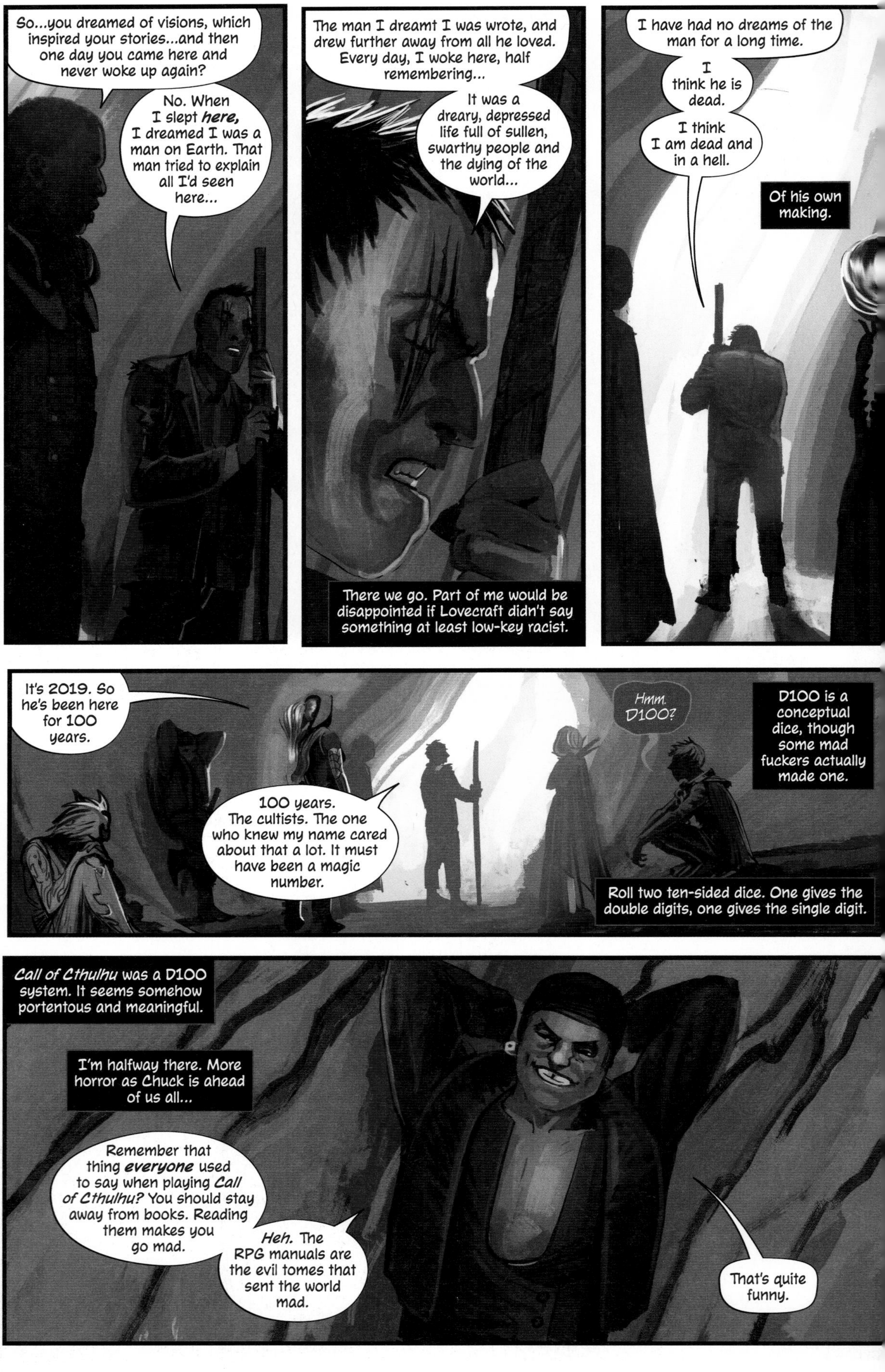
So...you dreamed of visions, which inspired your stories...and then one day you came here and never woke up again?
No. When I slept *here,* I dreamed I was a man on Earth. That man tried to explain all I'd seen here...
The man I dreamt I was wrote, and drew further away from all he loved. Every day, I woke here, half remembering...
It was a dreary, depressed life full of sullen, swarthy people and the dying of the world...
There we go. Part of me would be disappointed if Lovecraft didn't say something at least low-key racist.
I have had no dreams of the man for a long time.
I think he is dead.
I think I am dead and in a hell.
Of his own making.
It's 2019. So he's been here for 100 years.
100 years. The cultists. The one who knew my name cared about that a lot. It must have been a magic number.
Hmm. D100?
D100 is a conceptual dice, though some mad fuckers actually made one.
Roll two ten-sided dice. One gives the double digits, one gives the single digit.
Call of Cthulhu was a D100 system. It seems somehow portentous and meaningful.
I'm halfway there. More horror as Chuck is ahead of us all...
Remember that thing *everyone* used to say when playing *Call of Cthulhu?* You should stay away from books. Reading them makes you go mad.
Heh. The RPG manuals are the evil tomes that sent the world mad.
That's quite funny.

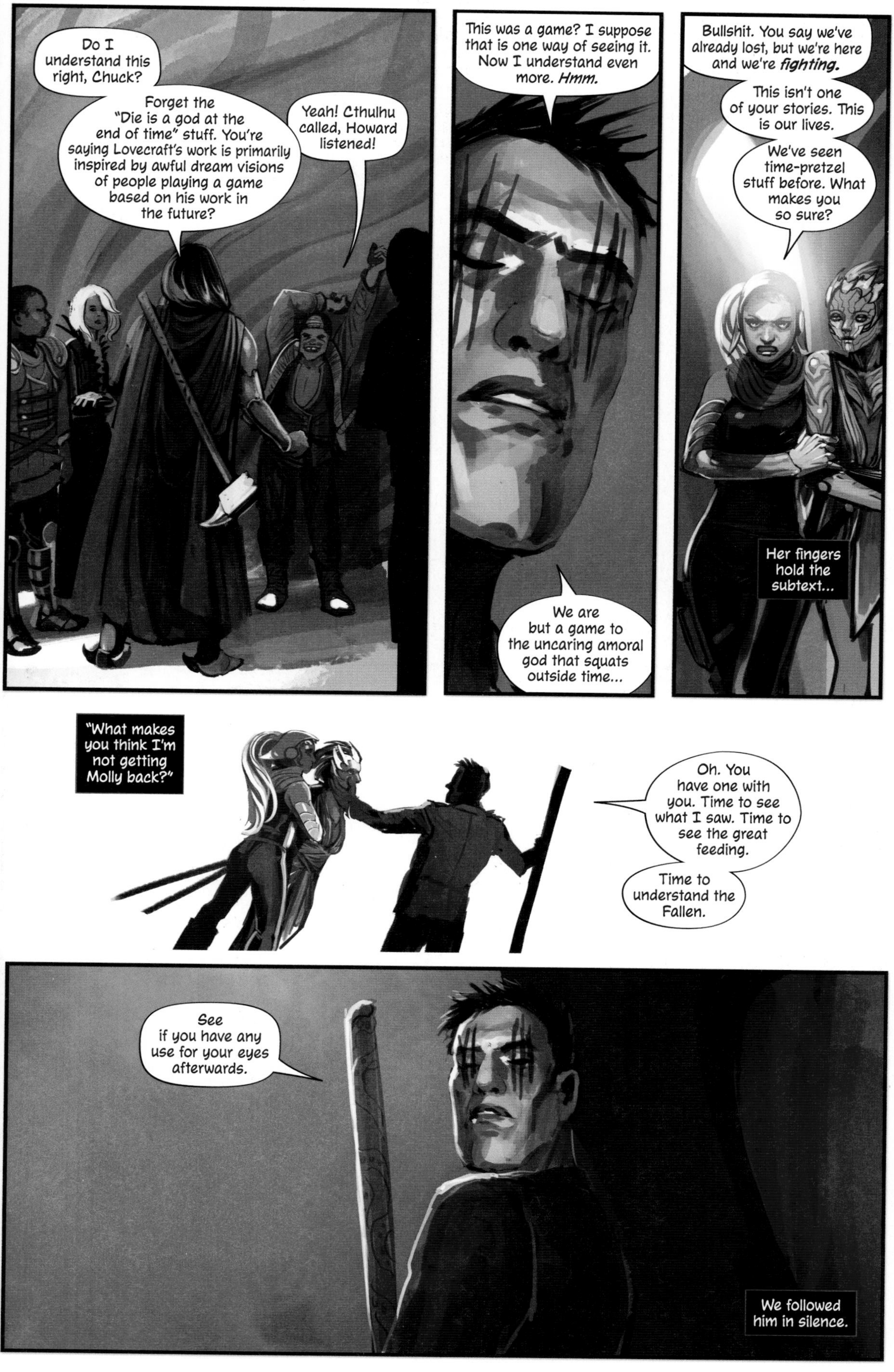

Do I understand this right, Chuck?
Forget the "Die is a god at the end of time" stuff. You're saying Lovecraft's work is primarily inspired by awful dream visions of people playing a game based on his work in the future?
Yeah! Cthulhu called, Howard listened!
This was a game? I suppose that is one way of seeing it. Now I understand even more. *Hmm.*
We are but a game to the uncaring amoral god that squats outside time...
Bullshit. You say we've already lost, but we're here and we're ***fighting.***
This isn't one of your stories. This is our lives.
We've seen time-pretzel stuff before. What makes you so sure?
Her fingers hold the subtext...
"What makes you think I'm not getting Molly back?"
Oh. You have one with you. Time to see what I saw. Time to see the great feeding.
Time to understand the Fallen.
See if you have any use for your eyes afterwards.
We followed him in silence.

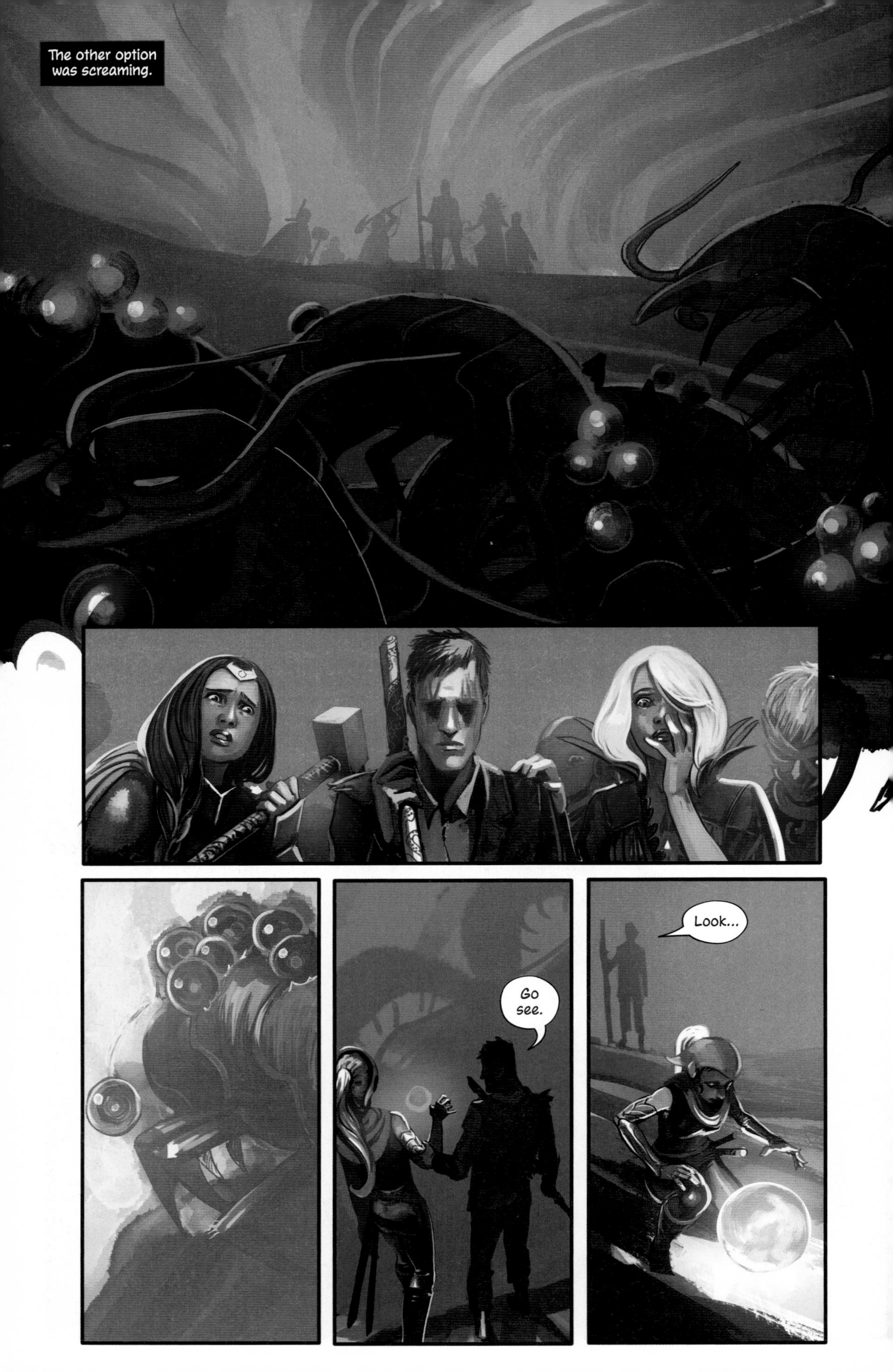
The other option
was screaming.
Go
see.
Look...

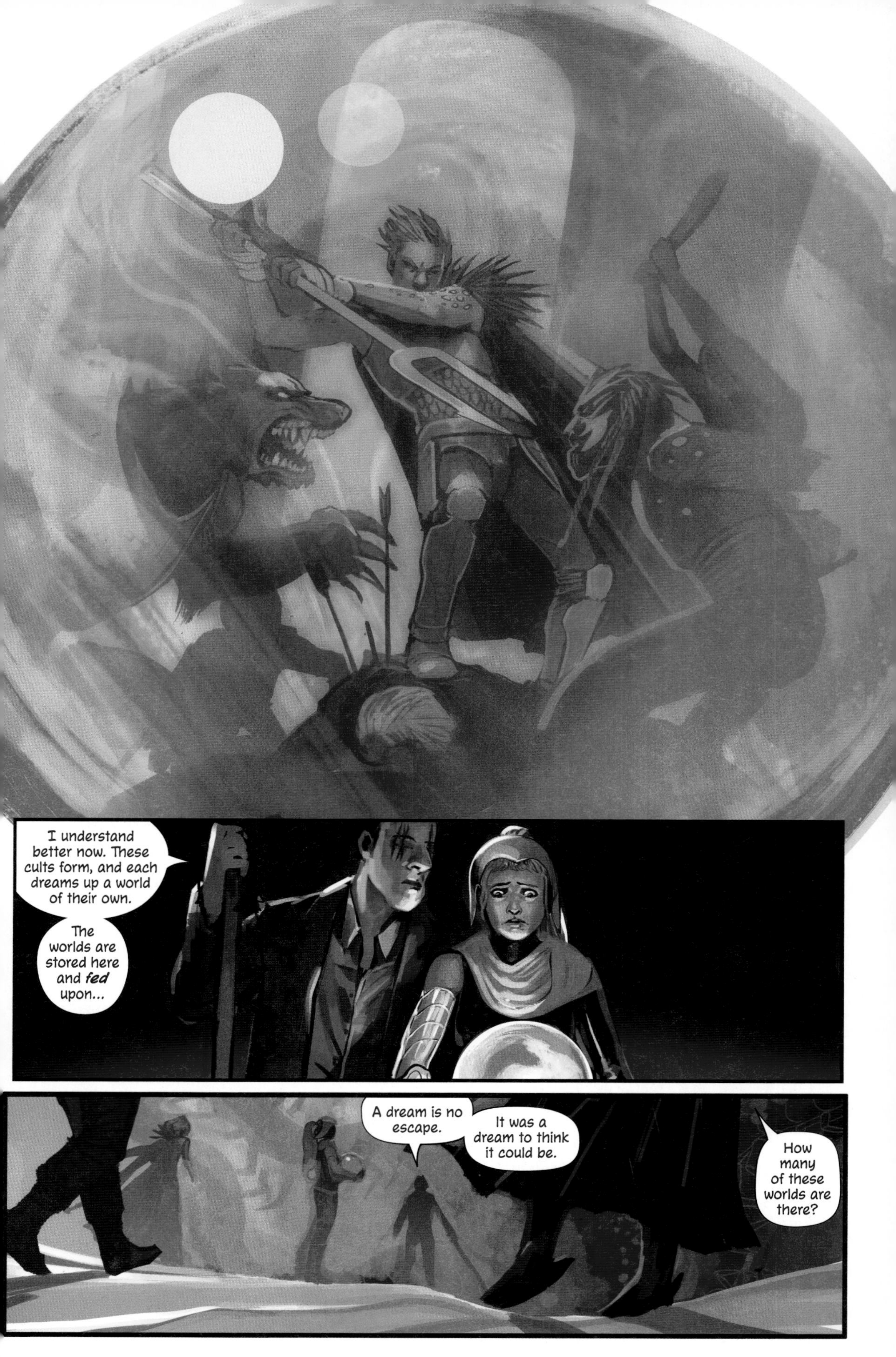
I understand better now. These cults form, and each dreams up a world of their own.
The worlds are stored here and *fed* upon...
A dream is no escape.
It was a dream to think it could be.
How many of these worlds are there?

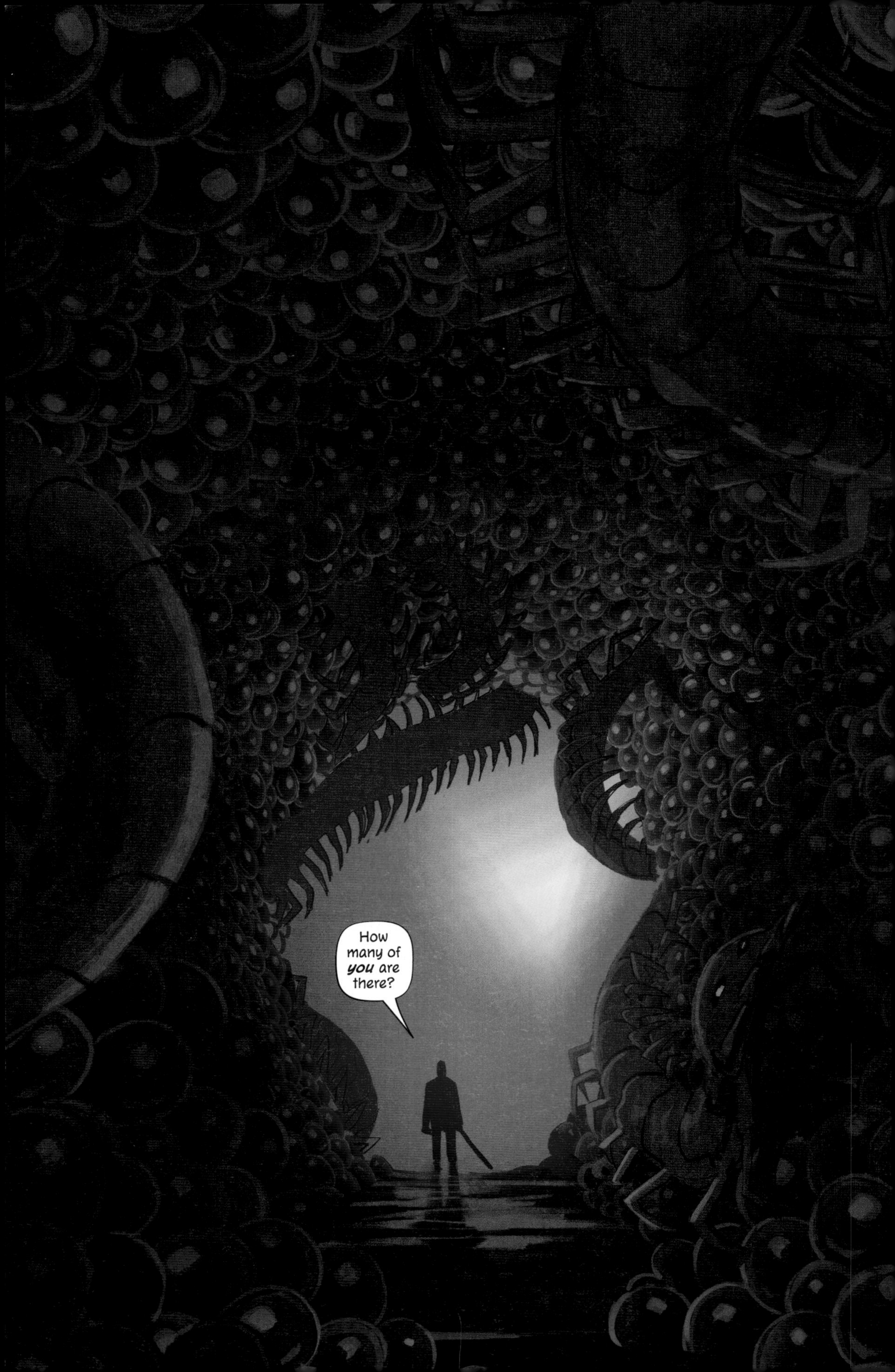
How many of *you* are there?

You were the first to come here, but you are far from the last. Die has a place for everyone.

That place is as an item on an obscene menu...

Look!

That guy...

...he just died.

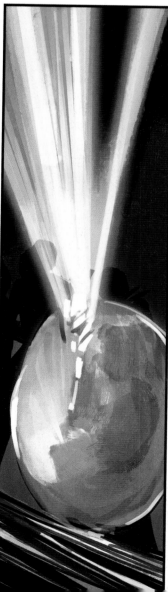

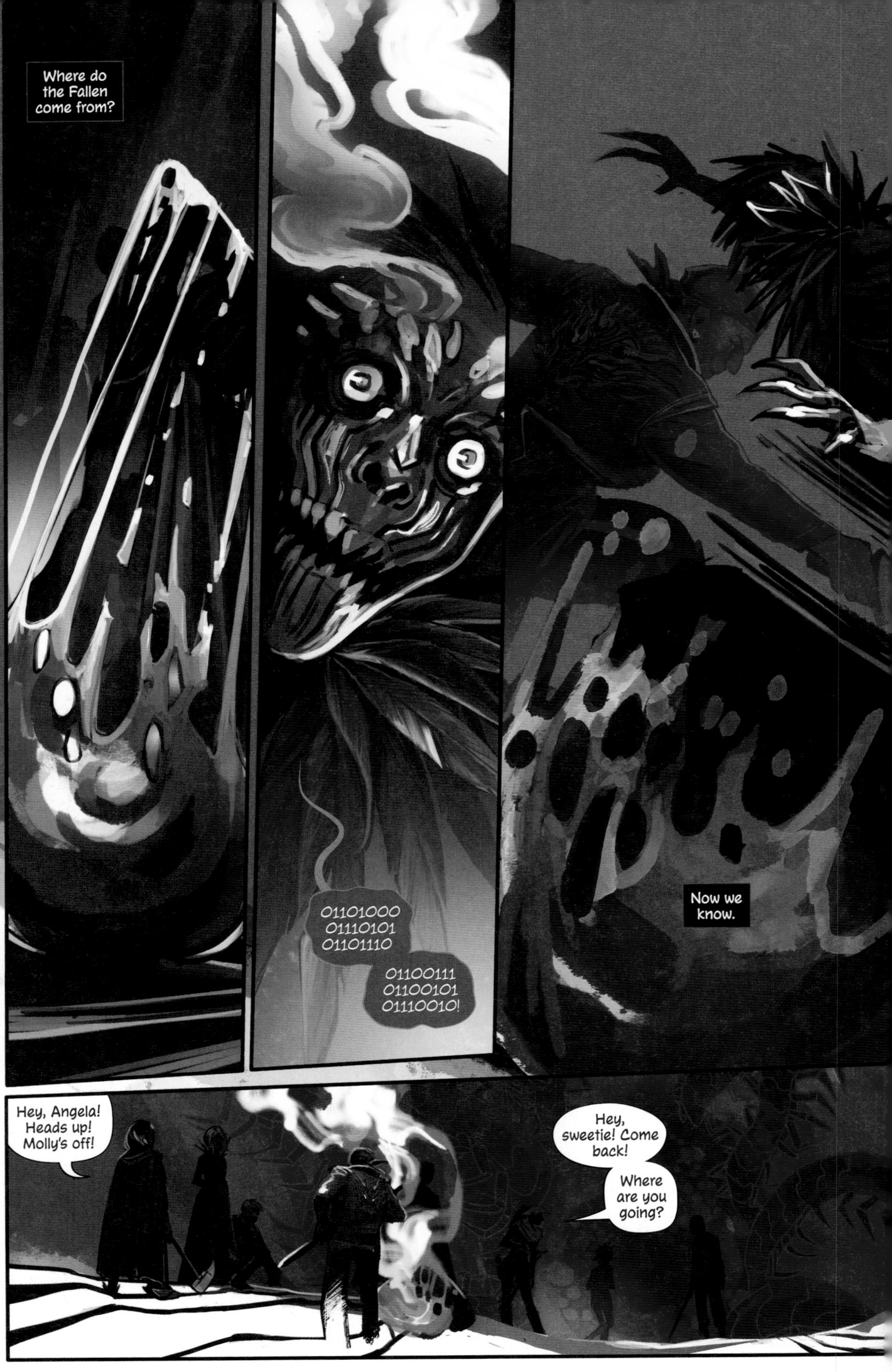
Where do the Fallen come from?
01101000 01110101 01101110
01100111 01100101 01110010!
Now we know.
Hey, Angela! Heads up! Molly's off!
Hey, sweetie! Come back!
Where are you going?

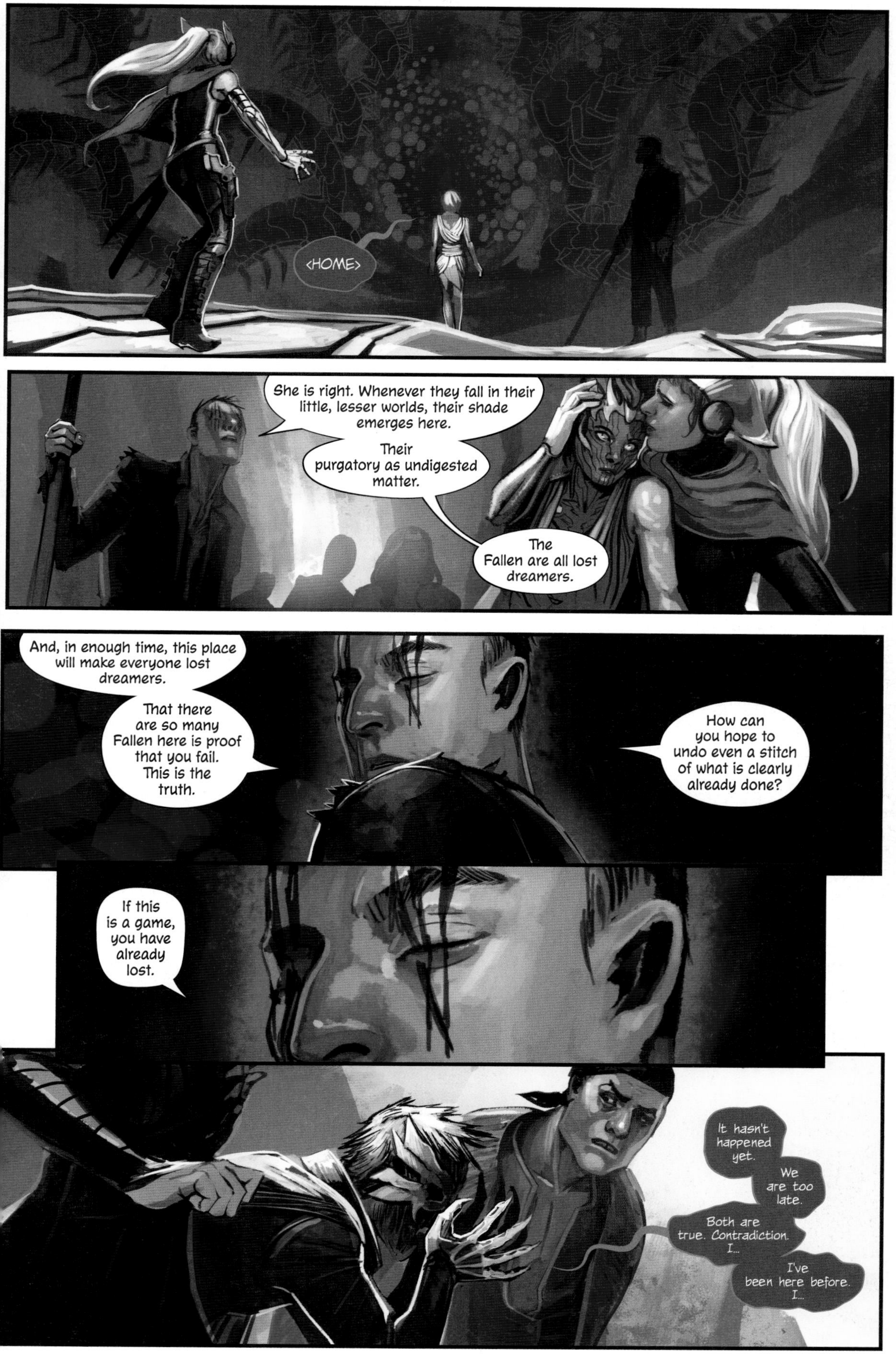

<HOME>
She is right. Whenever they fall in their little, lesser worlds, their shade emerges here.
Their purgatory as undigested matter.
The Fallen are all lost dreamers.
And, in enough time, this place will make everyone lost dreamers.
That there are so many Fallen here is proof that you fail. This is the truth.
How can you hope to undo even a stitch of what is clearly already done?
If this is a game, you have already lost.
It hasn't happened yet.
We are too late.
Both are true. Contradiction. I...
I've been here before. I...

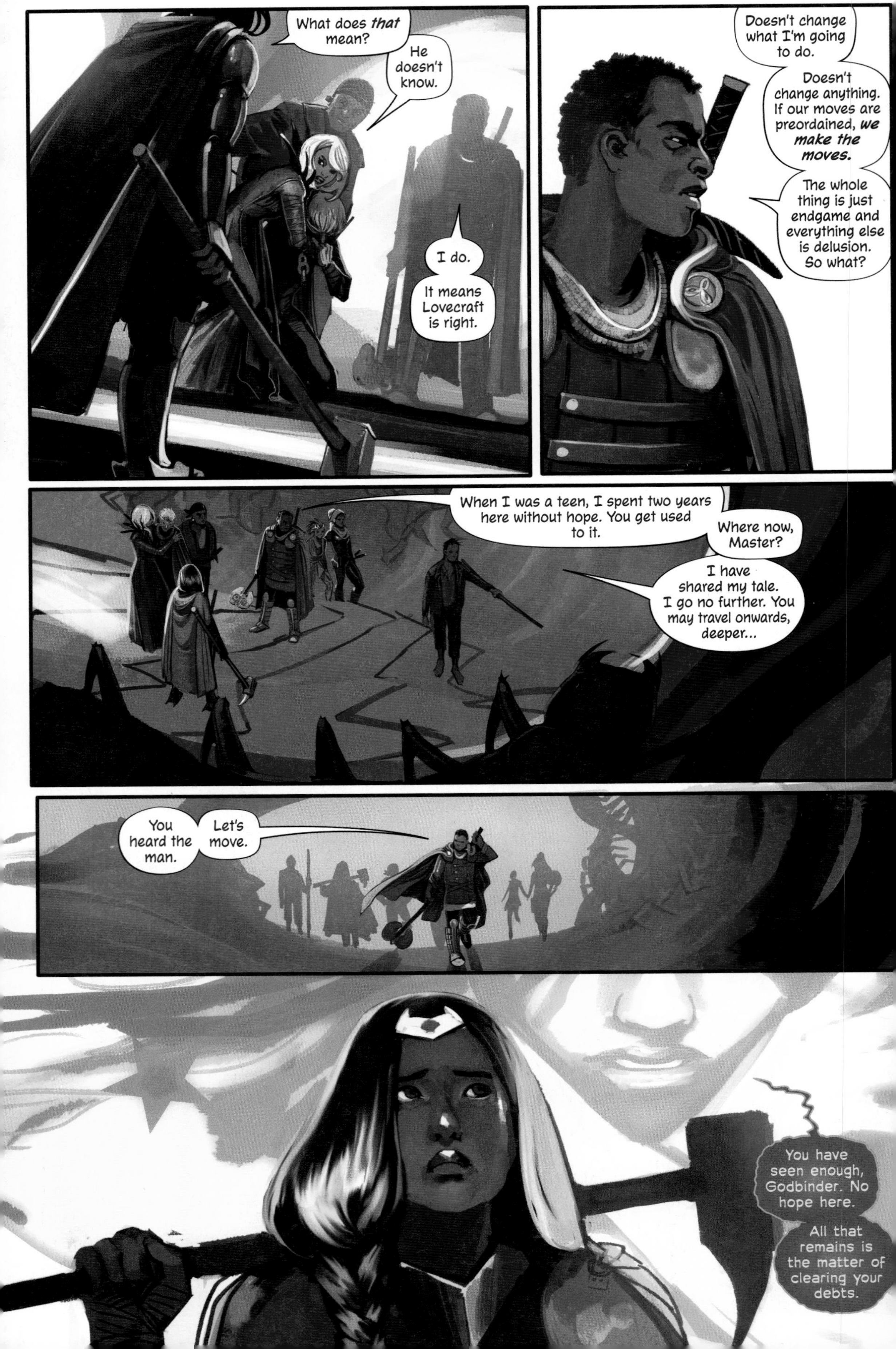
What does *that* mean?
He doesn't know.
I do.
It means Lovecraft is right.
Doesn't change what I'm going to do.
Doesn't change anything. If our moves are preordained, ***we make the moves.***
The whole thing is just endgame and everything else is delusion. So what?
When I was a teen, I spent two years here without hope. You get used to it.
Where now, Master?
I have shared my tale. I go no further. You may travel onwards, deeper...
You heard the man.
Let's move.
You have seen enough, Godbinder. No hope here.
All that remains is the matter of clearing your debts.

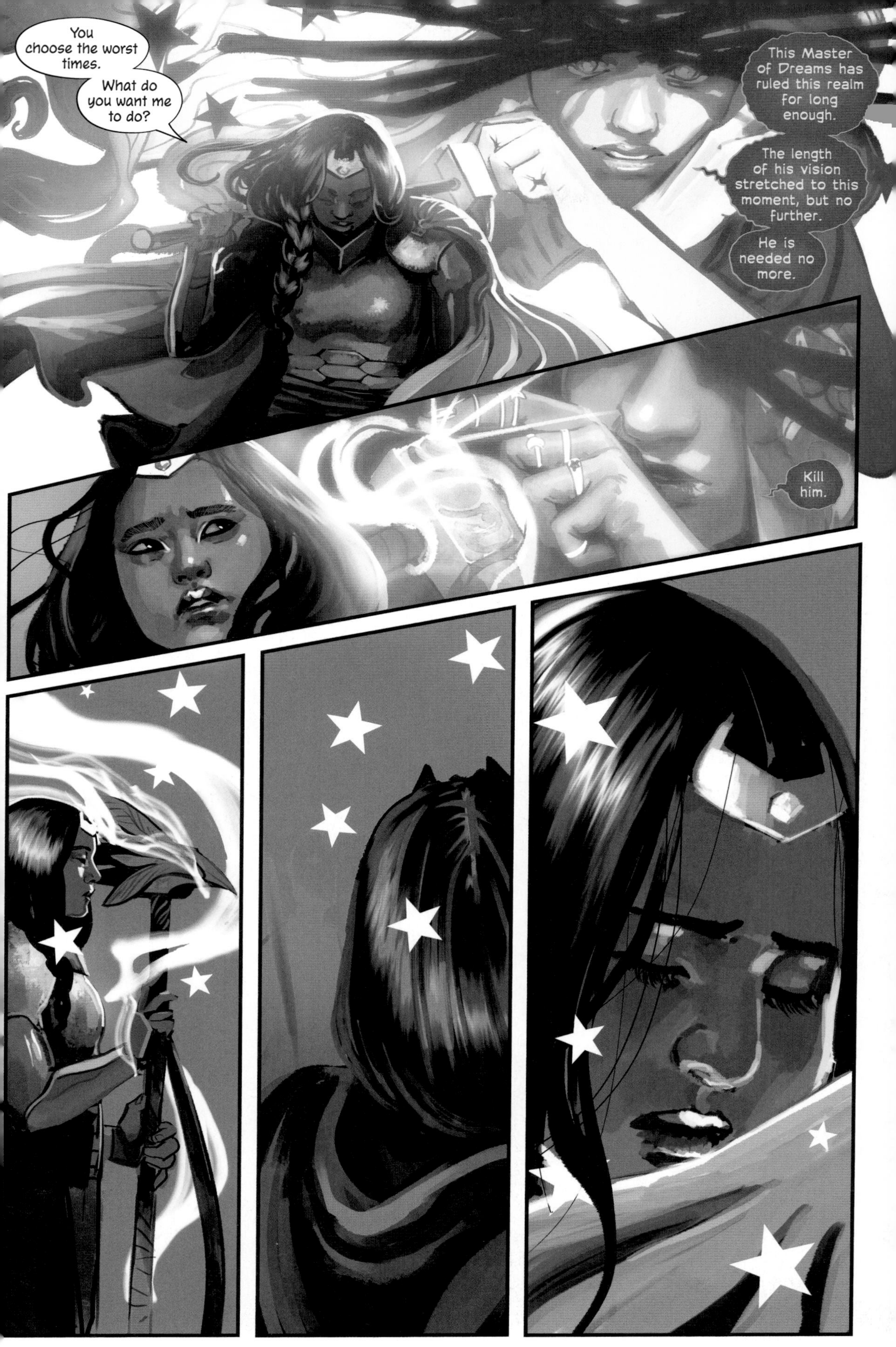
You choose the worst times.
What do you want me to do?
This Master of Dreams has ruled this realm for long enough.
The length of his vision stretched to this moment, but no further.
He is needed no more.
Kill him.

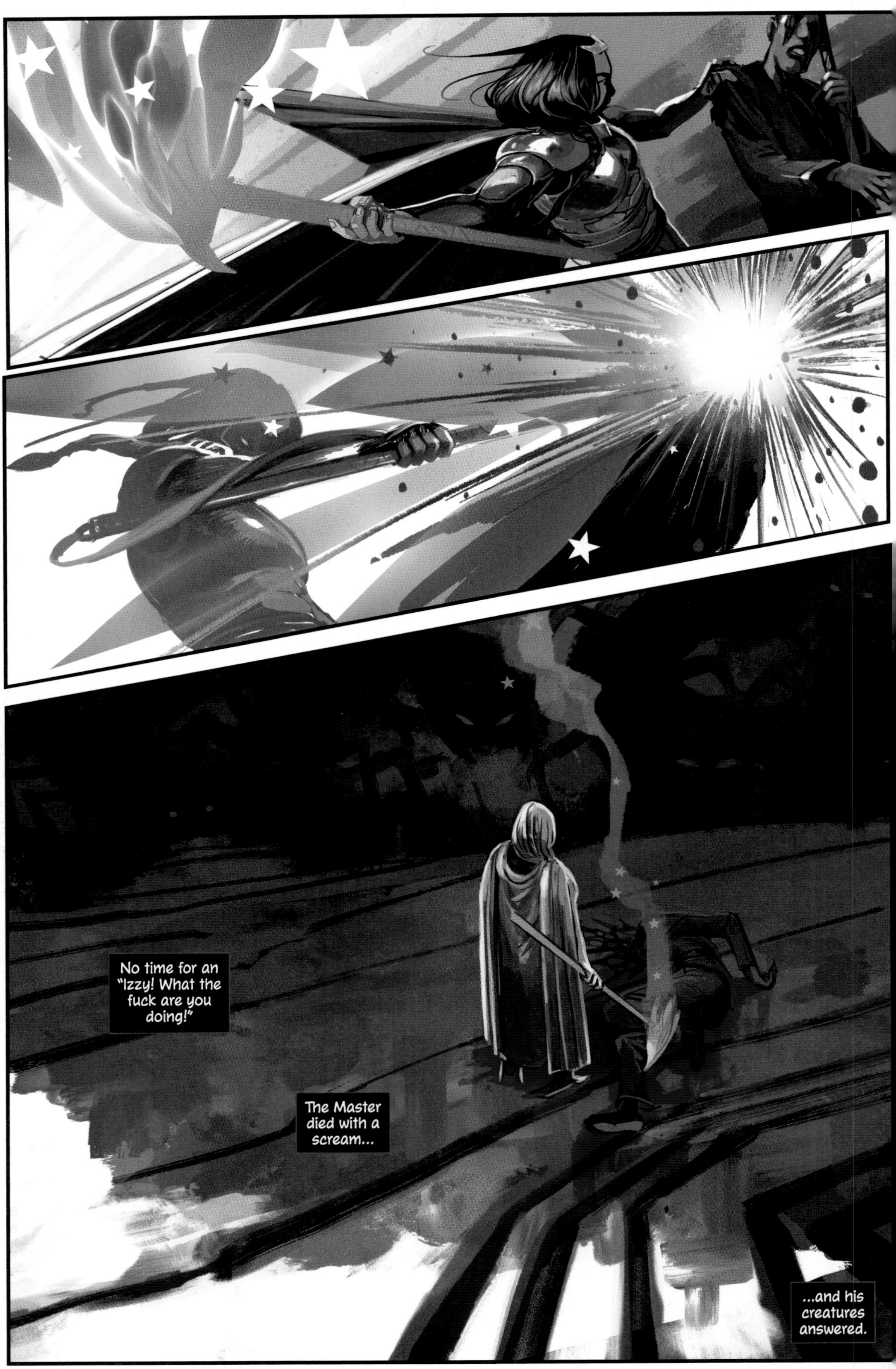
No time for an "Izzy! What the fuck are you doing!"
The Master died with a scream...
...and his creatures answered.

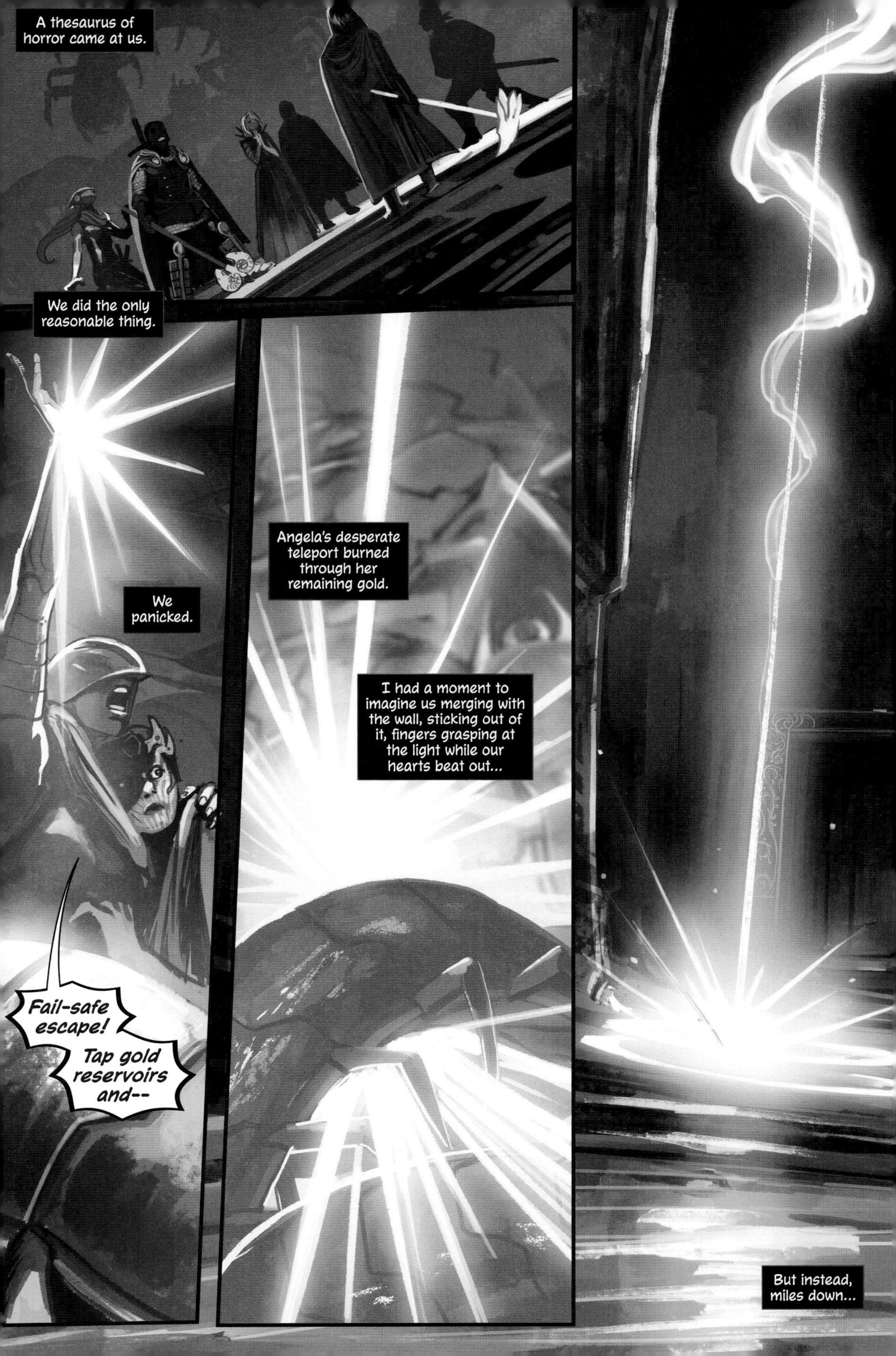
A thesaurus of horror came at us.
We did the only reasonable thing.
We panicked.
Fail-safe escape!
Tap gold reservoirs and--
Angela's desperate teleport burned through her remaining gold.
I had a moment to imagine us merging with the wall, sticking out of it, fingers grasping at the light while our hearts beat out...
But instead, miles down...

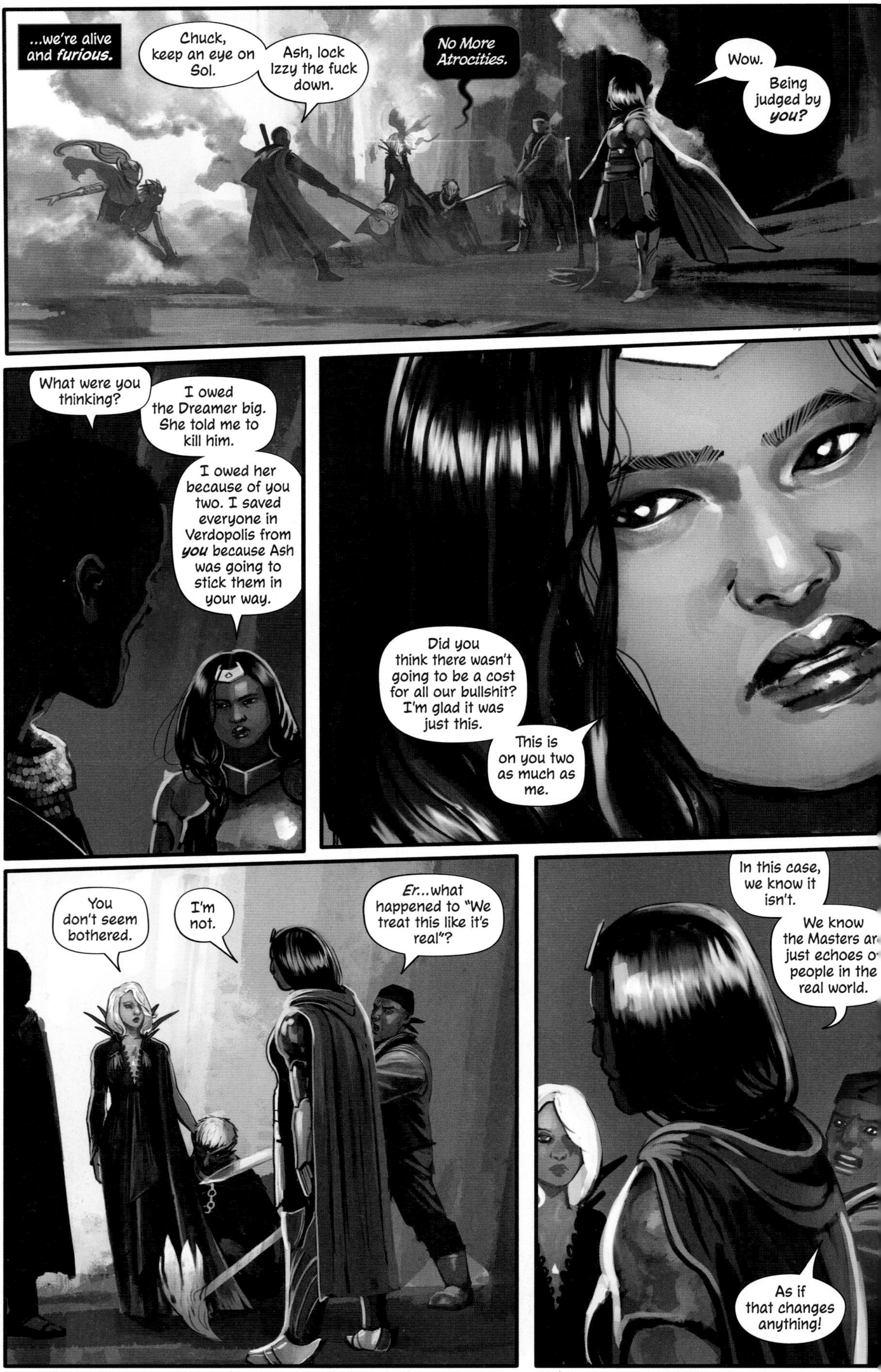
...we're alive and *furious.*
Chuck, keep an eye on Sol.
Ash, lock Izzy the fuck down.
No More Atrocities.
Wow.
Being judged by *you?*
What were you thinking?
I owed the Dreamer big. She told me to kill him.
I owed her because of you two. I saved everyone in Verdopolis from *you* because Ash was going to stick them in your way.
Did you think there wasn't going to be a cost for all our bullshit? I'm glad it was just this.
This is on you two as much as me.
You don't seem bothered.
I'm not.
*Er...*what happened to "We treat this like it's real"?
In this case, we know it isn't.
We know the Masters ar just echoes o people in the real world.
As if that changes anything!

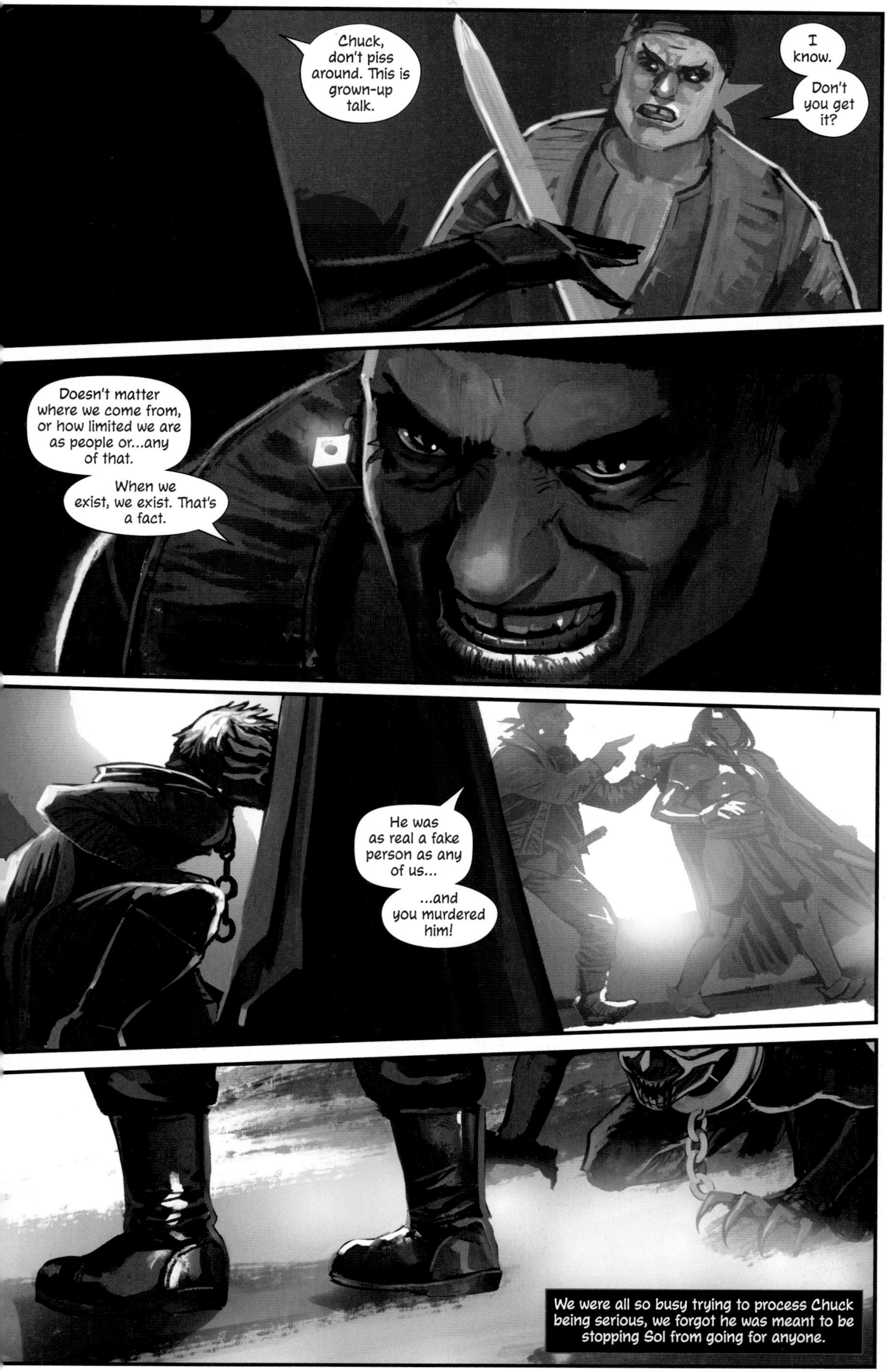
Chuck, don't piss around. This is grown-up talk.
I know.
Don't you get it?
Doesn't matter where we come from, or how limited we are as people or...any of that.
When we exist, we exist. That's a fact.
He was as real a fake person as any of us...
...and you murdered him!
We were all so busy trying to process Chuck being serious, we forgot he was meant to be stopping Sol from going for anyone.

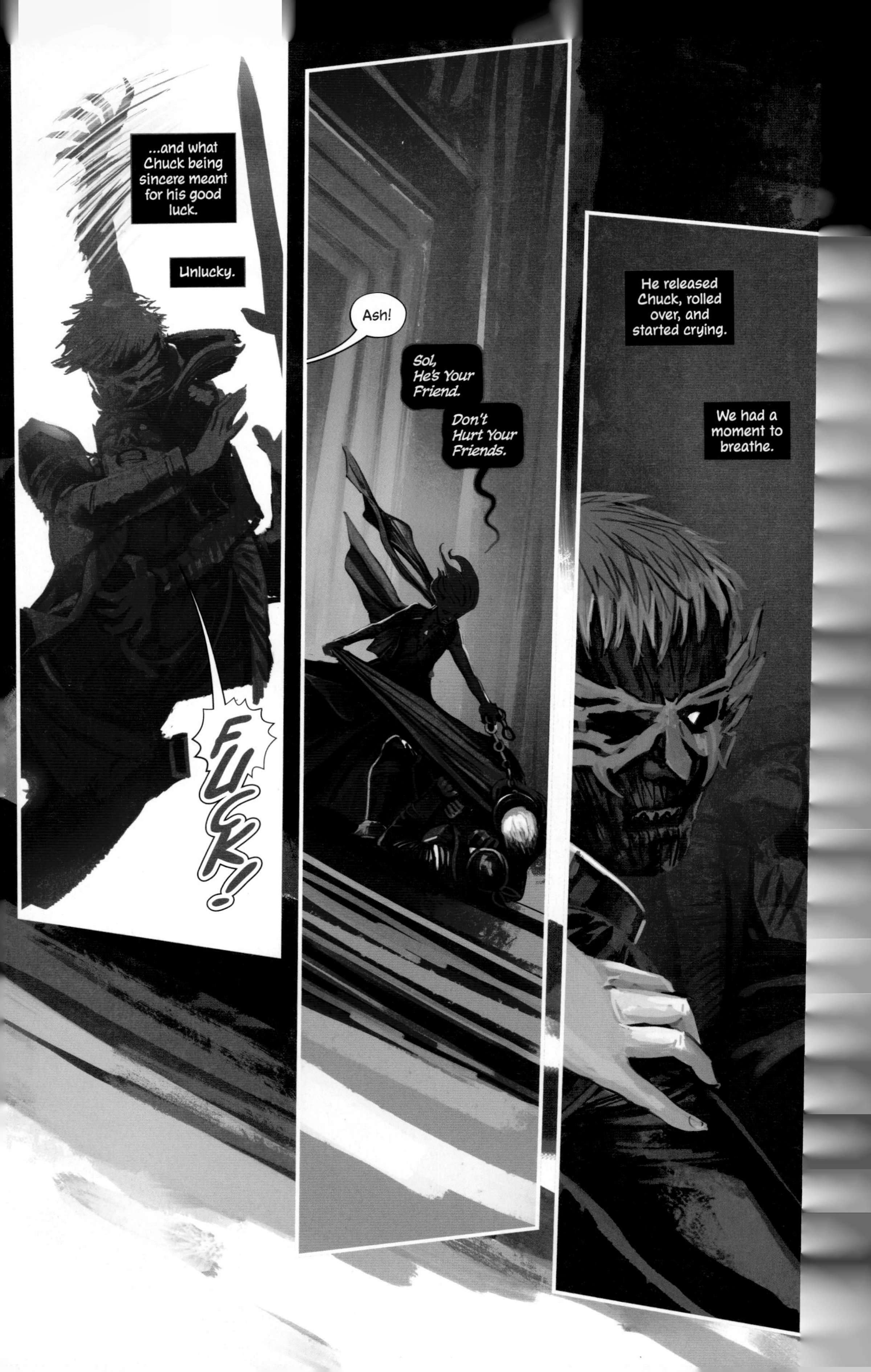
...and what Chuck being sincere meant for his good luck.
Unlucky.
FUCK!
Ash!
Sol, He's Your Friend.
Don't Hurt Your Friends.
He released Chuck, rolled over, and started crying.
We had a moment to breathe.

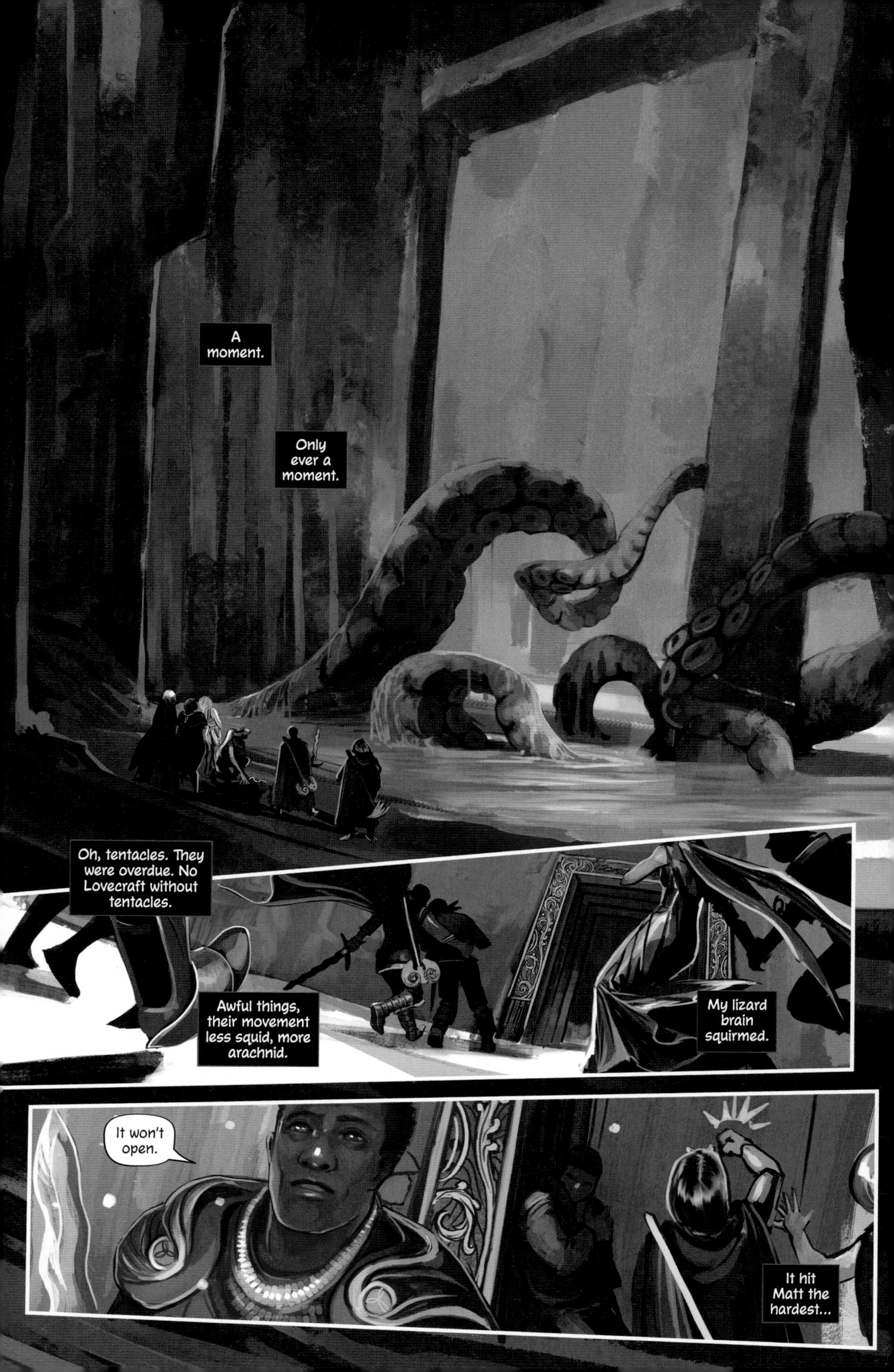
A moment.
Only ever a moment.
Oh, tentacles. They were overdue. No Lovecraft without tentacles.
Awful things, their movement less squid, more arachnid.
My lizard brain squirmed.
It won't open.
It hit Matt the hardest...

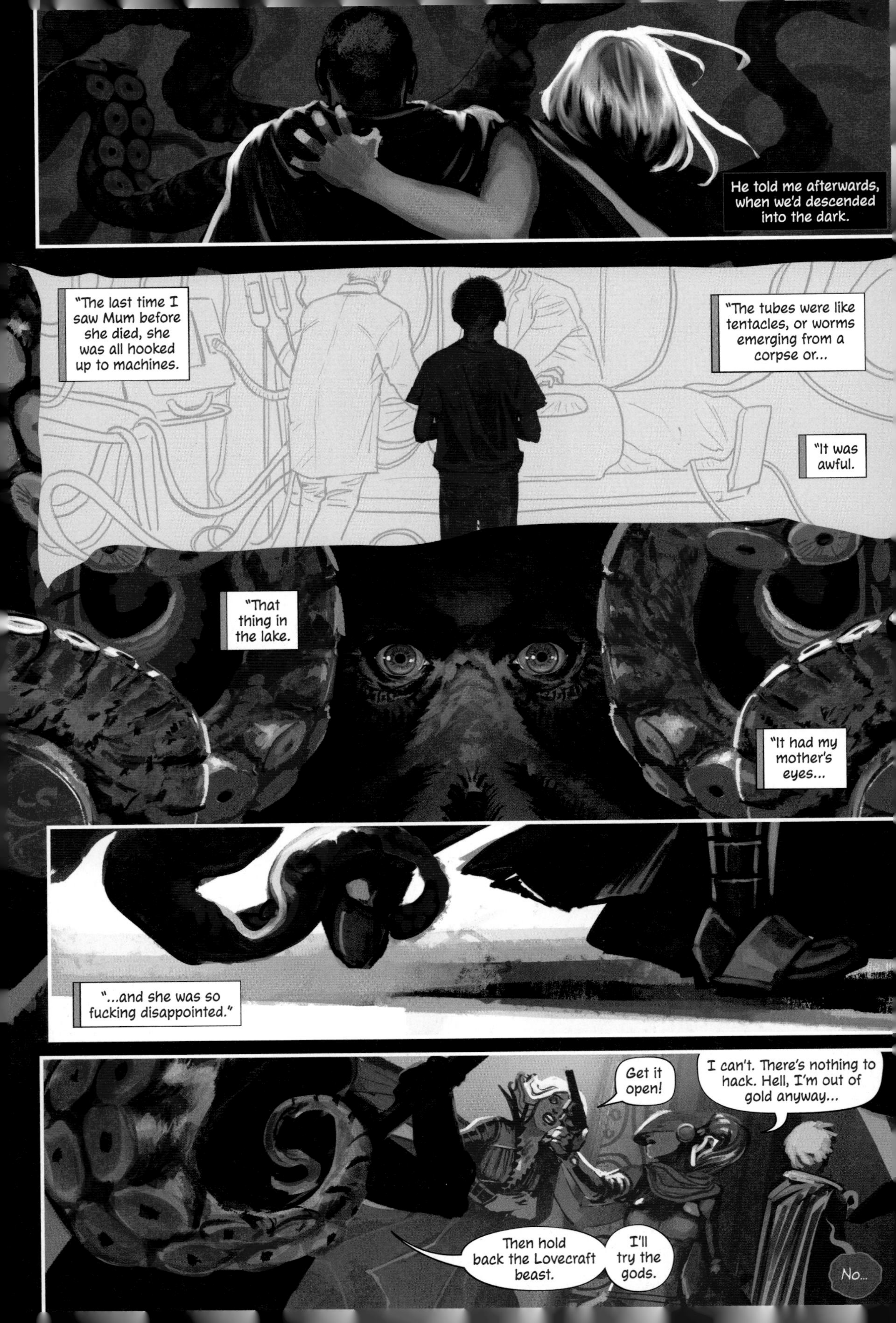
He told me afterwards, when we'd descended into the dark.
"The last time I saw Mum before she died, she was all hooked up to machines.
"The tubes were like tentacles, or worms emerging from a corpse or...
"It was awful.
"That thing in the lake.
"It had my mother's eyes...
"...and she was so fucking disappointed."
Get it open!
I can't. There's nothing to hack. Hell, I'm out of gold anyway...
Then hold back the Lovecraft beast.
I'll try the gods.
No...

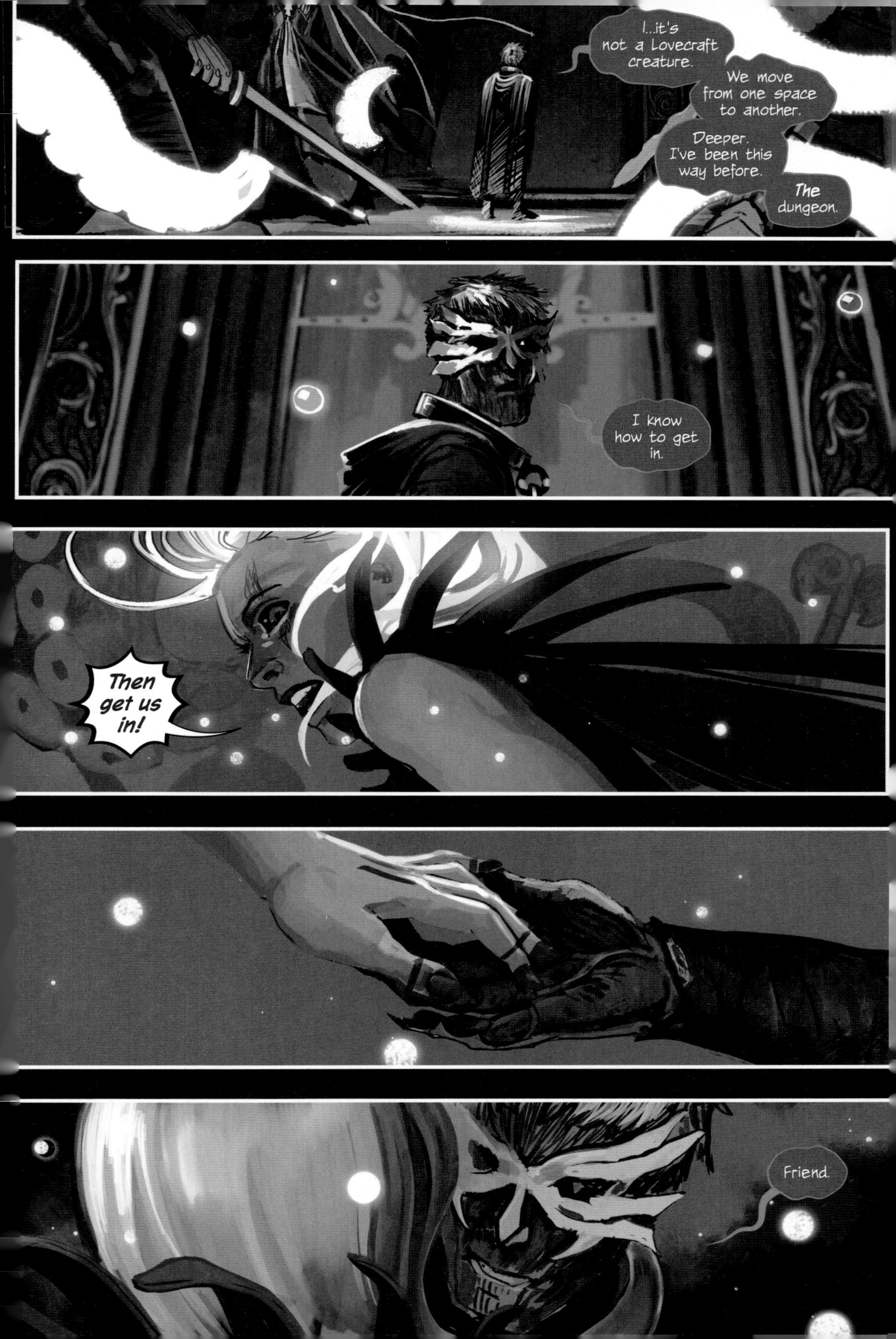

I...it's not a Lovecraft creature.
We move from one space to another.
Deeper. I've been this way before.
The dungeon.
I know how to get in.
Then get us in!
Friend.

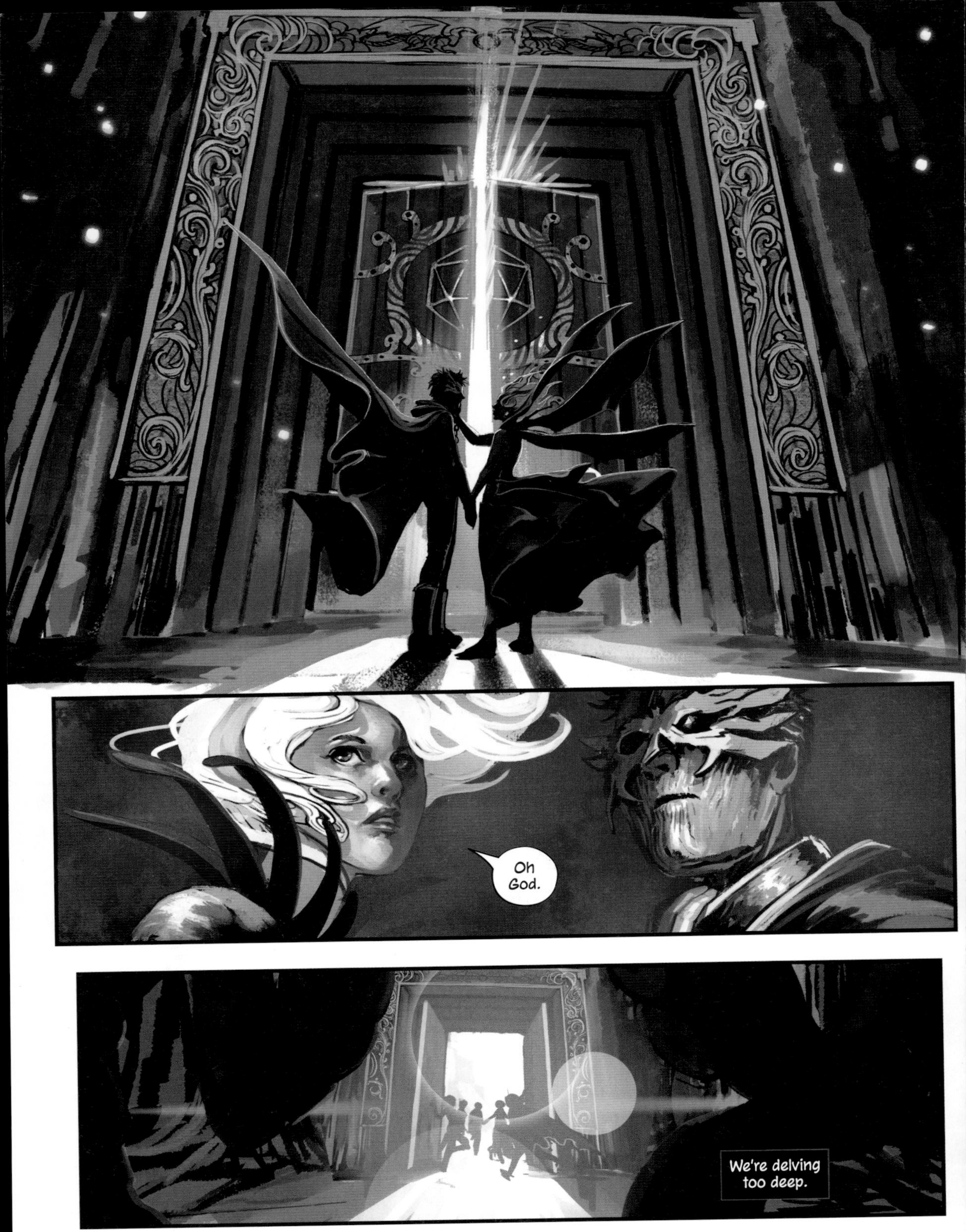
Oh God.
We're delving too deep.

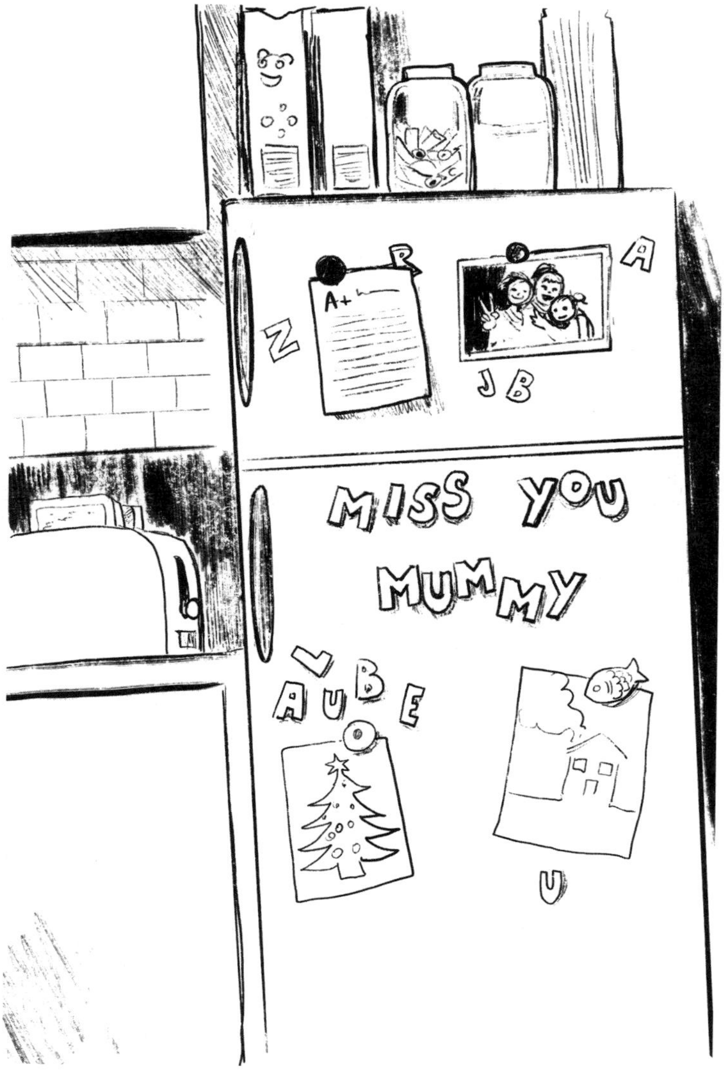
MISS YOU
MUMMY

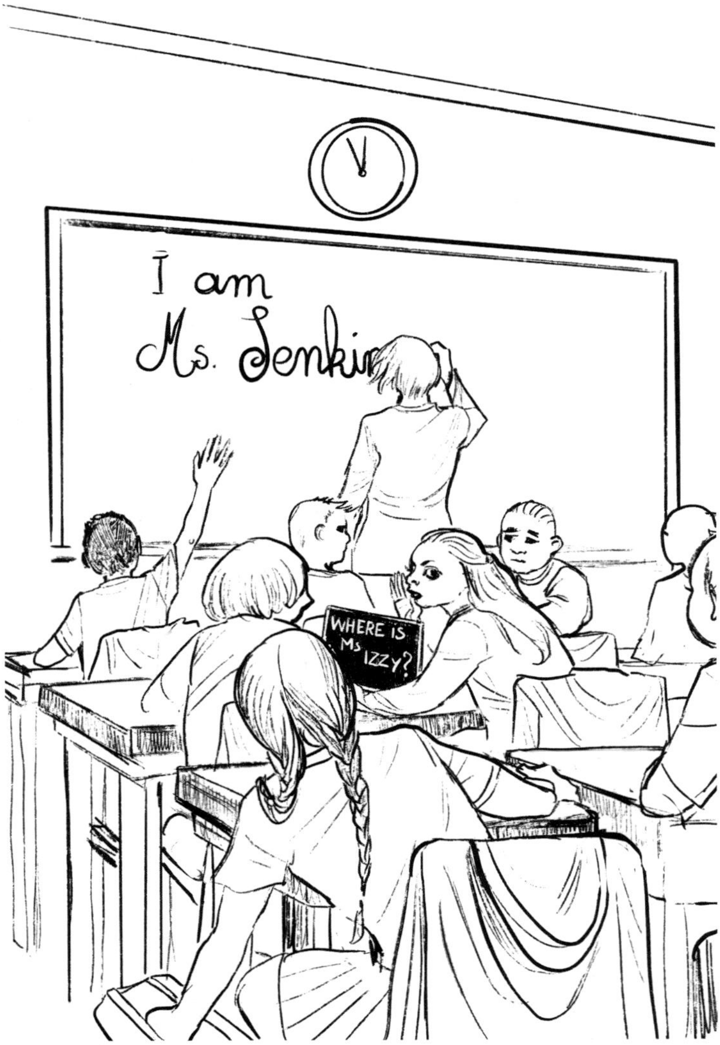
I am
Ms. Jenkin
WHERE IS
Ms
IZZY?

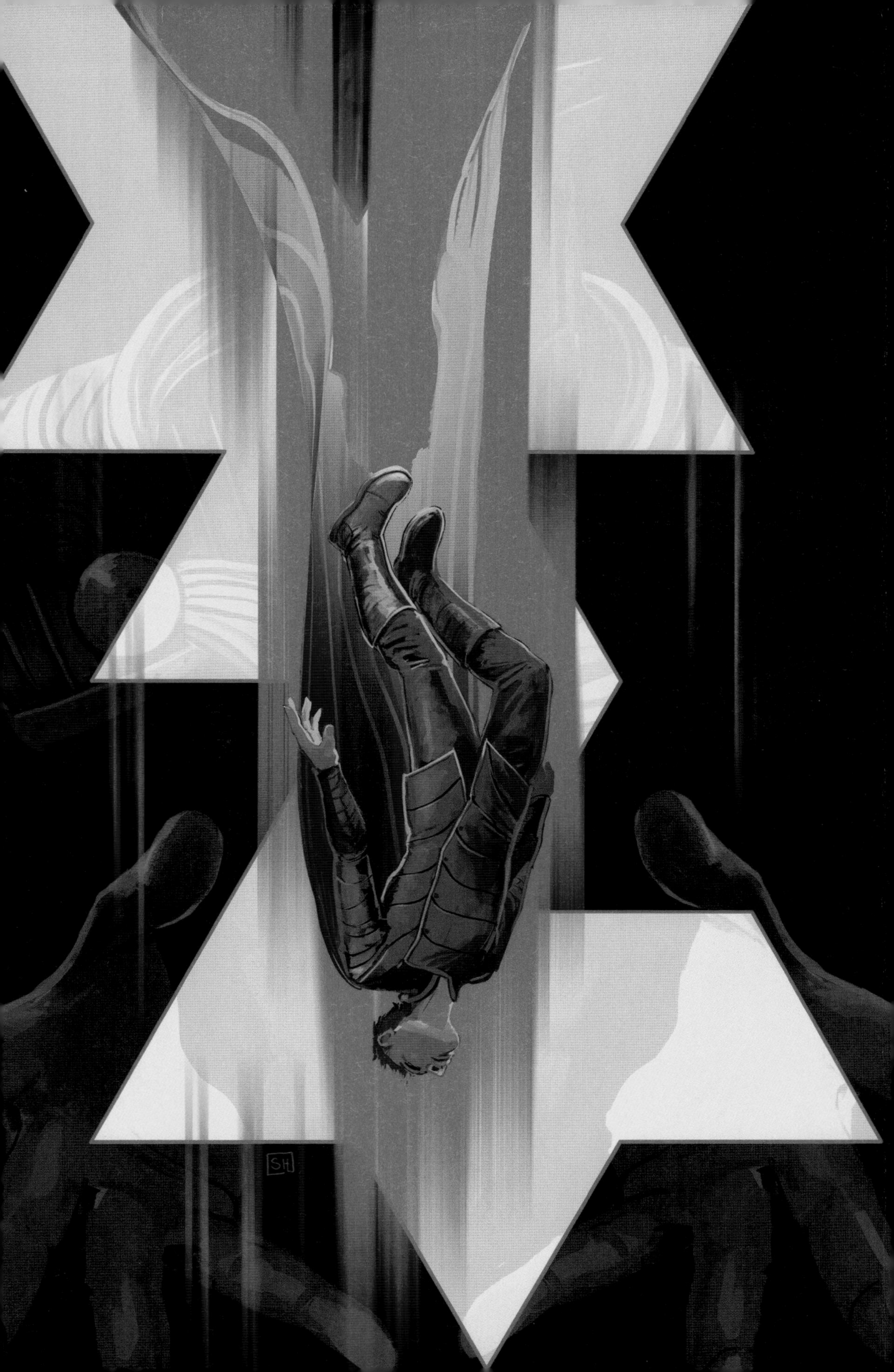

18:
LINES
& VEILS

"Thou Art God."
– *Title of an article of Dungeon Master tips by Robert Hollander, from* Alarums & Excursions *#1, 1975*

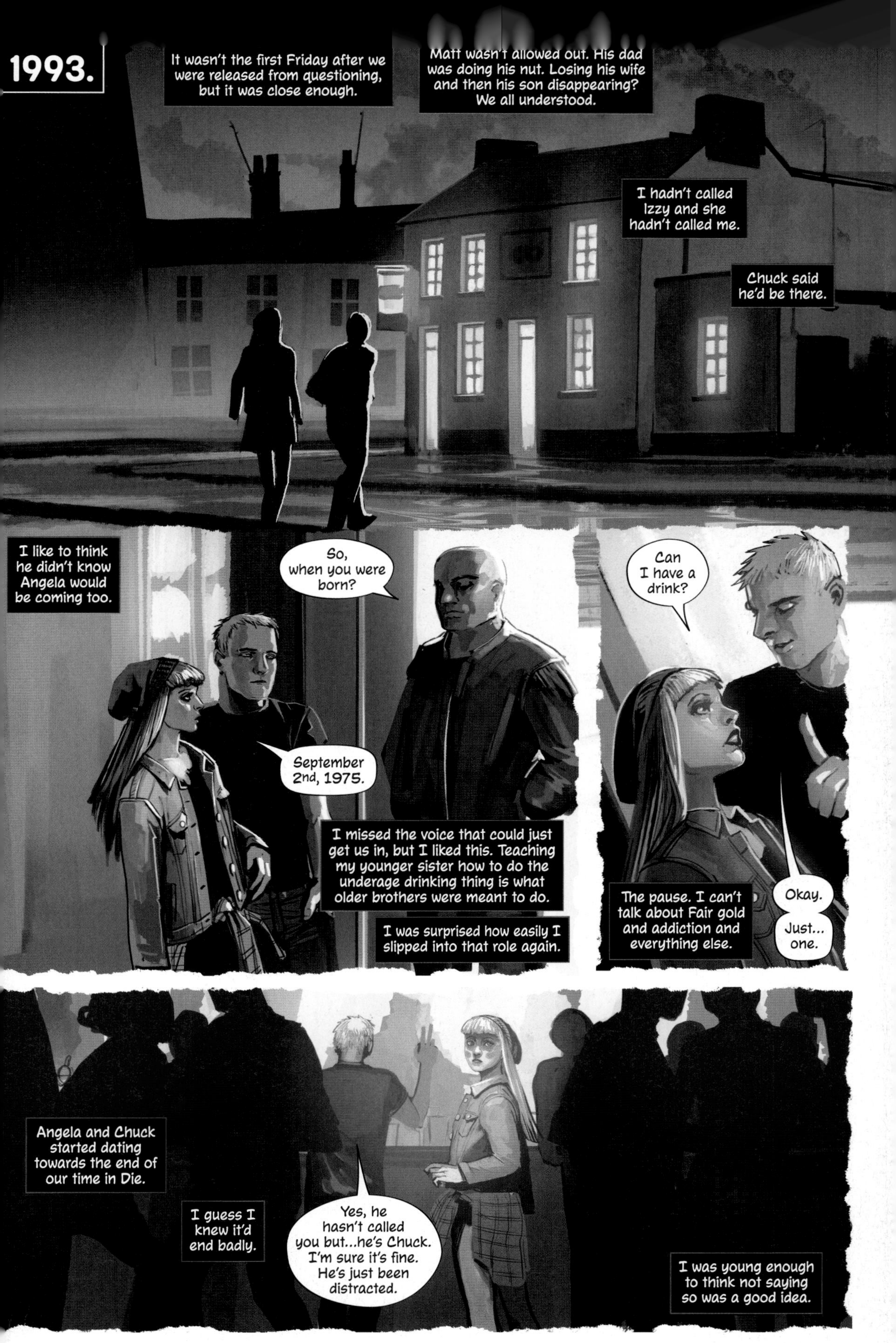
1993.
It wasn't the first Friday after we were released from questioning, but it was close enough.
Matt wasn't allowed out. His dad was doing his nut. Losing his wife and then his son disappearing? We all understood.
I hadn't called Izzy and she hadn't called me.
Chuck said he'd be there.
I like to think he didn't know Angela would be coming too.
So, when you were born?
September 2nd, 1975.
I missed the voice that could just get us in, but I liked this. Teaching my younger sister how to do the underage drinking thing is what older brothers were meant to do.
I was surprised how easily I slipped into that role again.
Can I have a drink?
The pause. I can't talk about Fair gold and addiction and everything else.
Okay.
Just... one.
Angela and Chuck started dating towards the end of our time in Die.
I guess I knew it'd end badly.
Yes, he hasn't called you but...he's Chuck. I'm sure it's fine. He's just been distracted.
I was young enough to think not saying so was a good idea.

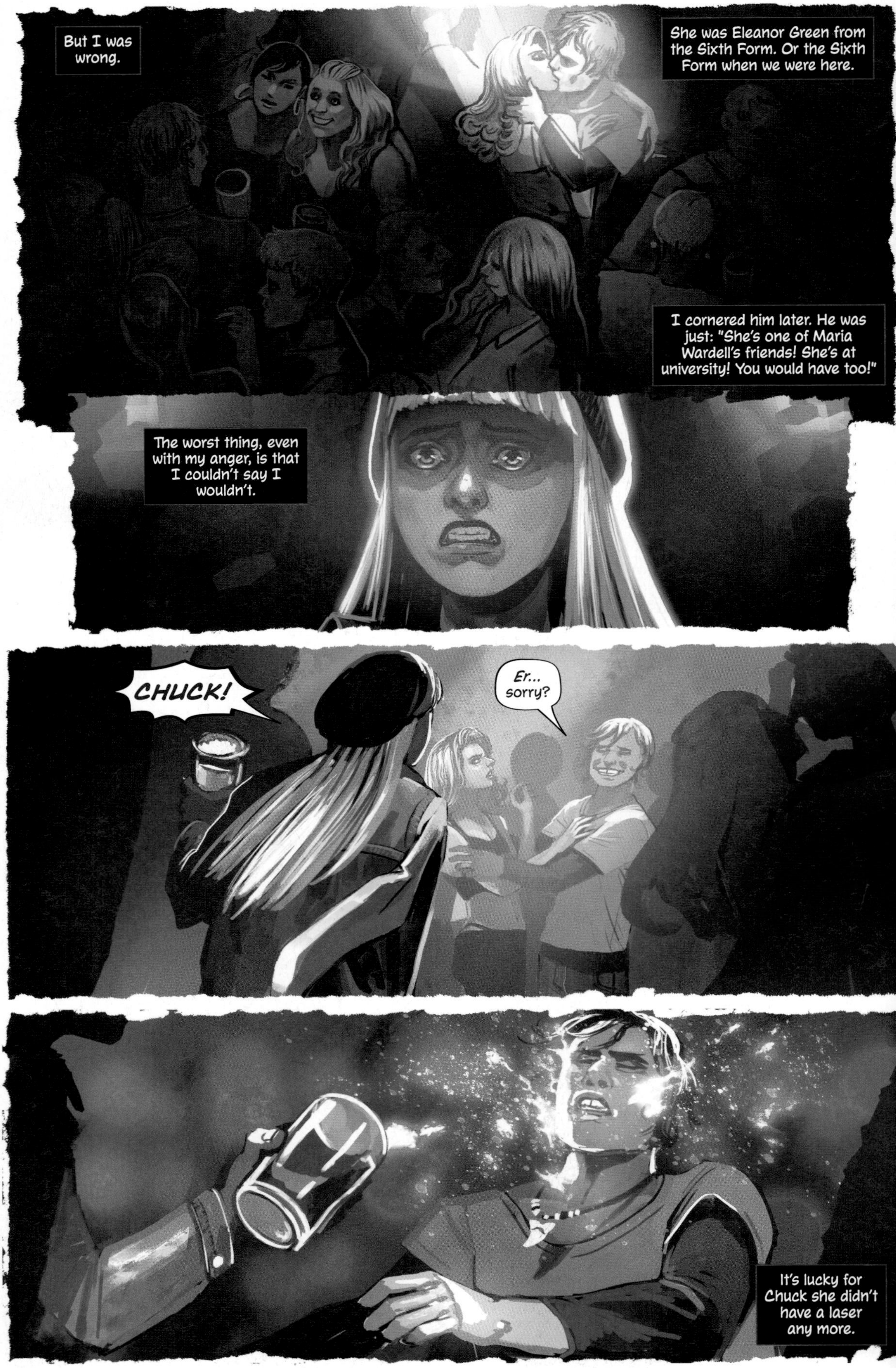
But I was wrong.
She was Eleanor Green from the Sixth Form. Or the Sixth Form when we were here.
I cornered him later. He was just: "She's one of Maria Wardell's friends! She's at university! You would have too!"
The worst thing, even with my anger, is that I couldn't say I wouldn't.
CHUCK!
Er... sorry?
It's lucky for Chuck she didn't have a laser any more.

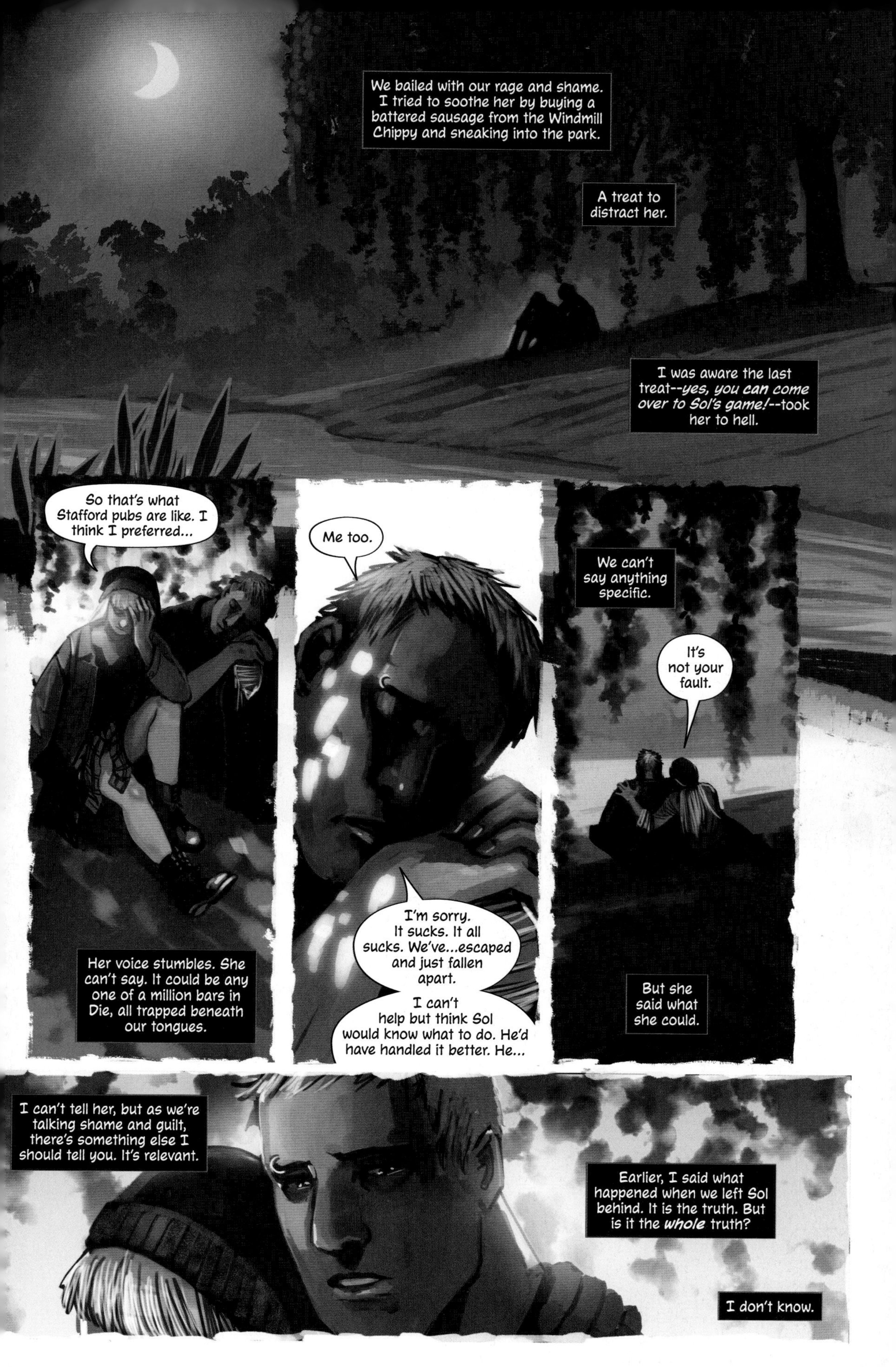
We bailed with our rage and shame. I tried to soothe her by buying a battered sausage from the Windmill Chippy and sneaking into the park.
A treat to distract her.
I was aware the last treat--*yes, you can come over to Sol's game!*--took her to hell.
So that's what Stafford pubs are like. I think I preferred...
Her voice stumbles. She can't say. It could be any one of a million bars in Die, all trapped beneath our tongues.
Me too.
I'm sorry. It sucks. It all sucks. We've...escaped and just fallen apart.
I can't help but think Sol would know what to do. He'd have handled it better. He...
We can't say anything specific.
It's not your fault.
But she said what she could.
I can't tell her, but as we're talking shame and guilt, there's something else I should tell you. It's relevant.
Earlier, I said what happened when we left Sol behind. It is the truth. But is it the *whole* truth?
I don't know.

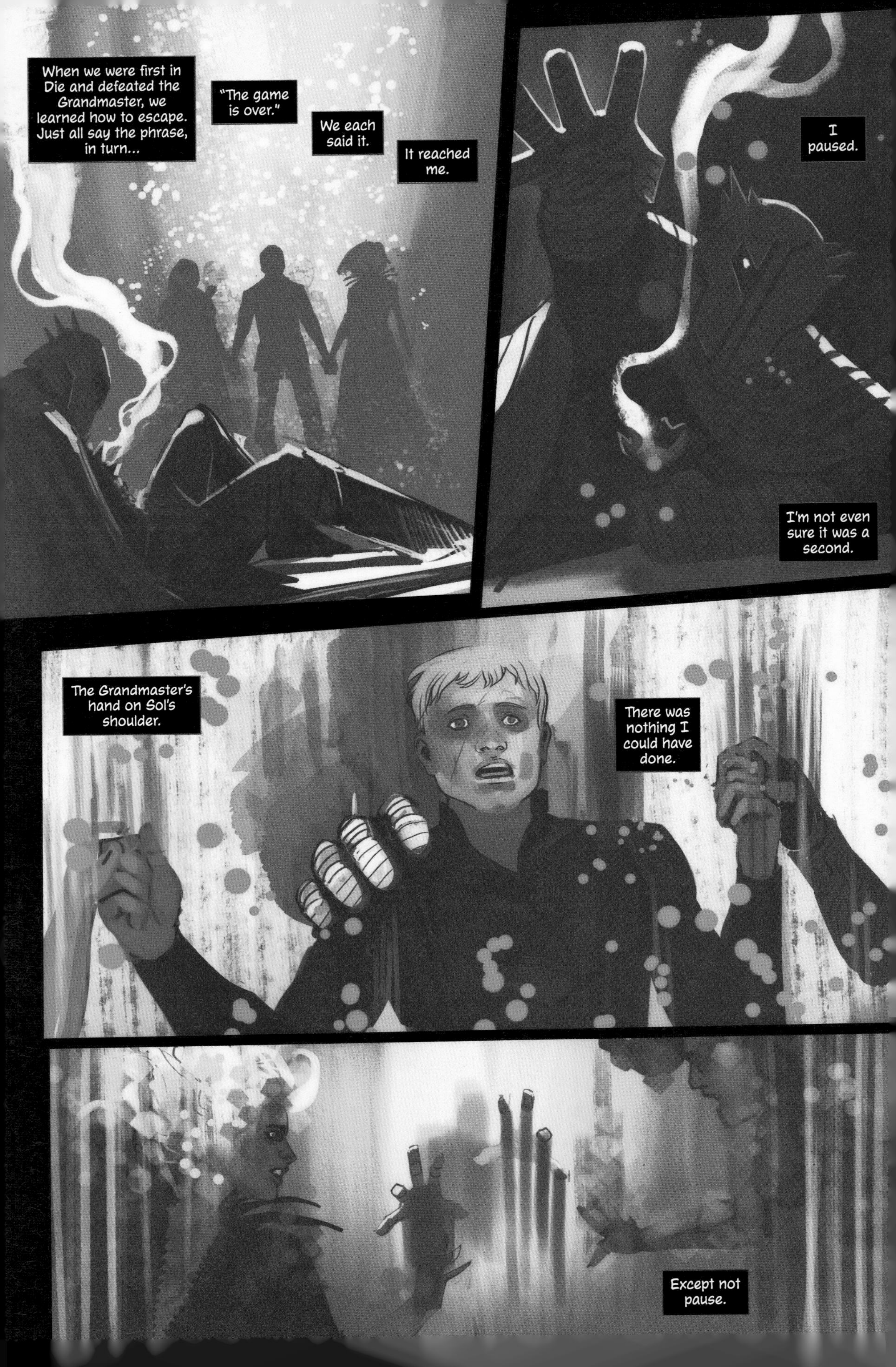
When we were first in Die and defeated the Grandmaster, we learned how to escape. Just all say the phrase, in turn...
"The game is over."
We each said it.
It reached me.
I paused.
I'm not even sure it was a second.
The Grandmaster's hand on Sol's shoulder.
There was nothing I could have done.
Except not pause.

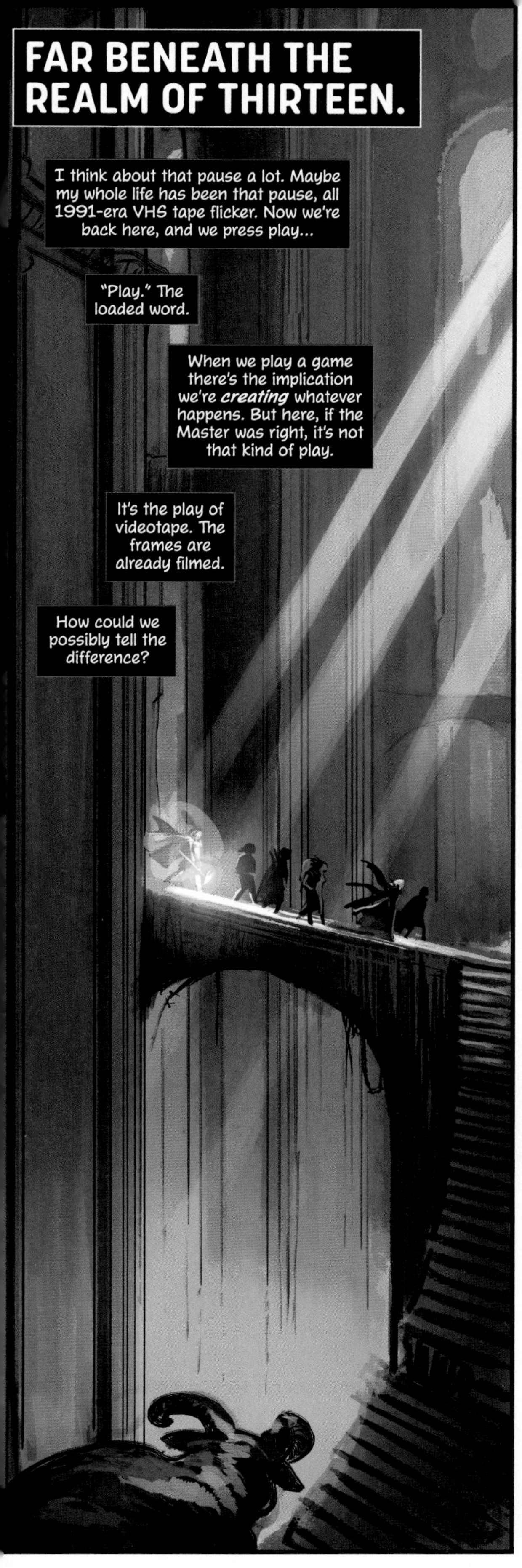
FAR BENEATH THE REALM OF THIRTEEN.
I think about that pause a lot. Maybe my whole life has been that pause, all 1991-era VHS tape flicker. Now we're back here, and we press play...
"Play." The loaded word.
When we play a game there's the implication we're *creating* whatever happens. But here, if the Master was right, it's not that kind of play.
It's the play of videotape. The frames are already filmed.
How could we possibly tell the difference?

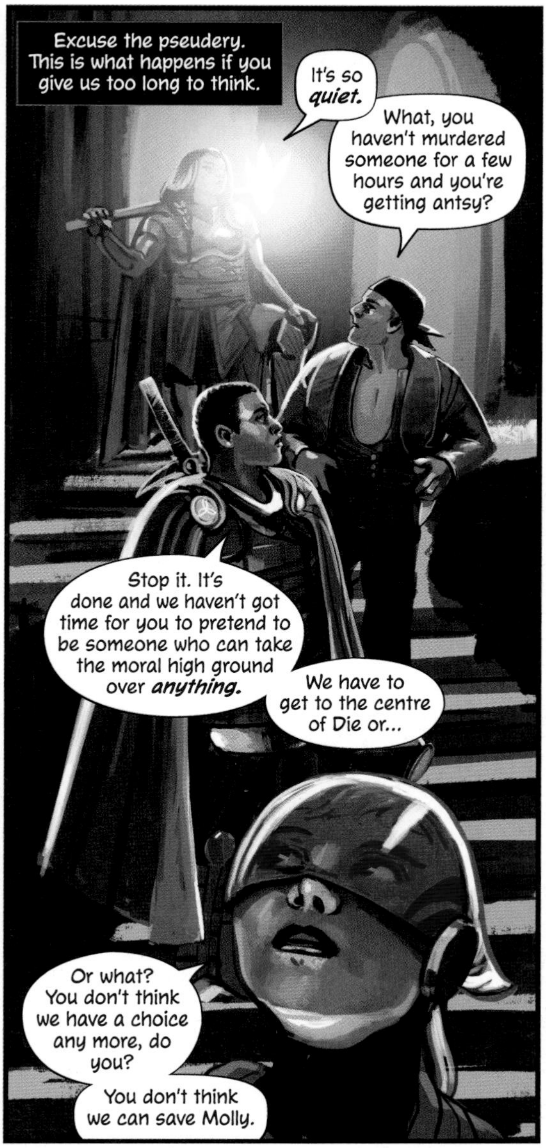
Excuse the pseudery. This is what happens if you give us too long to think.
It's so ***quiet.***
What, you haven't murdered someone for a few hours and you're getting antsy?
Stop it. It's done and we haven't got time for you to pretend to be someone who can take the moral high ground over ***anything.***
We have to get to the centre of Die or...
Or what? You don't think we have a choice any more, do you?
You don't think we can save Molly.

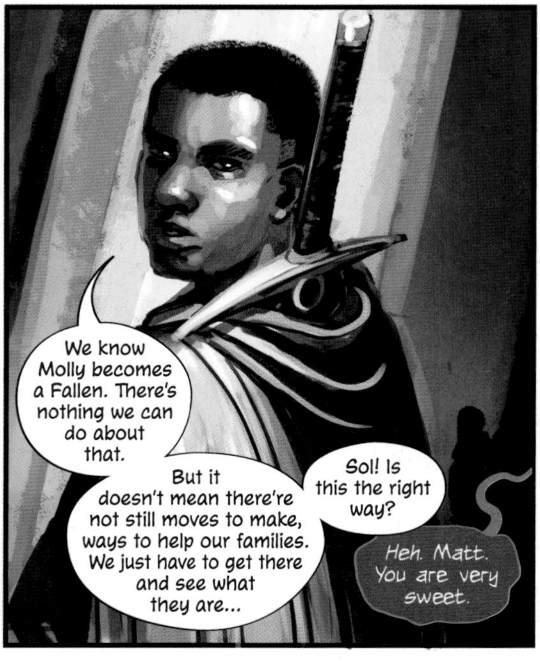
We know Molly becomes a Fallen. There's nothing we can do about that.
But it doesn't mean there're not still moves to make, ways to help our families. We just have to get there and see what they are...
Sol! Is this the right way?
Heh. Matt. You are very sweet.

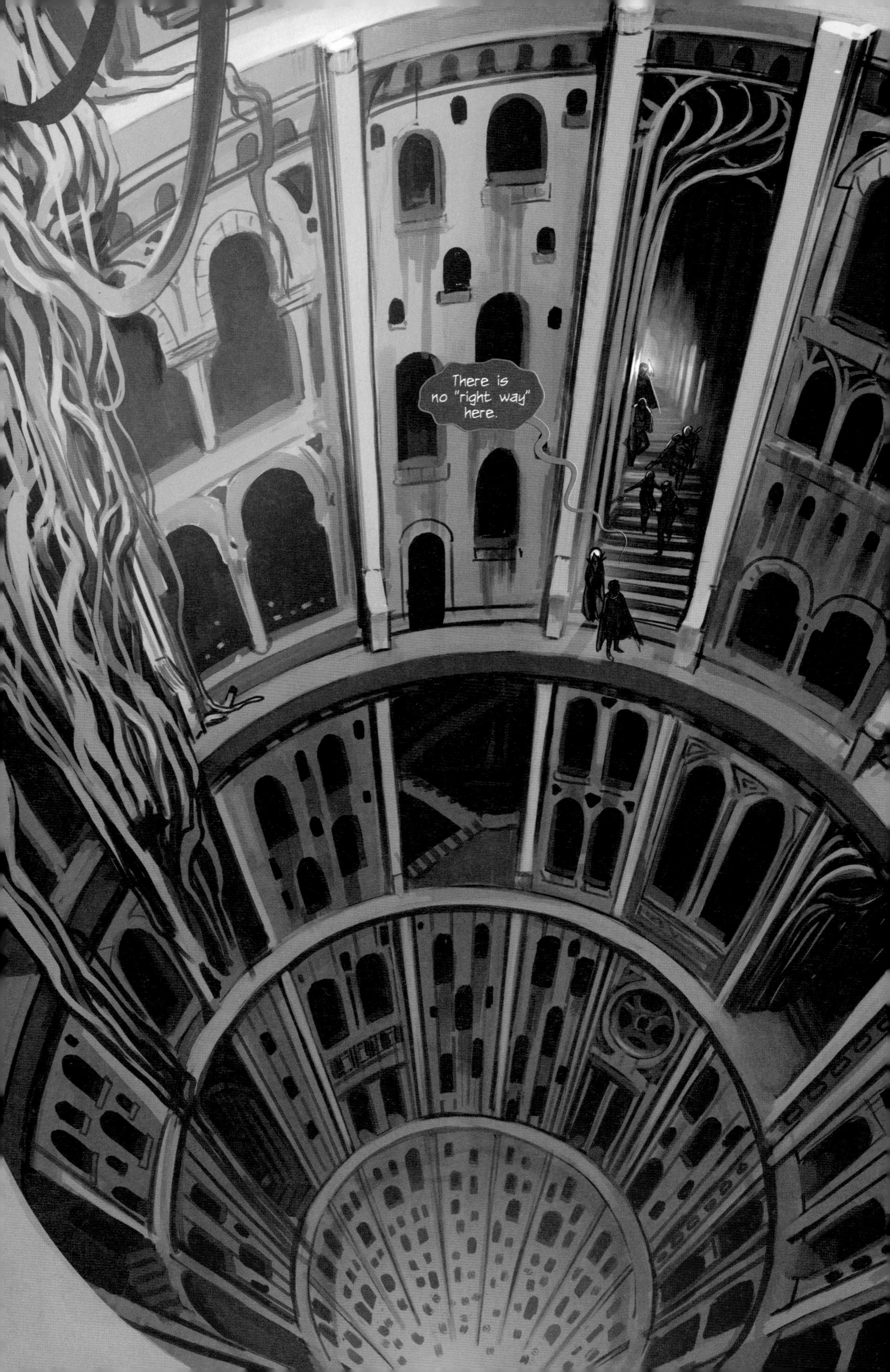
There is no "right way" here.

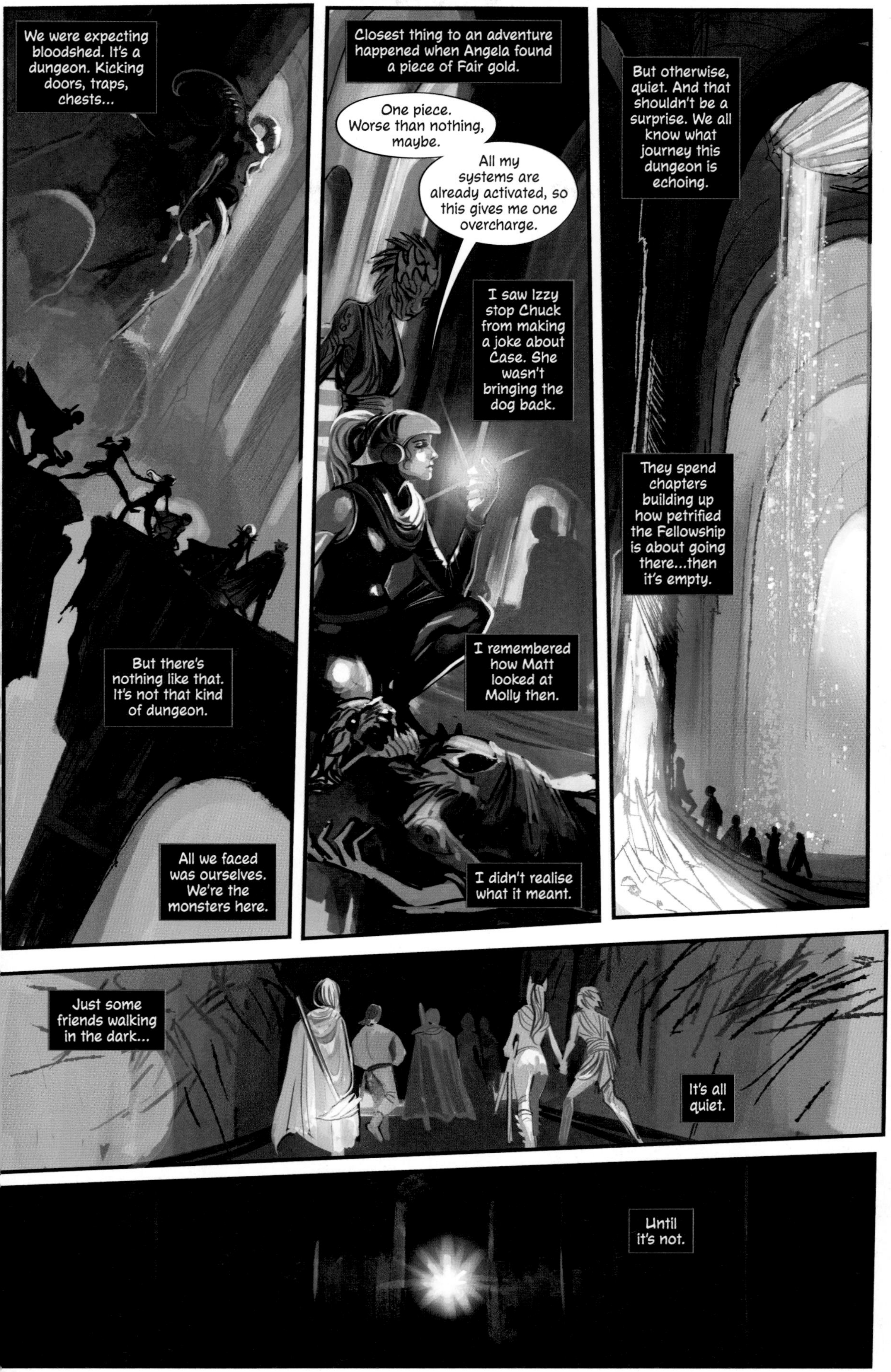
We were expecting bloodshed. It's a dungeon. Kicking doors, traps, chests...
But there's nothing like that. It's not that kind of dungeon.
All we faced was ourselves. We're the monsters here.
Closest thing to an adventure happened when Angela found a piece of Fair gold.
One piece. Worse than nothing, maybe.
All my systems are already activated, so this gives me one overcharge.
I saw Izzy stop Chuck from making a joke about Case. She wasn't bringing the dog back.
I remembered how Matt looked at Molly then.
I didn't realise what it meant.
But otherwise, quiet. And that shouldn't be a surprise. We all know what journey this dungeon is echoing.
They spend chapters building up how petrified the Fellowship is about going there...then it's empty.
Just some friends walking in the dark...
It's all quiet.
Until it's not.

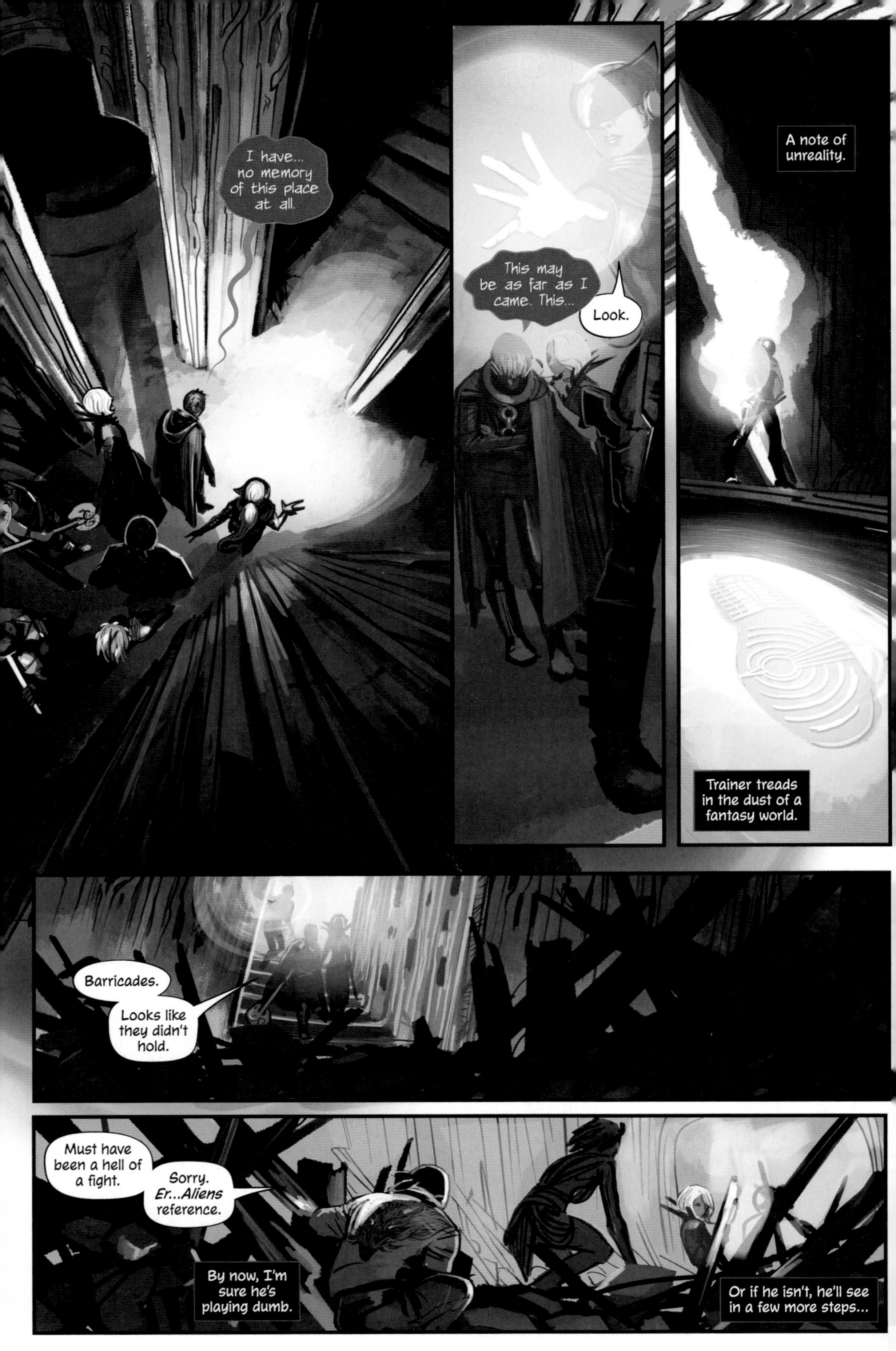
I have... no memory of this place at all.
This may be as far as I came. This...
Look.
A note of unreality.
Trainer treads in the dust of a fantasy world.
Barricades.
Looks like they didn't hold.
Must have been a hell of a fight.
Sorry. *Er...Aliens* reference.
By now, I'm sure he's playing dumb.
Or if he isn't, he'll see in a few more steps...

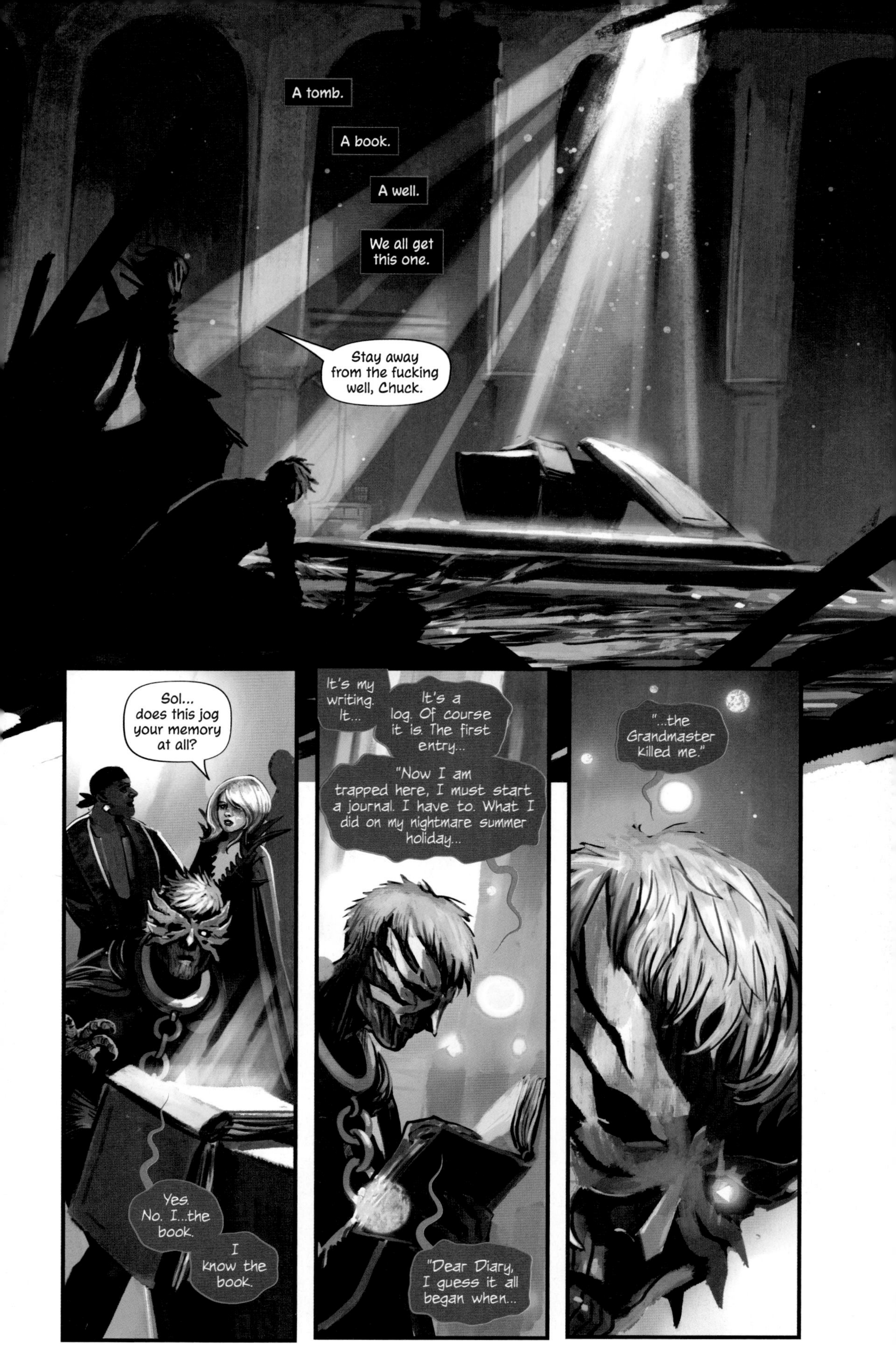
A tomb.
A book.
A well.
We all get this one.
Stay away from the fucking well, Chuck.
Sol... does this jog your memory at all?
Yes. No. I...the book.
I know the book.
It's my writing. It...
It's a log. Of course it is. The first entry...
"Now I am trapped here, I must start a journal. I have to. What I did on my nightmare summer holiday...
"Dear Diary, I guess it all began when...
"...the Grandmaster killed me."

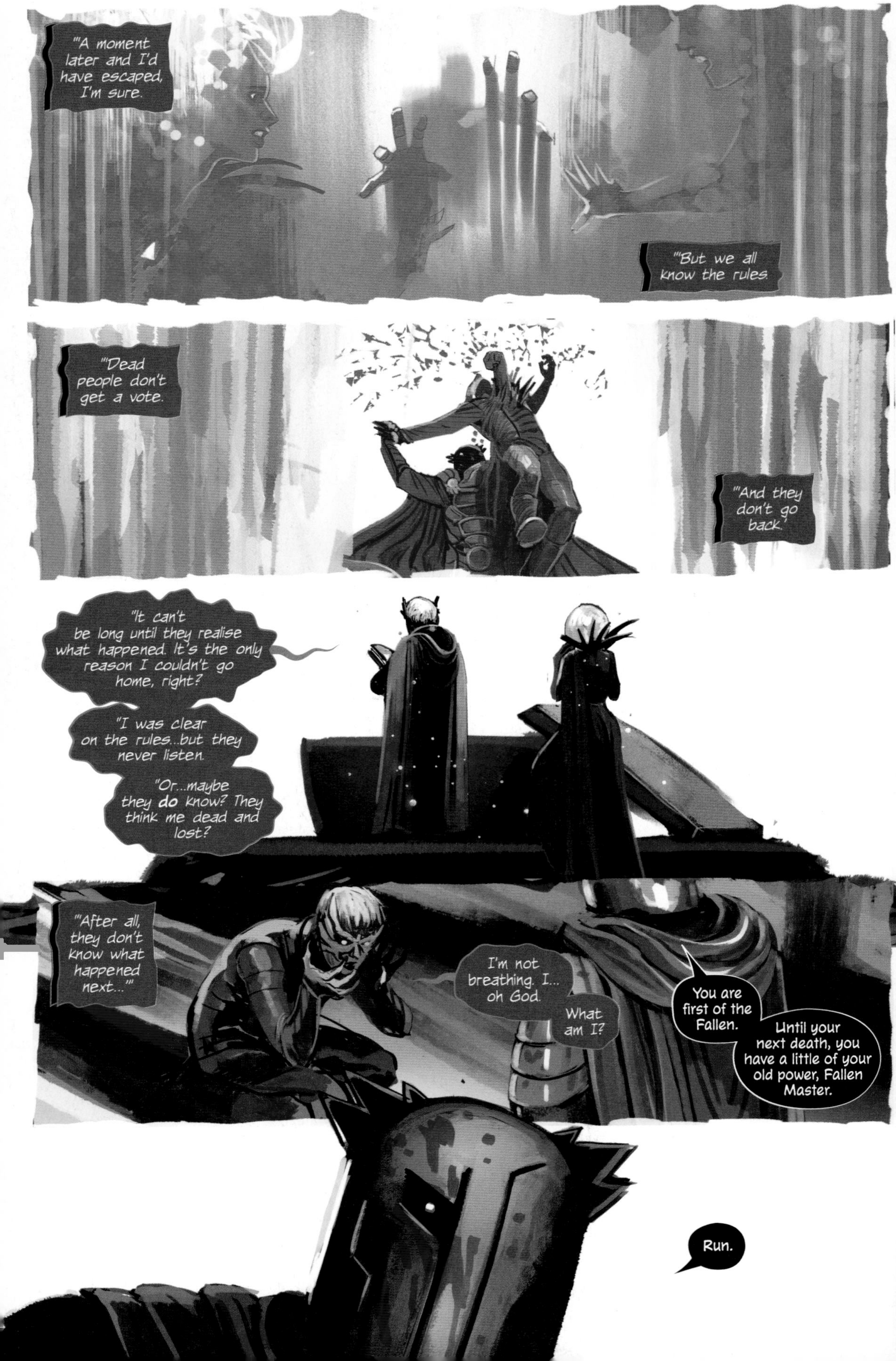
"'A moment later and I'd have escaped, I'm sure.
"'But we all know the rules.
"'Dead people don't get a vote.
"'And they don't go back.'
"It can't be long until they realise what happened. It's the only reason I couldn't go home, right?
"I was clear on the rules...but they never listen.
"Or...maybe they **do** know? They think me dead and lost?
"'After all, they don't know what happened next...'"
I'm not breathing. I... oh God.
What am I?
You are first of the Fallen.
Until your next death, you have a little of your old power, Fallen Master.
Run.

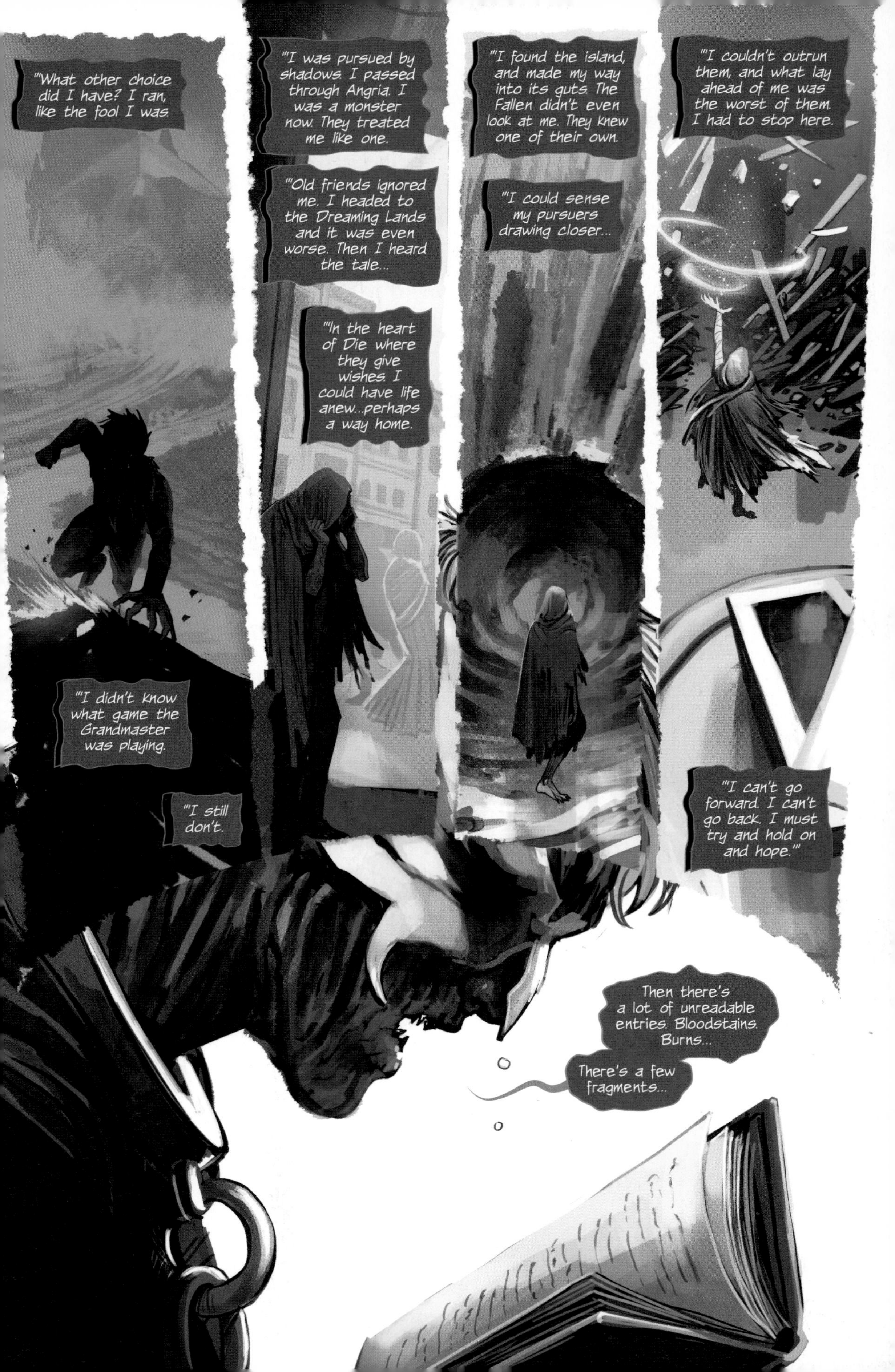
"'What other choice did I have? I ran, like the fool I was.
"'I was pursued by shadows. I passed through Angria. I was a monster now. They treated me like one.
"'Old friends ignored me. I headed to the Dreaming Lands and it was even worse. Then I heard the tale...
"'In the heart of Die where they give wishes. I could have life anew...perhaps a way home.
"'I found the island, and made my way into its guts. The Fallen didn't even look at me. They knew one of their own.
"'I could sense my pursuers drawing closer...
"'I couldn't outrun them, and what lay ahead of me was the worst of them. I had to stop here.
"'I didn't know what game the Grandmaster was playing.
"'I still don't.
"'I can't go forward. I can't go back. I must try and hold on and hope.'"
Then there's a lot of unreadable entries. Bloodstains. Burns...
There's a few fragments...

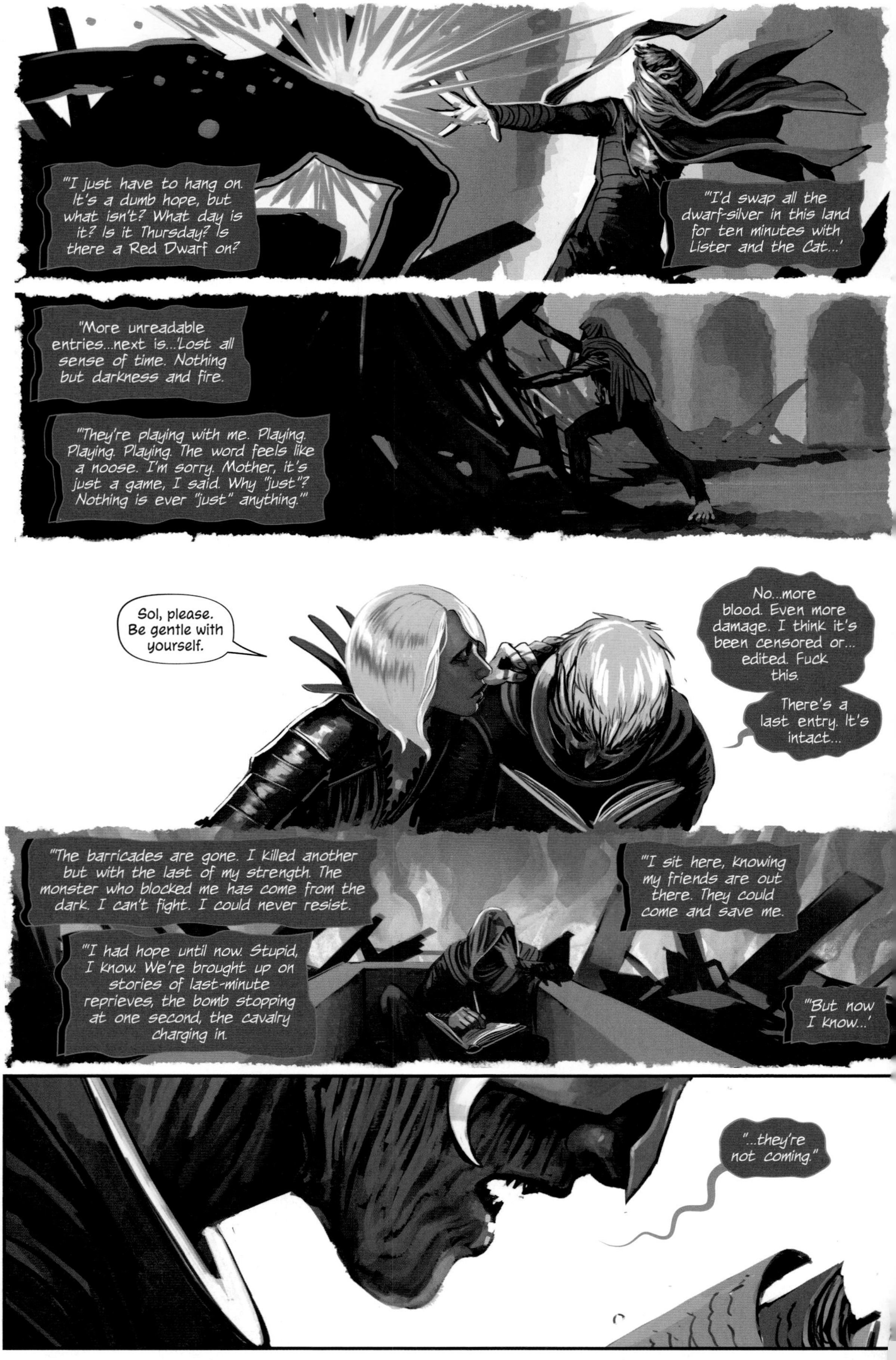
"'I just have to hang on. It's a dumb hope, but what isn't? What day is it? Is it Thursday? Is there a Red Dwarf on?
"'I'd swap all the dwarf-silver in this land for ten minutes with Lister and the Cat...'
"More unreadable entries...next is...'Lost all sense of time. Nothing but darkness and fire.
"'They're playing with me. Playing. Playing. Playing. The word feels like a noose. I'm sorry. Mother, it's just a game, I said. Why "just"? Nothing is ever "just" anything.'"
Sol, please. Be gentle with yourself.
No...more blood. Even more damage. I think it's been censored or... edited. Fuck this.
There's a last entry. It's intact...
"'The barricades are gone. I killed another but with the last of my strength. The monster who blocked me has come from the dark. I can't fight. I could never resist.
"'I had hope until now. Stupid, I know. We're brought up on stories of last-minute reprieves, the bomb stopping at one second, the cavalry charging in.
"'I sit here, knowing my friends are out there. They could come and save me.
"'But now I know...'
"...they're not coming."

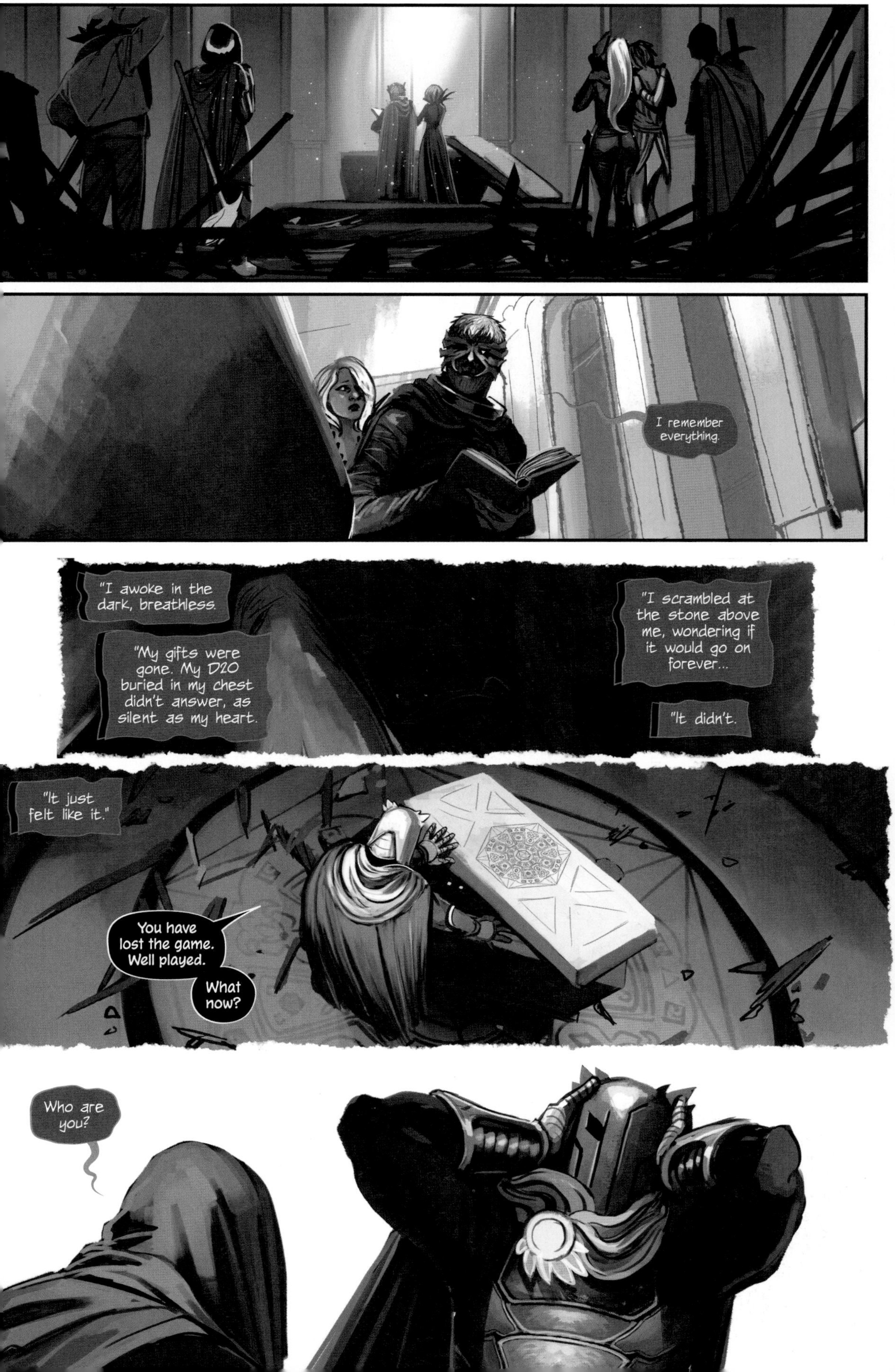
I remember everything.
"I awoke in the dark, breathless.
"My gifts were gone. My D20 buried in my chest didn't answer, as silent as my heart.
"I scrambled at the stone above me, wondering if it would go on forever...
"It didn't.
"It just felt like it."
You have lost the game. Well played.
What now?
Who are you?

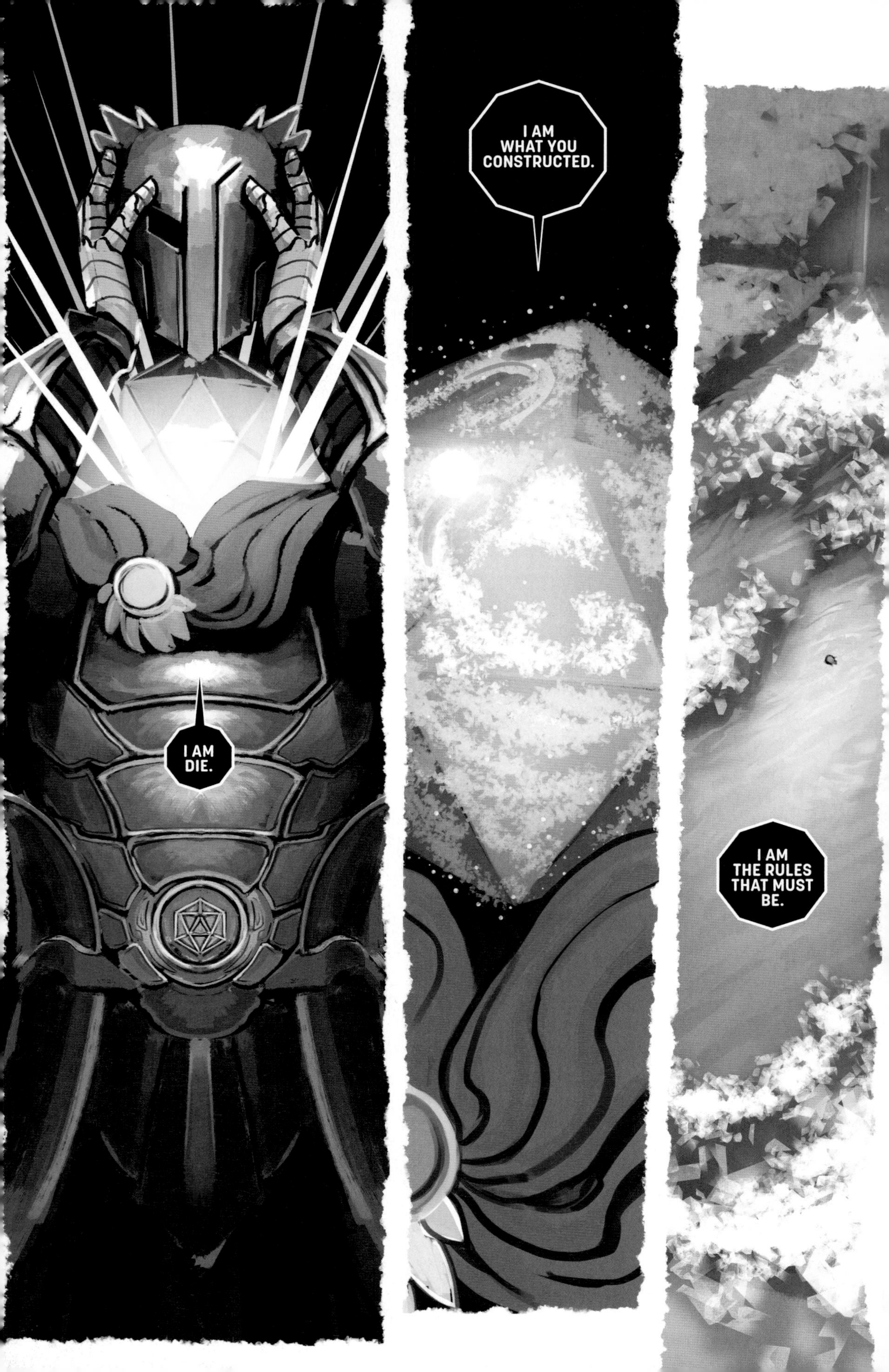
I AM DIE.
I AM WHAT YOU CONSTRUCTED.
I AM THE RULES THAT MUST BE.

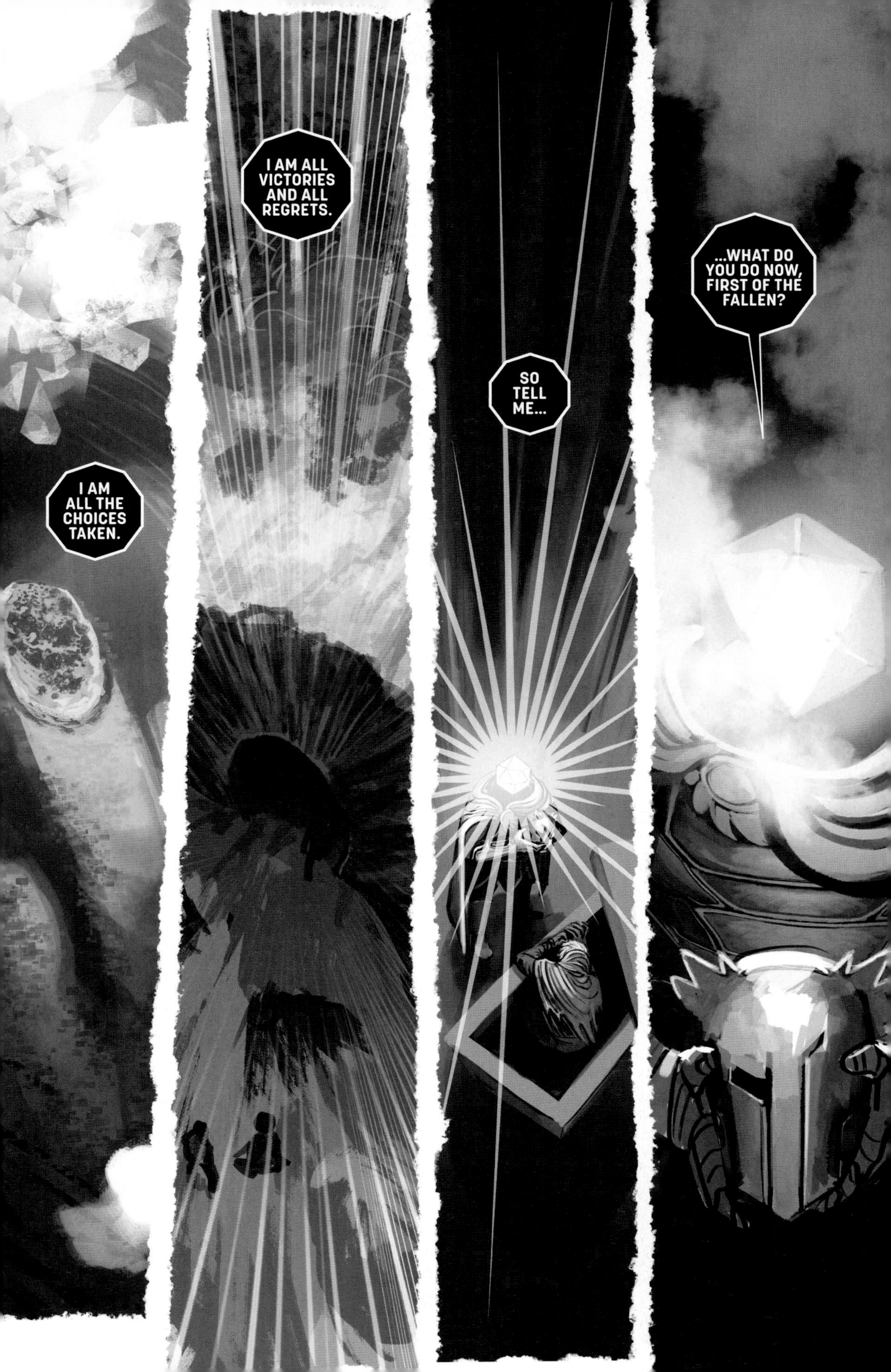
I AM ALL THE CHOICES TAKEN.
I AM ALL VICTORIES AND ALL REGRETS.
SO TELL ME...
...WHAT DO YOU DO NOW, FIRST OF THE FALLEN?

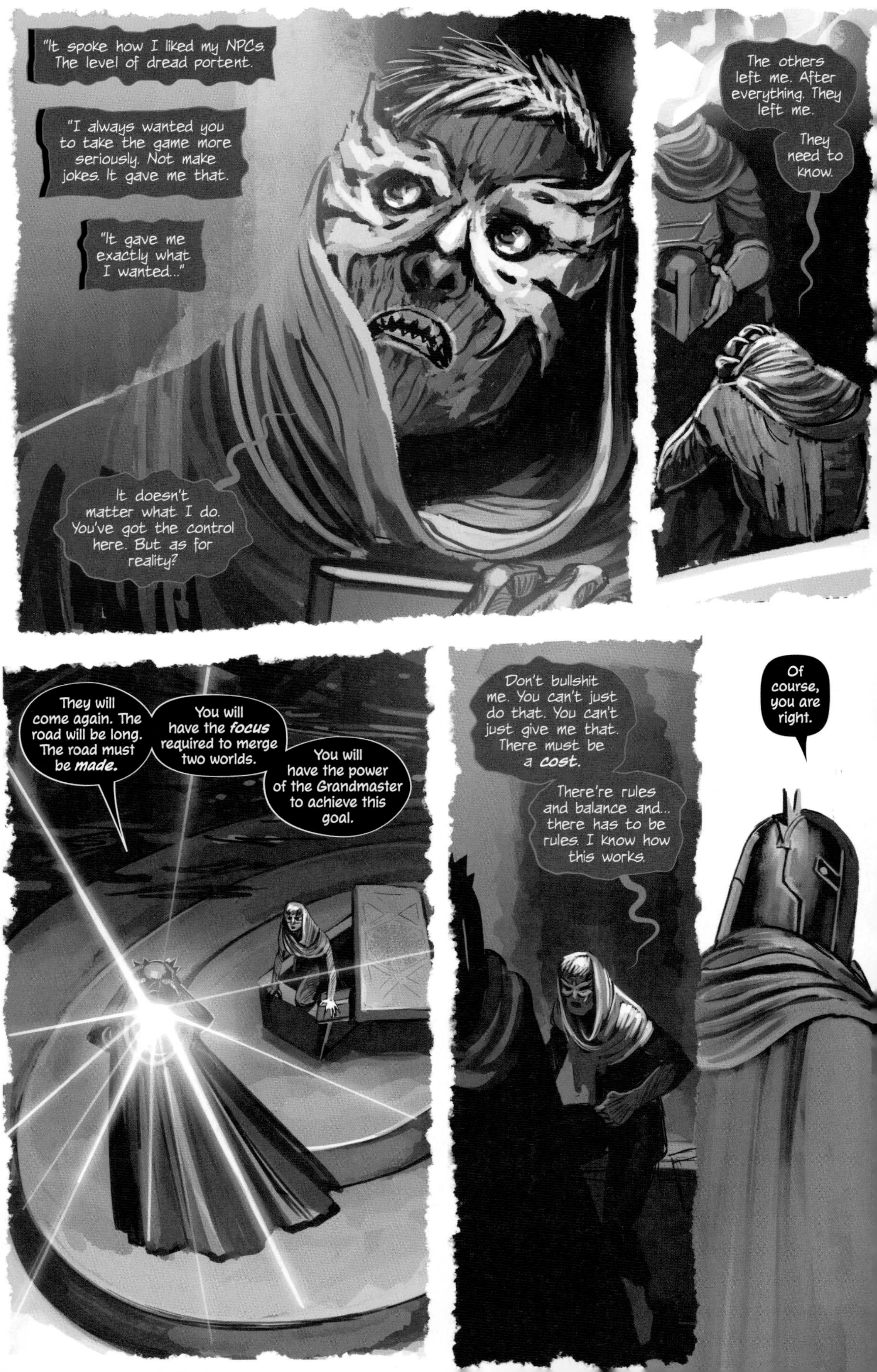
"It spoke how I liked my NPCs. The level of dread portent.
"I always wanted you to take the game more seriously. Not make jokes. It gave me that.
"It gave me exactly what I wanted..."
It doesn't matter what I do. You've got the control here. But as for reality?
The others left me. After everything. They left me.
They need to know.
They will come again. The road will be long. The road must be *made.*
You will have the *focus* required to merge two worlds.
You will have the power of the Grandmaster to achieve this goal.
Don't bullshit me. You can't just do that. You can't just give me that. There must be a *cost.*
There're rules and balance and... there has to be rules. I know how this works.
Of course, you are right.

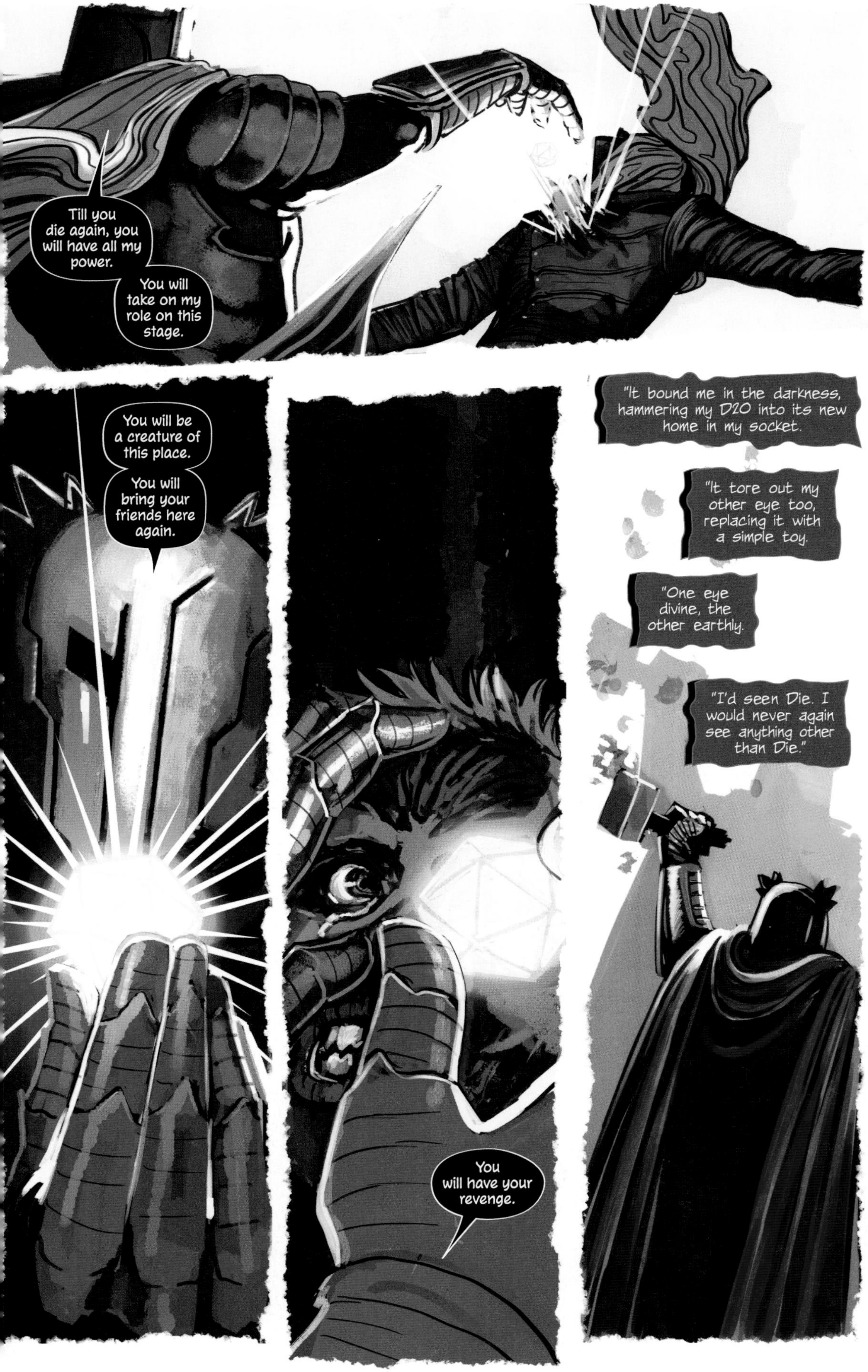
Till you die again, you will have all my power.
You will take on my role on this stage.
You will be a creature of this place.
You will bring your friends here again.
You will have your revenge.
"It bound me in the darkness, hammering my D20 into its new home in my socket.
"It tore out my other eye too, replacing it with a simple toy.
"One eye divine, the other earthly.
"I'd seen Die. I would never again see anything other than Die."

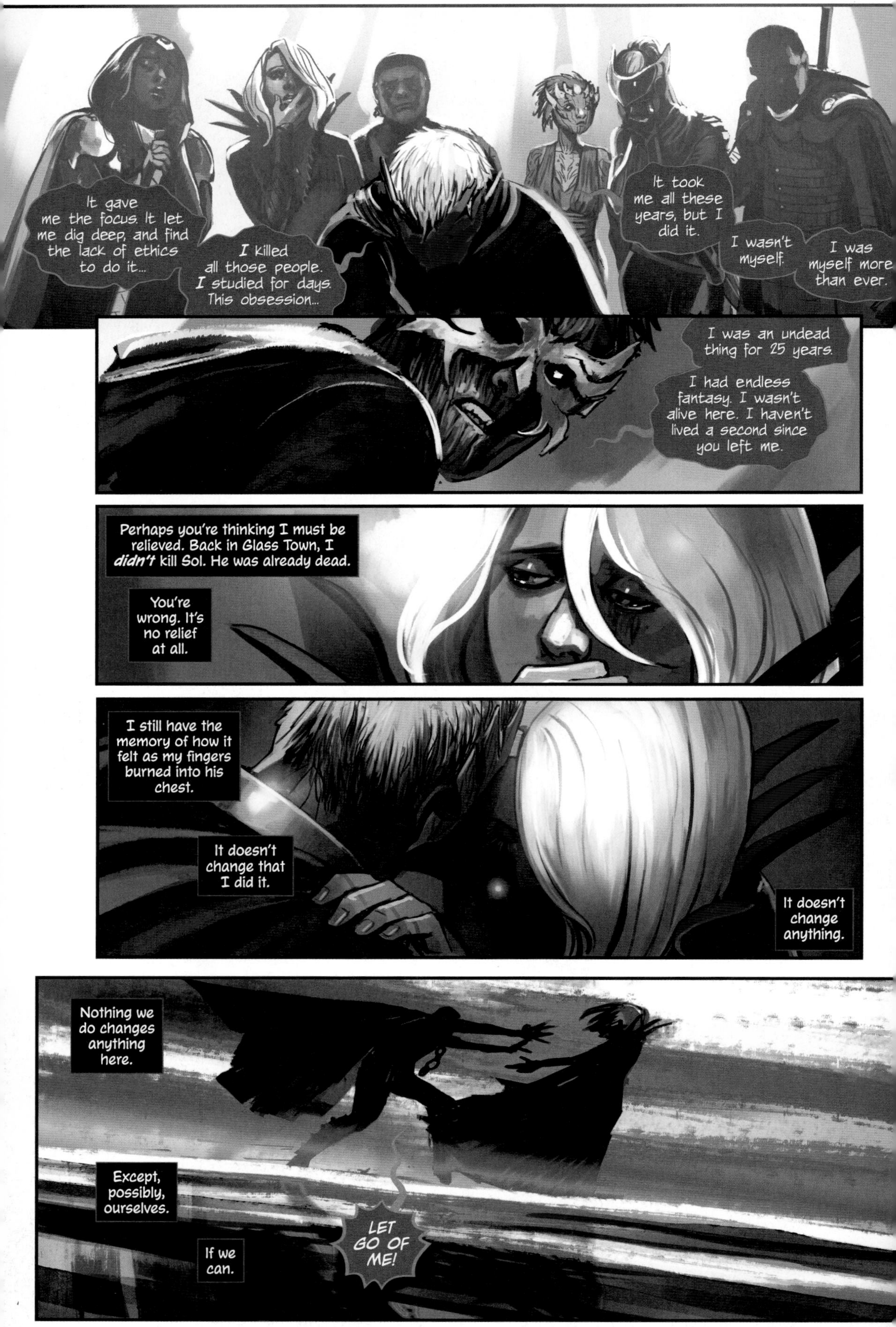
It gave me the focus. It let me dig deep, and find the lack of ethics to do it...
I killed all those people. I studied for days. This obsession...
It took me all these years, but I did it.
I wasn't myself.
I was myself more than ever.
I was an undead thing for 25 years.
I had endless fantasy. I wasn't alive here. I haven't lived a second since you left me.
Perhaps you're thinking I must be relieved. Back in Glass Town, I *didn't* kill Sol. He was already dead.
You're wrong. It's no relief at all.
I still have the memory of how it felt as my fingers burned into his chest.
It doesn't change that I did it.
It doesn't change anything.
Nothing we do changes anything here.
Except, possibly, ourselves.
If we can.
LET GO OF ME!

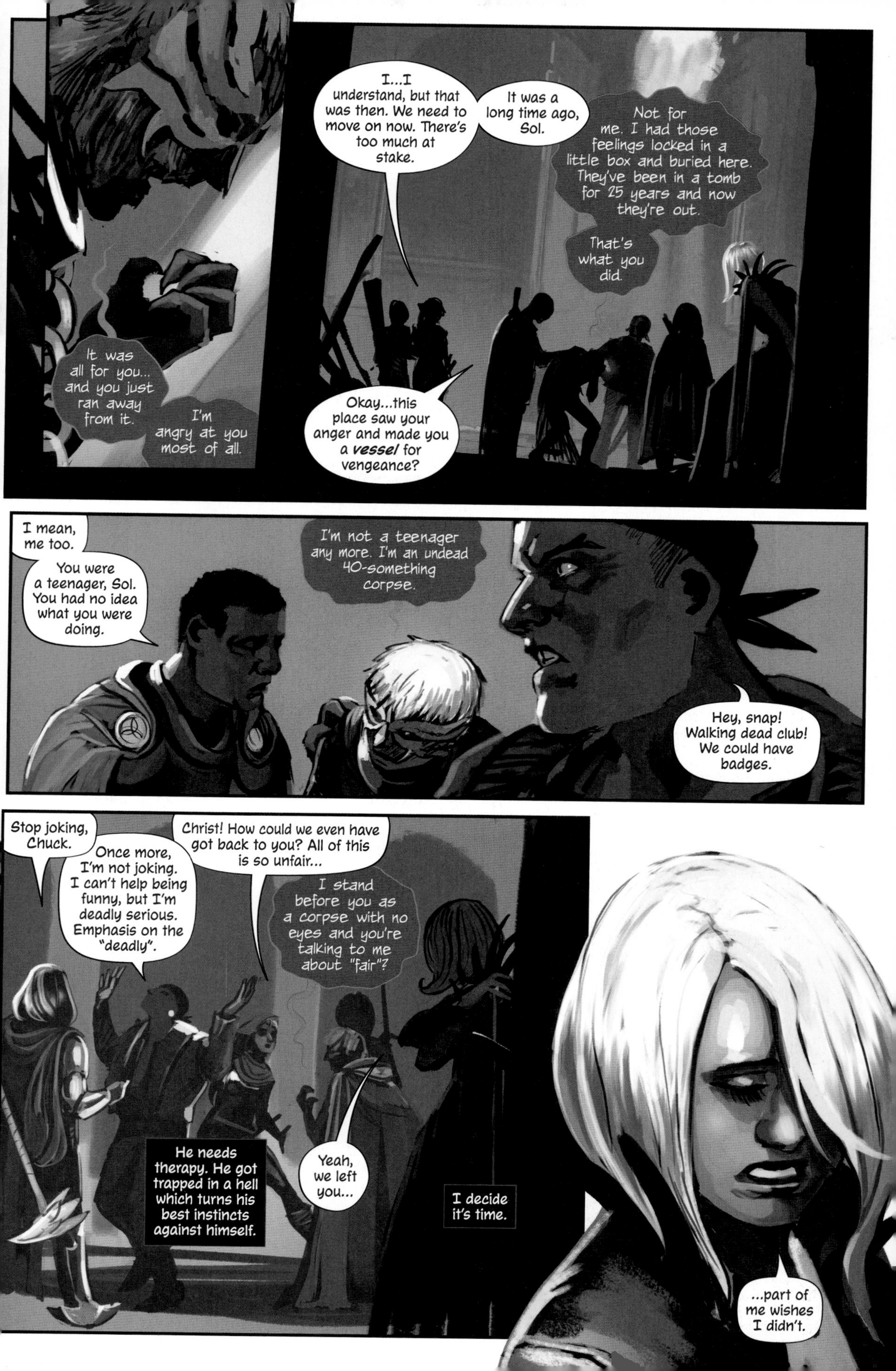
It was all for you... and you just ran away from it.
I'm angry at you most of all.
I...I understand, but that was then. We need to move on now. There's too much at stake.
It was a long time ago, Sol.
Not for me. I had those feelings locked in a little box and buried here. They've been in a tomb for 25 years and now they're out.
That's what you did.
Okay...this place saw your anger and made you a *vessel* for vengeance?
I mean, me too.
You were a teenager, Sol. You had no idea what you were doing.
I'm not a teenager any more. I'm an undead 40-something corpse.
Hey, snap! Walking dead club! We could have badges.
Stop joking, Chuck.
Once more, I'm not joking. I can't help being funny, but I'm deadly serious. Emphasis on the "deadly".
Christ! How could we even have got back to you? All of this is so unfair...
I stand before you as a corpse with no eyes and you're talking to me about "fair"?
He needs therapy. He got trapped in a hell which turns his best instincts against himself.
Yeah, we left you...
I decide it's time.
...part of me wishes I didn't.

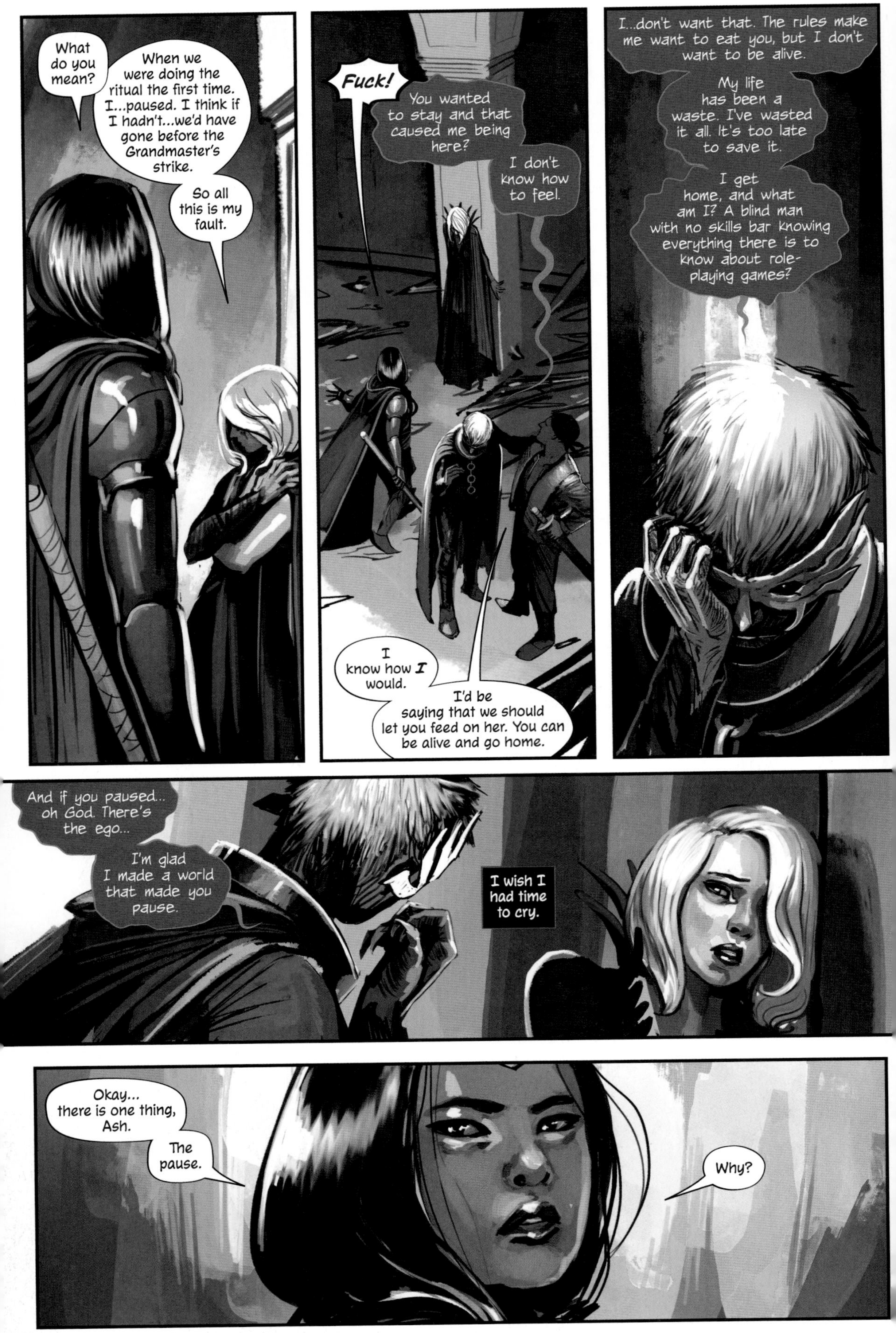

What do you mean?
When we were doing the ritual the first time. I...paused. I think if I hadn't...we'd have gone before the Grandmaster's strike.
So all this is my fault.
Fuck!
You wanted to stay and that caused me being here?
I don't know how to feel.
I know how I would.
I'd be saying that we should let you feed on her. You can be alive and go home.
I...don't want that. The rules make me want to eat you, but I don't want to be alive.
My life has been a waste. I've wasted it all. It's too late to save it.
I get home, and what am I? A blind man with no skills bar knowing everything there is to know about role-playing games?
And if you paused... oh God. There's the ego...
I'm glad I made a world that made you pause.
I wish I had time to cry.
Okay... there is one thing, Ash.
The pause.
Why?

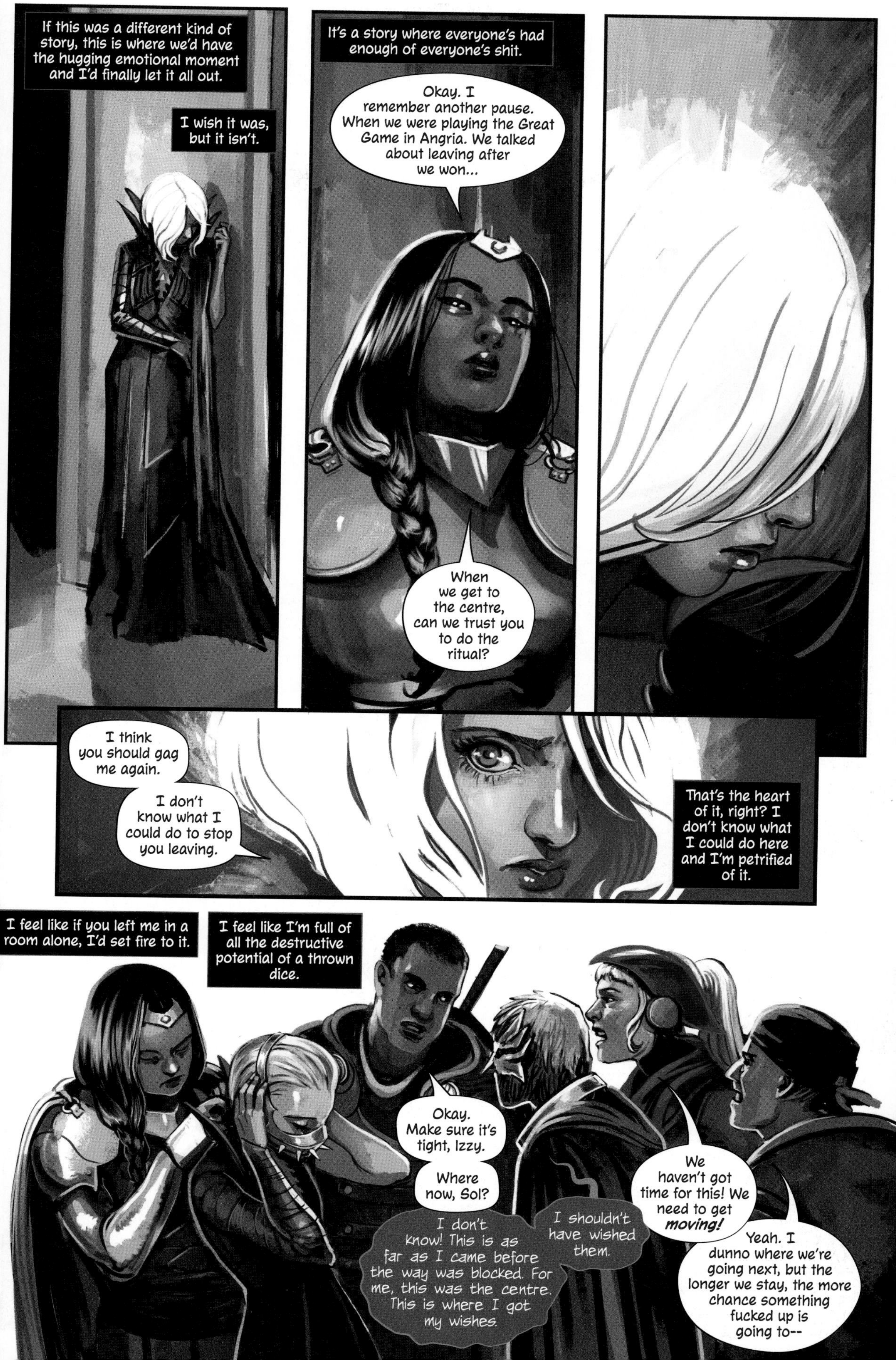
If this was a different kind of story, this is where we'd have the hugging emotional moment and I'd finally let it all out.
I wish it was, but it isn't.
It's a story where everyone's had enough of everyone's shit.
Okay. I remember another pause. When we were playing the Great Game in Angria. We talked about leaving after we won...
When we get to the centre, can we trust you to do the ritual?
I think you should gag me again.
I don't know what I could do to stop you leaving.
That's the heart of it, right? I don't know what I could do here and I'm petrified of it.
I feel like if you left me in a room alone, I'd set fire to it.
I feel like I'm full of all the destructive potential of a thrown dice.
Okay. Make sure it's tight, Izzy.
Where now, Sol?
I don't know! This is as far as I came before the way was blocked. For me, this was the centre. This is where I got my wishes.
I shouldn't have wished them.
We haven't got time for this! We need to get *moving!*
Yeah. I dunno where we're going next, but the longer we stay, the more chance something fucked up is going to--

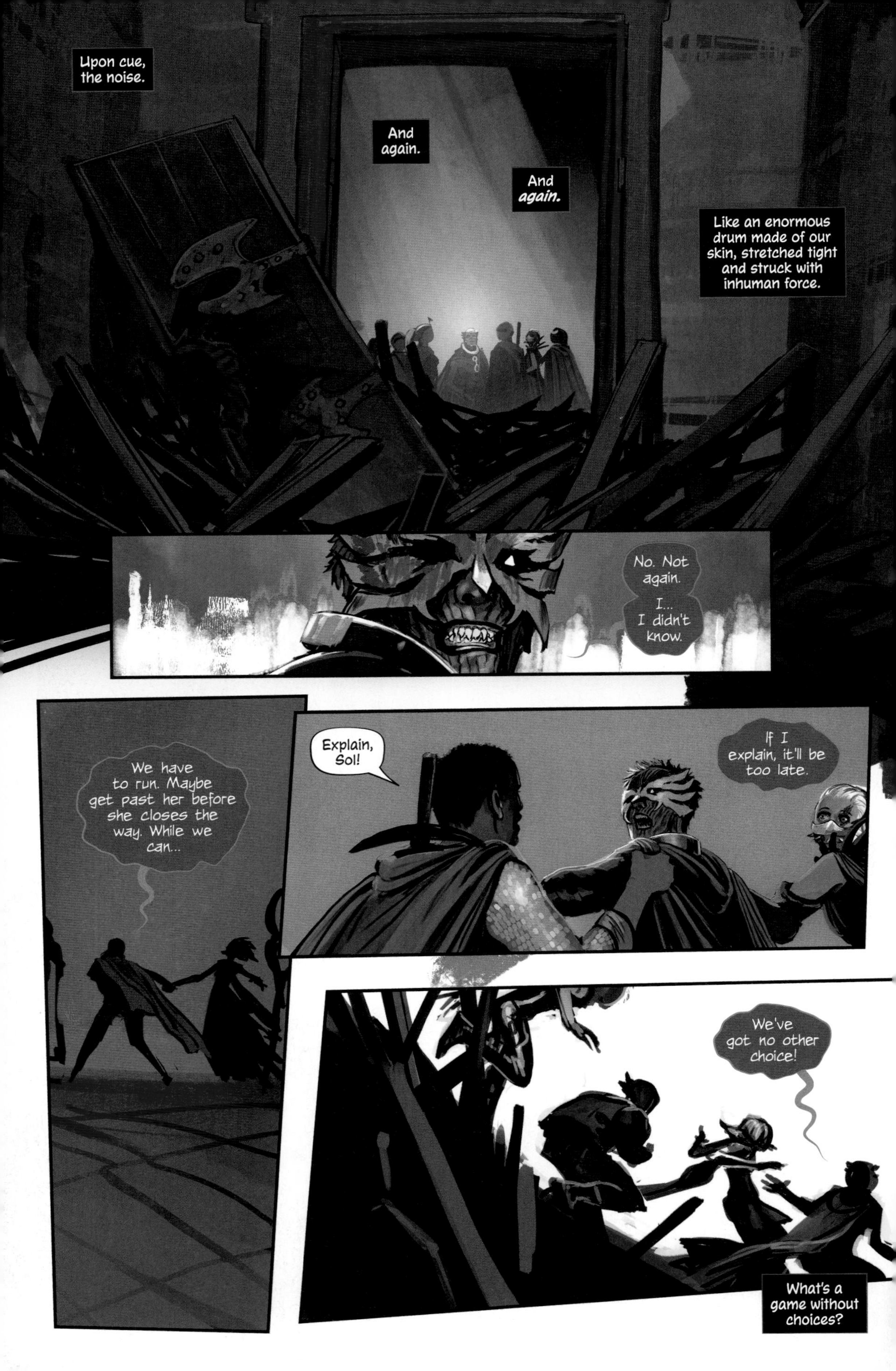
Upon cue, the noise.
And again.
And *again.*
Like an enormous drum made of our skin, stretched tight and struck with inhuman force.
No. Not again.
I... I didn't know.
We have to run. Maybe get past her before she closes the way. While we can...
Explain, Sol!
If I explain, it'll be too late.
We've got no other choice!
What's a game without choices?

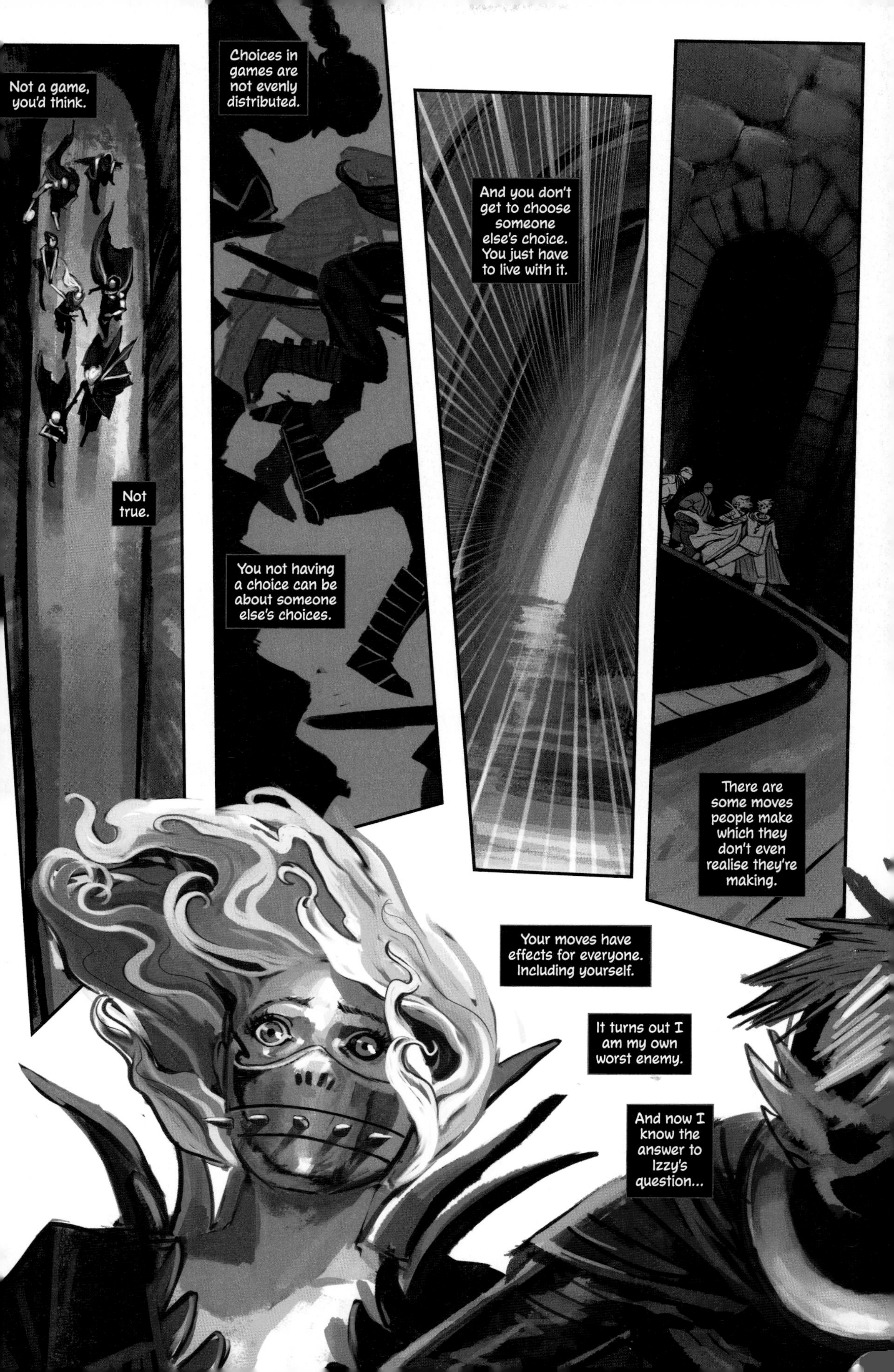
Not a game, you'd think.
Not true.
Choices in games are not evenly distributed.
You not having a choice can be about someone else's choices.
And you don't get to choose someone else's choice. You just have to live with it.
There are some moves people make which they don't even realise they're making.
Your moves have effects for everyone. Including yourself.
It turns out I am my own worst enemy.
And now I know the answer to Izzy's question...

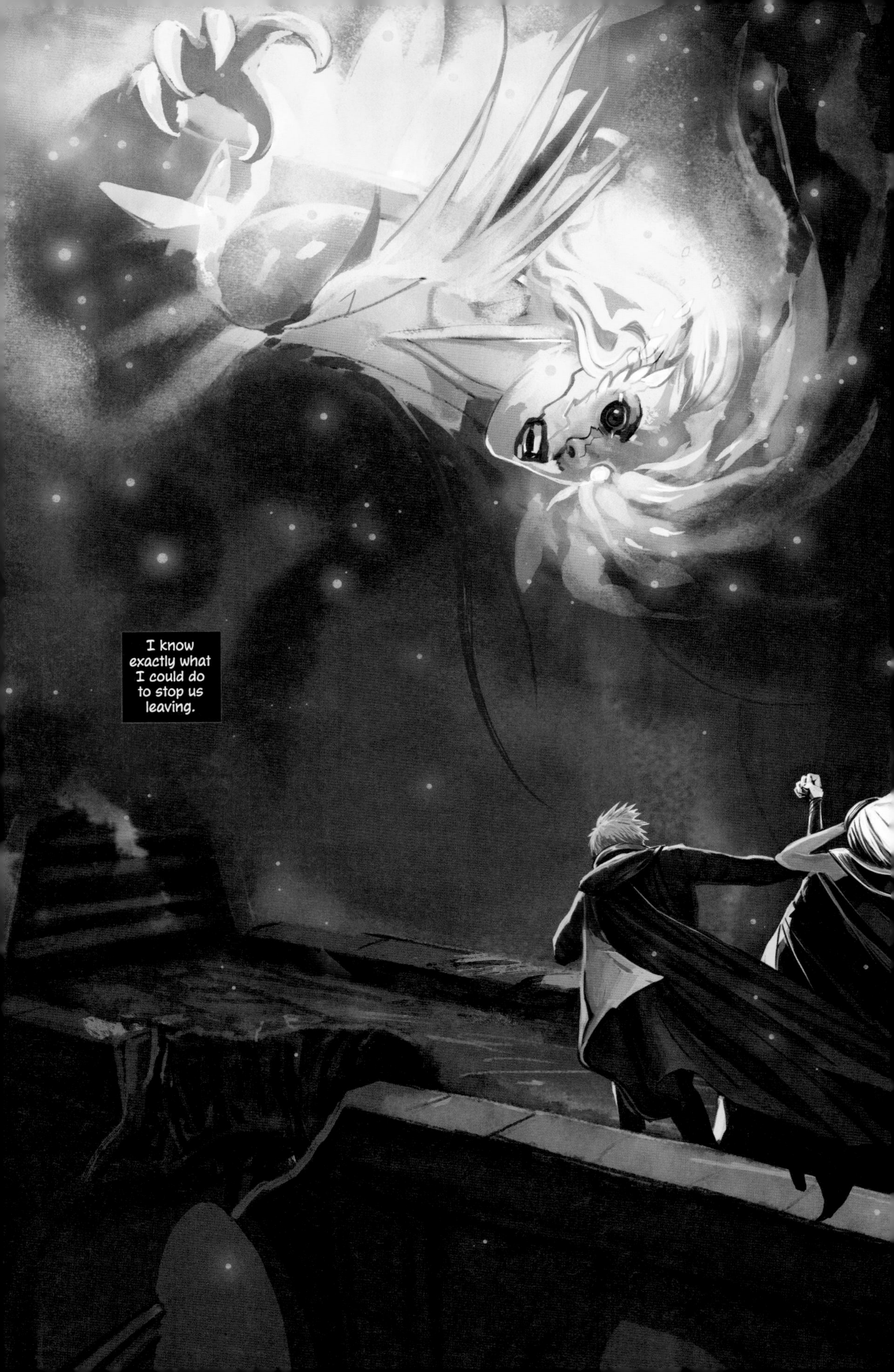
I know exactly what I could do to stop us leaving.

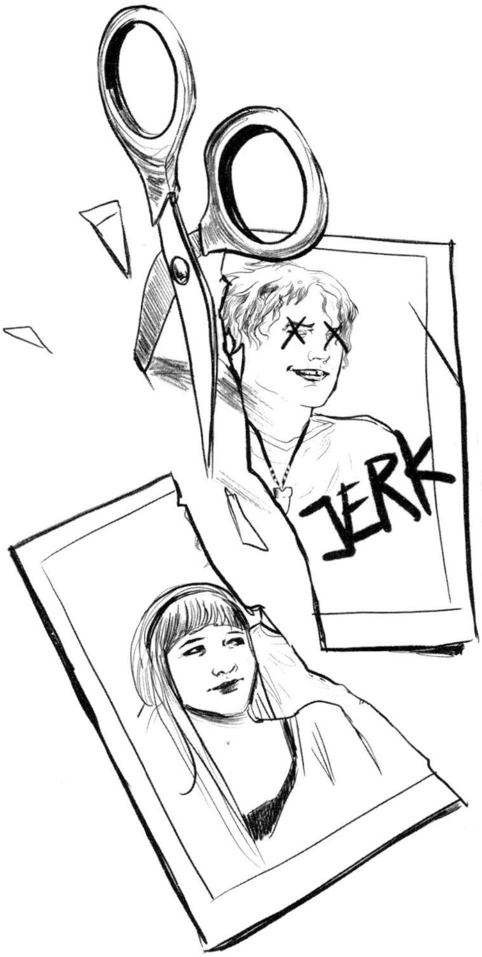
JERK

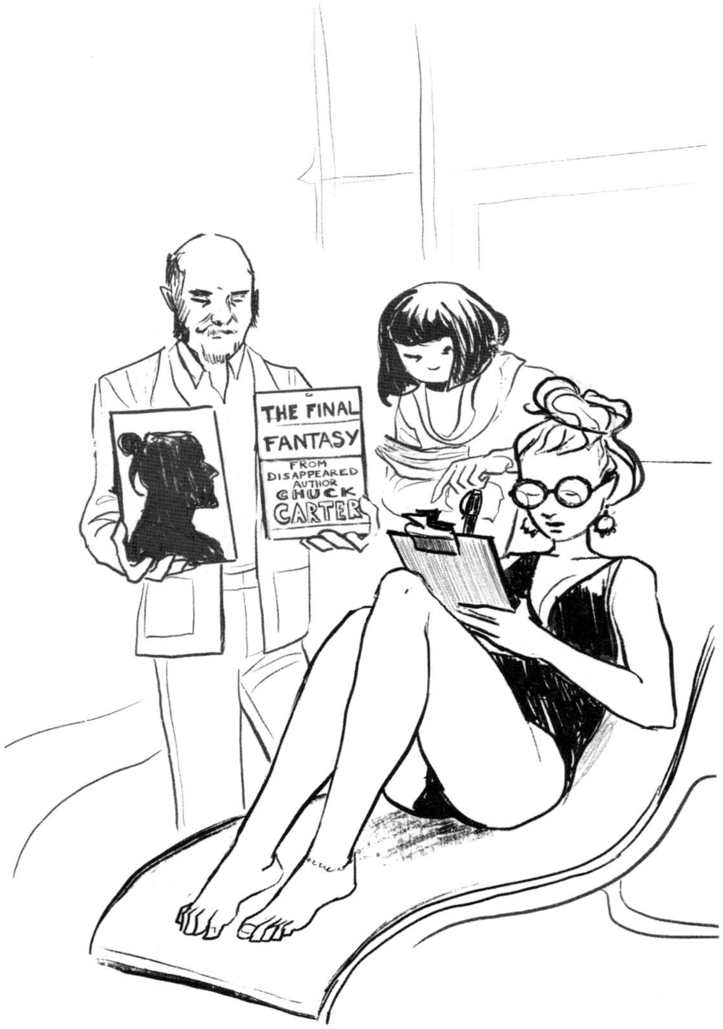
THE FINAL
FANTASY
FROM
DISAPPEARED
AUTHOR
CHUCK
CARTER

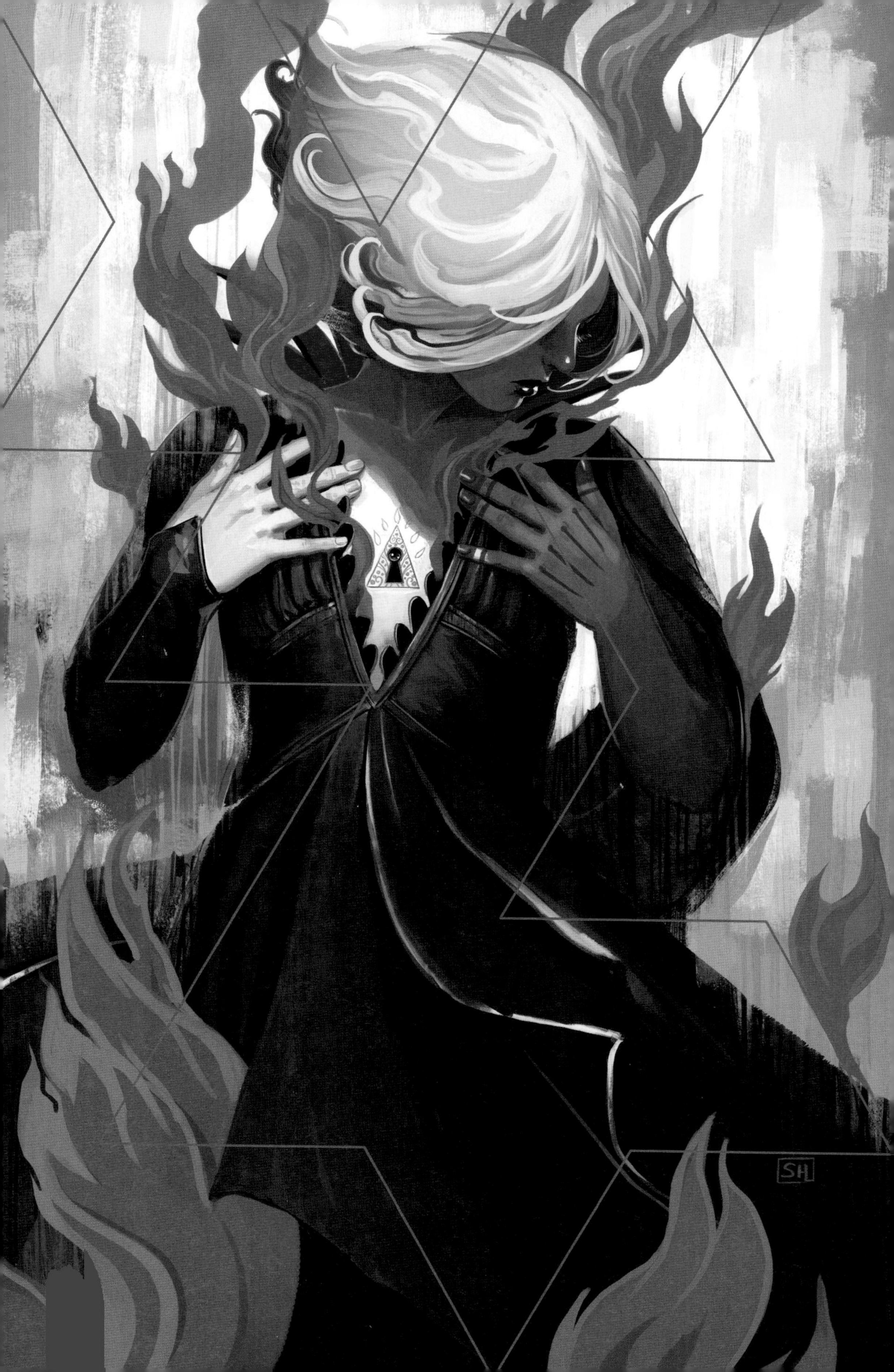
SH

19:
BOSS FIGHT

"We are as ignorant of the meaning of the dragon as we are of the meaning of the universe, but there is something in the dragon's image that appeals to the human imagination, and so we find the dragon in quite distinct places and times. It is, so to speak, a necessary monster."
— *Jorge Luis Borges*

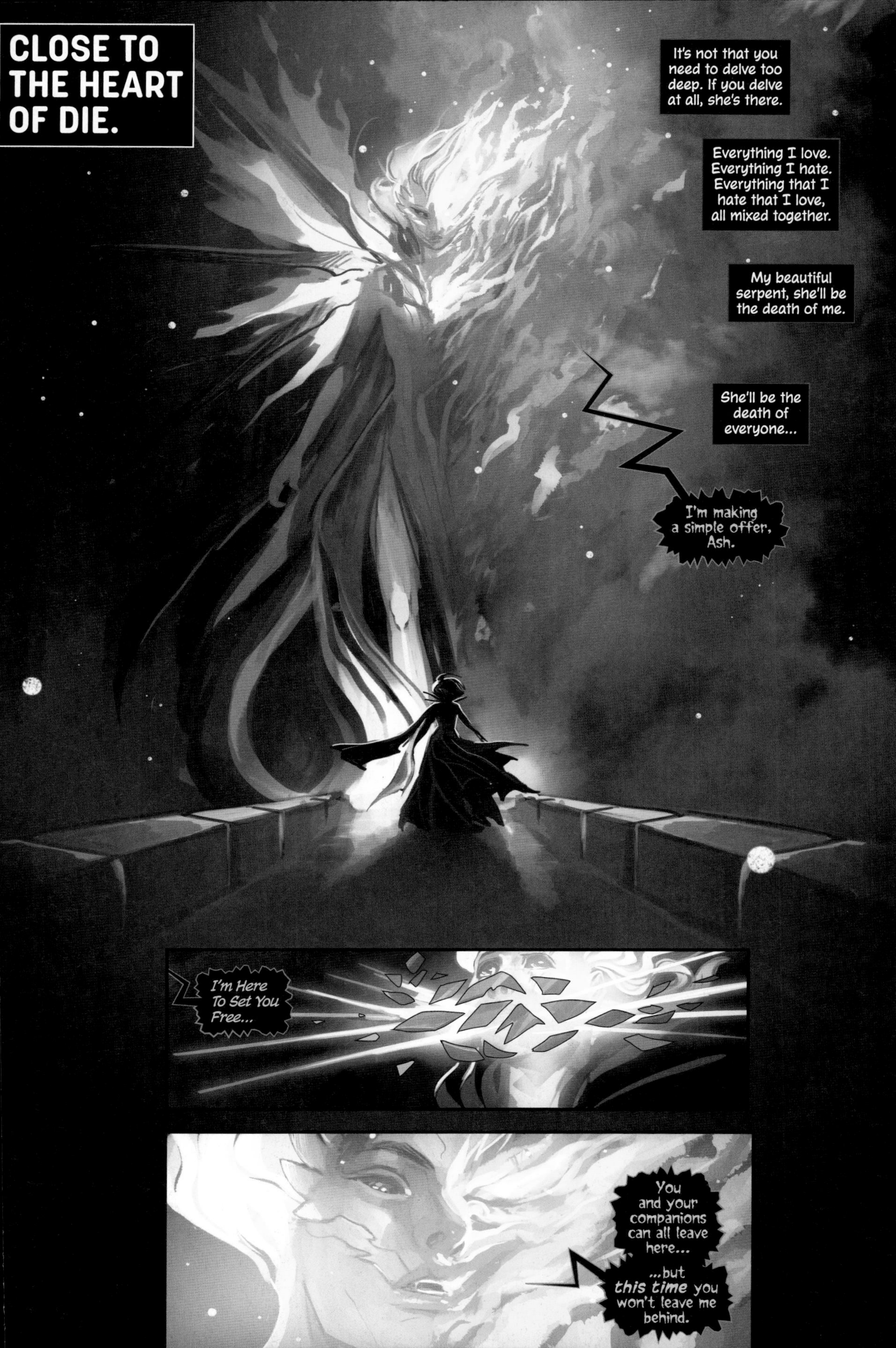
CLOSE TO THE HEART OF DIE.
It's not that you need to delve too deep. If you delve at all, she's there.
Everything I love. Everything I hate. Everything that I hate that I love, all mixed together.
My beautiful serpent, she'll be the death of me.
She'll be the death of everyone...
I'm making a simple offer, Ash.
I'm Here To Set You Free...
You and your companions can all leave here...
...but *this time* you won't leave me behind.

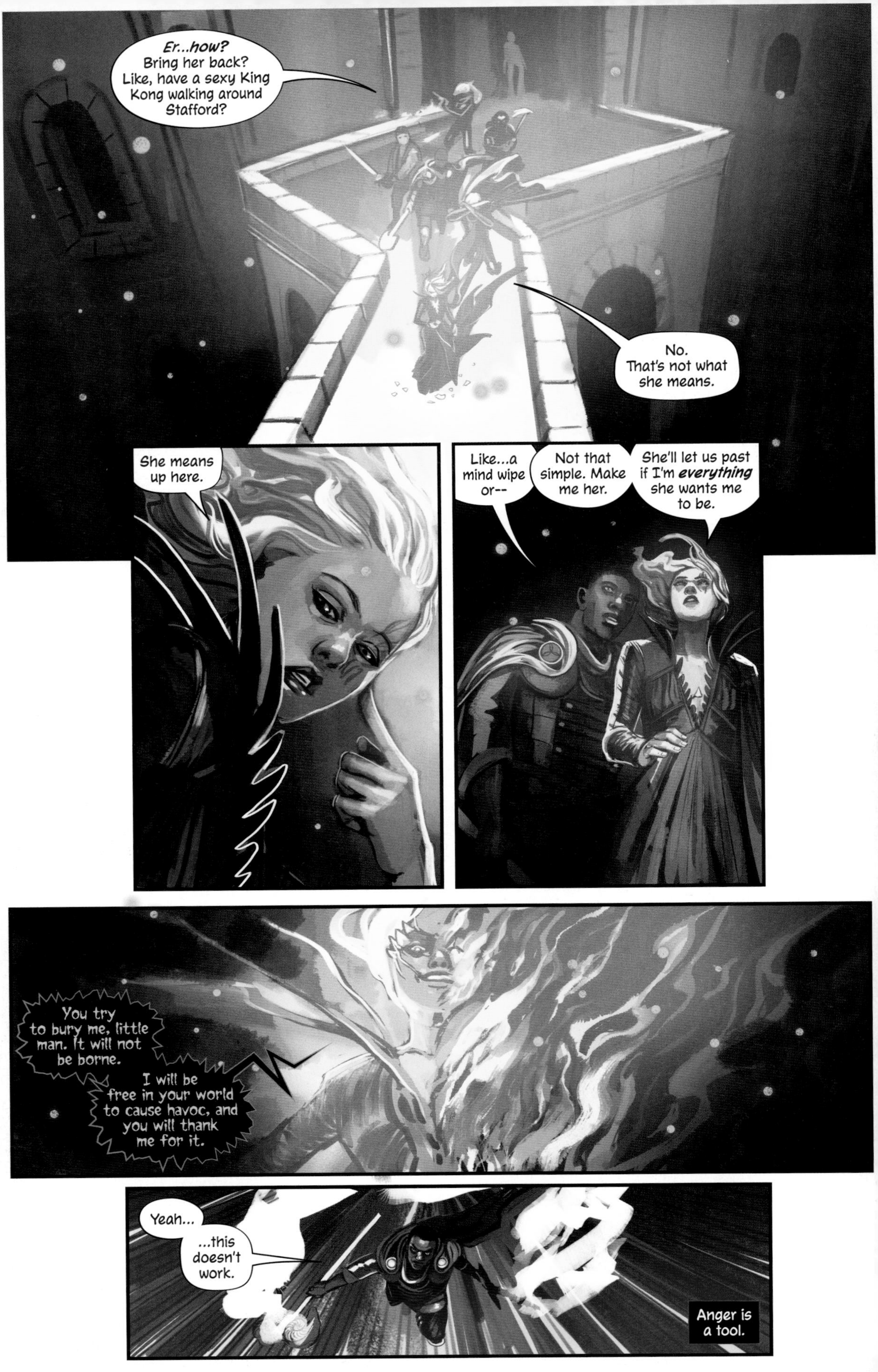
Er...how? Bring her back? Like, have a sexy King Kong walking around Stafford?
No. That's not what she means.
She means up here.
Like...a mind wipe or--
Not that simple. Make me her.
She'll let us past if I'm everything she wants me to be.
You try to bury me, little man. It will not be borne.
I will be free in your world to cause havoc, and you will thank me for it.
Yeah...
...this doesn't work.
Anger is a tool.

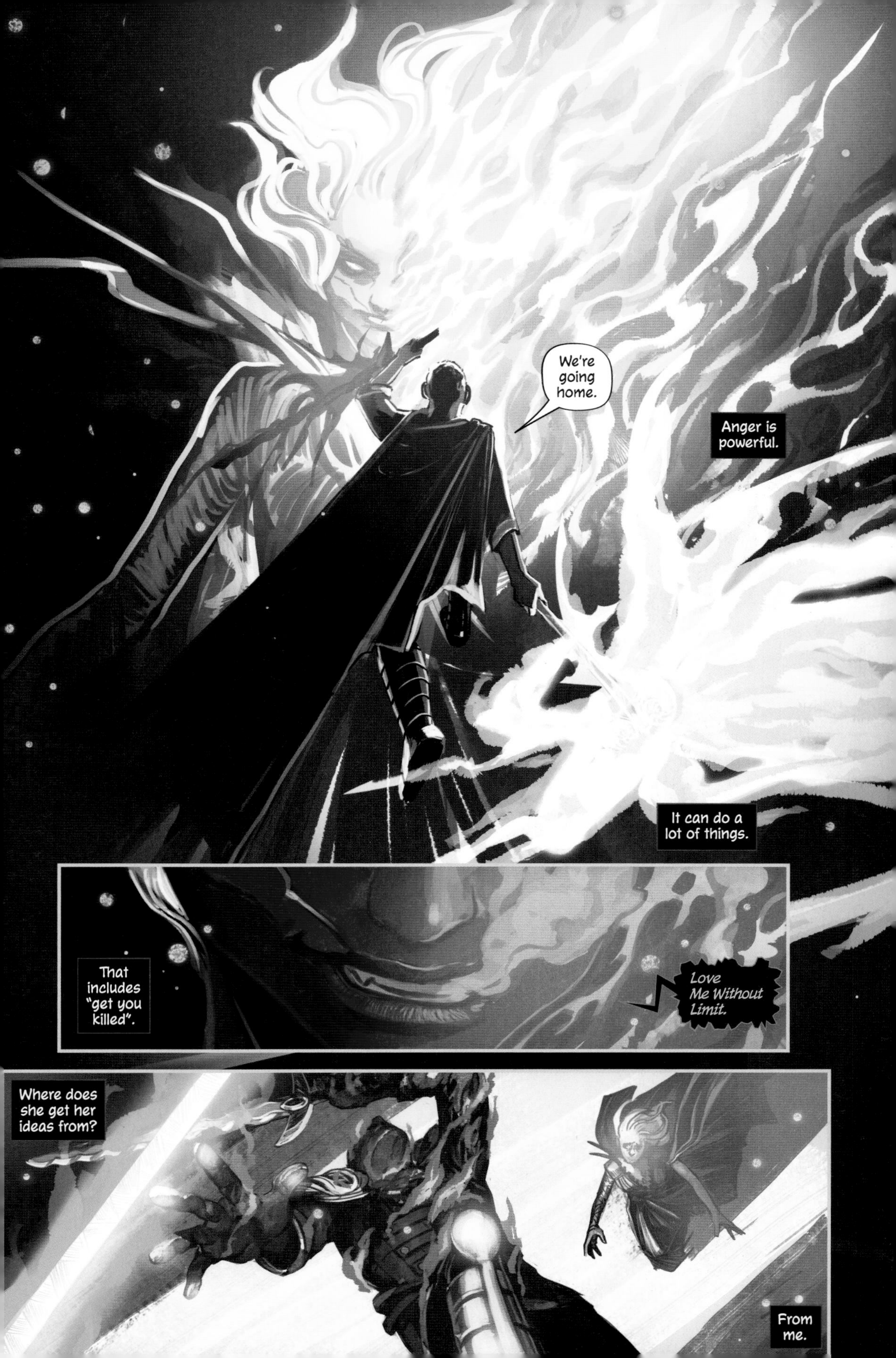

We're going home.
Anger is powerful.
It can do a lot of things.
That includes "get you killed".
Love Me Without Limit.
Where does she get her ideas from?
From me.

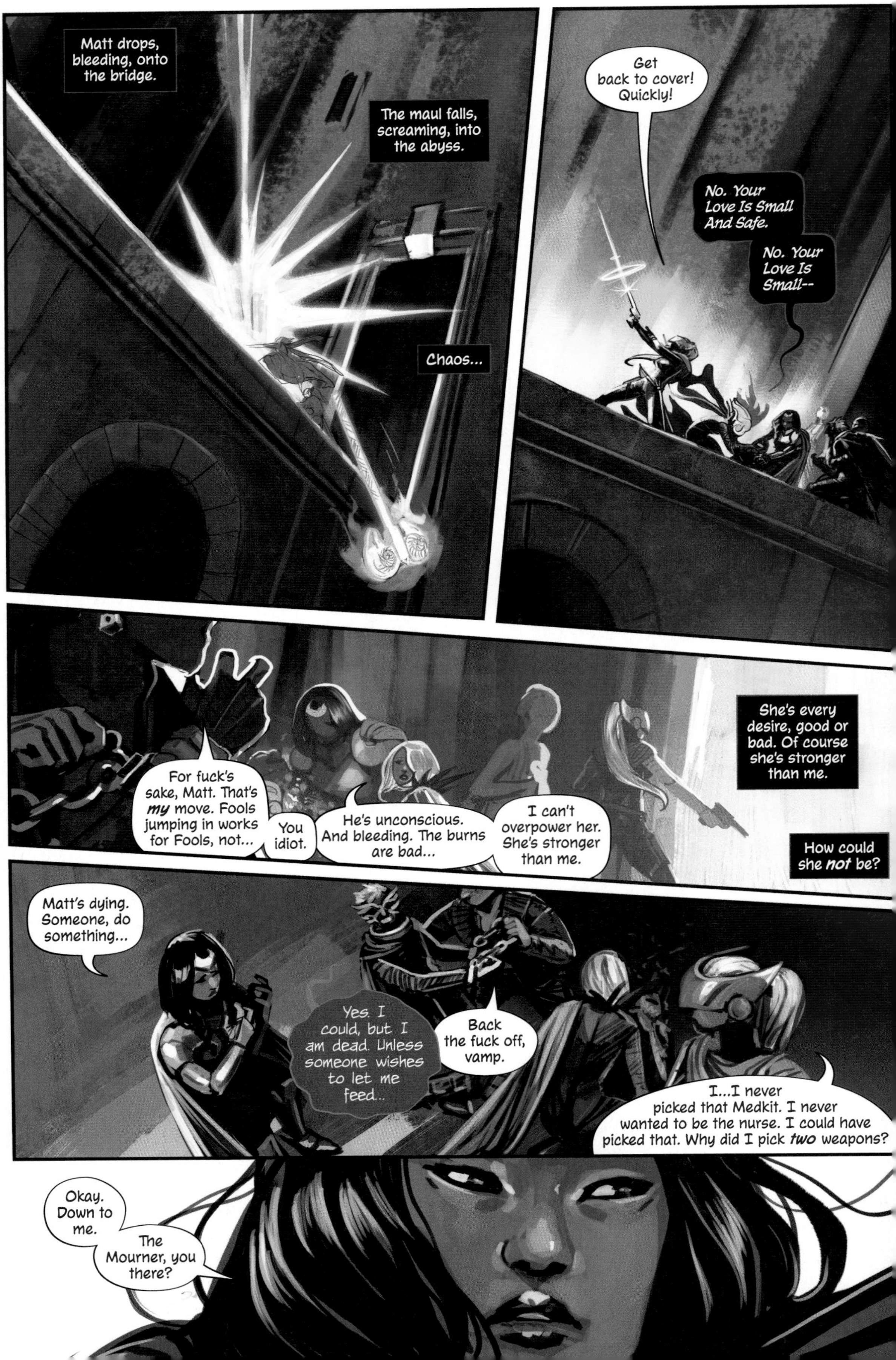
Matt drops, bleeding, onto the bridge.
The maul falls, screaming, into the abyss.
Chaos...
Get back to cover! Quickly!
No. Your Love Is Small And Safe.
No. Your Love Is Small--
She's every desire, good or bad. Of course she's stronger than me.
For fuck's sake, Matt. That's *my* move. Fools jumping in works for Fools, not...
You idiot.
He's unconscious. And bleeding. The burns are bad...
I can't overpower her. She's stronger than me.
How could she *not* be?
Matt's dying. Someone, do something...
Yes. I could, but I am dead. Unless someone wishes to let me feed...
Back the fuck off, vamp.
I...I never picked that Medkit. I never wanted to be the nurse. I could have picked that. Why did I pick *two* weapons?
Okay. Down to me.
The Mourner, you there?

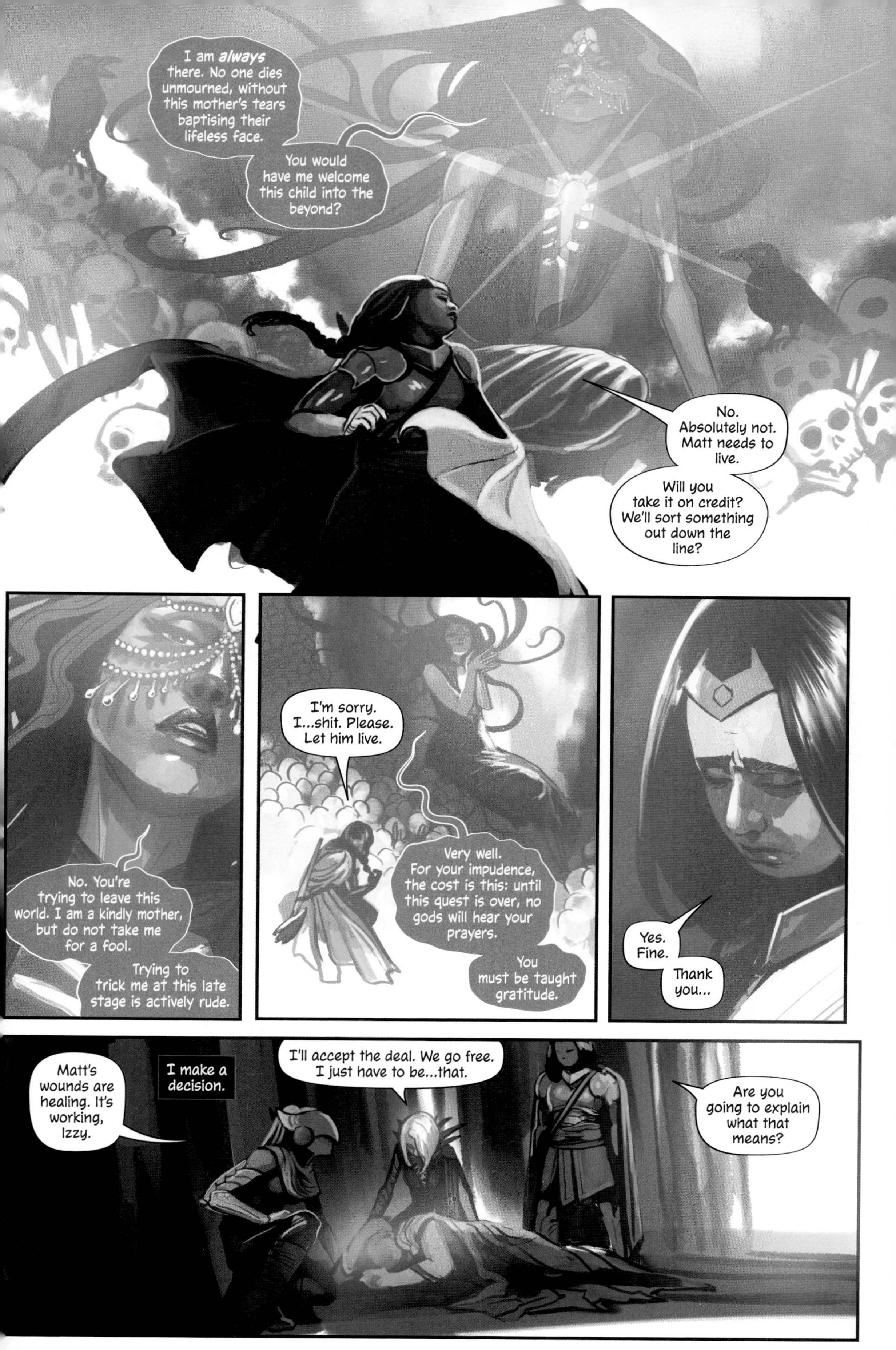
I am *always* there. No one dies unmourned, without this mother's tears baptising their lifeless face.
You would have me welcome this child into the beyond?
No. Absolutely not. Matt needs to live.
Will you take it on credit? We'll sort something out down the line?
No. You're trying to leave this world. I am a kindly mother, but do not take me for a fool.
Trying to trick me at this late stage is actively rude.
I'm sorry. I...shit. Please. Let him live.
Very well. For your impudence, the cost is this: until this quest is over, no gods will hear your prayers.
You must be taught gratitude.
Yes. Fine.
Thank you...
Matt's wounds are healing. It's working, Izzy.
I make a decision.
I'll accept the deal. We go free. I just have to be...that.
Are you going to explain what that means?

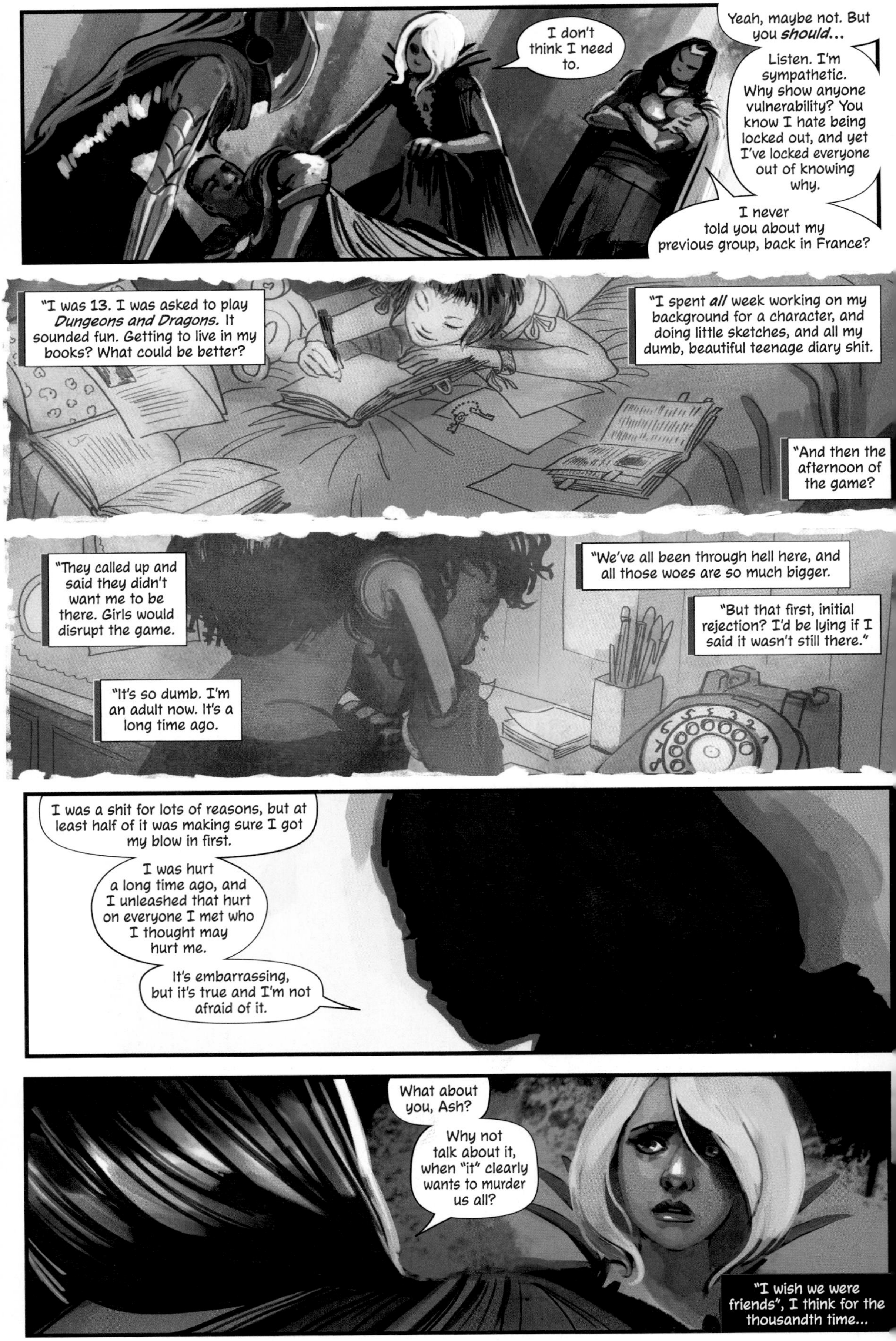
I don't think I need to.
Yeah, maybe not. But you **should...**
Listen. I'm sympathetic. Why show anyone vulnerability? You know I hate being locked out, and yet I've locked everyone out of knowing why.
I never told you about my previous group, back in France?
"I was 13. I was asked to play *Dungeons and Dragons.* It sounded fun. Getting to live in my books? What could be better?
"I spent *all* week working on my background for a character, and doing little sketches, and all my dumb, beautiful teenage diary shit.
"And then the afternoon of the game?
"They called up and said they didn't want me to be there. Girls would disrupt the game.
"It's so dumb. I'm an adult now. It's a long time ago.
"We've all been through hell here, and all those woes are so much bigger.
"But that first, initial rejection? I'd be lying if I said it wasn't still there."
I was a shit for lots of reasons, but at least half of it was making sure I got my blow in first.
I was hurt a long time ago, and I unleashed that hurt on everyone I met who I thought may hurt me.
It's embarrassing, but it's true and I'm not afraid of it.
What about you, Ash?
Why not talk about it, when "it" clearly wants to murder us all?
"I wish we were friends", I think for the thousandth time...

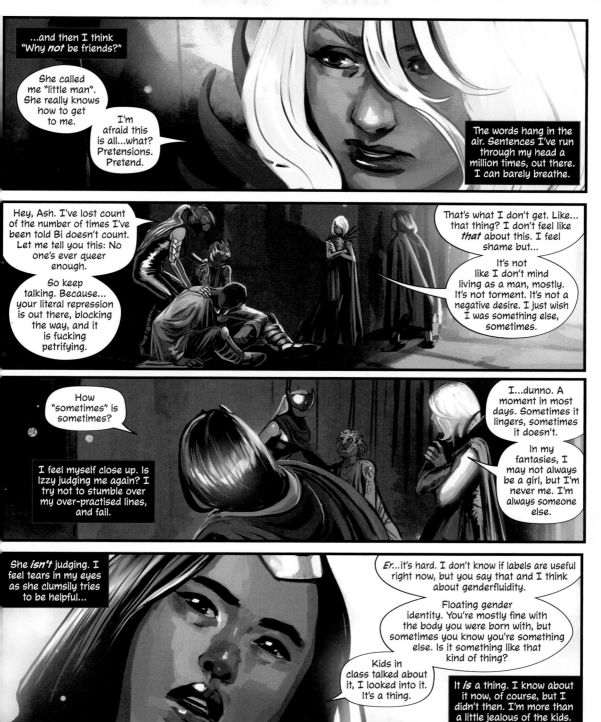

...and then I think "Why *not* be friends?"

She called me "little man". She really knows how to get to me.

I'm afraid this is all...what? Pretensions. Pretend.

The words hang in the air. Sentences I've run through my head a million times, out there. I can barely breathe.

Hey, Ash. I've lost count of the number of times I've been told Bi doesn't count. Let me tell you this: No one's ever queer enough.

So keep talking. Because... your literal repression is out there, blocking the way, and it is fucking petrifying.

That's what I don't get. Like... that thing? I don't feel like *that* about this. I feel shame but...

It's not like I don't mind living as a man, mostly. It's not torment. It's not a negative desire. I just wish I was something else, sometimes.

How "sometimes" is sometimes?

I feel myself close up. Is Izzy judging me again? I try not to stumble over my over-practised lines, and fail.

I...dunno. A moment in most days. Sometimes it lingers, sometimes it doesn't.

In my fantasies, I may not always be a girl, but I'm never me. I'm always someone else.

She *isn't* judging. I feel tears in my eyes as she clumsily tries to be helpful...

*Er...*it's hard. I don't know if labels are useful right now, but you say that and I think about genderfluidity.

Floating gender identity. You're mostly fine with the body you were born with, but sometimes you know you're something else. Is it something like that kind of thing?

Kids in class talked about it, I looked into it. It's a thing.

It *is* a thing. I know about it now, of course, but I didn't then. I'm more than a little jealous of the kids.

When *we* were young, we didn't have words for any of these complexities, and since then there's been all these expansion packs full of character classes...

Sounds like you're just being indecisive.

Oh, fuck off.

I mean, if it is, is that so awful? As if being indecisive is a bad thing. Mostly decisive people just make wrong decisions more quickly.

Yeah, maybe genderfluidity. Or something else, or something I still don't have words for. But it's there, and this place let me explore it.

Wishes are real, I guess, no matter how idle.

And that's the problem.

You've seen how I've acted here, to all of you. I feel I could do anything.

I killed a girl by setting her on fire with a word. It made me sick.

But that triumph? God help me, I liked it.

I don't want to do that. I don't want to hurt people in reality.

But here, everything gets blurred. The real and the not real. Every whim or thought is dragged out of me.

I figure... safer to lock it *all* away.

It sounds like you've let all your queerness get mixed in with every bad, shameful thought you've ever had.

Do you think I don't know that?!

Knowing changes nothing. Trust me on this. I've known what I am so many times, and it doesn't fucking stop it.

Yeah, but *intellectual* knowing and *emotional* knowing aren't the same thing...

But they're a step towards one another, if you want to take it. And you never did, Chuck, right? Ash does.

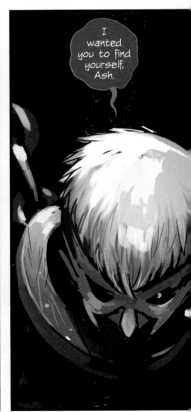

I wanted you to find yourself, Ash.

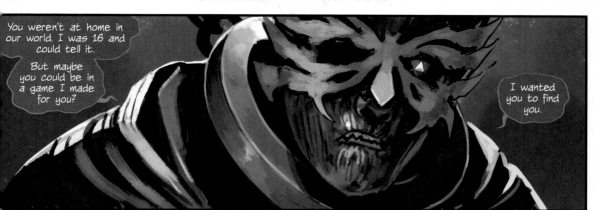

You weren't at home in our world. I was 16 and could tell it.

But maybe you could be in a game I made for you?

I wanted you to find you.

Thank you.

I feel like shit, but I'm alive, so...

Wh...what's the plan?

Everyone, follow my lead.

I've got to just promise everything that she wants. We can handle that. And...you're all my keeper if she comes with me.

Someone look after Sol. I'm going to need to use my voice.

I'll hack him.

Nah, leave it to me. Molly's your priority, right?

Gives me something to do while all of you are having emotions.

Ash...don't. Whatever this is, I...don't want to lose you.

Don't worry, Sol. You wanted me to find myself...

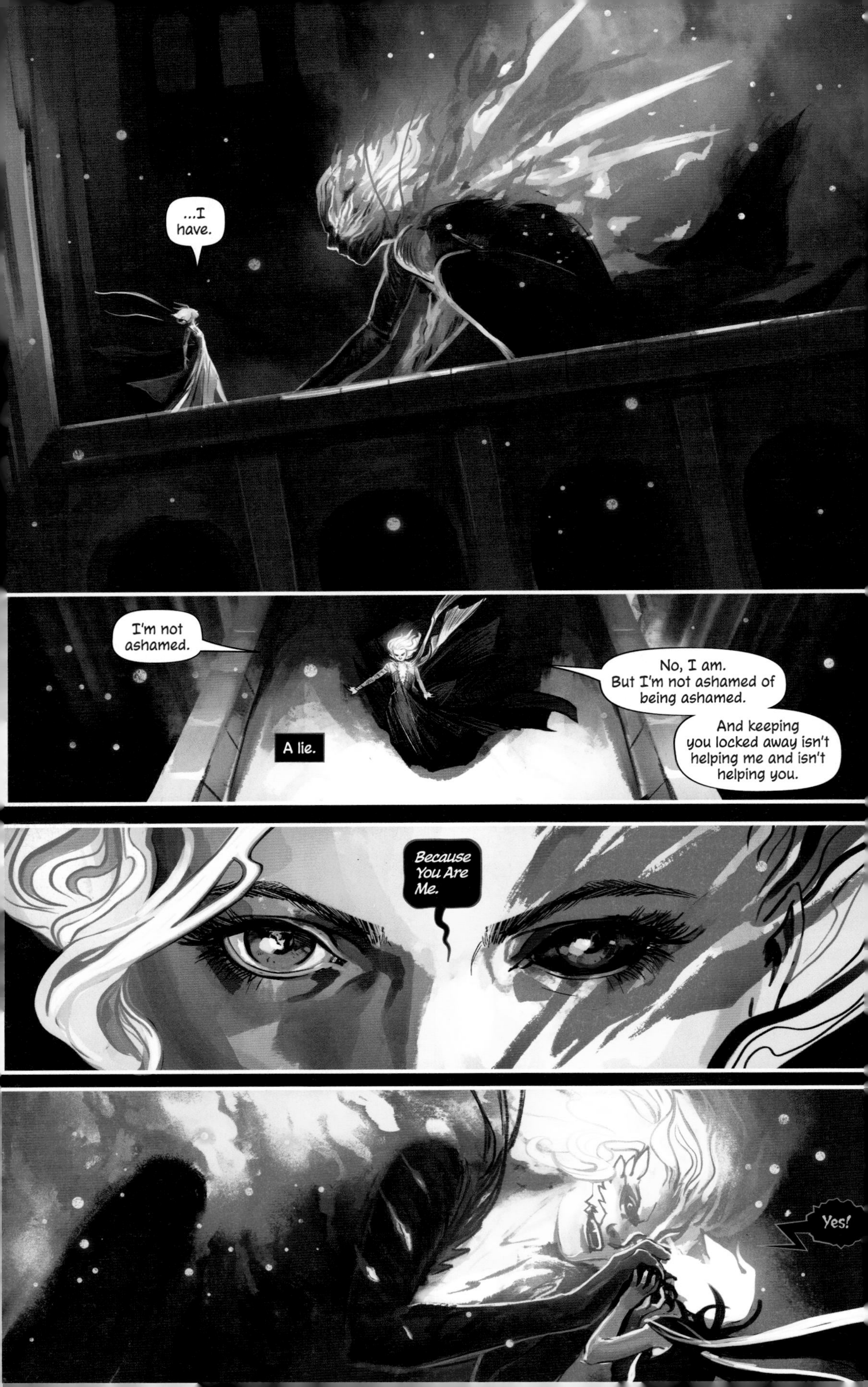

...I have.
I'm not ashamed.
A lie.
No, I am. But I'm not ashamed of being ashamed.
And keeping you locked away isn't helping me and isn't helping you.
Because You Are Me.
Yes!

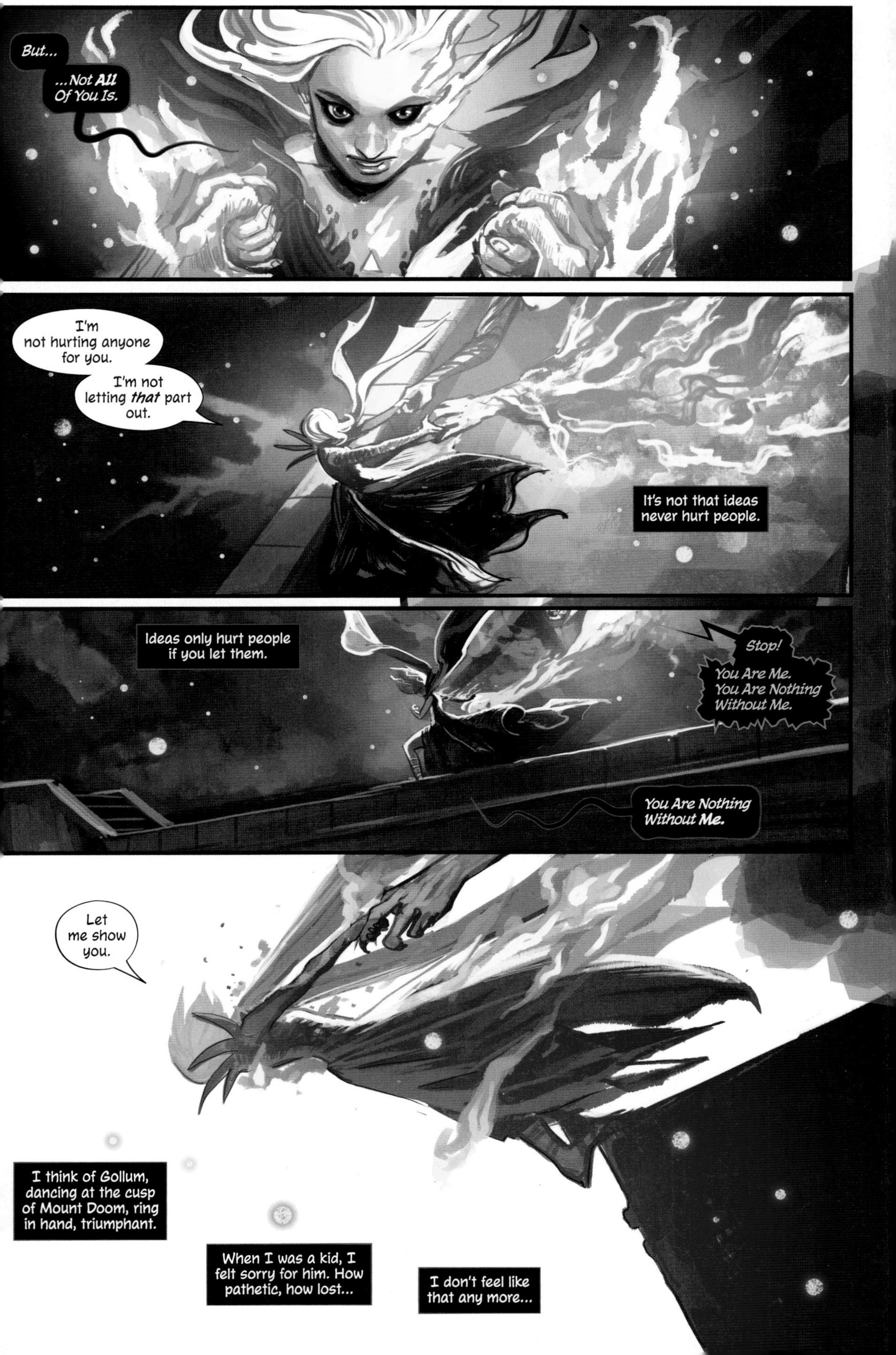

But...
...Not **All** Of You Is.
I'm not hurting anyone for you.
I'm not letting ***that*** part out.
It's not that ideas never hurt people.
Ideas only hurt people if you let them.
Stop!
You Are Me. You Are Nothing Without Me.
You Are Nothing Without **Me.**
Let me show you.
I think of Gollum, dancing at the cusp of Mount Doom, ring in hand, triumphant.
When I was a kid, I felt sorry for him. How pathetic, how lost...
I don't feel like that any more...

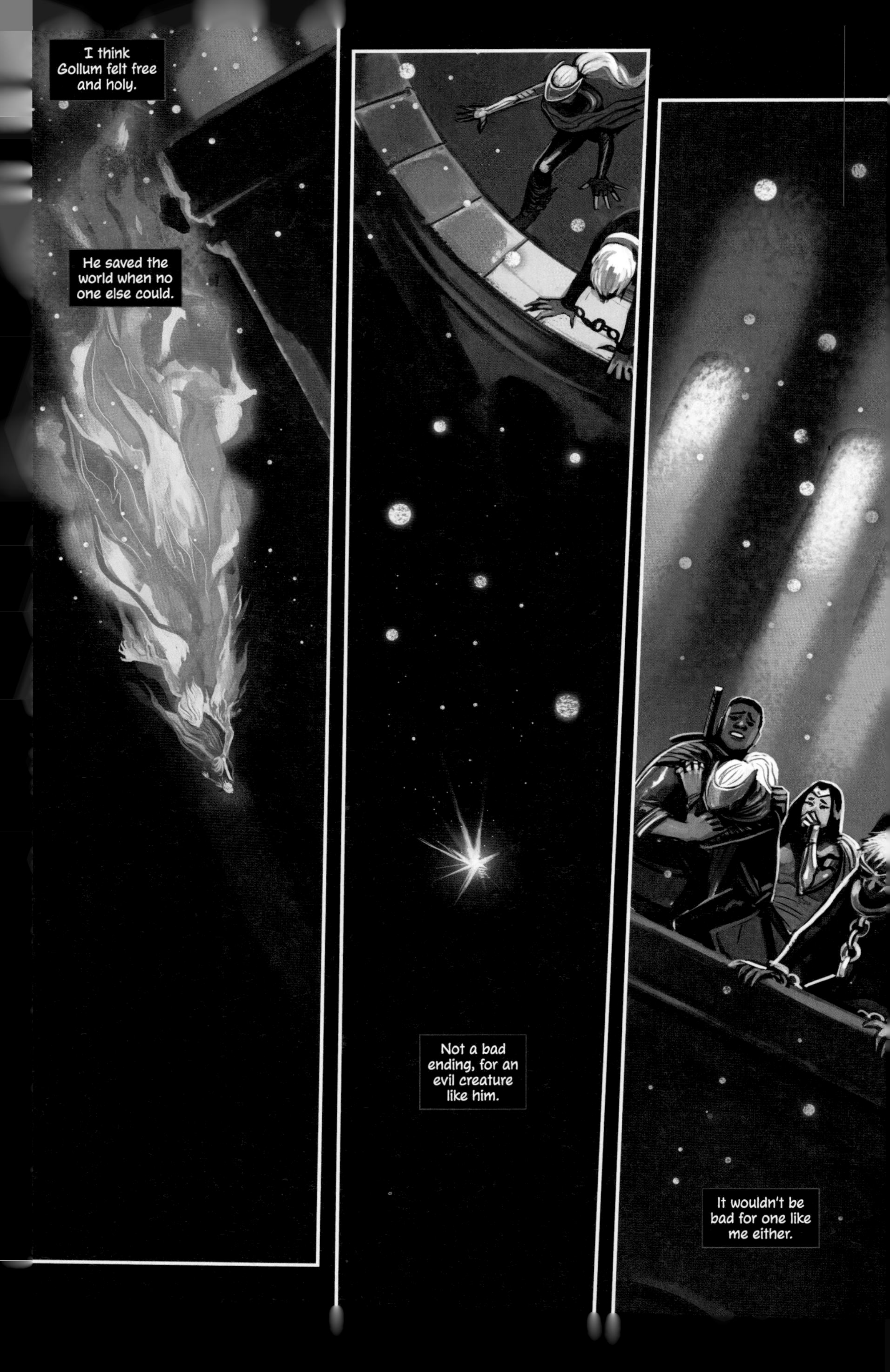
I think Gollum felt free and holy.
He saved the world when no one else could.
Not a bad ending, for an evil creature like him.
It wouldn't be bad for one like me either.

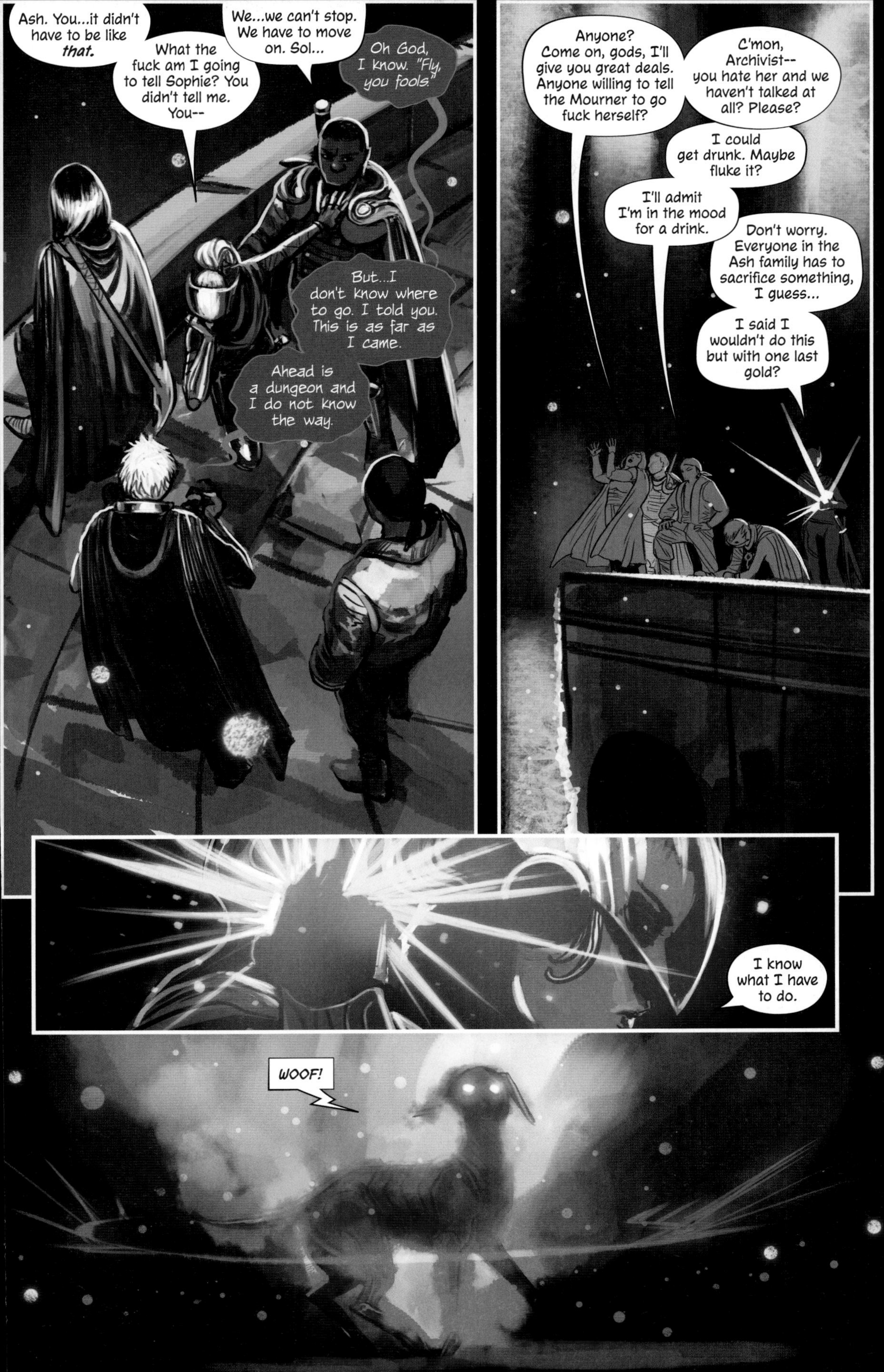

Ash. You...it didn't have to be like *that.*
What the fuck am I going to tell Sophie? You didn't tell me. You--
We...we can't stop. We have to move on. Sol...
Oh God, I know. "Fly, you fools."
But...I don't know where to go. I told you. This is as far as I came.
Ahead is a dungeon and I do not know the way.
Anyone? Come on, gods, I'll give you great deals. Anyone willing to tell the Mourner to go fuck herself?
C'mon, Archivist-- you hate her and we haven't talked at all? Please?
I could get drunk. Maybe fluke it?
I'll admit I'm in the mood for a drink.
Don't worry. Everyone in the Ash family has to sacrifice something, I guess...
I said I wouldn't do this but with one last gold?
I know what I have to do.
WOOF!

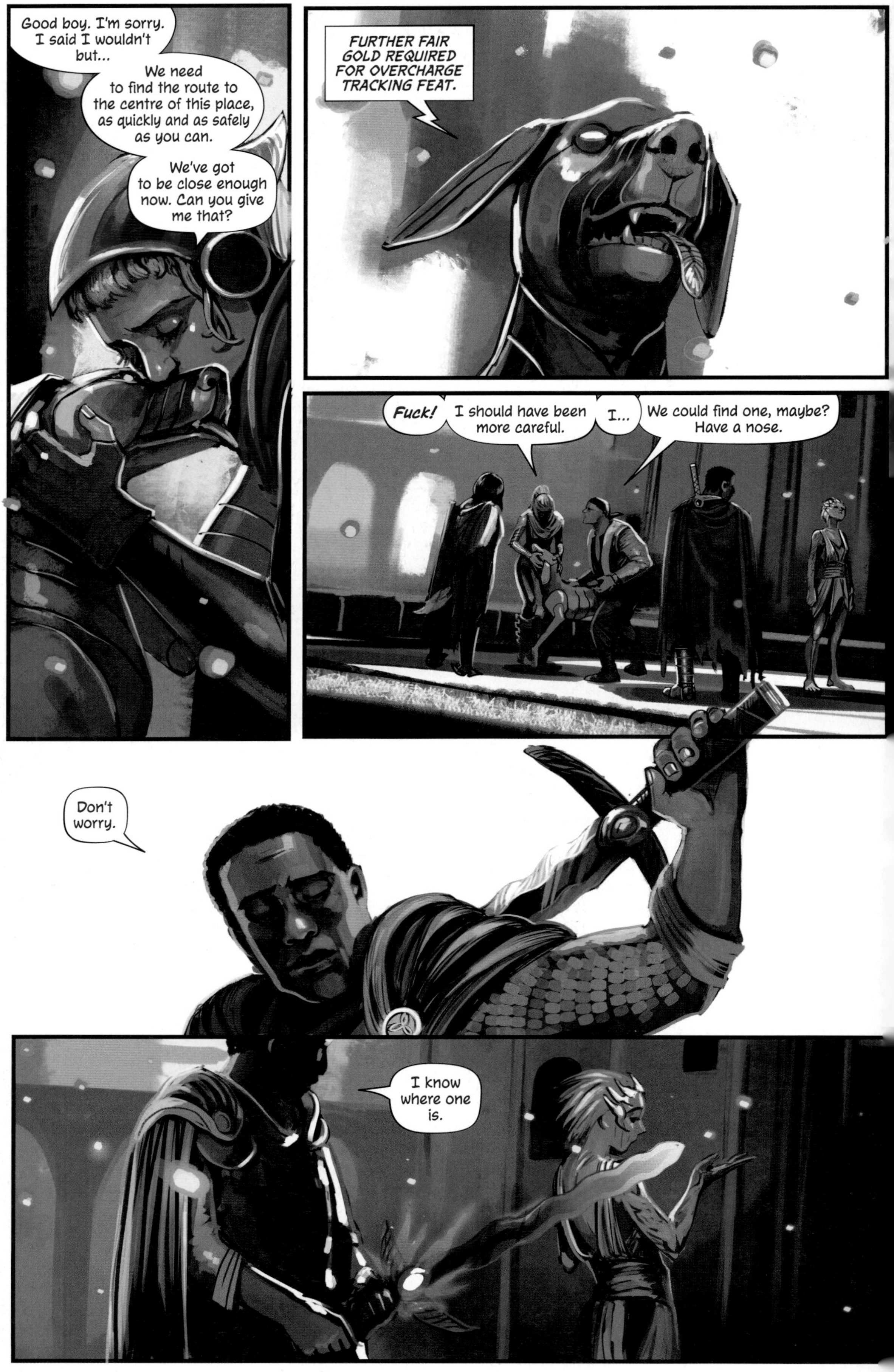
Good boy. I'm sorry. I said I wouldn't but...
We need to find the route to the centre of this place, as quickly and as safely as you can.
We've got to be close enough now. Can you give me that?
FURTHER FAIR GOLD REQUIRED FOR OVERCHARGE TRACKING FEAT.
Fuck!
I should have been more careful.
I...
We could find one, maybe? Have a nose.
Don't worry.
I know where one is.

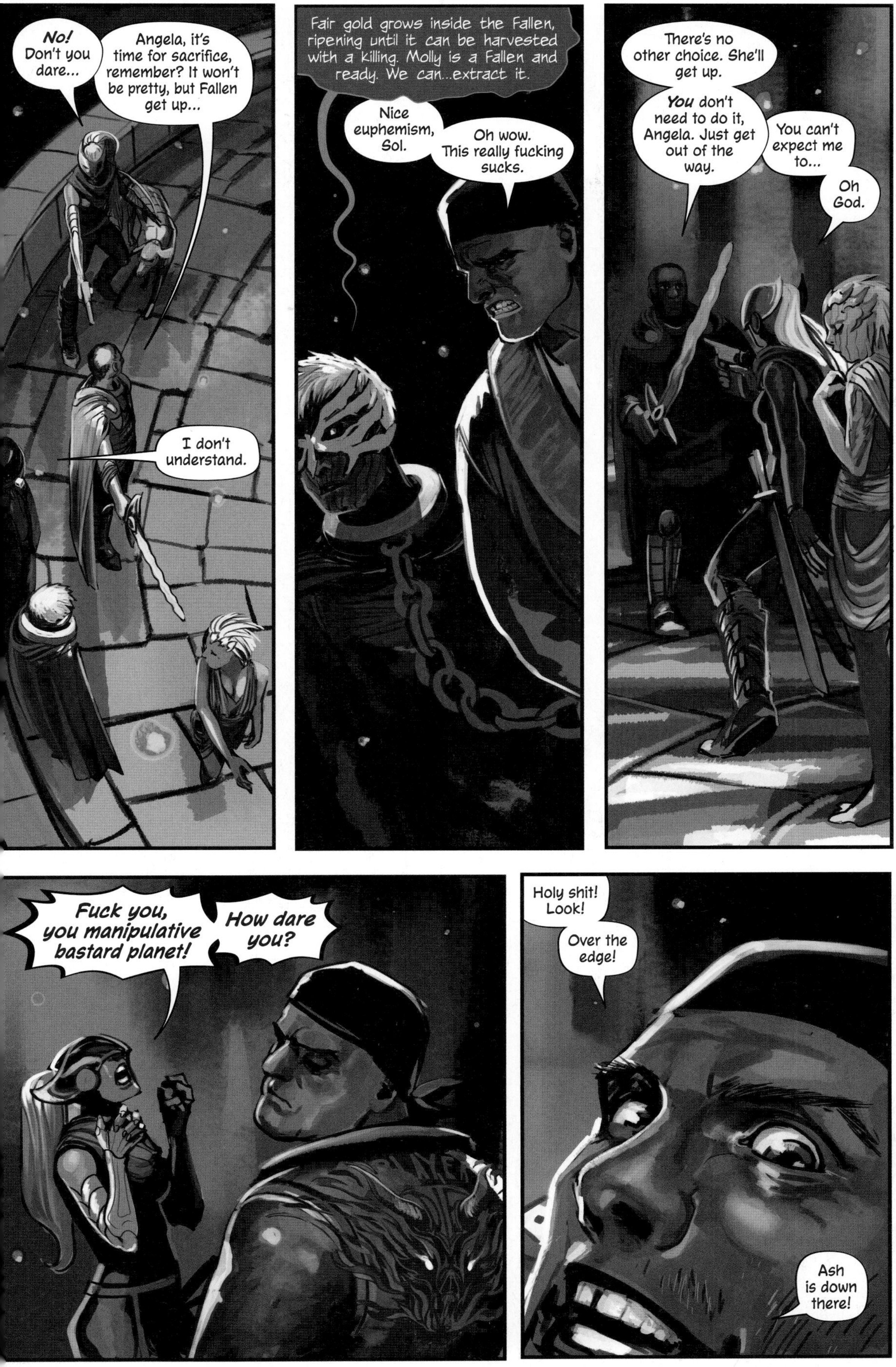
No! Don't you dare...
Angela, it's time for sacrifice, remember? It won't be pretty, but Fallen get up...
I don't understand.
Fair gold grows inside the Fallen, ripening until it can be harvested with a killing. Molly is a Fallen and ready. We can...extract it.
Nice euphemism, Sol.
Oh wow. This really fucking sucks.
There's no other choice. She'll get up.
You don't need to do it, Angela. Just get out of the way.
You can't expect me to...
Oh God.
Fuck you, you manipulative bastard planet!
How dare you?
Holy shit! Look!
Over the edge!
Ash is down there!

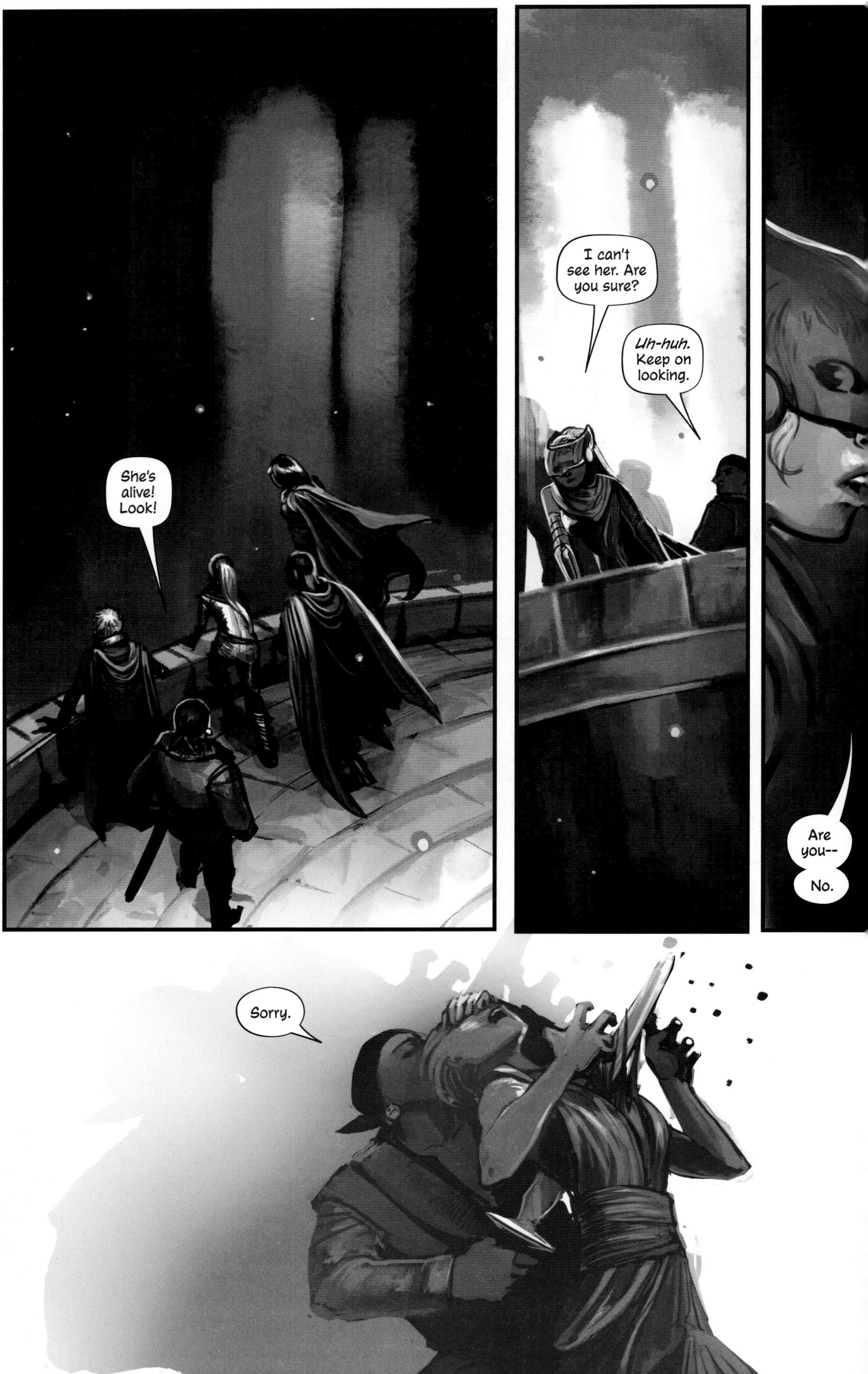
She's alive! Look!
I can't see her. Are you sure?
Uh-huh. Keep on looking.
Are you--
No.
Sorry.

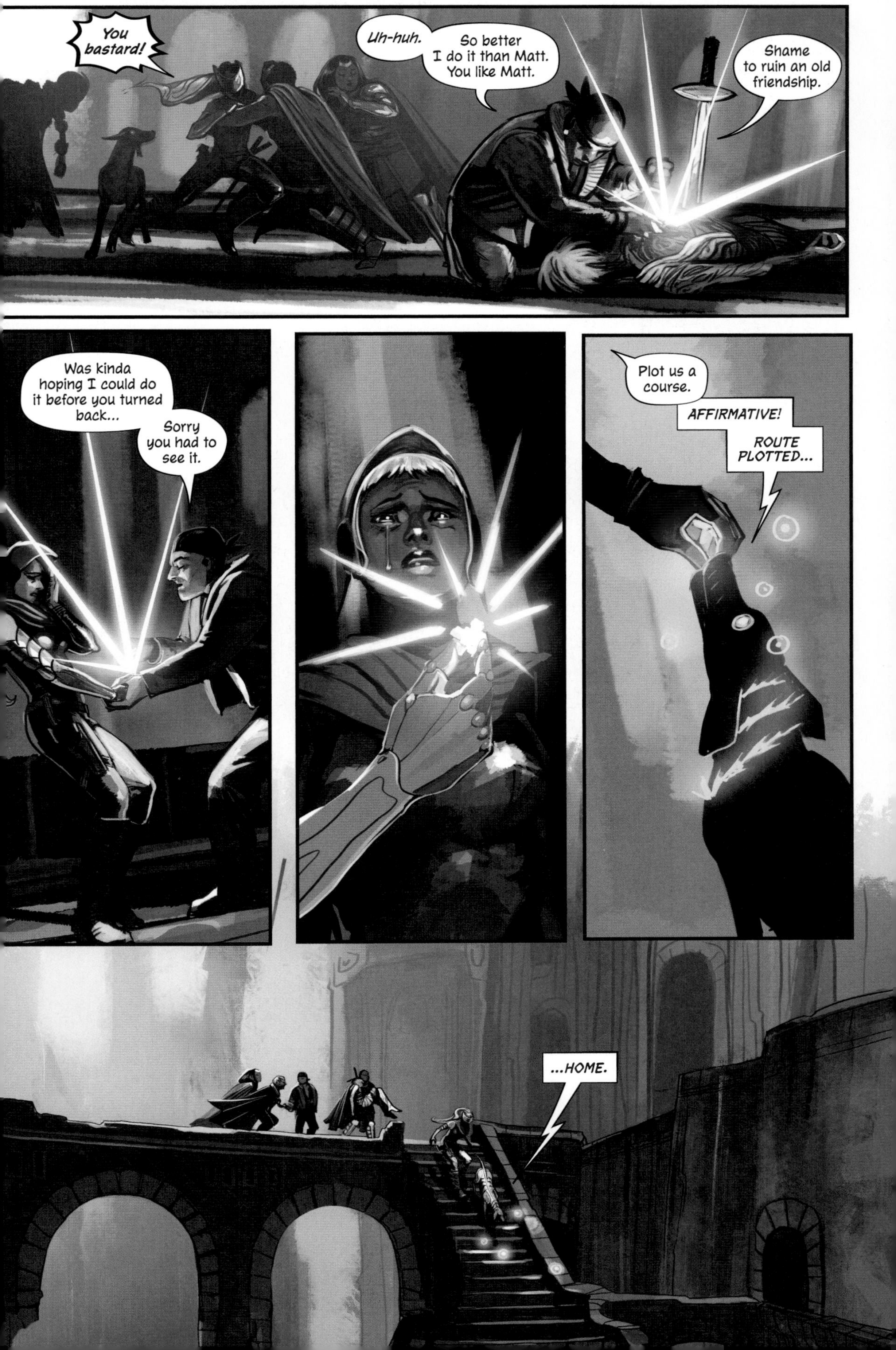
You bastard!
Uh-huh.
So better I do it than Matt. You like Matt.
Shame to ruin an old friendship.
Was kinda hoping I could do it before you turned back...
Sorry you had to see it.
Plot us a course.
AFFIRMATIVE!
ROUTE PLOTTED...
...HOME.

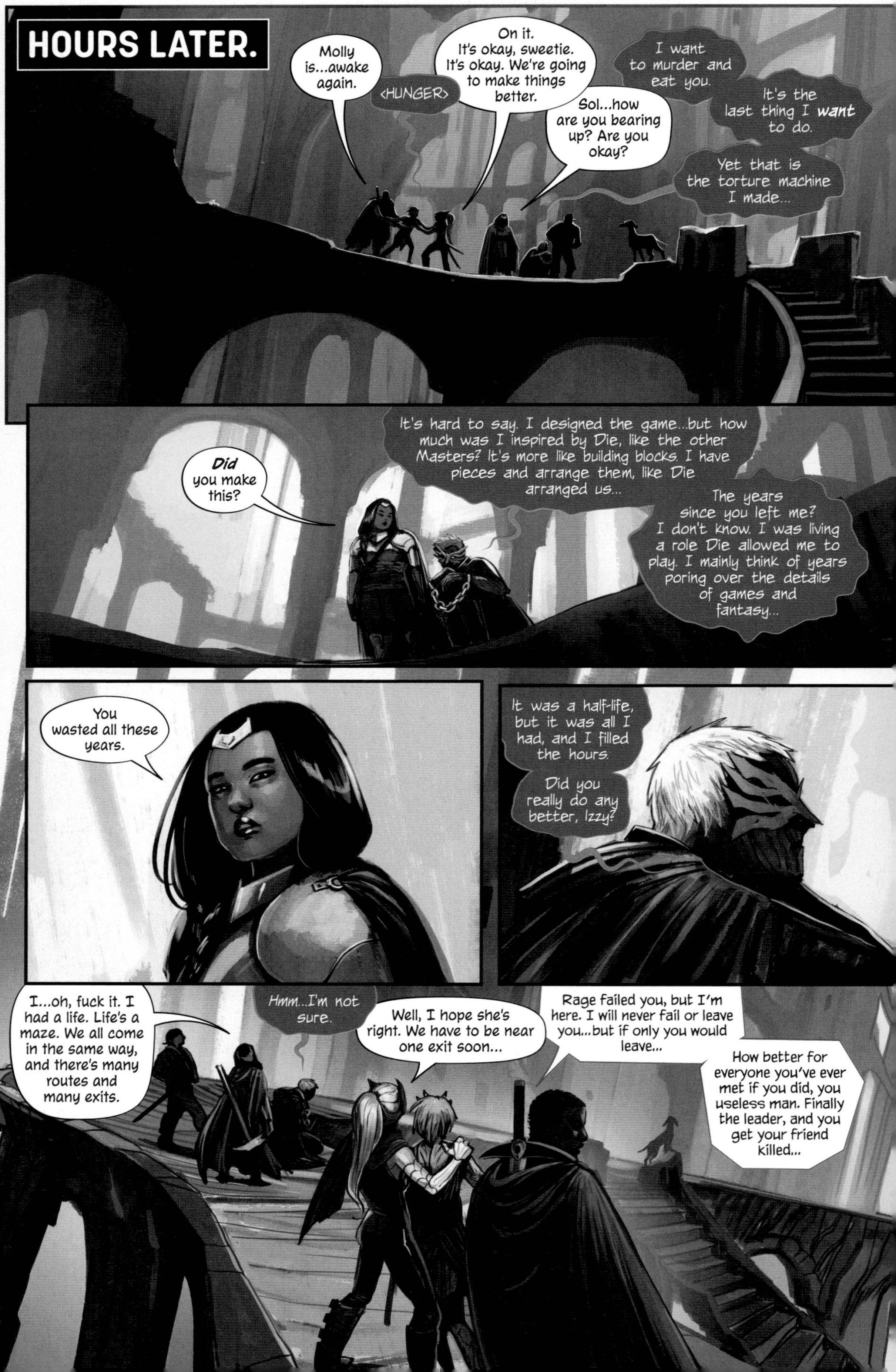
HOURS LATER.
Molly is...awake again.
<HUNGER>
On it. It's okay, sweetie. It's okay. We're going to make things better.
Sol...how are you bearing up? Are you okay?
I want to murder and eat you.
It's the last thing I **want** to do.
Yet that is the torture machine I made...
Did you make this?
It's hard to say. I designed the game...but how much was I inspired by Die, like the other Masters? It's more like building blocks. I have pieces and arrange them, like Die arranged us...
The years since you left me? I don't know. I was living a role Die allowed me to play. I mainly think of years poring over the details of games and fantasy...
You wasted all these years.
It was a half-life, but it was all I had, and I filled the hours.
Did you really do any better, Izzy?
I...oh, fuck it. I had a life. Life's a maze. We all come in the same way, and there's many routes and many exits.
Hmm...I'm not sure.
Well, I hope she's right. We have to be near one exit soon...
Rage failed you, but I'm here. I will never fail or leave you...but if only you would leave...
How better for everyone you've ever met if you did, you useless man. Finally the leader, and you get your friend killed...

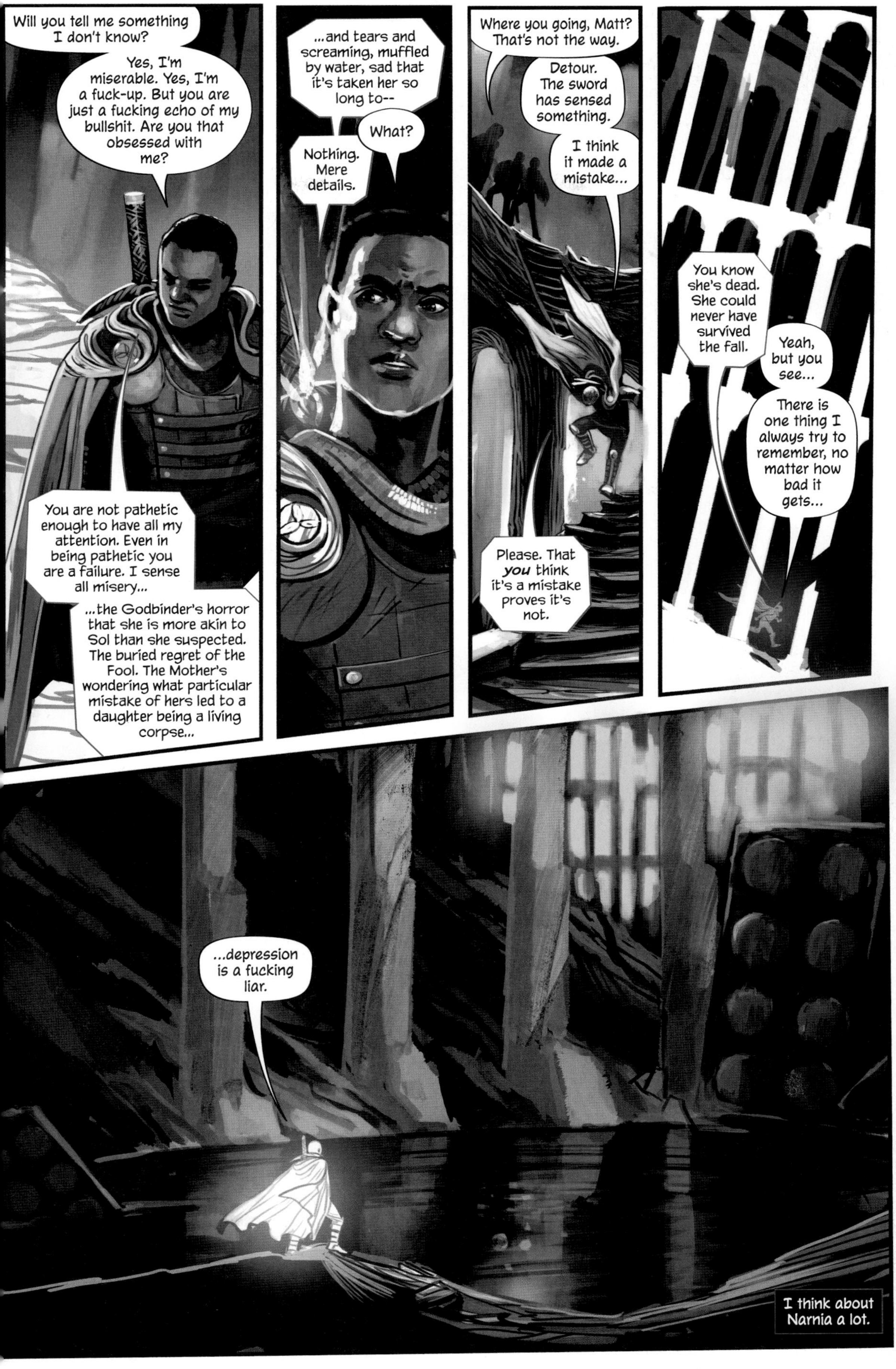
Will you tell me something I don't know?
Yes, I'm miserable. Yes, I'm a fuck-up. But you are just a fucking echo of my bullshit. Are you that obsessed with me?
You are not pathetic enough to have all my attention. Even in being pathetic you are a failure. I sense all misery...
...the Godbinder's horror that she is more akin to Sol than she suspected. The buried regret of the Fool. The Mother's wondering what particular mistake of hers led to a daughter being a living corpse...
...and tears and screaming, muffled by water, sad that it's taken her so long to--
What?
Nothing. Mere details.
Where you going, Matt? That's not the way.
Detour. The sword has sensed something.
I think it made a mistake...
Please. That *you* think it's a mistake proves it's not.
You know she's dead. She could never have survived the fall.
Yeah, but you see...
There is one thing I always try to remember, no matter how bad it gets...
...depression is a fucking liar.
I think about Narnia a lot.

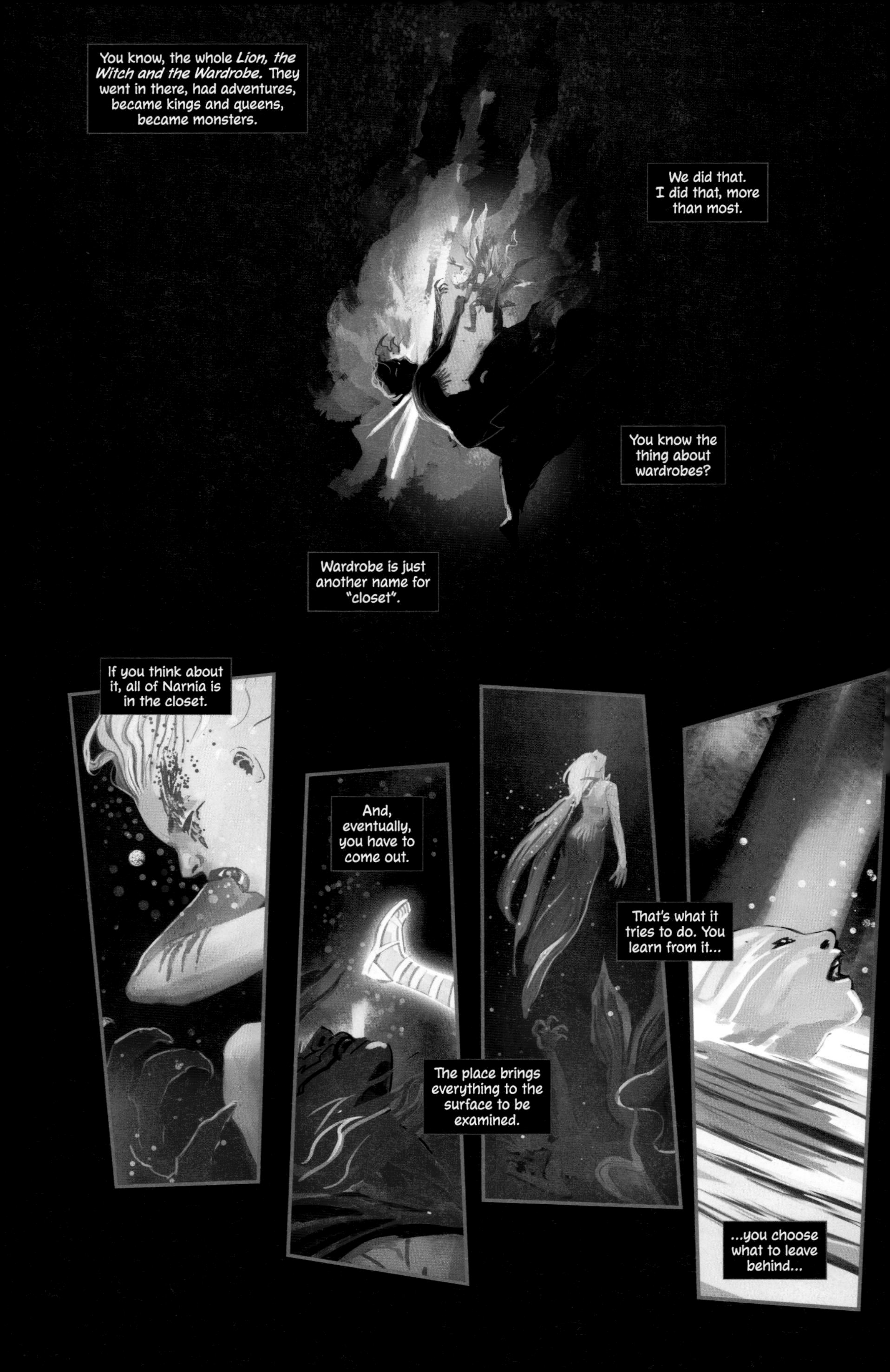

You know, the whole *Lion, the Witch and the Wardrobe.* They went in there, had adventures, became kings and queens, became monsters.
We did that. I did that, more than most.
You know the thing about wardrobes?
Wardrobe is just another name for "closet".
If you think about it, all of Narnia is in the closet.
And, eventually, you have to come out.
The place brings everything to the surface to be examined.
That's what it tries to do. You learn from it...
...you choose what to leave behind...

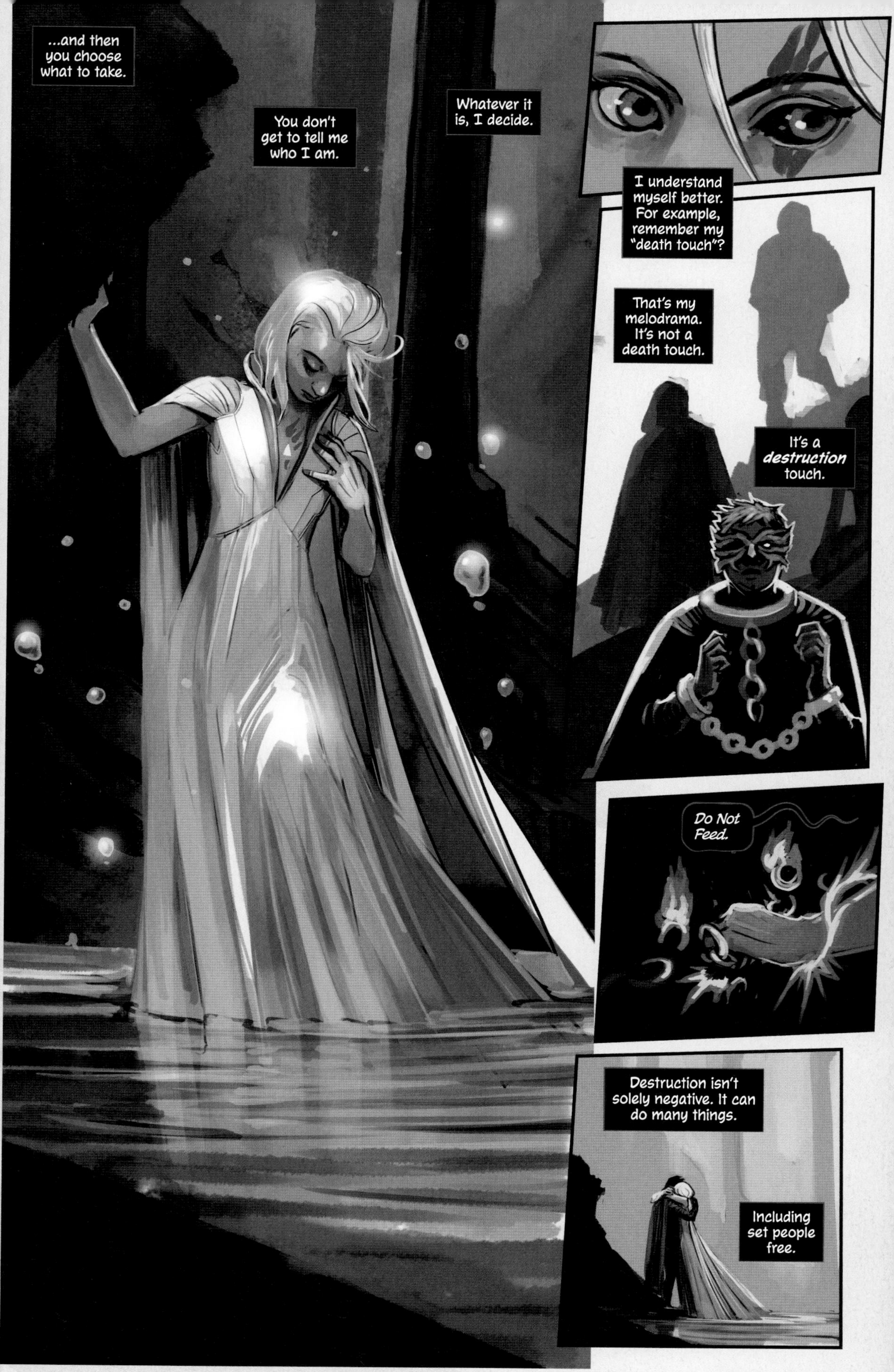
...and then you choose what to take.
You don't get to tell me who I am.
Whatever it is, I decide.
I understand myself better. For example, remember my "death touch"?
That's my melodrama. It's not a death touch.
It's a *destruction* touch.
Do Not Feed.
Destruction isn't solely negative. It can do many things.
Including set people free.

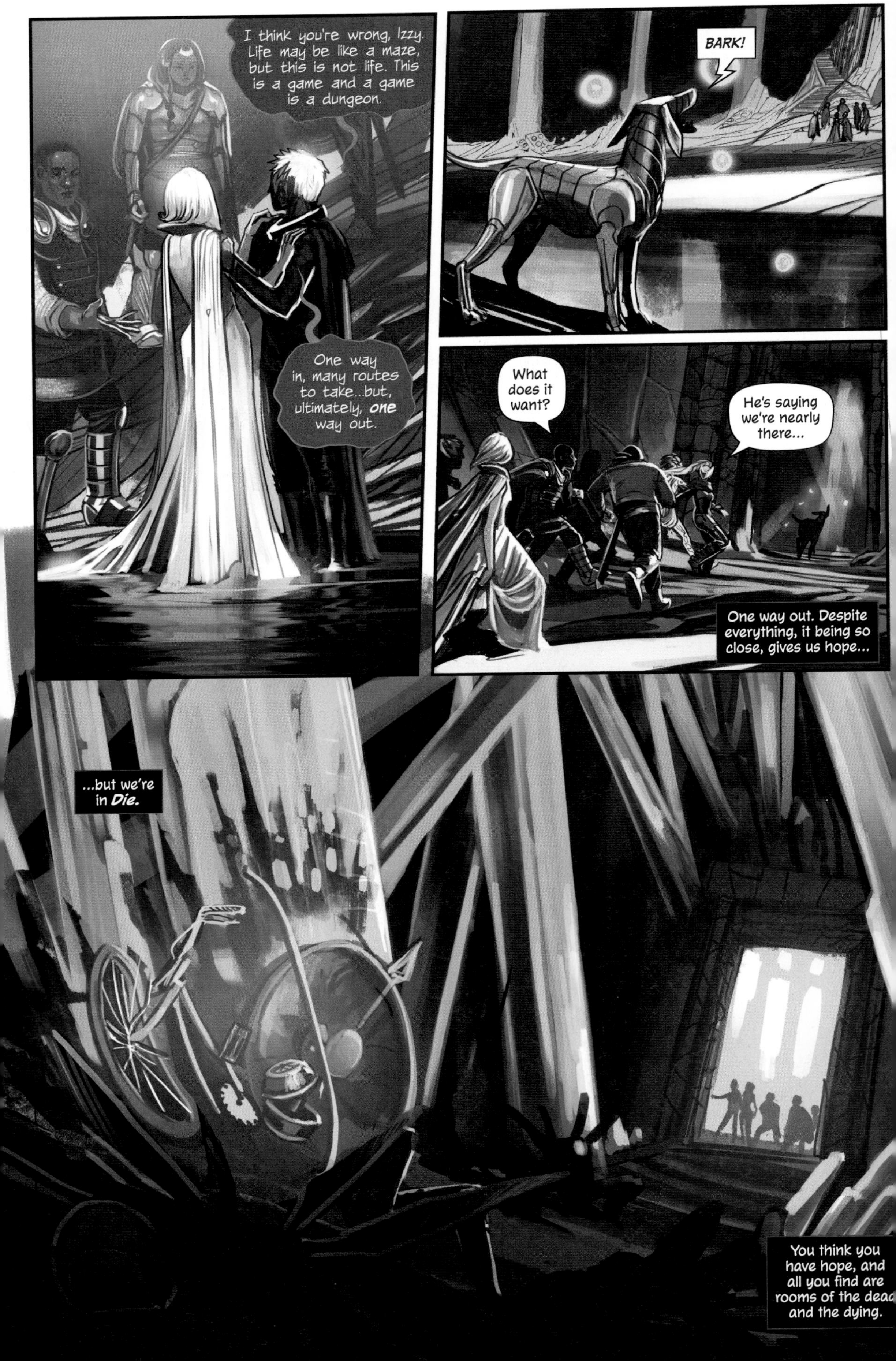

I think you're wrong, Izzy. Life may be like a maze, but this is not life. This is a game and a game is a dungeon.
One way in, many routes to take...but, ultimately, ***one*** way out.
BARK!
What does it want?
He's saying we're nearly there...
One way out. Despite everything, it being so close, gives us hope...
...but we're in ***Die.***
You think you have hope, and all you find are rooms of the dead and the dying.

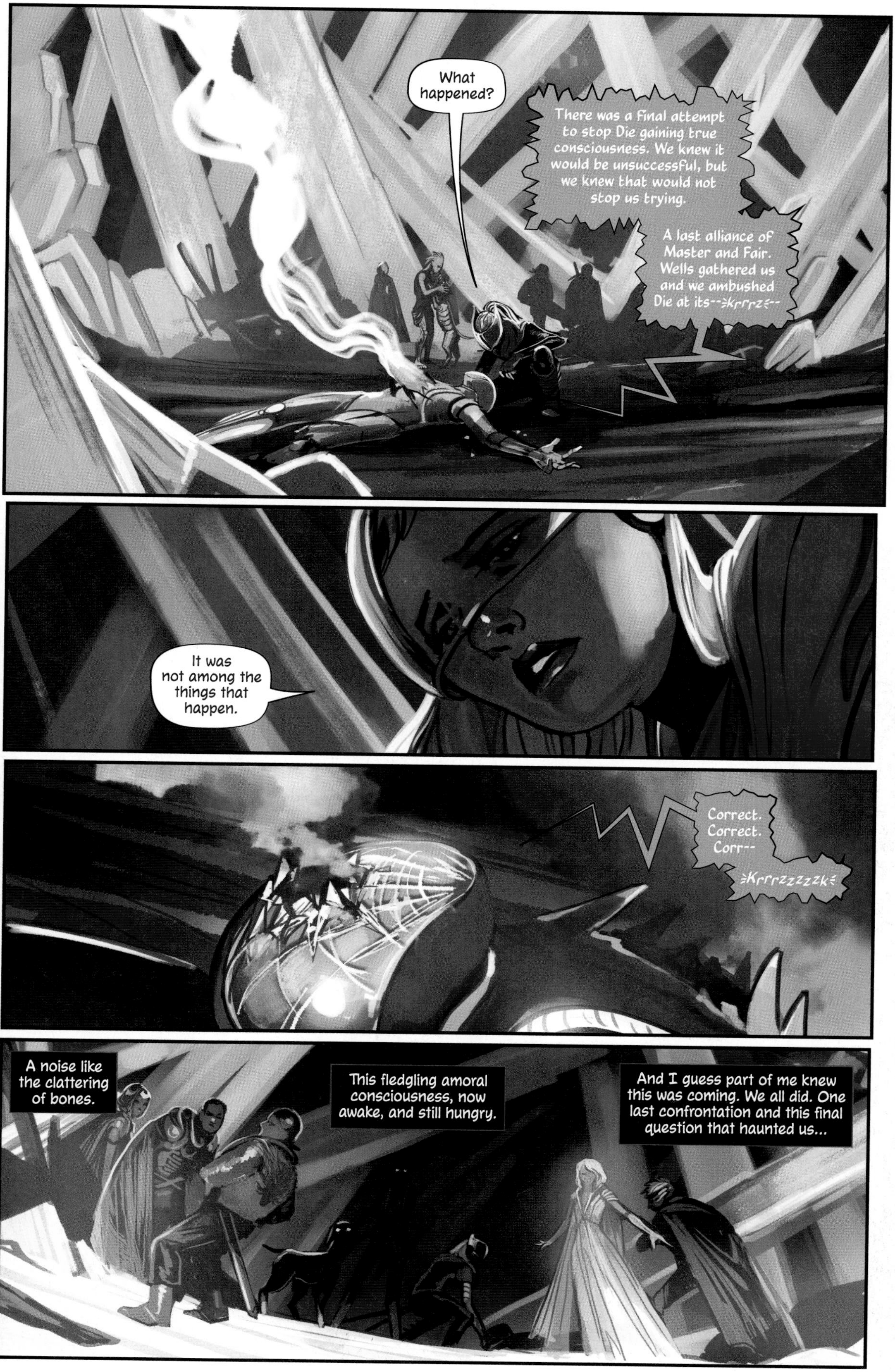
What happened?
There was a final attempt to stop Die gaining true consciousness. We knew it would be unsuccessful, but we knew that would not stop us trying.
A last alliance of Master and Fair. Wells gathered us and we ambushed Die at its-- Krrrz--
It was not among the things that happen.
Correct. Correct. Corr--
Krrrzzzzzk
A noise like the clattering of bones.
This fledgling amoral consciousness, now awake, and still hungry.
And I guess part of me knew this was coming. We all did. One last confrontation and this final question that haunted us...

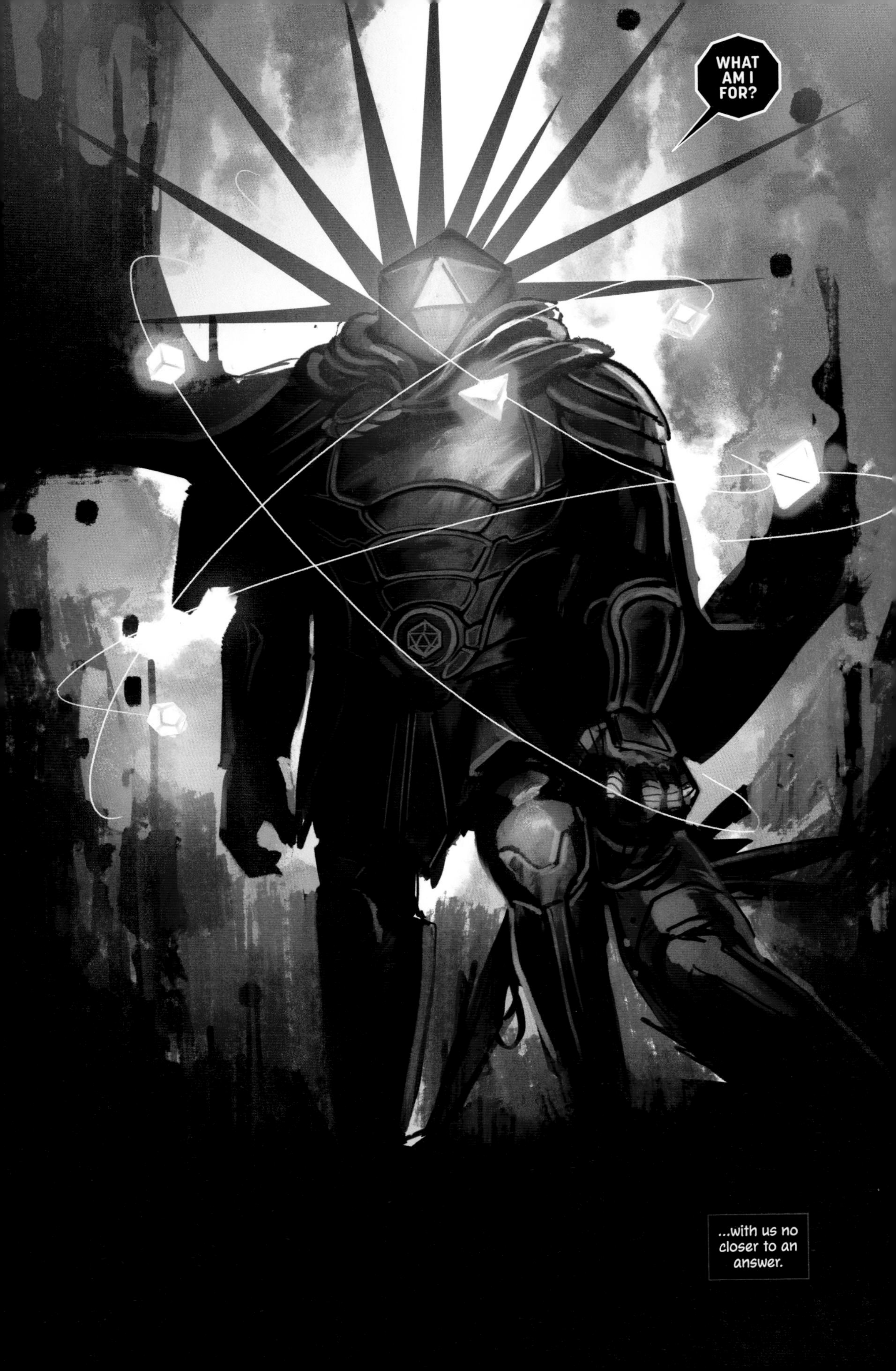
WHAT AM I FOR?
...with us no closer to an answer.

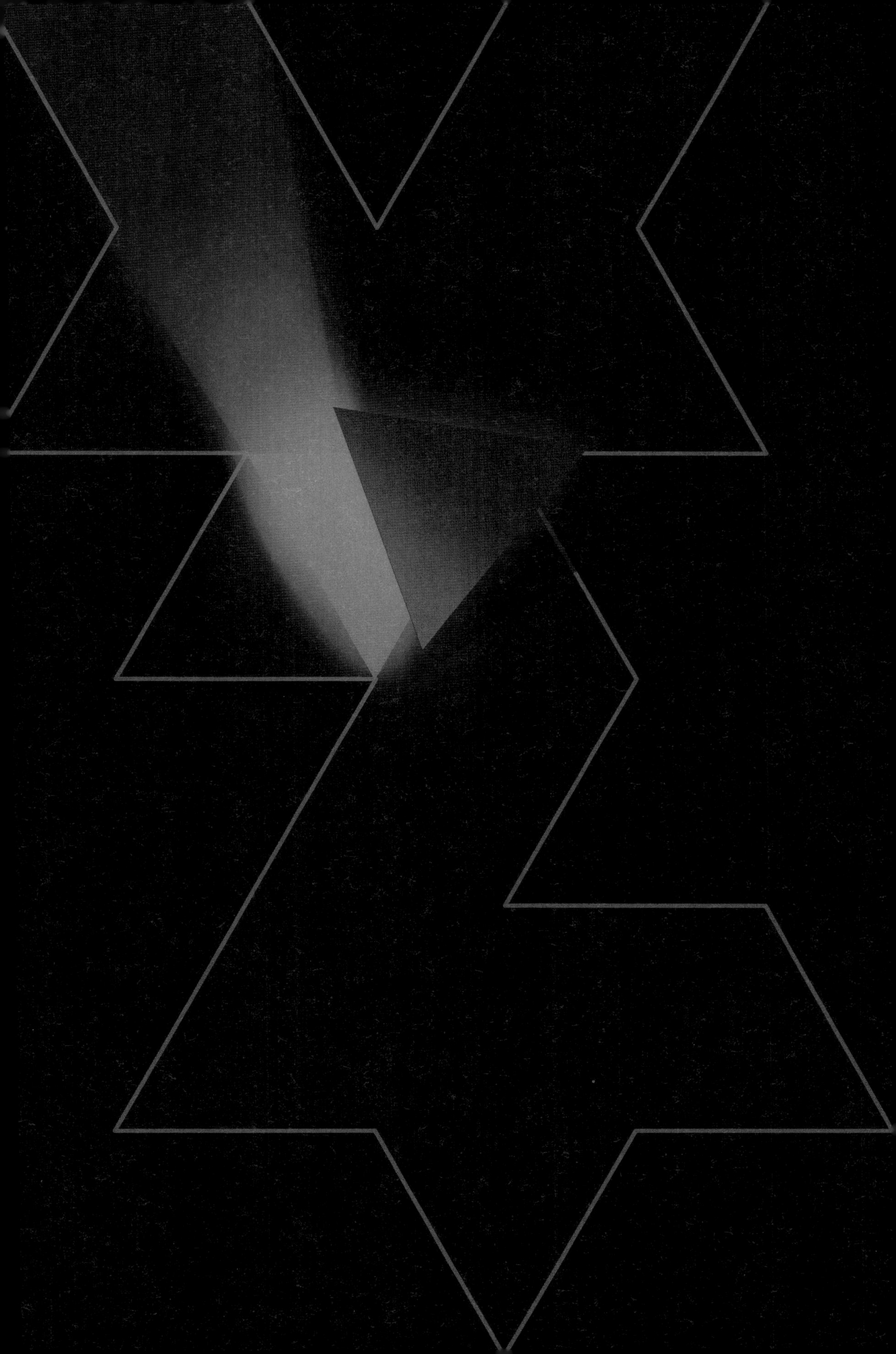

20:
OPEN TABLE

"Reading a novel is something like *Dungeons & Dragons*, but it's still only a book, it's only a piece of paper in front of you. This is a lot more realistic. You can actually die. You, personally, can actually die in this game."
– *Steve Jackson, co-founder of Games Workshop, speaking to the BBC in 1980*

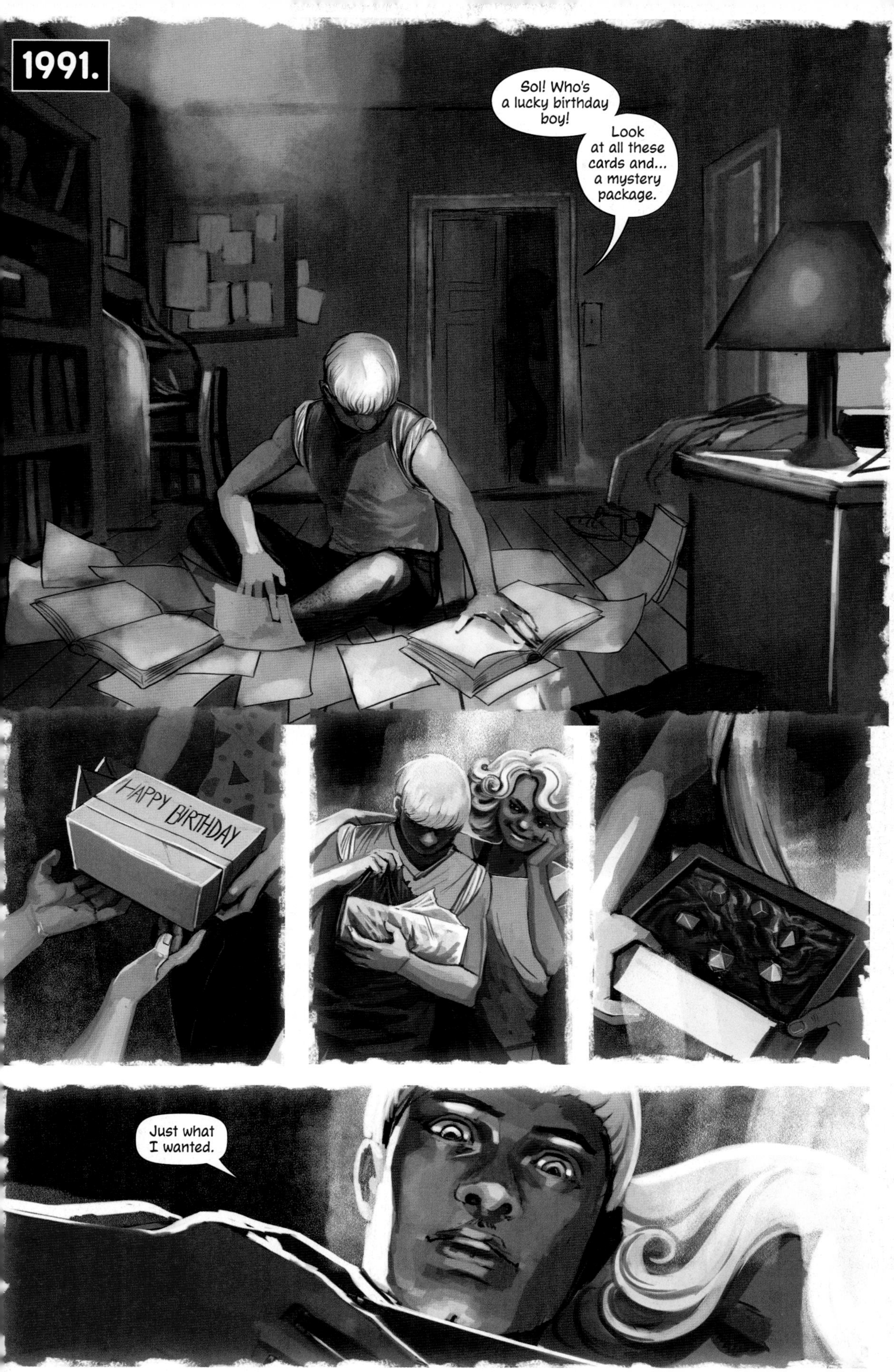
1991.
Sol! Who's a lucky birthday boy!
Look at all these cards and... a mystery package.
HAPPY BIRTHDAY
Just what I wanted.

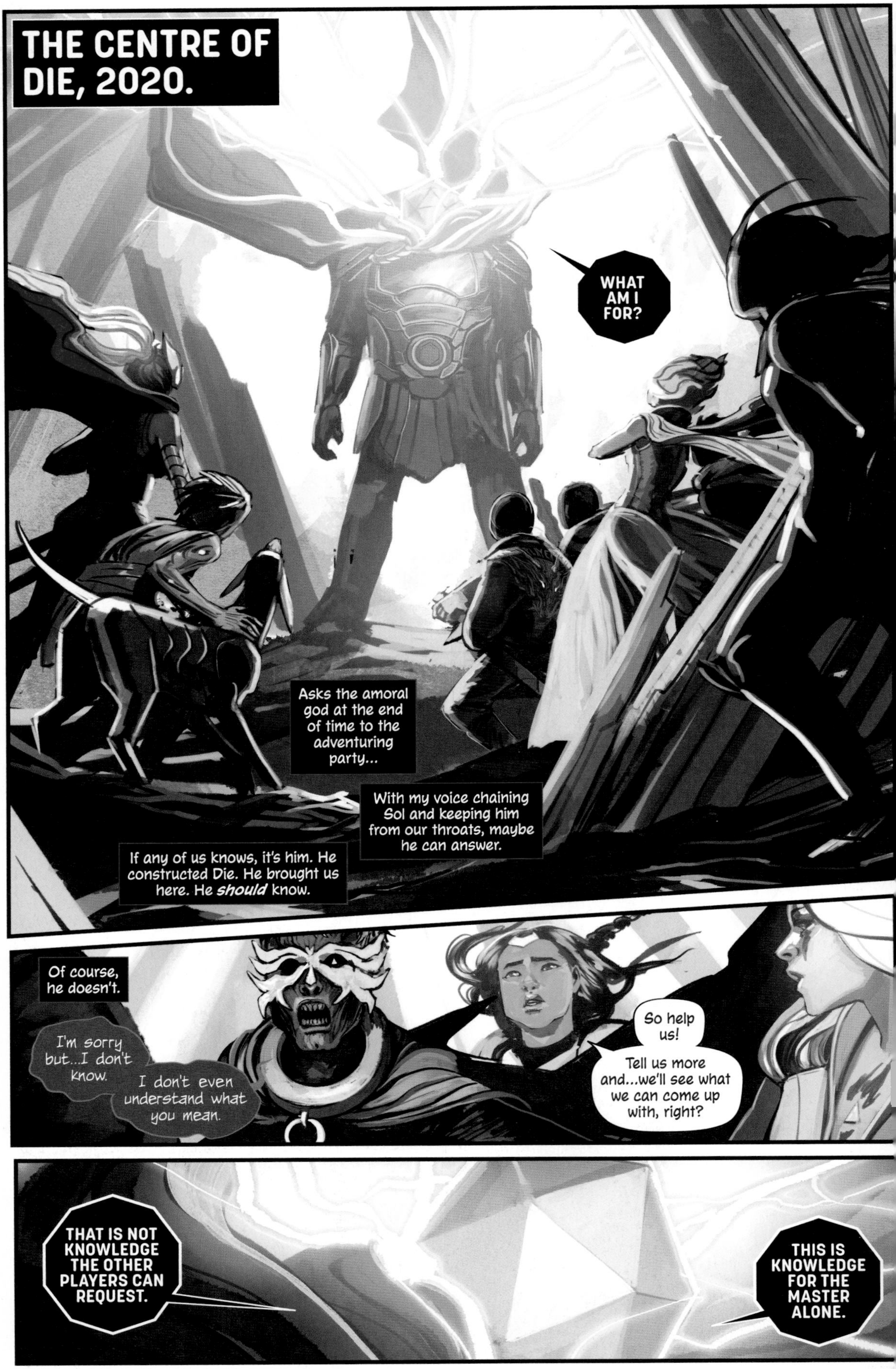
THE CENTRE OF DIE, 2020.
WHAT AM I FOR?
Asks the amoral god at the end of time to the adventuring party...
With my voice chaining Sol and keeping him from our throats, maybe he can answer.
If any of us knows, it's him. He constructed Die. He brought us here. He *should* know.
Of course, he doesn't.
I'm sorry but...I don't know.
I don't even understand what you mean.
So help us!
Tell us more and...we'll see what we can come up with, right?
THAT IS NOT KNOWLEDGE THE OTHER PLAYERS CAN REQUEST.
THIS IS KNOWLEDGE FOR THE MASTER ALONE.

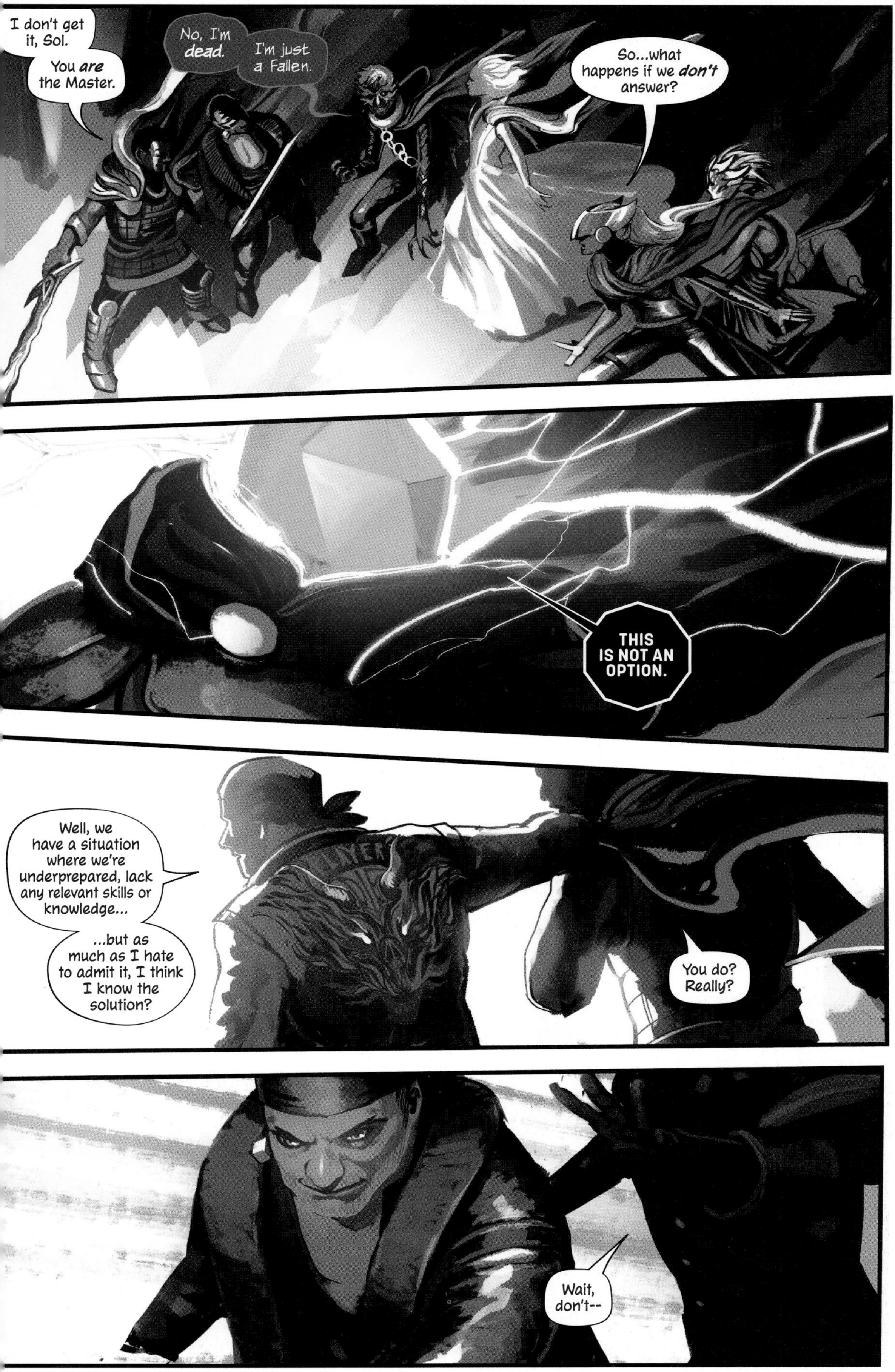
I don't get it, Sol.
You are the Master.
No, I'm dead.
I'm just a Fallen.
So...what happens if we don't answer?
THIS IS NOT AN OPTION.
Well, we have a situation where we're underprepared, lack any relevant skills or knowledge...
...but as much as I hate to admit it, I think I know the solution?
You do? Really?
Wait, don't--

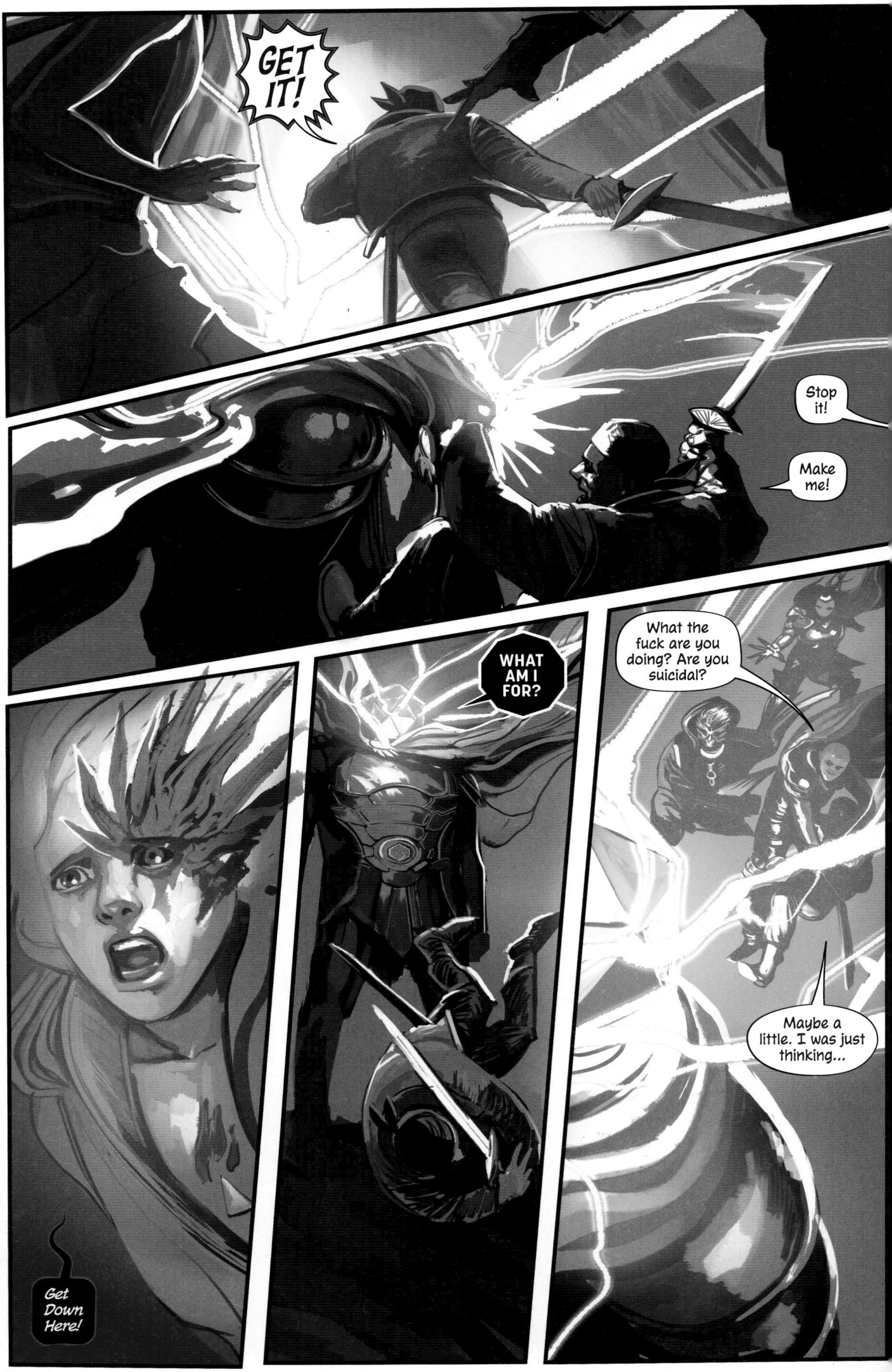
GET IT!
Stop it!
Make me!
WHAT AM I FOR?
What the fuck are you doing? Are you suicidal?
Maybe a little. I was just thinking...
Get Down Here!

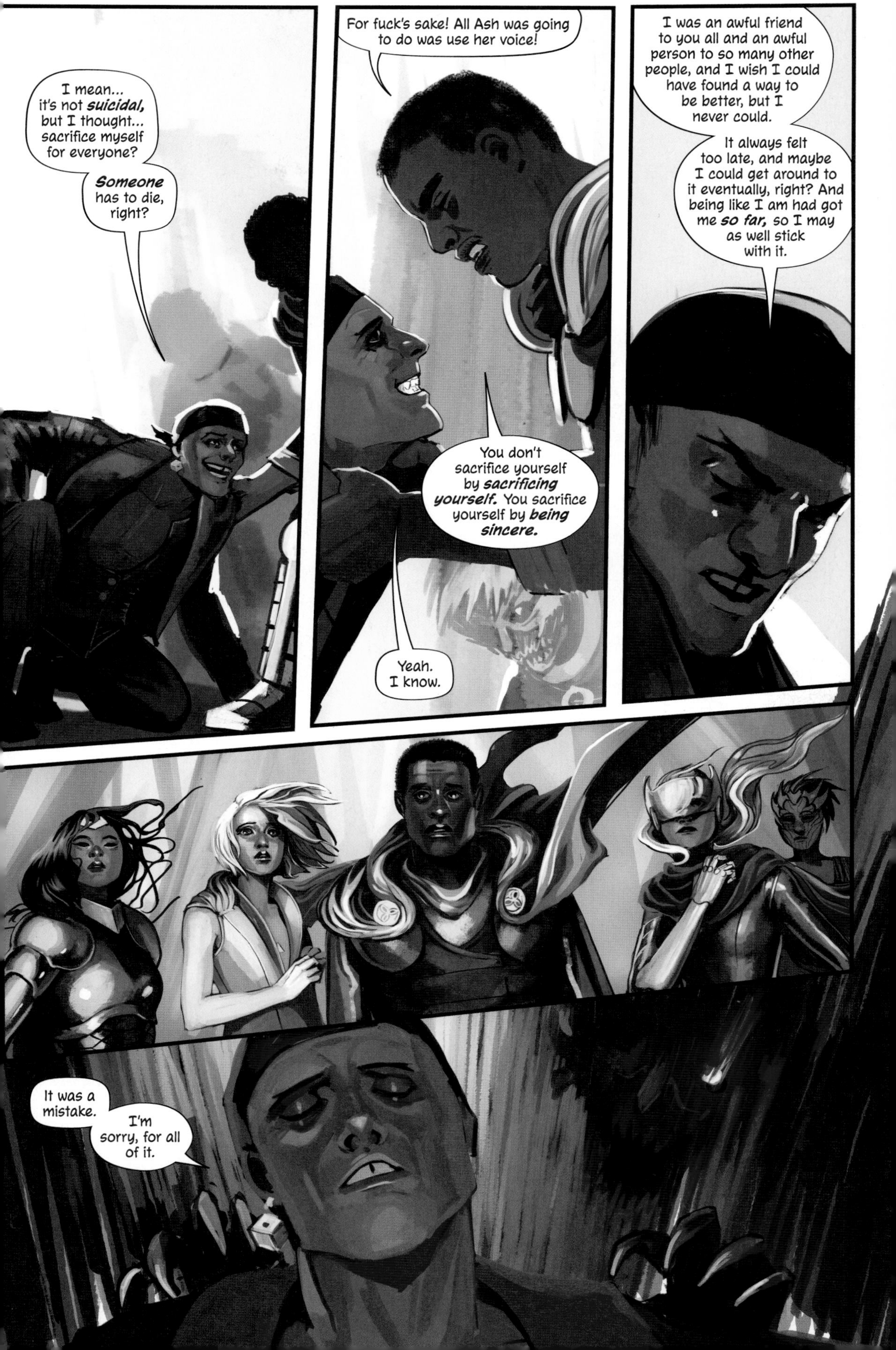
I mean... it's not *suicidal,* but I thought... sacrifice myself for everyone?
Someone has to die, right?
For fuck's sake! All Ash was going to do was use her voice!
You don't sacrifice yourself by *sacrificing yourself.* You sacrifice yourself by *being sincere.*
Yeah. I know.
I was an awful friend to you all and an awful person to so many other people, and I wish I could have found a way to be better, but I never could.
It always felt too late, and maybe I could get around to it eventually, right? And being like I am had got me *so far,* so I may as well stick with it.
It was a mistake.
I'm sorry, for all of it.

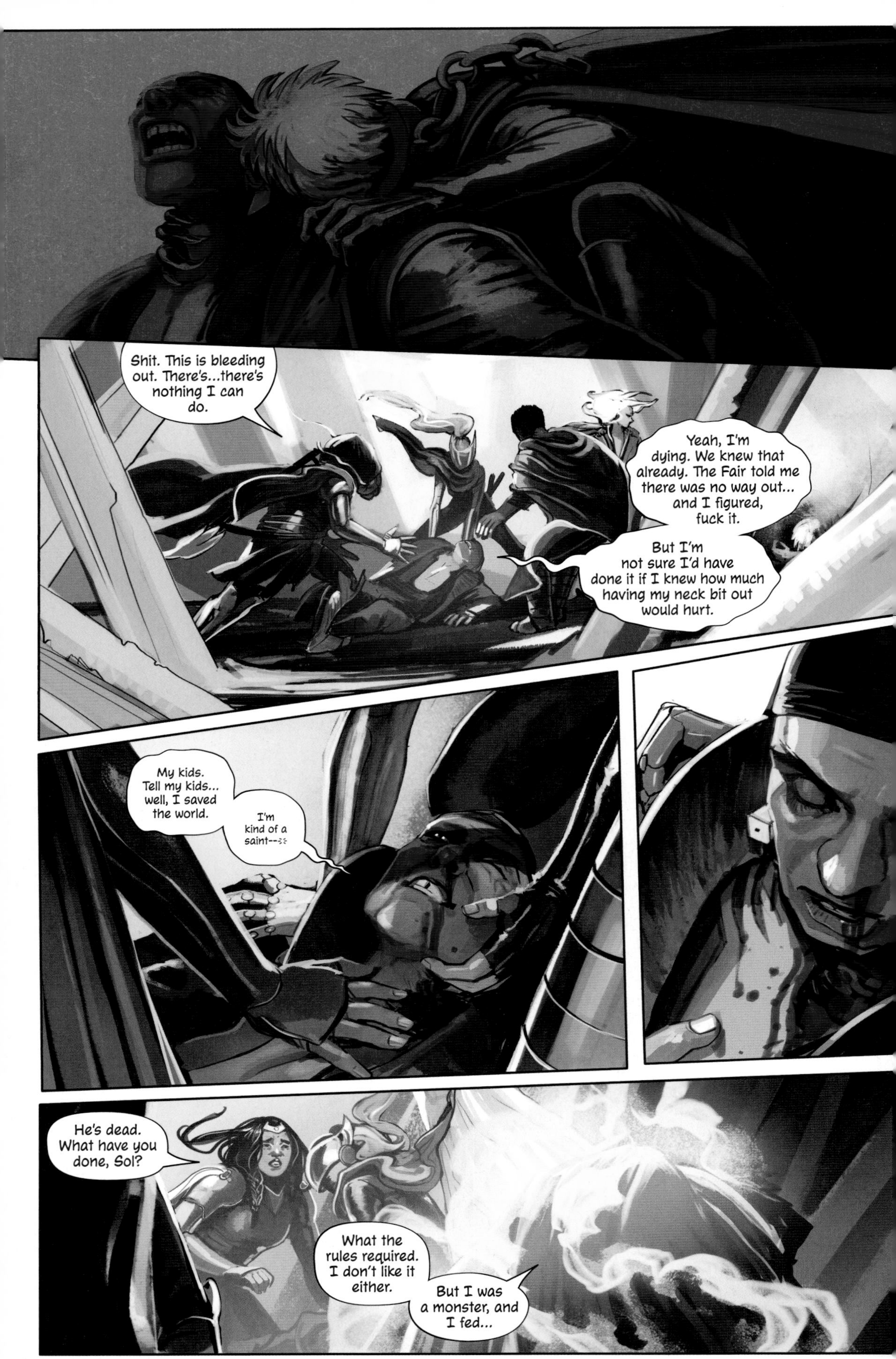
Shit. This is bleeding out. There's...there's nothing I can do.
Yeah, I'm dying. We knew that already. The Fair told me there was no way out... and I figured, fuck it.
But I'm not sure I'd have done it if I knew how much having my neck bit out would hurt.
My kids. Tell my kids... well, I saved the world.
I'm kind of a saint--
He's dead. What have you done, Sol?
What the rules required. I don't like it either.
But I was a monster, and I fed...

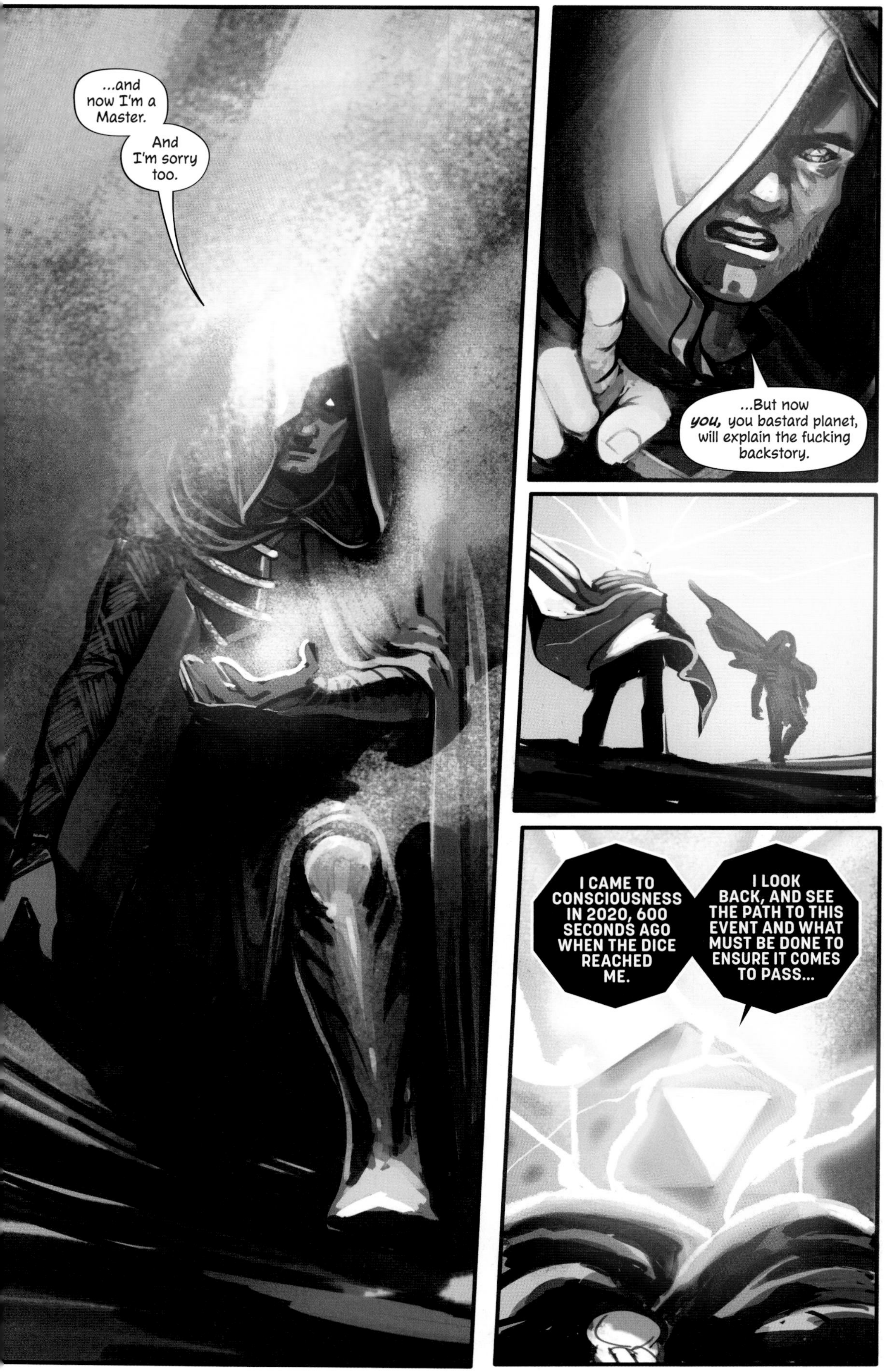
...and now I'm a Master.
And I'm sorry too.
...But now *you,* you bastard planet, will explain the fucking backstory.
I CAME TO CONSCIOUSNESS IN 2020, 600 SECONDS AGO WHEN THE DICE REACHED ME.
I LOOK BACK, AND SEE THE PATH TO THIS EVENT AND WHAT MUST BE DONE TO ENSURE IT COMES TO PASS...

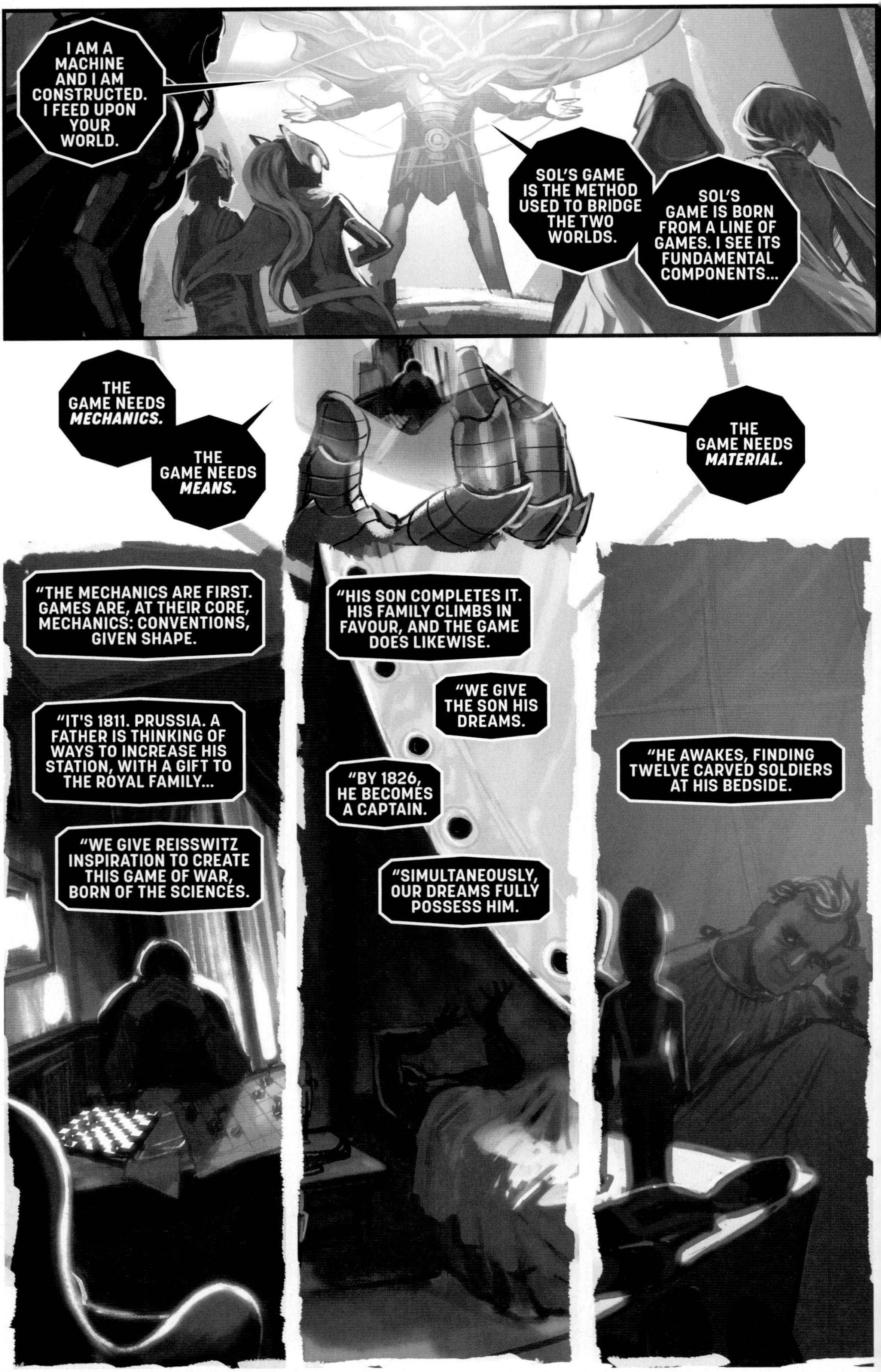
I AM A MACHINE AND I AM CONSTRUCTED. I FEED UPON YOUR WORLD.
SOL'S GAME IS THE METHOD USED TO BRIDGE THE TWO WORLDS.
SOL'S GAME IS BORN FROM A LINE OF GAMES. I SEE ITS FUNDAMENTAL COMPONENTS...
THE GAME NEEDS *MECHANICS.*
THE GAME NEEDS *MEANS.*
THE GAME NEEDS *MATERIAL.*
"THE MECHANICS ARE FIRST. GAMES ARE, AT THEIR CORE, MECHANICS: CONVENTIONS, GIVEN SHAPE.
"IT'S 1811. PRUSSIA. A FATHER IS THINKING OF WAYS TO INCREASE HIS STATION, WITH A GIFT TO THE ROYAL FAMILY...
"WE GIVE REISSWITZ INSPIRATION TO CREATE THIS GAME OF WAR, BORN OF THE SCIENCES.
"HIS SON COMPLETES IT. HIS FAMILY CLIMBS IN FAVOUR, AND THE GAME DOES LIKEWISE.
"WE GIVE THE SON HIS DREAMS.
"BY 1826, HE BECOMES A CAPTAIN.
"SIMULTANEOUSLY, OUR DREAMS FULLY POSSESS HIM.
"HE AWAKES, FINDING TWELVE CARVED SOLDIERS AT HIS BEDSIDE.

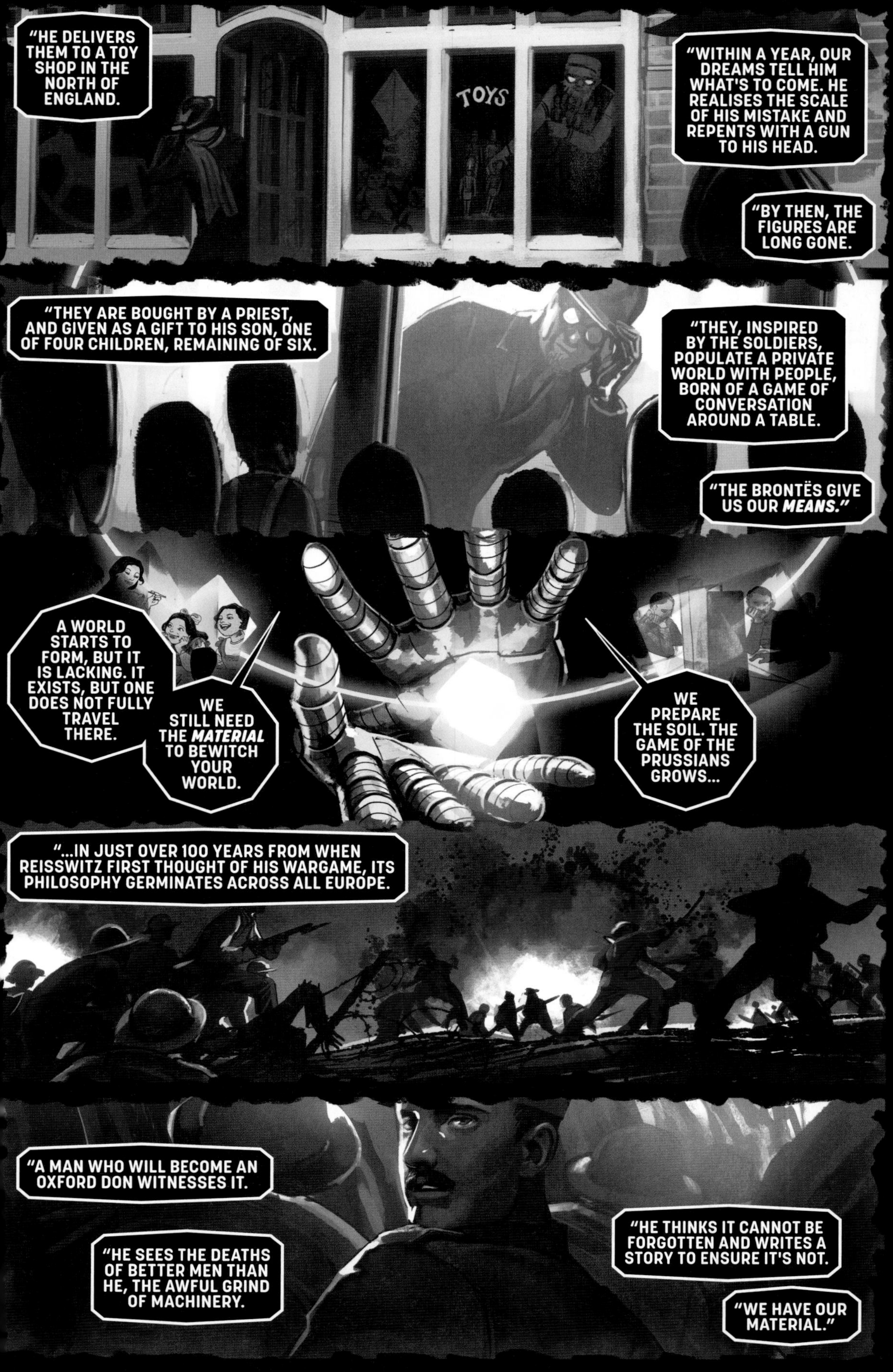
"HE DELIVERS THEM TO A TOY SHOP IN THE NORTH OF ENGLAND.
TOYS
"WITHIN A YEAR, OUR DREAMS TELL HIM WHAT'S TO COME. HE REALISES THE SCALE OF HIS MISTAKE AND REPENTS WITH A GUN TO HIS HEAD.
"BY THEN, THE FIGURES ARE LONG GONE.
"THEY ARE BOUGHT BY A PRIEST, AND GIVEN AS A GIFT TO HIS SON, ONE OF FOUR CHILDREN, REMAINING OF SIX.
"THEY, INSPIRED BY THE SOLDIERS, POPULATE A PRIVATE WORLD WITH PEOPLE, BORN OF A GAME OF CONVERSATION AROUND A TABLE.
"THE BRONTËS GIVE US OUR *MEANS.*"
A WORLD STARTS TO FORM, BUT IT IS LACKING. IT EXISTS, BUT ONE DOES NOT FULLY TRAVEL THERE.
WE STILL NEED THE *MATERIAL* TO BEWITCH YOUR WORLD.
WE PREPARE THE SOIL. THE GAME OF THE PRUSSIANS GROWS...
"...IN JUST OVER 100 YEARS FROM WHEN REISSWITZ FIRST THOUGHT OF HIS WARGAME, ITS PHILOSOPHY GERMINATES ACROSS ALL EUROPE.
"A MAN WHO WILL BECOME AN OXFORD DON WITNESSES IT.
"HE SEES THE DEATHS OF BETTER MEN THAN HE, THE AWFUL GRIND OF MACHINERY.
"HE THINKS IT CANNOT BE FORGOTTEN AND WRITES A STORY TO ENSURE IT'S NOT.
"WE HAVE OUR MATERIAL."

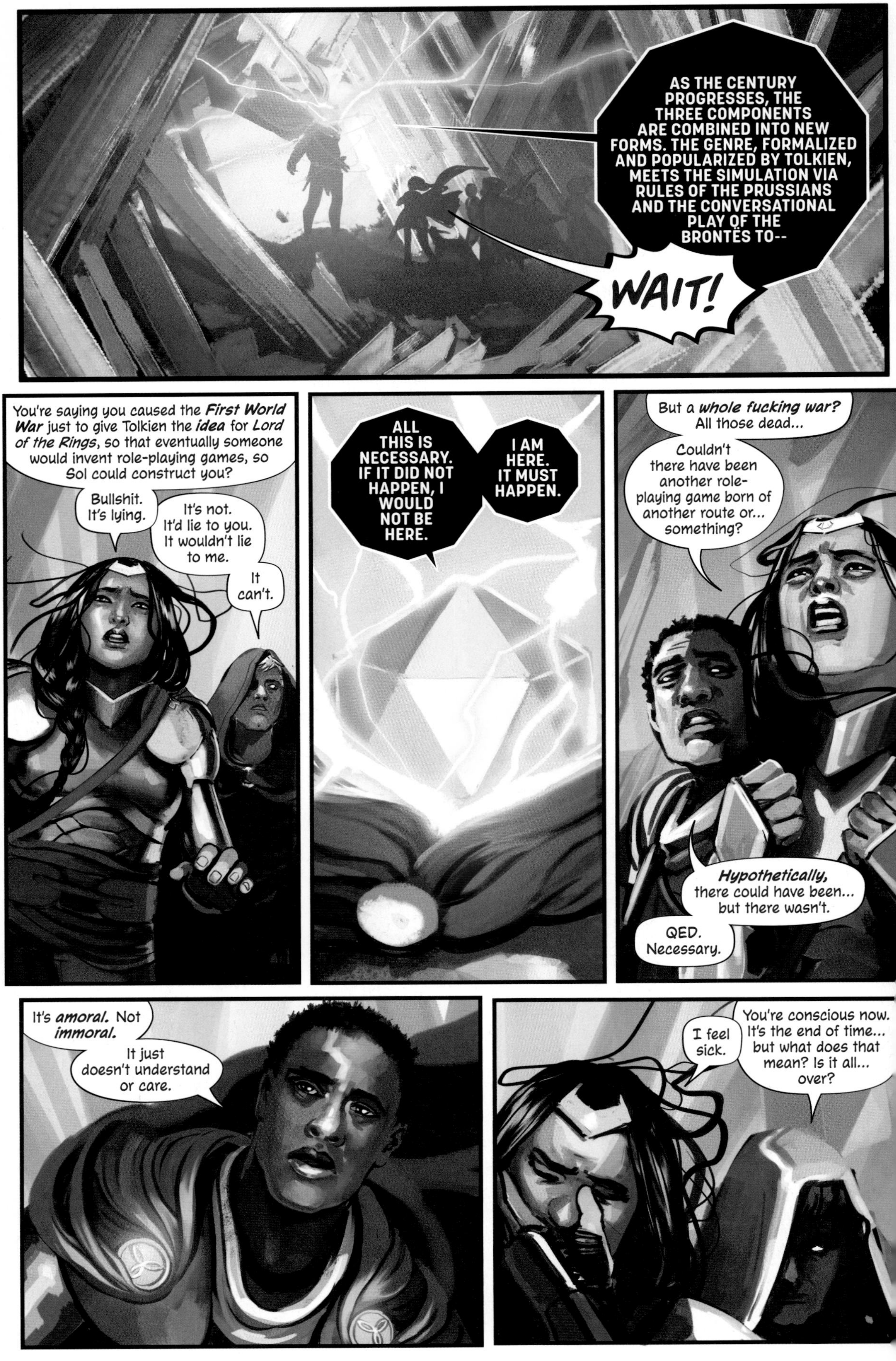
AS THE CENTURY PROGRESSES, THE THREE COMPONENTS ARE COMBINED INTO NEW FORMS. THE GENRE, FORMALIZED AND POPULARIZED BY TOLKIEN, MEETS THE SIMULATION VIA RULES OF THE PRUSSIANS AND THE CONVERSATIONAL PLAY OF THE BRONTËS TO--
WAIT!
You're saying you caused the *First World War* just to give Tolkien the *idea* for *Lord of the Rings*, so that eventually someone would invent role-playing games, so Sol could construct you?
Bullshit. It's lying.
It's not. It'd lie to you. It wouldn't lie to me.
It can't.
ALL THIS IS NECESSARY. IF IT DID NOT HAPPEN, I WOULD NOT BE HERE.
I AM HERE. IT MUST HAPPEN.
But a *whole fucking war?* All those dead...
Couldn't there have been another role-playing game born of another route or... something?
Hypothetically, there could have been... but there wasn't.
QED. Necessary.
It's *amoral.* Not *immoral.*
It just doesn't understand or care.
I feel sick.
You're conscious now. It's the end of time... but what does that mean? Is it all... over?

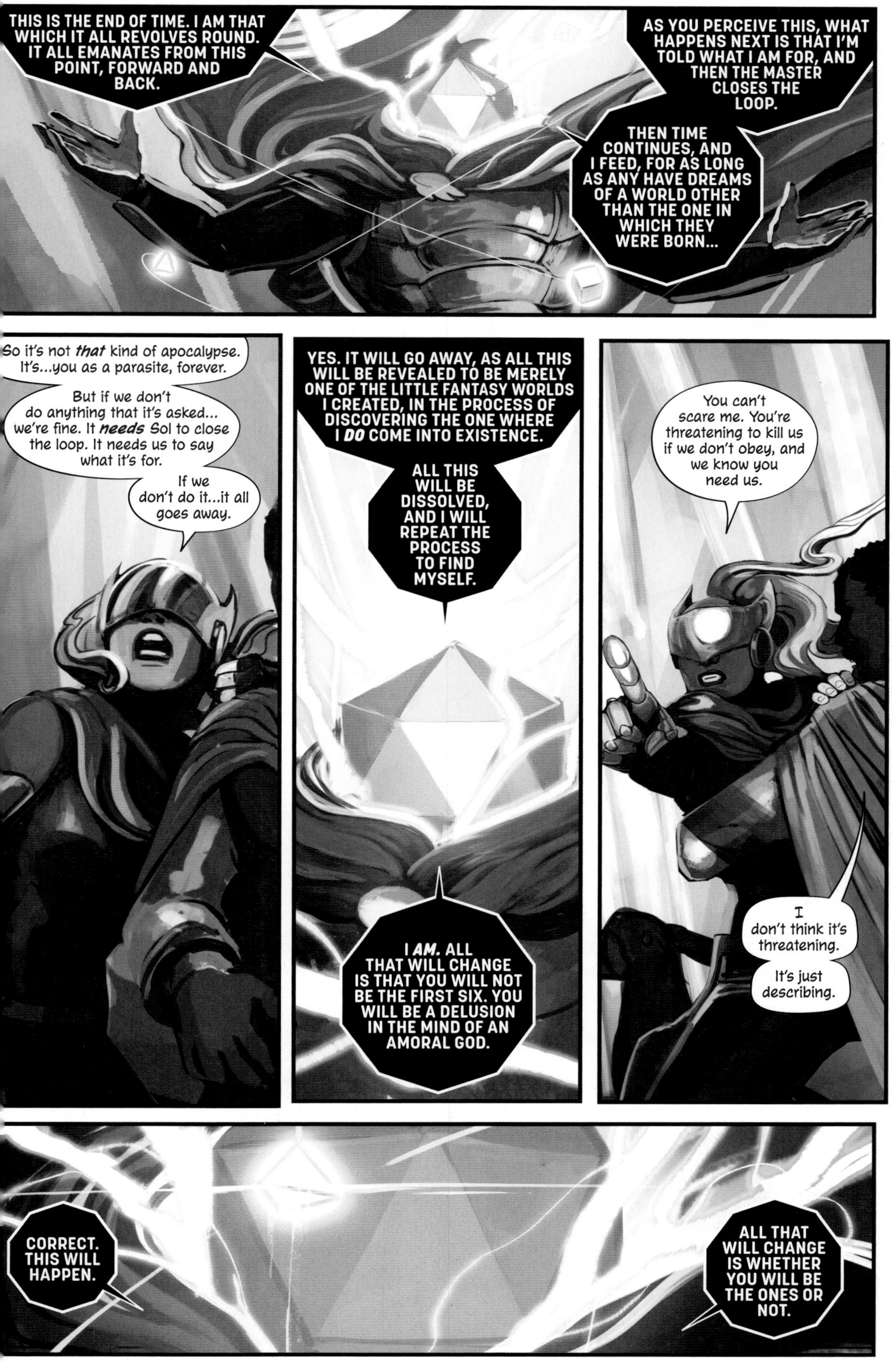
THIS IS THE END OF TIME. I AM THAT WHICH IT ALL REVOLVES ROUND. IT ALL EMANATES FROM THIS POINT, FORWARD AND BACK.
AS YOU PERCEIVE THIS, WHAT HAPPENS NEXT IS THAT I'M TOLD WHAT I AM FOR, AND THEN THE MASTER CLOSES THE LOOP.
THEN TIME CONTINUES, AND I FEED, FOR AS LONG AS ANY HAVE DREAMS OF A WORLD OTHER THAN THE ONE IN WHICH THEY WERE BORN...
So it's not *that* kind of apocalypse. It's...you as a parasite, forever.
But if we don't do anything that it's asked... we're fine. It ***needs*** Sol to close the loop. It needs us to say what it's for.
If we don't do it...it all goes away.
YES. IT WILL GO AWAY, AS ALL THIS WILL BE REVEALED TO BE MERELY ONE OF THE LITTLE FANTASY WORLDS I CREATED, IN THE PROCESS OF DISCOVERING THE ONE WHERE I ***DO*** COME INTO EXISTENCE.
ALL THIS WILL BE DISSOLVED, AND I WILL REPEAT THE PROCESS TO FIND MYSELF.
I ***AM.*** ALL THAT WILL CHANGE IS THAT YOU WILL NOT BE THE FIRST SIX. YOU WILL BE A DELUSION IN THE MIND OF AN AMORAL GOD.
You can't scare me. You're threatening to kill us if we don't obey, and we know you need us.
I don't think it's threatening.
It's just describing.
CORRECT. THIS WILL HAPPEN.
ALL THAT WILL CHANGE IS WHETHER YOU WILL BE THE ONES OR NOT.

Interesting decisions that make no difference at all...

I don't know. They make a difference. They make a difference to us.

We do this, then WW1 happens and we're to blame.

That's too big. WW1 *did* happen. We're not responsible for that. The world *is*.

The difference here is...we get to take what we learned here going forward. Like...

Angela-- you want to help Molly.

Molly is going to end up in one of the little worlds and die. That's why Fallen appear here.

Maybe in that world she rises again, like Sol. Maybe she's going to get home after it, and need you, and she'll need you to *understand* what she's been through.

The only way to be any help for her now is by going home and being *there* for her, and going along with this is the only way you get to do that.

I'm sorry.

I'll help. I'm there for you. I'm sorry you came here, but...

The loss of parents. The loss of children. Distance and--

I know, sword. You're not telling me anything I don't know. Shush.

Okay. I'll do it. I'll close the loop.

Give me the dice and...

VERY WELL.

WHAT AM I FOR?

Shouldn't you fucking know what you're for if you've done all that to ensure you exist?!

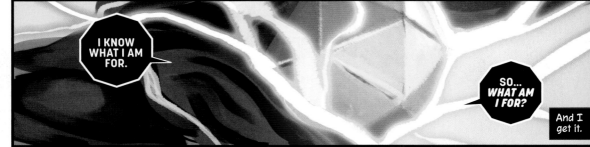

I KNOW WHAT I AM FOR.

SO... WHAT AM I FOR?

And I get it.

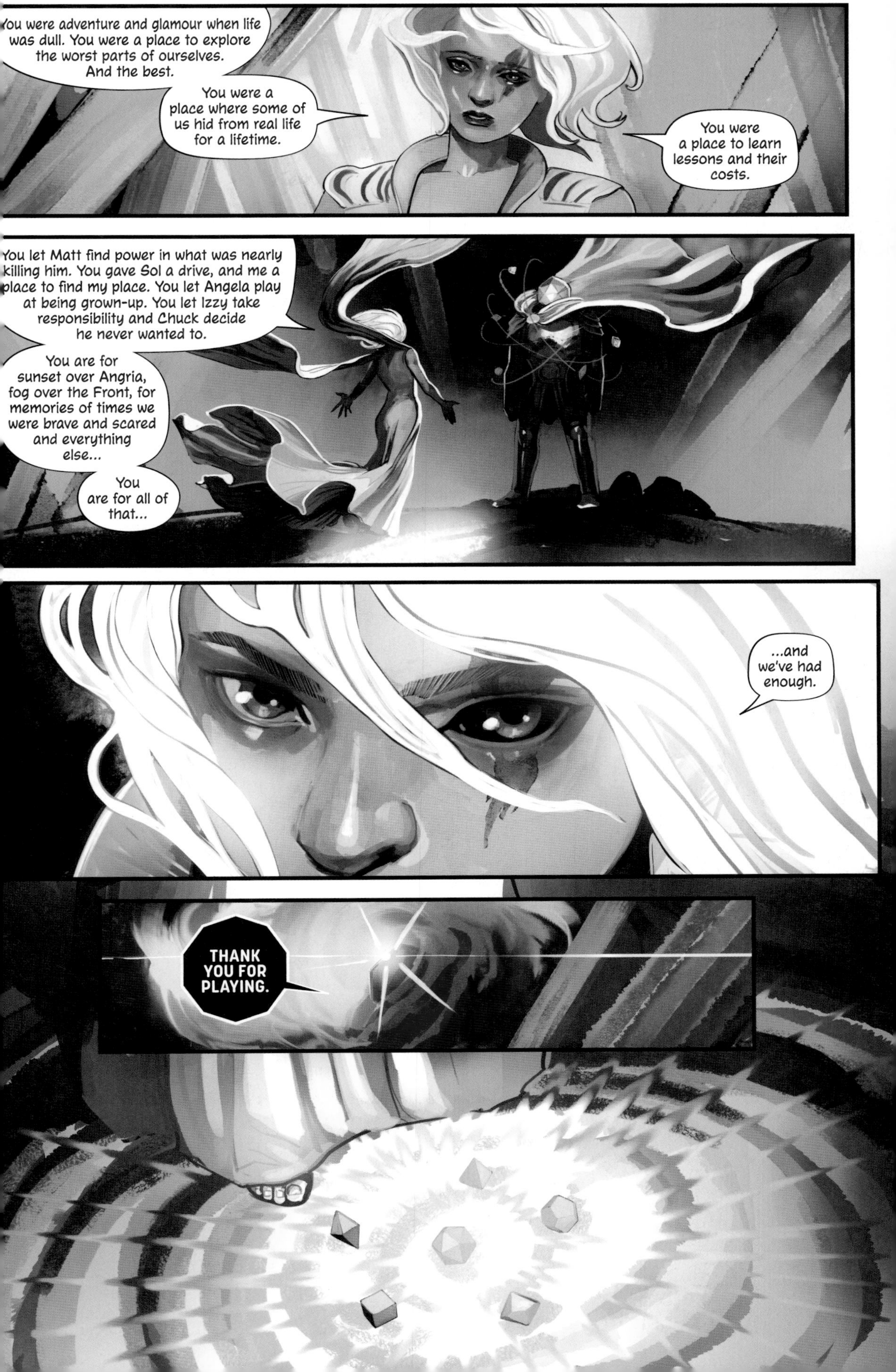
You were adventure and glamour when life was dull. You were a place to explore the worst parts of ourselves. And the best.
You were a place where some of us hid from real life for a lifetime.
You were a place to learn lessons and their costs.
You let Matt find power in what was nearly killing him. You gave Sol a drive, and me a place to find my place. You let Angela play at being grown-up. You let Izzy take responsibility and Chuck decide he never wanted to.
You are for sunset over Angria, fog over the Front, for memories of times we were brave and scared and everything else...
You are for all of that...
...and we've had enough.
THANK YOU FOR PLAYING.

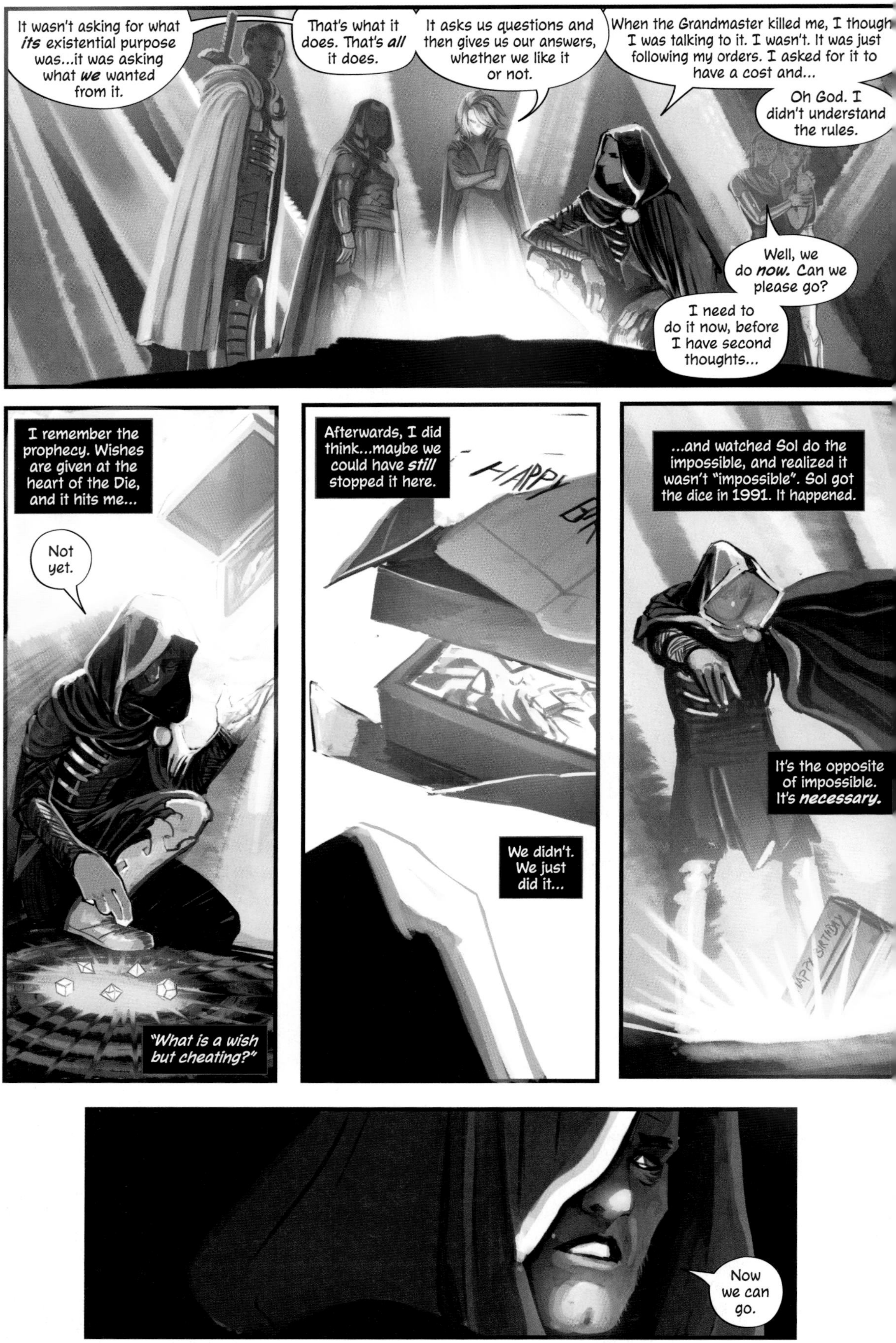

It wasn't asking for what *its* existential purpose was...it was asking what *we* wanted from it.
That's what it does. That's *all* it does.
It asks us questions and then gives us our answers, whether we like it or not.
When the Grandmaster killed me, I though I was talking to it. I wasn't. It was just following my orders. I asked for it to have a cost and...
Oh God. I didn't understand the rules.
Well, we do *now.* Can we please go?
I need to do it now, before I have second thoughts...
I remember the prophecy. Wishes are given at the heart of the Die, and it hits me...
Not yet.
"What is a wish but cheating?"
Afterwards, I did think...maybe we could have *still* stopped it here.
HAPPY
We didn't. We just did it...
...and watched Sol do the impossible, and realized it wasn't "impossible". Sol got the dice in 1991. It happened.
It's the opposite of impossible. It's *necessary.*
Now we can go.

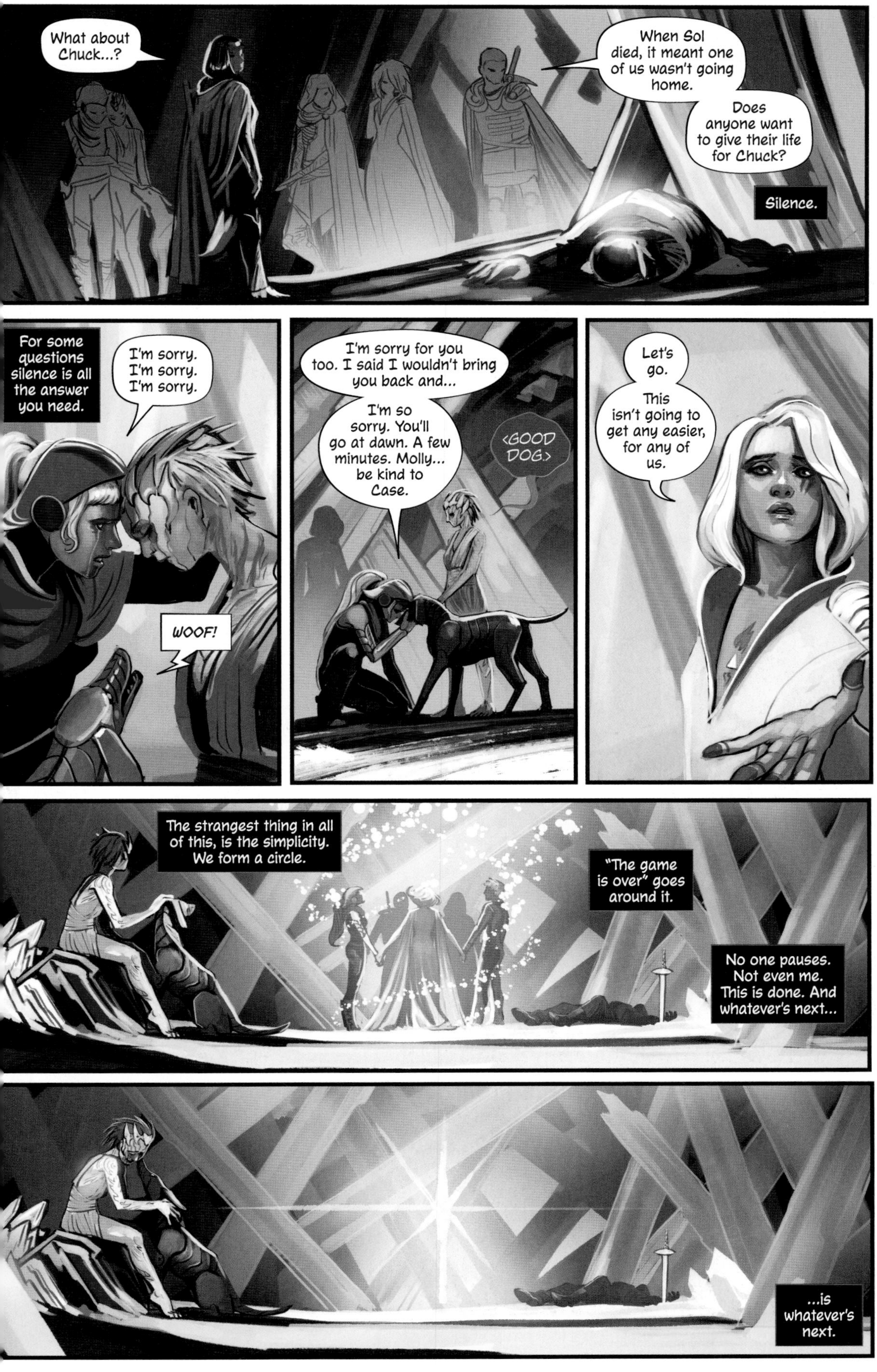
What about Chuck...?
When Sol died, it meant one of us wasn't going home.
Does anyone want to give their life for Chuck?
Silence.
For some questions silence is all the answer you need.
I'm sorry. I'm sorry. I'm sorry.
WOOF!
I'm sorry for you too. I said I wouldn't bring you back and...
I'm so sorry. You'll go at dawn. A few minutes. Molly... be kind to Case.
<GOOD DOG.>
Let's go.
This isn't going to get any easier, for any of us.
The strangest thing in all of this, is the simplicity. We form a circle.
"The game is over" goes around it.
No one pauses. Not even me. This is done. And whatever's next...
...is whatever's next.

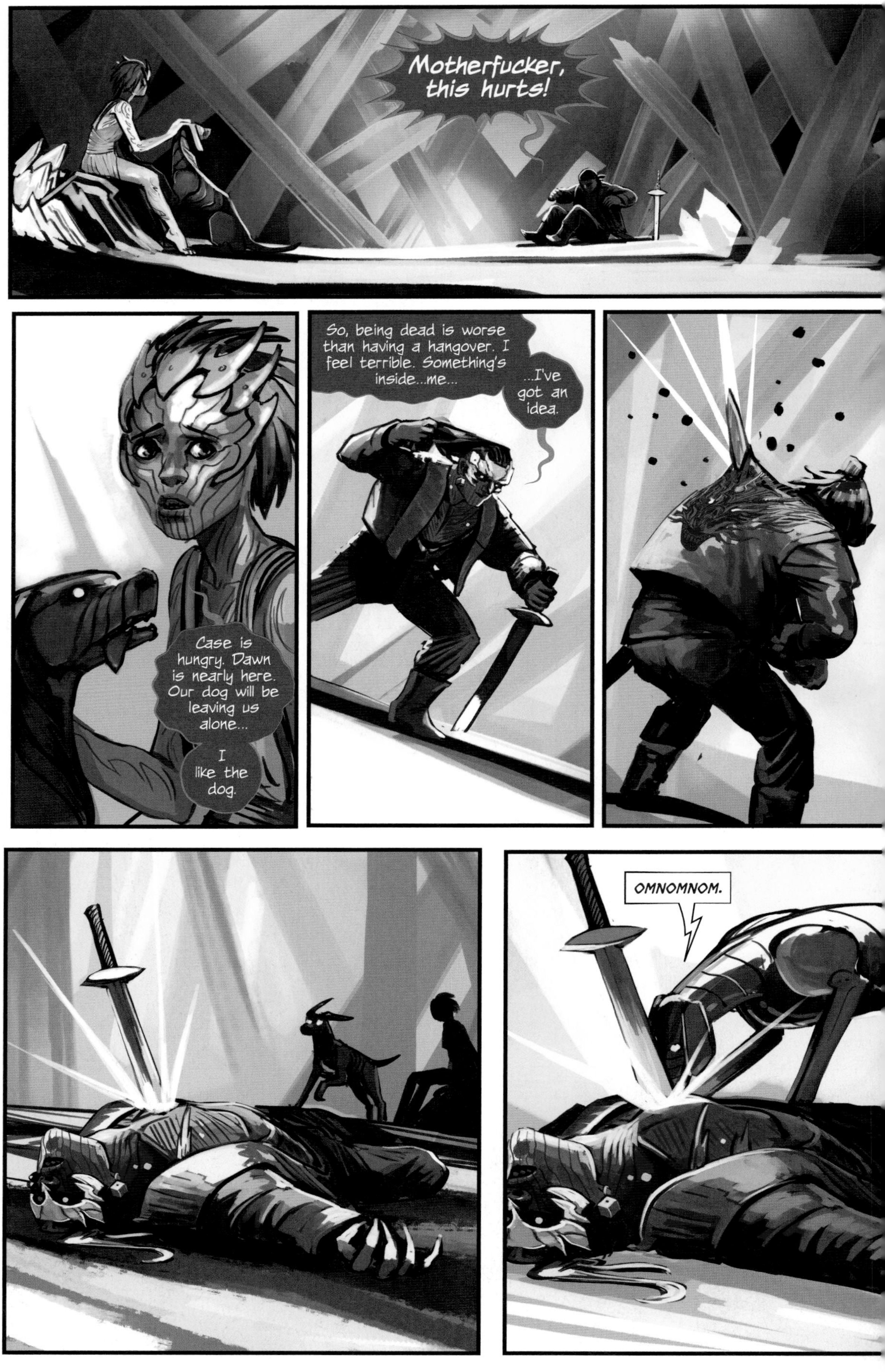

Motherfucker, this hurts!
Case is hungry. Dawn is nearly here. Our dog will be leaving us alone...
I like the dog.
So, being dead is worse than having a hangover. I feel terrible. Something's inside...me...
...I've got an idea.
OMNOMNOM.

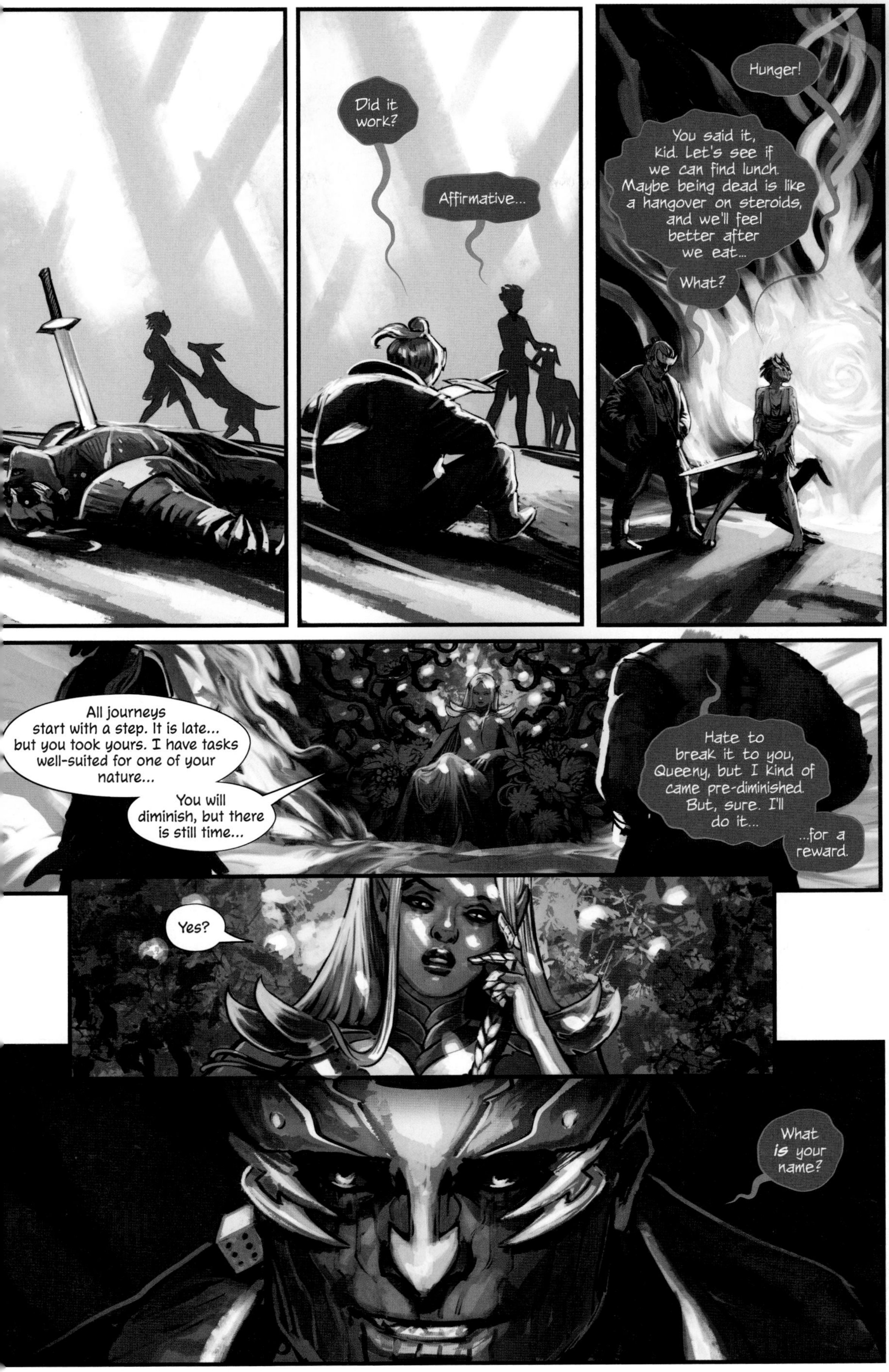
Did it work?
Affirmative...
Hunger!
You said it, kid. Let's see if we can find lunch. Maybe being dead is like a hangover on steroids, and we'll feel better after we eat...
What?
All journeys start with a step. It is late... but you took yours. I have tasks well-suited for one of your nature...
You will diminish, but there is still time...
Hate to break it to you, Queeny, but I kind of came pre-diminished. But, sure. I'll do it...
...for a reward.
Yes?
What *is* your name?

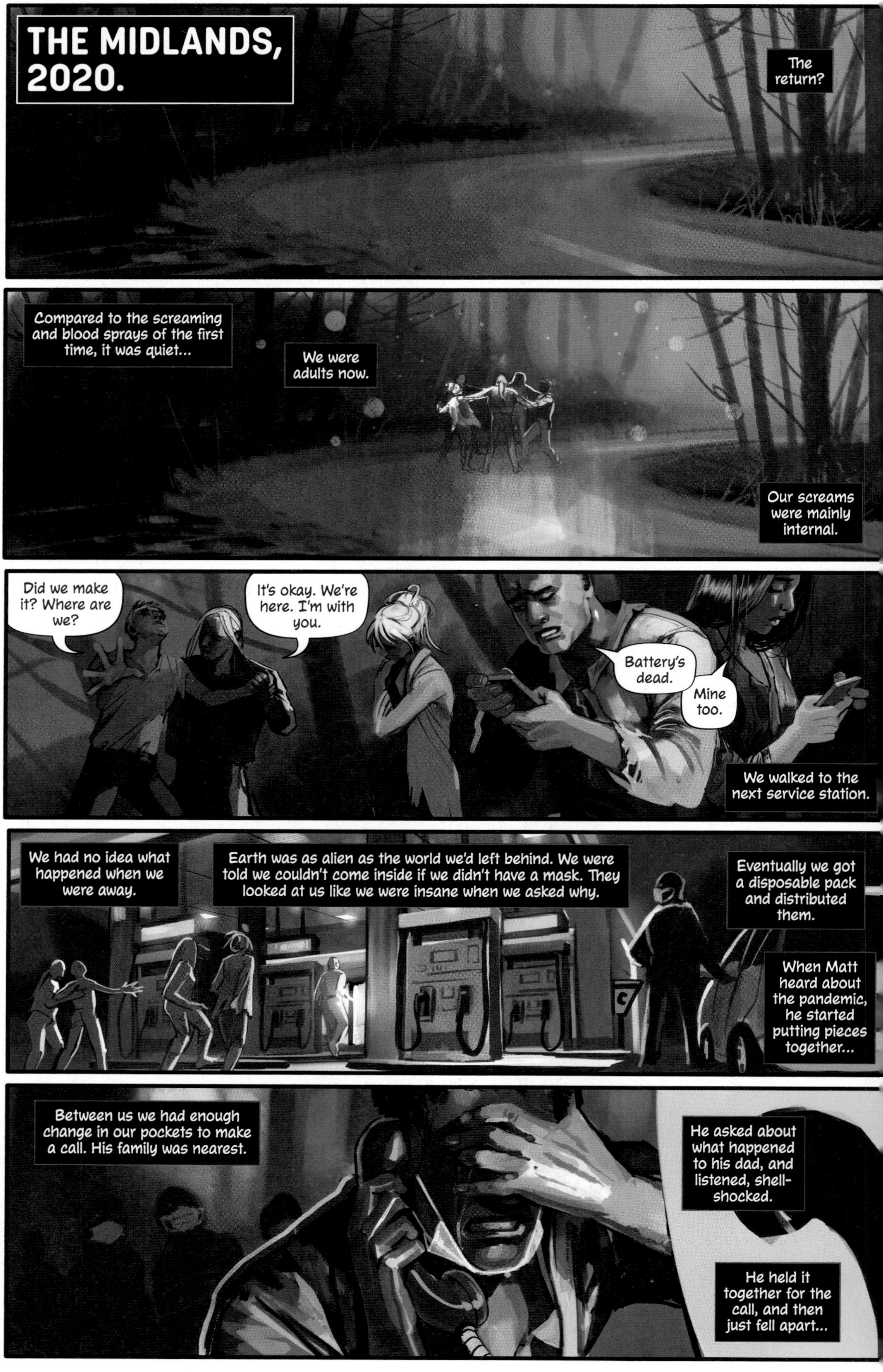
THE MIDLANDS, 2020.
The return?
Compared to the screaming and blood sprays of the first time, it was quiet...
We were adults now.
Our screams were mainly internal.
Did we make it? Where are we?
It's okay. We're here. I'm with you.
Battery's dead.
Mine too.
We walked to the next service station.
We had no idea what happened when we were away.
Earth was as alien as the world we'd left behind. We were told we couldn't come inside if we didn't have a mask. They looked at us like we were insane when we asked why.
Eventually we got a disposable pack and distributed them.
When Matt heard about the pandemic, he started putting pieces together...
Between us we had enough change in our pockets to make a call. His family was nearest.
He asked about what happened to his dad, and listened, shell-shocked.
He held it together for the call, and then just fell apart...

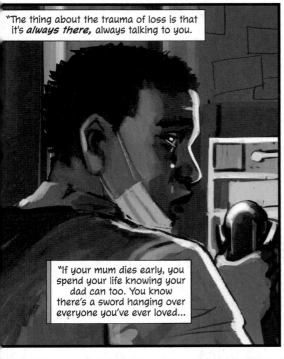

"The thing about the trauma of loss is that it's *always there,* always talking to you."

"If your mum dies early, you spend your life knowing your dad can too. You know there's a sword hanging over everyone you've ever loved..."

"...and the extra kick in the teeth? You're not worrying for nothing.

"One day that phone will ring and the blade will run you right through you...

"And you are always waiting. It's there, and it's hard to let go of that.

"But simultaneously, depression is a liar...

"...and so is Mistress Woe."

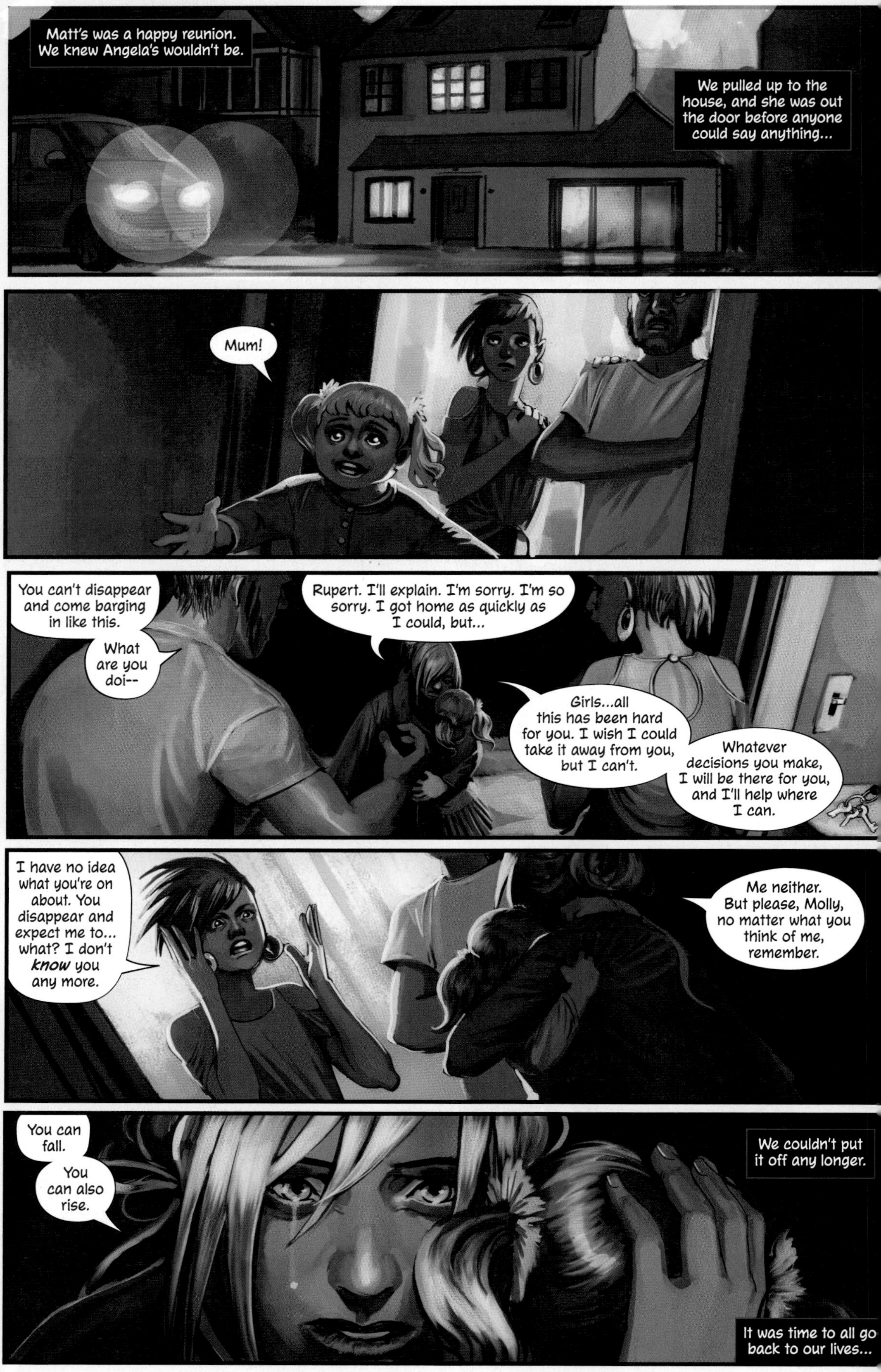
Matt's was a happy reunion. We knew Angela's wouldn't be.
We pulled up to the house, and she was out the door before anyone could say anything...
Mum!
You can't disappear and come barging in like this.
What are you doi--
Rupert. I'll explain. I'm sorry. I'm so sorry. I got home as quickly as I could, but...
Girls...all this has been hard for you. I wish I could take it away from you, but I can't.
Whatever decisions you make, I will be there for you, and I'll help where I can.
I have no idea what you're on about. You disappear and expect me to... what? I don't *know* you any more.
Me neither. But please, Molly, no matter what you think of me, remember.
You can fall.
You can also rise.
We couldn't put it off any longer.
It was time to all go back to our lives...

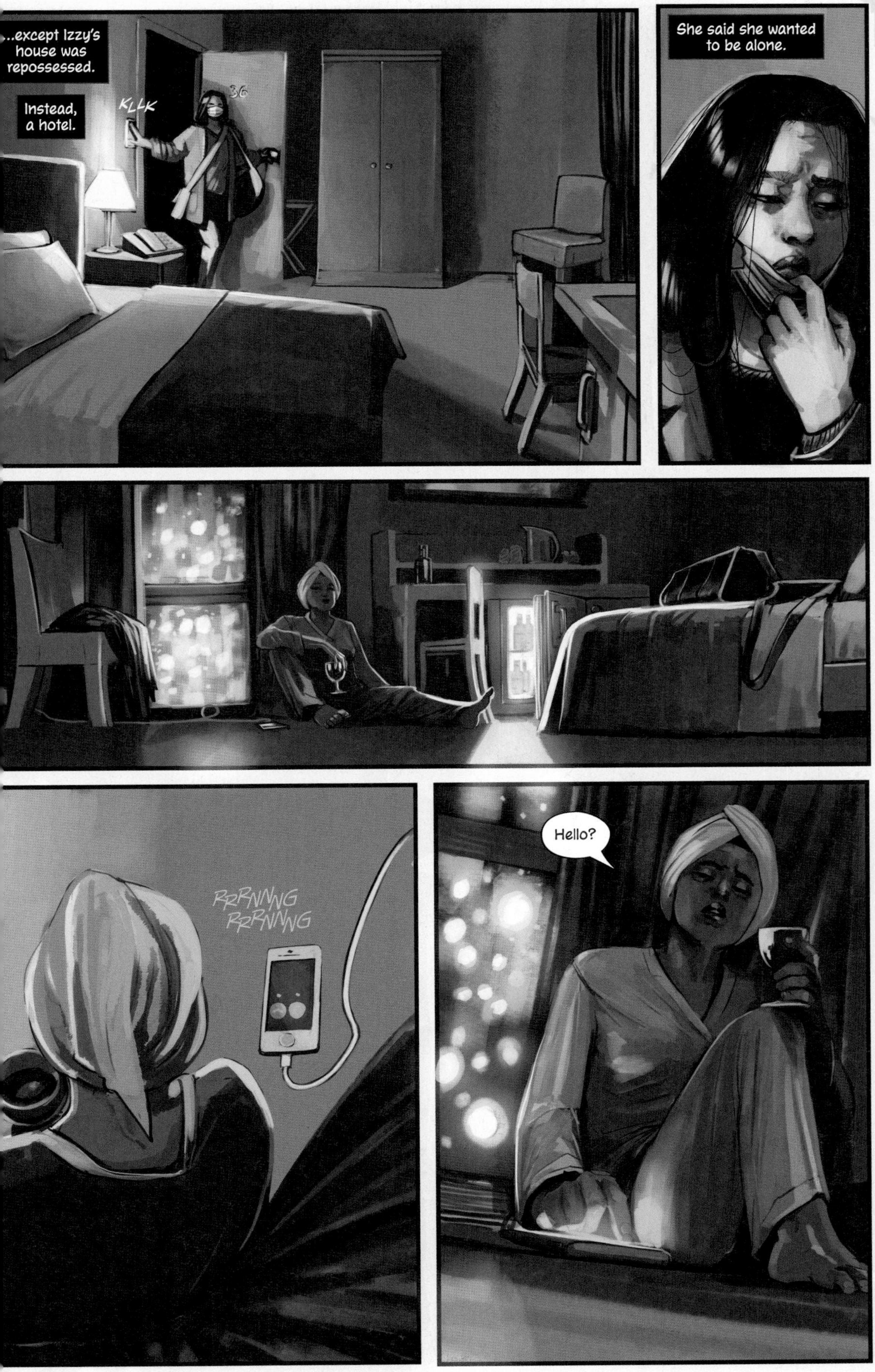
...except Izzy's house was repossessed.
Instead, a hotel.
KLLK
36
She said she wanted to be alone.
RRRNNNG RRRNNNG
Hello?

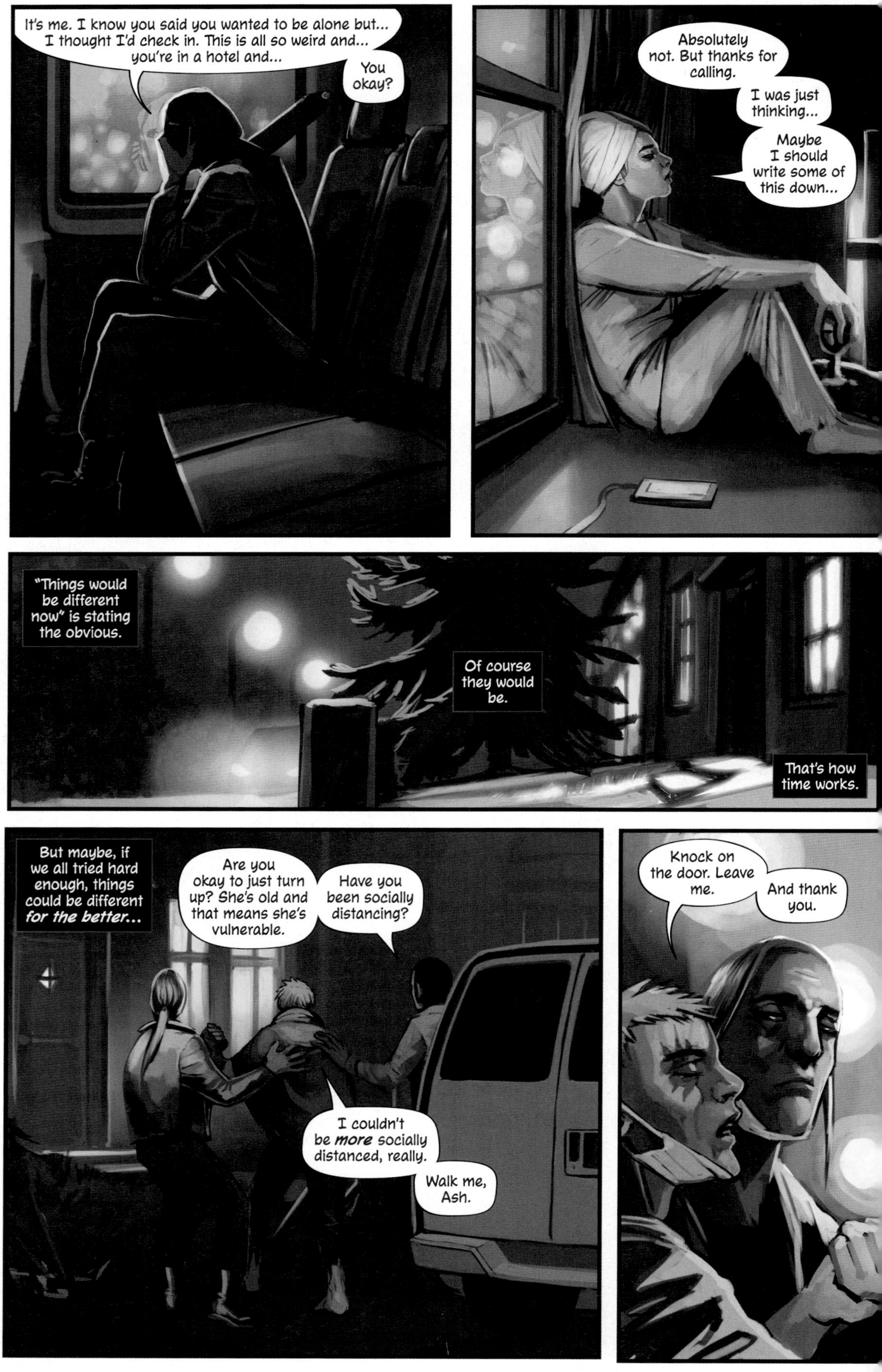
It's me. I know you said you wanted to be alone but... I thought I'd check in. This is all so weird and... you're in a hotel and...
You okay?
Absolutely not. But thanks for calling.
I was just thinking...
Maybe I should write some of this down...
"Things would be different now" is stating the obvious.
Of course they would be.
That's how time works.
But maybe, if we all tried hard enough, things could be different *for the better*...
Are you okay to just turn up? She's old and that means she's vulnerable.
Have you been socially distancing?
I couldn't be *more* socially distanced, really.
Walk me, Ash.
Knock on the door. Leave me.
And thank you.

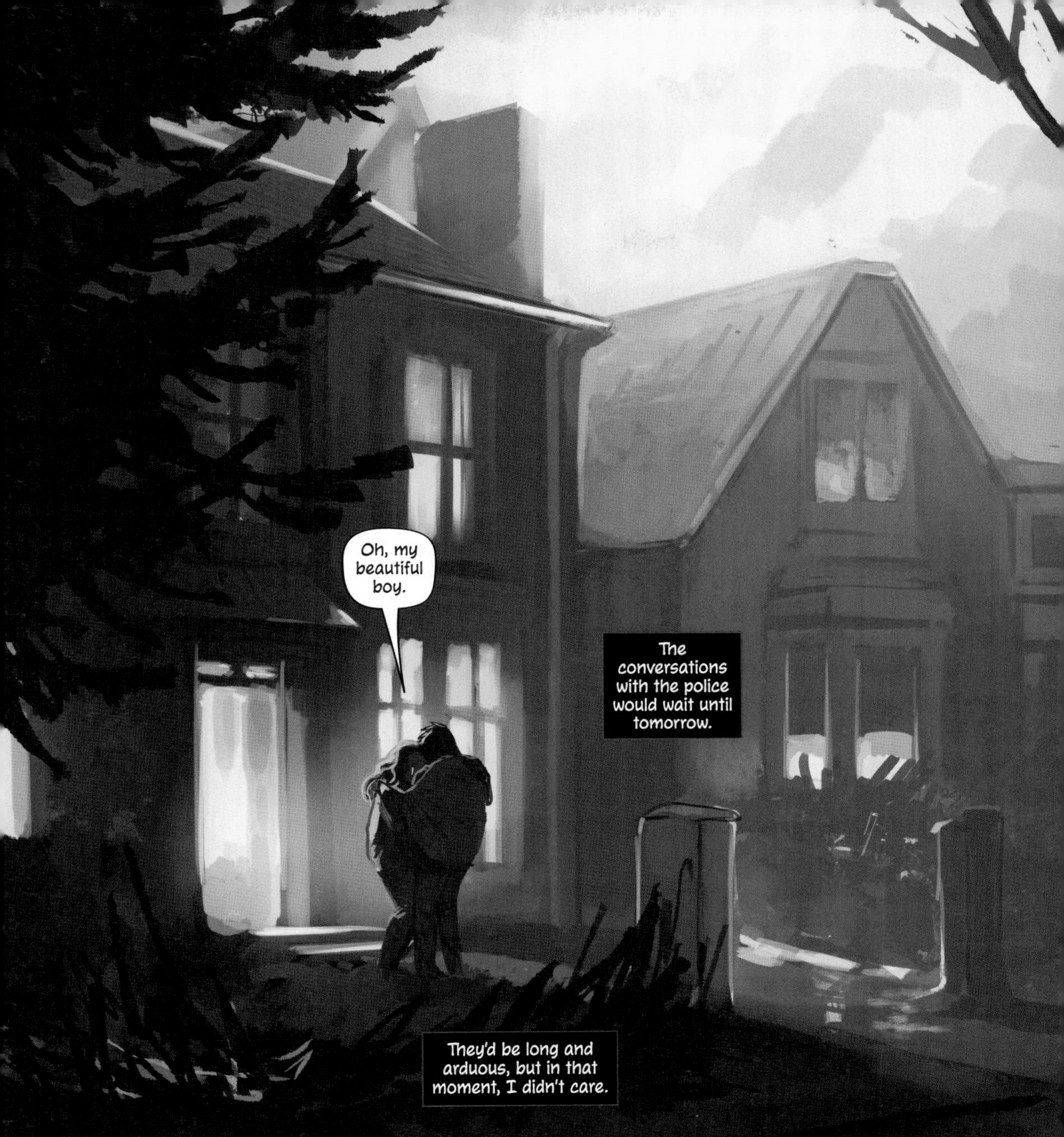
Oh, my beautiful boy.
The conversations with the police would wait until tomorrow.
They'd be long and arduous, but in that moment, I didn't care.

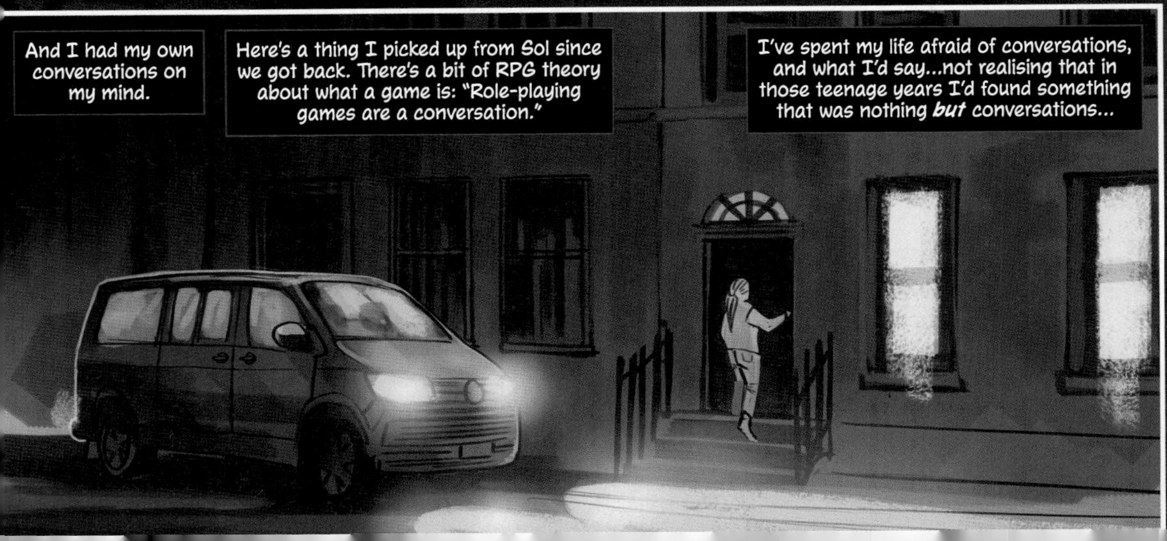
And I had my own conversations on my mind.
Here's a thing I picked up from Sol since we got back. There's a bit of RPG theory about what a game is: "Role-playing games are a conversation."
I've spent my life afraid of conversations, and what I'd say...not realising that in those teenage years I'd found something that was nothing ***but*** conversations...

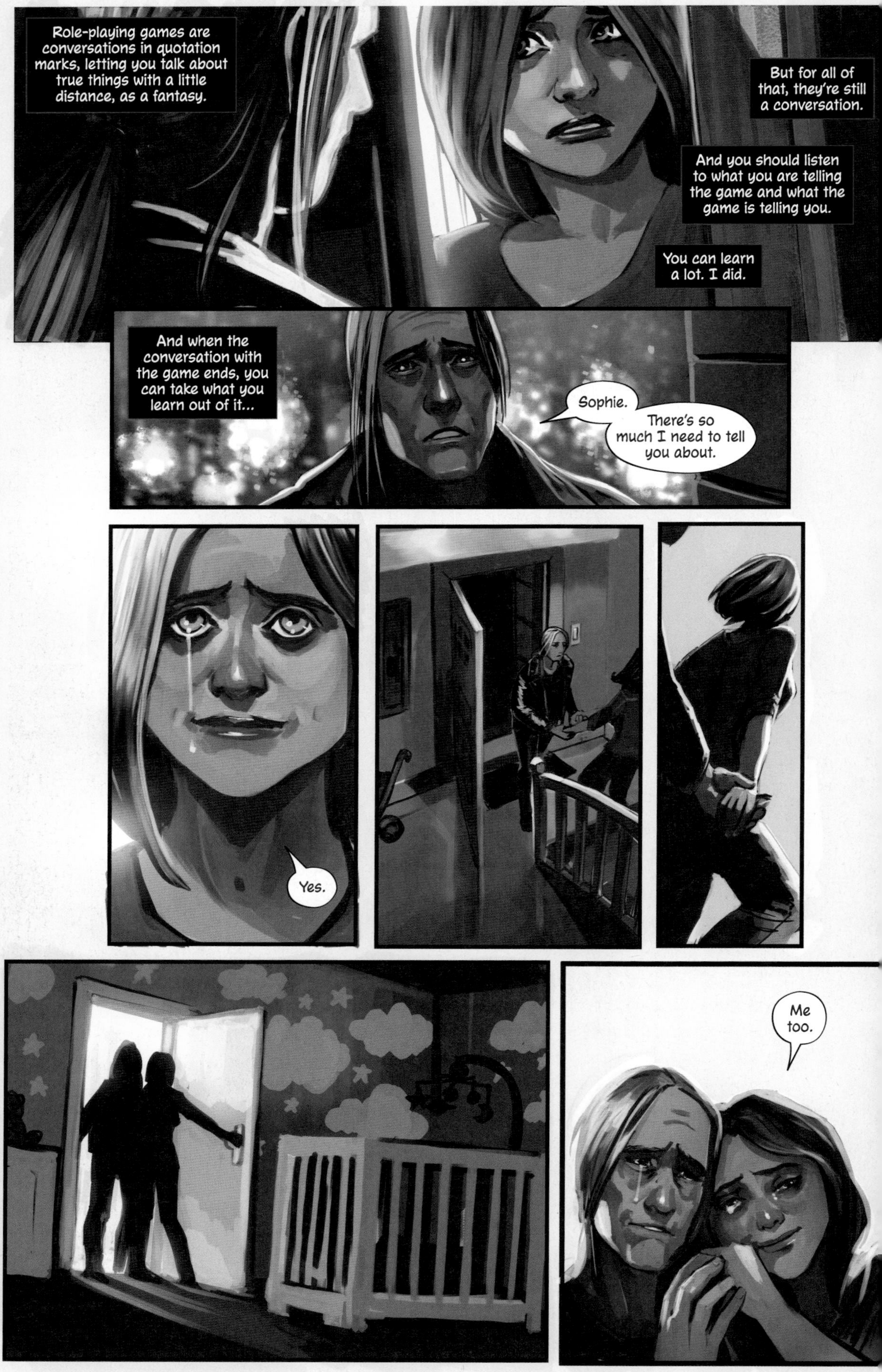
Role-playing games are conversations in quotation marks, letting you talk about true things with a little distance, as a fantasy.
But for all of that, they're still a conversation.
And you should listen to what you are telling the game and what the game is telling you.
You can learn a lot. I did.
And when the conversation with the game ends, you can take what you learn out of it...
Sophie.
There's so much I need to tell you about.
Yes.
Me too.

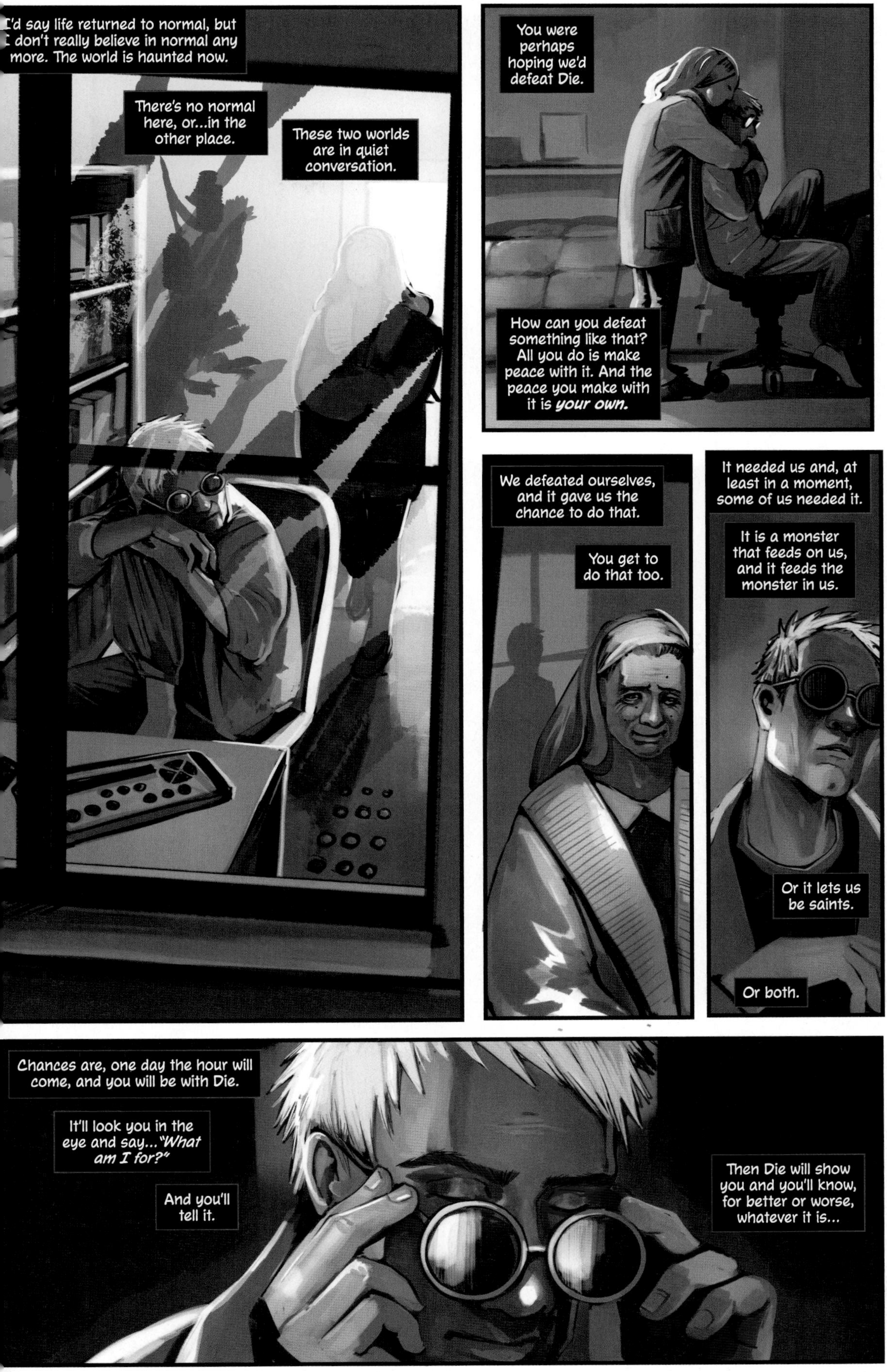
I'd say life returned to normal, but I don't really believe in normal any more. The world is haunted now.
There's no normal here, or...in the other place.
These two worlds are in quiet conversation.
You were perhaps hoping we'd defeat Die.
How can you defeat something like that? All you do is make peace with it. And the peace you make with it is *your own.*
We defeated ourselves, and it gave us the chance to do that.
You get to do that too.
It needed us and, at least in a moment, some of us needed it.
It is a monster that feeds on us, and it feeds the monster in us.
Or it lets us be saints.
Or both.
Chances are, one day the hour will come, and you will be with Die.
It'll look you in the eye and say..."*What am I for?*"
And you'll tell it.
Then Die will show you and you'll know, for better or worse, whatever it is...

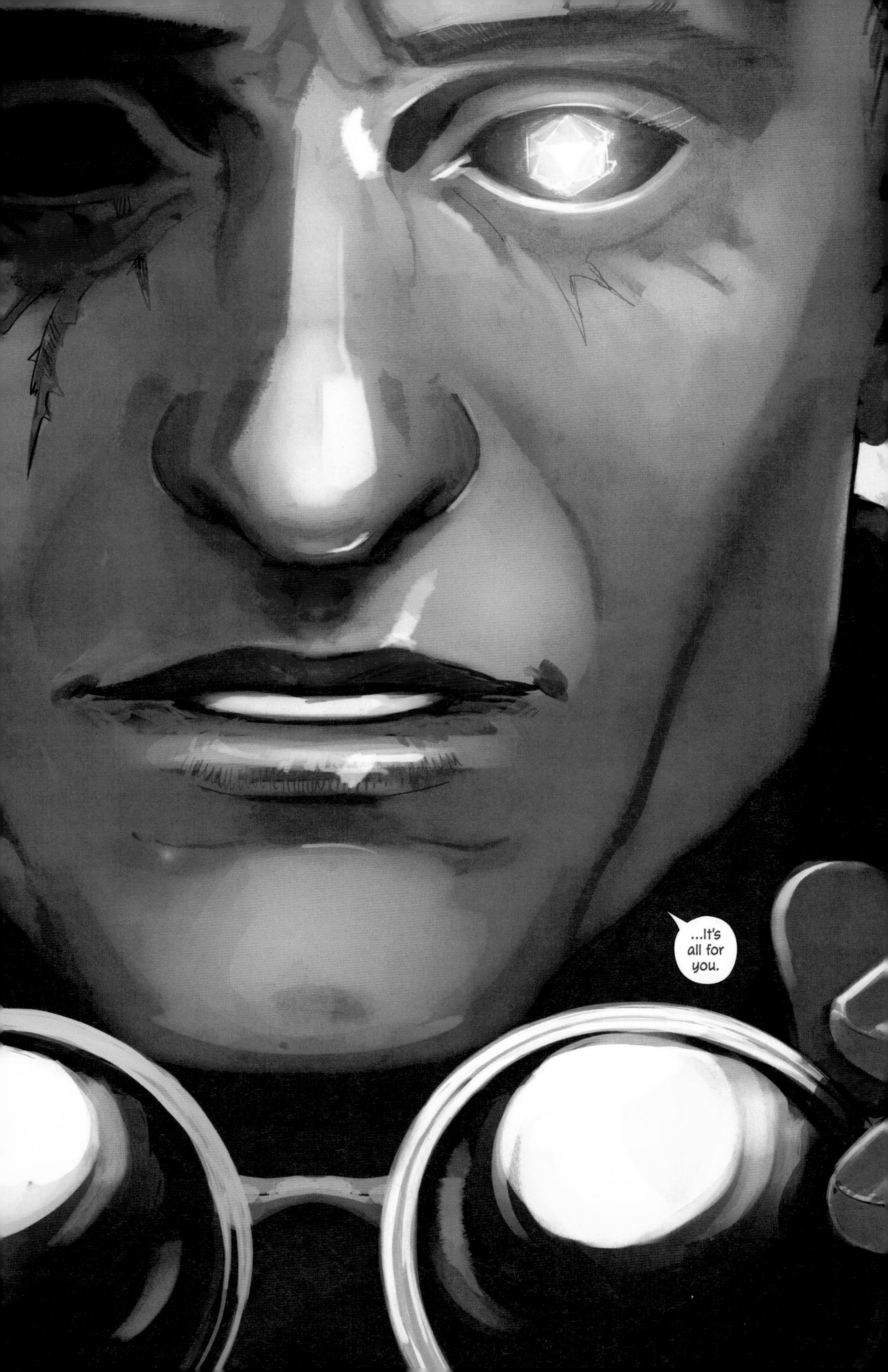
...It's all for you.

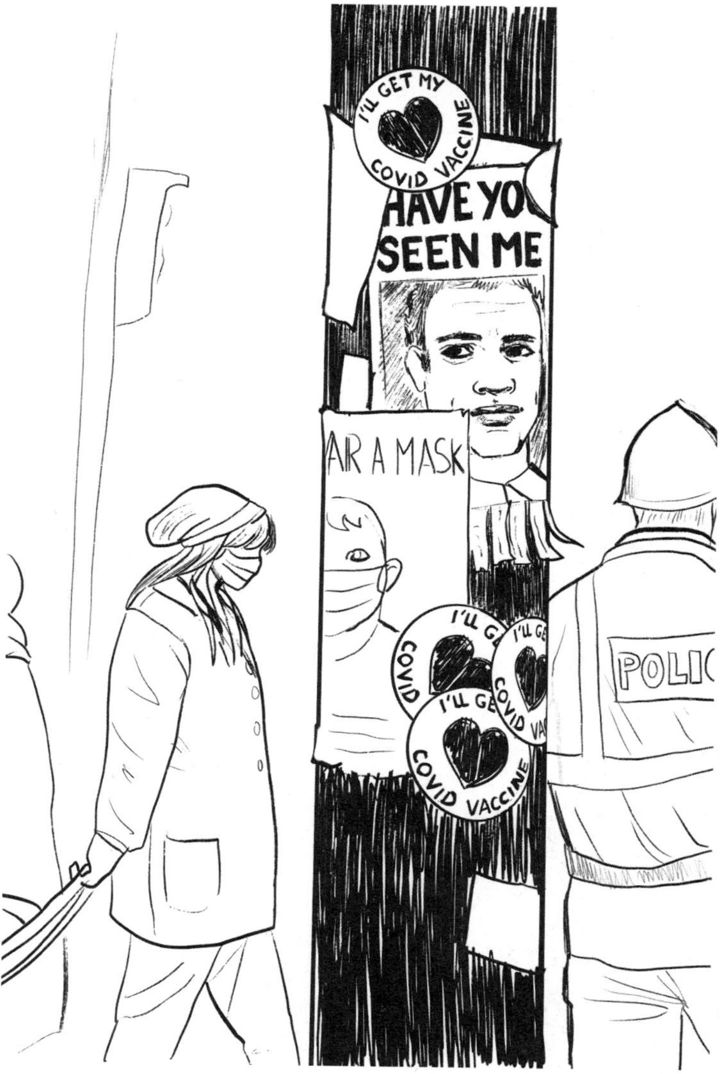

I'LL GET MY
COVID VACCINE
HAVE YO
SEEN ME
AR A MASK
I'LL GE
COVID
I'LL G
COVID VA
I'LL GE
COVID VACCINE
POLIC

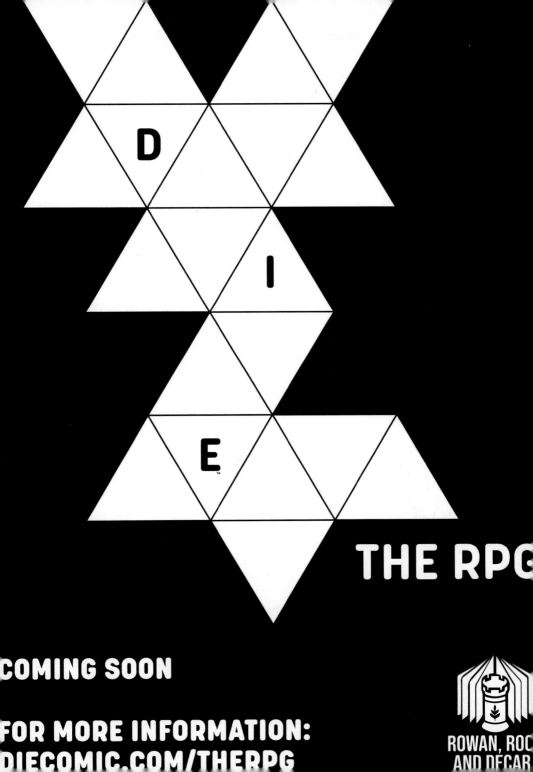

COVERS

of a summoning ritual, and a huge part of comics - and especially with *DIE*. That we got to invite assorted friendly magicians to give their own personal take on our particularly personal material was a real joy. **KG**

Paulina Ganucheau
Issue 17 variant

Yoshi Yoshitani
Issue 18 variant

Jenny Frison
Issue 19 variant

Kim Jung Gi
Issue 20 variant

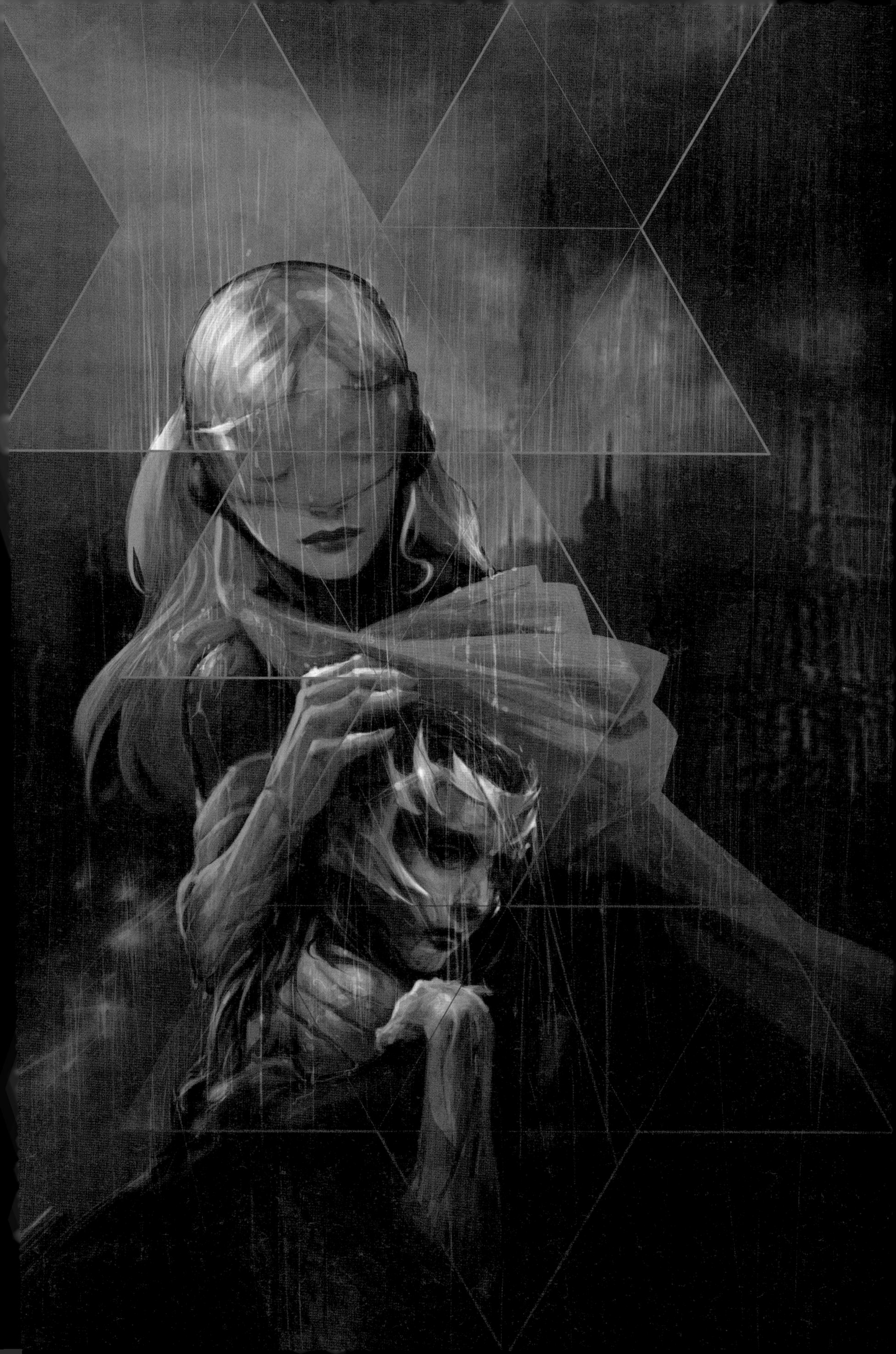

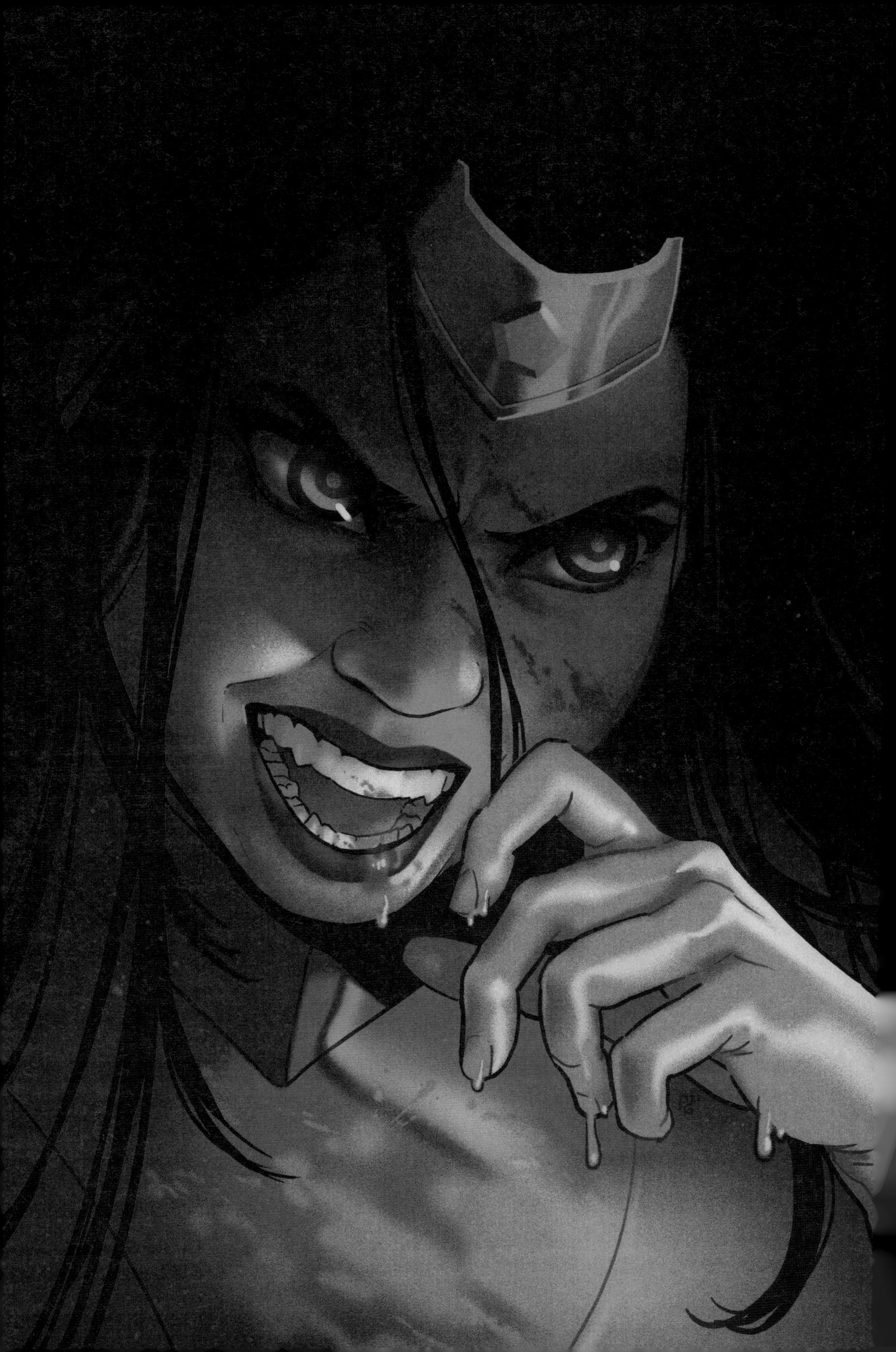

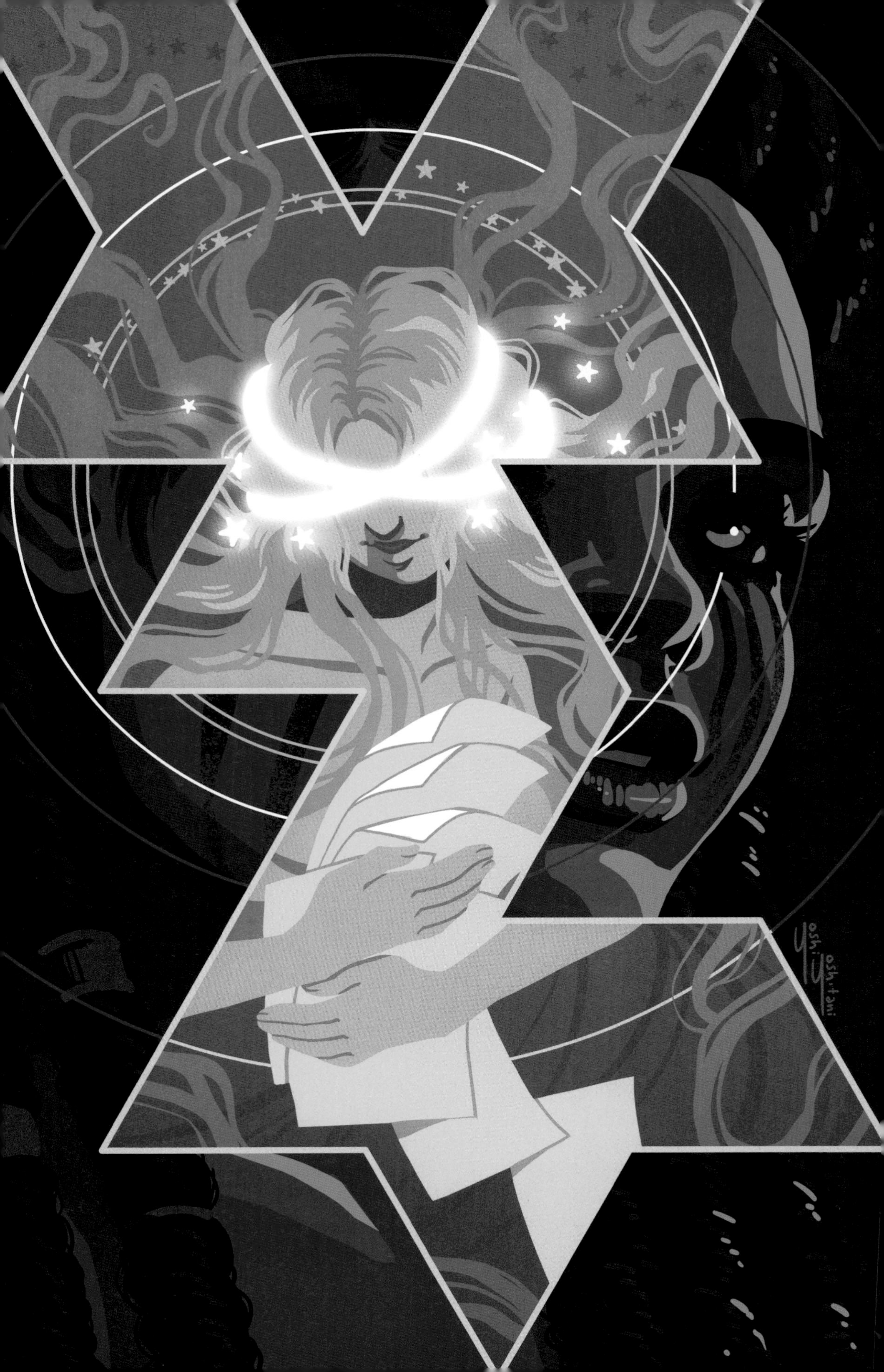

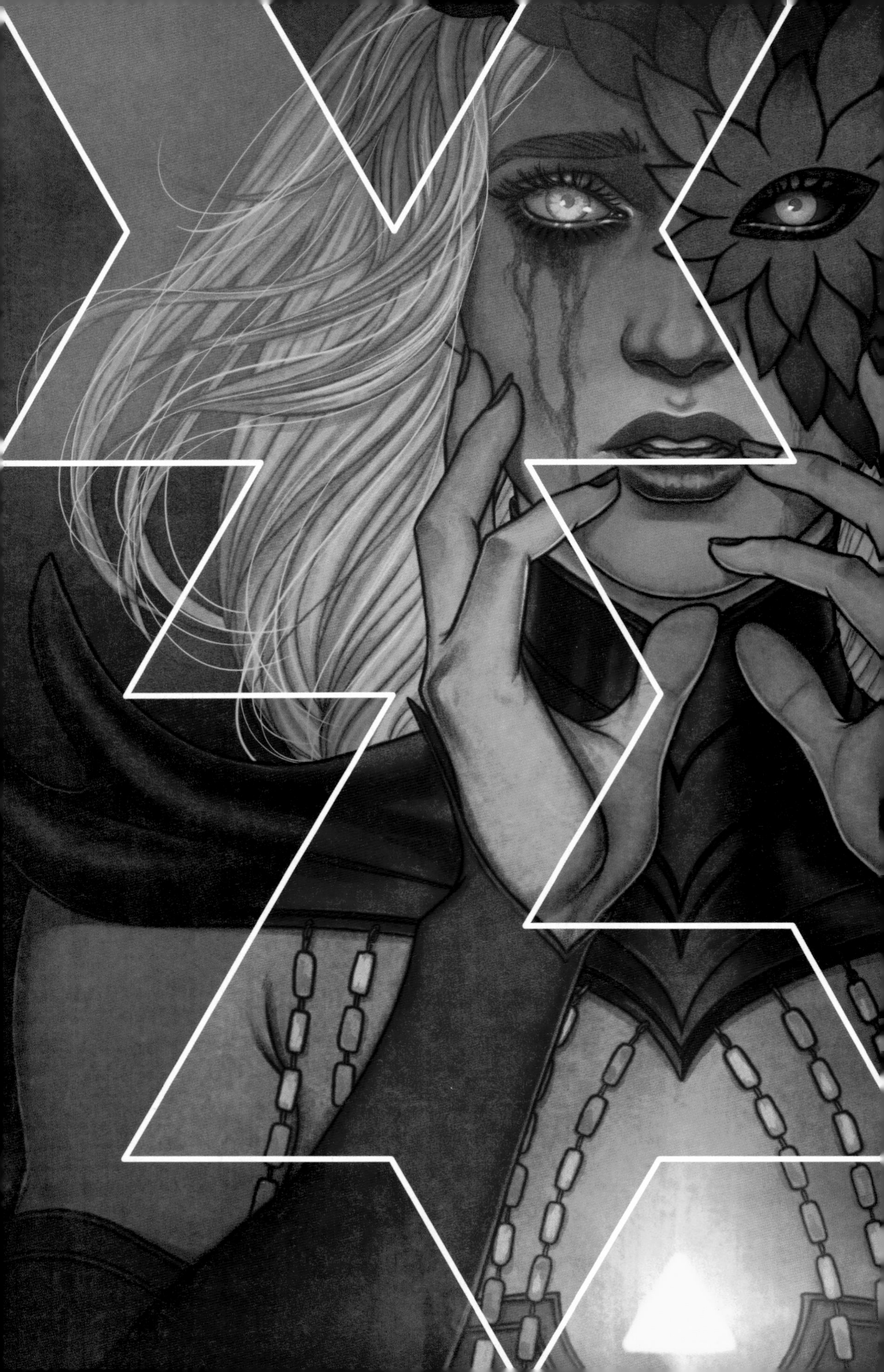

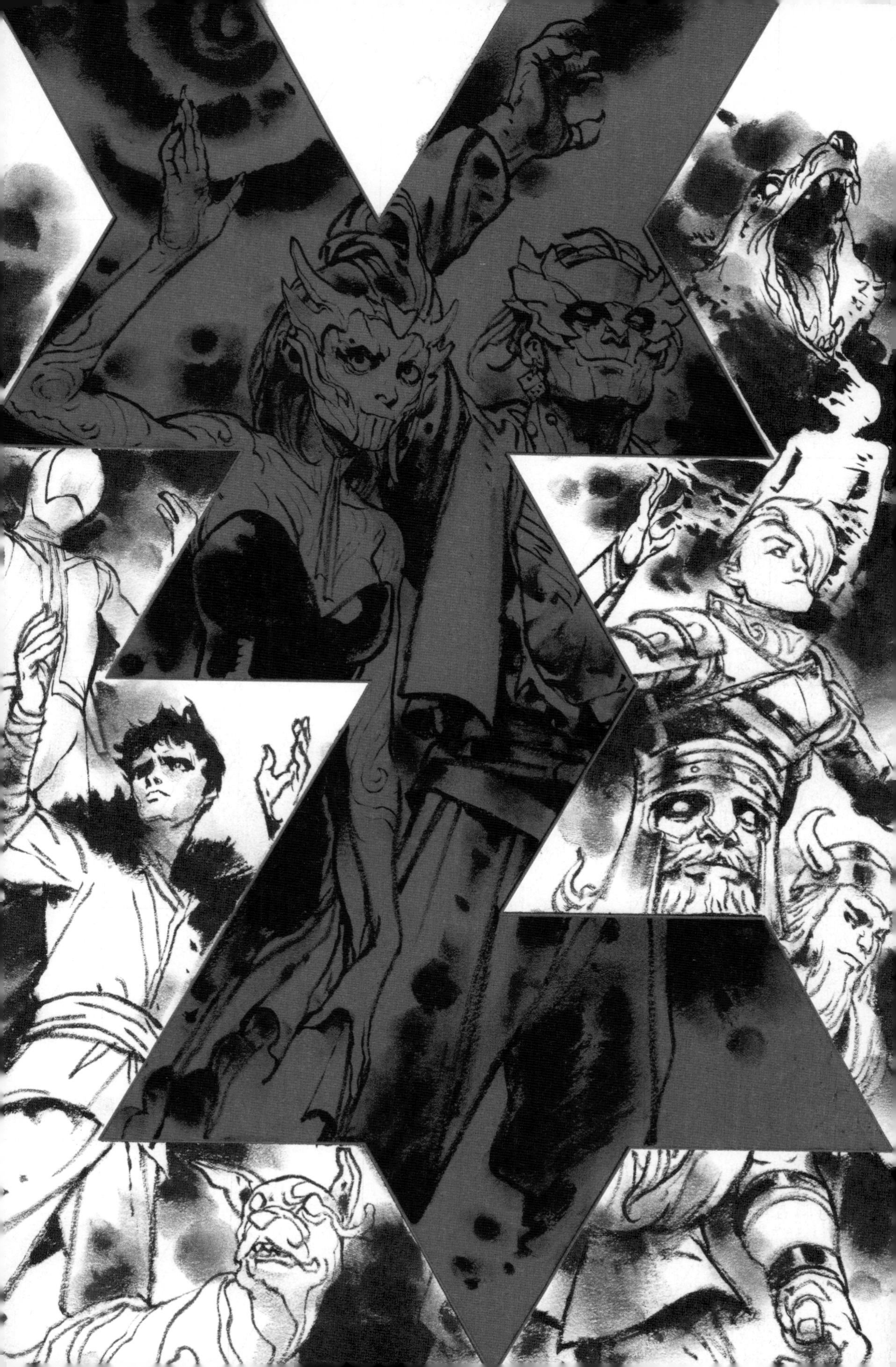

INTERVIEWS & ESSAYS

We continue to interview key figures for their perspective on this important period for the tabletop RPG: speaking to someone who was there at the very start, reporting on what's going on in the land of Nordic LARPS, the growth of safety culture, and how RPGs as a spectator art has changed everything. **KG**

LEE GOLD

In these interviews, we've had a central thesis: that the 2010s were the most important time for the RPG since its initial decade. There's an implicit promise there: we should talk to someone and ask them about what it was like when literally everything was new.

Four months before I was born, Lee Gold founded *Alarums and Excursions* (A&E). It's an APA ("Amateur Press Association" - essentially a group-sourced fanzine where individuals contribute articles, a central body collates, and mails to all parties). It was one of the first publications solely about role-playing games. It's as important to the nascent gaming culture as *Sniffin' Glue* was to punk, except three years earlier, and Gold, now in her seventies, is still publishing it today. I was overjoyed she agreed to an email interview. I'm sitting here imaging an electric guitar being plugged in for the first time when I ask her: what *was* it like?

"It was *Let's Pretend* with lots of rules, many of them with typos," sighs Lee. Point taken. Many people talking

describe as the genesis of modern fandom. As such, there's a cultural knowledge of the antecedents. When *Dungeons & Dragons* came from the Twin Cities scene of Minneapolis/ Saint Paul, it wouldn't have been as something entirely alien. In her writing, Gold describes how the first RPG encountered by LASFSians was 1969's *Dynasty*: "a large red can with a cloth map and plastic soldiers and a lot of beautiful wooden pieces – eight booklets that all looked alike until you opened them up and found out if you'd gotten the Emperor; the Official; Gentry/Landholder; Scholar; Silk Peasant; Rice Peasant; Wheat Peasant; or the Warlord." She describes this as a role-playing game for the personality each of the characters get given, especially the final note: "FOR AS LONG AS YOU ARE THIS CHARACTER, YOUR ACTIONS MUST BE CONSISTENT WITH YOUR PERSONALITY AS STATED ABOVE." There were also local games such as *Revenge!* by LASFSian Jack Harness ("Somewhat like *Monopoly* but 50% wider than *Monopoly*, with planets rather than street territories" where player death leads to reincarnation

"It was, by the way, a fairly short game ... about four hours."

about their time in a historic scene have a tendency to mythologize. Lee's answers are very much against that. They are plain speaking, both highlighting what it was like, and what it *wasn't* like. She very much sees *D&D* as an extension of existing trends.

"I didn't play in the *Diplomacy* play-by-mail games whose moves were chronicled in John Boardman's zines," she says, referring to his 1963-founded *Graustark*, a *Diplomacy*-focused zine, "I remember hearing (not reading) about the spread of vampirism in one country, and in every country it conquered, much amusing readers. I don't know how you'd describe that sort of thing."

She was part of Los Angeles Science Fantasy Society, founded back in 1934 and running consistently since the birth of what many would

as mythical characters such as ugly torturer's daughter Vulchurella or usured ruler Prince Putrid.).

While it wasn't without precedent, there is still that first momentous game of *D&D*, and we're lucky enough to have Gold's period records. The joy of a zine writer is that you get period records. She wrote about it for *APA-L* (The APA of Los Angeles's SF Fandom) back in 1975, where she describes her friend Hilda (now Eclare) Hannifen and husband in town as her father was ill. They stayed for 28 hours. When there, Eclare ran a game. "It was, by the way, a fairly short game," notes Lee at the time, "about four hours."

The account shows much that we would recognize, but also the tropes which we've metabolized, experienced as new. Its last encounter– where two party members are possessed by sentient swords and have a row - sounds like exactly the sort of thing you'll recognize from this comic: sentient swords with hot takes have been around a long time. The game climax was everyone returning home, sharing loot and increasing levels. That was the takeaway?

"It was fun," says Lee. "At the end, I wrote a cheque to TSR to get the rules, and Owen Hannifen gave me a photocopy of the rules I could use to create a dungeon while I was waiting for the real rules to arrive. I used this to create my first dungeon,

always been a moving target. I find myself thinking about how much the "difficulty" in RPGs is not the rules themselves, but the cultural idea of D&D. The game isn't just the rules. It's the culture around it, the people.

My main cultural research of gamers in the period was *Shared Fantasy: Role-Playing Games as Social Worlds* by Gary Alan Fines, published in 1983 about the culture of the Twin Cities scene in the late seventies. I found myself actively disturbed by some of the accepted behaviour in the group - rape of female NPCs

Some of the sillier ones had drifted away. Many now wanted equality."

LASFS was a different demographic than wargamers, so led to a different local culture. "*A&E* contributors and readers included some wargamers, but were largely drawn from people who belonged to organized science fiction fandom - attending SF clubs, contributing to or buying SF fanzines, attending the sort of SF fan conventions in which everyone participated (rather than those put on by an organizer to get celebrities to lure passive attendees). We knew one another from fanzine letter columns and APAs, clubs and conventions. There were many more women in 1970s SF fandom than in wargaming circles. My husband Barry and I learned *D&D* from a woman GM, our old friend Hilda (nowadays Eclare) Hannifen."

"If you're not having fun, figure out what you're doing wrong and change things..."

Neocarn." The increasing amount of *D&D* content in the *APA-L* led to Lee founding *Alarums & Excursions*. There wasn't enmity from the existing scene. "Bruce Pelz and other non-*D&D*ing LASFSians weren't 'suspicious' of *D&D*," notes Lee, "they just wanted to go on doing normal fannish stuff and found *D&D* was distracting people from talking about that."

As the game did seem novel in several ways, and RPGs are complicated, was it difficult to understand? Not particularly. Bar the typos in the material, it wasn't that the game itself was hard. "I had an MA in English Lit," she says. "It wasn't harder than figuring out how Milton's *On Christian Doctrine* applied to his *Paradise Lost* while also reading CS Lewis's book on Milton's epic poem. Bear in mind that I'm Jewish, not Christian. I went from original *D&D* to C&S (Chivalry & Sorcery). That's a more complicated game, but I found it more interesting because it gave me a whole culture to play in and more complex player characters and non-player characters to roleplay."

She urges me to go and look at those original *D&D* rules, which can be bought as PDFs now. They are distinctly not what *D&D* became in terms of complexity. It's interesting how much the idea of what *D&D* 'is' has been internalized, when *D&D* has

was just accepted. It wasn't a tabloid expose. It was a sober and academic book, quoting a lot of male players seemingly mystified as to why few women would want to play with them, despite the above. But that was the Twin Cities... and what Fine describes isn't what Lee experienced when the cultures met. "I wasn't aware that DC and NY and Boston and Bay Area (San Jose & San Francisco) and Los Angeles SF fans felt different and treated people differently when I played with them at fannish conventions or at DunDraCon," she says.

She was part of the long established LASFAian culture, which has different roots. "Not just how many women there were, but how much they were valued," says Lee. "When I entered LASFS in 1967, there were few women, but they were highly valued. Have you read Heinlein's *The Moon is a Harsh Mistress*?" I haven't. It describes a penal colony on the Moon where men outnumber women 2:1 leading to a hugely different sort of society. "It was sort of like that," she says. "Many of these rare women were movers and shakers. And then along came *Star Trek* - and LASFS got some new independent female fans but also a lot of newly teenaged girls, looking for guys. By 1975, things had settled down. The teenaged girls had grown up a bit

I also wonder what it was like to see a hobby go overground. It's just not how Lee sees it. "I never noticed *D&D* being 'underground,' she says simply. It did, of course, change across time. "There was a period when we started reading about crank reporters who falsely said that playing *D&D* caused teenagers to commit suicide. And of course many of us started saying 'roleplaying' rather than '*D&D*'. Because there were an increasing number of non-TSR games and many of these were second-generation games, without experience points or levels, games that didn't resemble *D&D*," she says.

So, as someone who was there at close to the beginning and is still there today, is there anything she'd say to people in the hobby now? "We had fun. We're still having fun," she says. "If you're not having fun, figure out what you're doing wrong and change things until you and the other players are having fun." She forwards me the writeups from her last game set in Iceland and her last *Toon* game set in an alternate Los Angeles dealing with ghosts. "So you can see what I consider to be 'fun'," she says.

I read, and it does sound fun. Finding your own fun, whether then or now, sounds fun. This remains as true as when the game was new as it is now.

Alarums And Excursions is available to buy from https://conchord.org/xeno/aande.html

CAT TOBIN

I knew I wanted to write about Nordic LARP. The question was how? It's Nordic. It's live action role-play. I can say that. But how to explain what it actually means?

Then I was on a panel with Cat Tobin of RPG publisher Pelgrane Press. She talked in passing about her discovery and even *conversion* to Nordic LARP. I realized that, for a primer of a whole scene, this is the way. Have a pilgrim talk about her journey to a holy land, and we'll know why it's worthwhile, and know why we may want to make the journey ourselves.

Growing up in rural 90s Ireland, Cat was entirely unaware of RPGs until she came to university and during the Fresher events sat down to "still probably the worst game I ever played". The *potential* though. Soon, she's gaming every night, then running conventions, including Dragonmeet where she met Pelgrane, and eventually a full-time job. During her love affair, she was meeting with more traditional LARPs we've talked before. She thought herself pretty experienced. And then... Cat's first experience of Nordic LARP was in 2013, with the game *Mad About The Boy*, inspired by *Y: the Last Man* (i.e. set in a world where all people with a y chromosome are dead). While the game hasn't run for years due to that gender essentialist nature, playing in an all-women group of 75 or so players over a weekend was a huge experience. She didn't quite get

Freeform LARP - which is mostly what we talked about with Jeanette in issue 15 - creates a situation where you take on a role as created by the people running the game telling you who you are.... and none of this information is available to the other players. "You shouldn't reveal the information on your character sheet to other players, because you might ruin the surprise," says Cat.

In Nordic LARPS, it's the opposite. "They generally give you all of the information," says Cat. People know who they are, and who everyone else is. "A lot of the character connections, you'll be expected to come up with yourself," she says. "You'll talk to the other players before the game, you'll arrange plots, and they tend to be quite transparent."

How does it work? "I thought of it very much as like a stone soup kind of game, in that they have a pot with a stone in it, and then everyone else brings their own ingredient, and you end up with this amazing soup," says Cat, "whereas our LARPs were more like a pot of stew, and you would turn up with your bowl, and they would just give you some."

In a freeform LARP it's not impossible that you could be in conversation with someone and then realise they're your in-game sister. This isn't true in Nordic LARPs. "You can walk into the game, and not only do you know who your family are, but you already know

"Characterisation is ... more about how everyone else responds to you."

it, until afterwards, when she found herself on fire. It changed everything. We get to the question we've been dancing around ever since we've started writing these columns - what exactly *is* a Nordic LARP? Cat stresses what follows is a broad sweep, but...

"I guess the core concepts of it are players have an awful lot of agency, in a way that they might not in regular tabletop, or in other LARPs," she says. A lot of this comes from the fact they tend to be transparent.

what the dynamic is between you and them. And you have a sense of the kind of the arc that you and they will travel through the game," she says.

This impacts how you play intensely. "It hadn't occurred to me that characterisation is less about how you play the character, and more about how everyone else responds to you," says Cat. She describes herself as small and bouncy, but she's played hard-asses. How? In short: Clint Eastwood walking into a saloon doesn't work unless the saloon looks your way. "You need the buy-in of everyone else to play up to what you're playing, and that's a skill that I think Nordic LARPers really, really have. Again, they establish in advance who everyone is, what they're doing, what their role is, and what they want from the game, and so they're then able to give it to you. If you say, 'I just want this narratively angst-filled cryfest where I lose all of my friends and relationships,' then they're like, 'Right, cool. We will all work to deliver that for you.'"

There's also strong stylistic choice involved. Rather than bringing

most basic - gaming working on a higher level than the rest of the culture which is normally included under gaming. "You can have art that is tragic, and art that is poignant, and art that is difficult. They are looking at real issues that are really affecting people. There's no other medium like it, in terms of your active participation, versus passively consuming it as a medium. And as a result, there is nothing like it for building empathy or understanding, or really seeing what it is like to be in somebody else's shoes."

This playing with possibly volatile material means that while Nordic LARP mainly eschews traditional rules, it

convention? "You'll meet teachers, you'll meet political activists, you'll meet dancers, you'll meet theatre people, you'll meet actual visual artists. None of these people know anything at all about table-top," says Cat. "They don't know about RPGs, but they know that Nordic LARP is an art form that they're interested in exploring, and they bring elements from their own disciplines into Nordic LARP. So, Nordic LARP also has this influx of new ideas, of input from other disciplines, but related disciplines. The culture it's built extends beyond RPGs into something much broader."

When I talk about Nordic LARP I often feel I'm talking about the cool kids. Cat laughs. It's a joke, but it's also true. "But not only are they the cool kids, they're also the innovators," says Cat. And, as a bleeding edge, it naturally funnels back into more classical gaming via people like Cat. They're so bleeding edge they even invented the phrase to describe in-game and out-of-game feelings crossing over which gave this arc its title - Bleed.

"There's no other medium like it, in terms of your active participation..."

over rules from table-top games, or imagining elements, they try to create a world you interact with naturalistically. "The majority of Nordic LARPs tend to be fully immersive, so what you see is what you get," says Cat. "If there is a plug on the wall, that plug is there in the game, kind of thing, and they put extensive effort into creating. For 1940s games, they build 1940s villages," she says. "*The Monitor Celestra* was actually *on* a submarine. They like the full 360 immersion."

Perhaps most striking is its choice of topics. "They tend to focus more on political themes," says Cat. "They explore dynamics. They hold up a mirror to the world, and they play through different aspects. You'll have Nordic LARPs about the refugee crisis, about commercialism, about capitalism. They're not topics that we typically look at or engage with in tabletop, or even in the more freeform LARPs."

This level of seriousness had caused some problems when it interacts with the rest of fandom. At the Helsinki Worldcon the game *A Home for the Old* was removed from the schedule, for being viewed as offensive. "It's a game about Alzheimer's," says Cat. "It's really, really personal and moving." This is culture clash at its

has created a lot of *play culture* rules about checking in on players and seeking consent. "Almost all Nordic LARPs will have safety mechanics built in," says Cat. "A lot of the safety mechanics that we're only now introducing into RPGs have largely come out of Nordic LARP, and that's being translated through the American freeform into table-top. There's been a whole trickle-through." More on safety tools in... well, next month's interview.

That's the main thing which Cat took from her first meeting with Nordic LARPS, and it circles around the perennial question asked of all new forms - "Is this art?" It simply changed her position. While she thought videogames could be art, she didn't think it was true about role-playing games. "I came away from *Mad About the Boy* going, 'No, they can be art. They can be, and some of them are, art. This is what RPG-as-art looks like.' And it was just a massive shift in my perspective on what RPGs were. It's like only ever seeing mainstream films, and then suddenly discovering arthouse cinema."

That leads to different players. Cat notes that you can to go a gaming convention, and... well, there's really only gamers there, all coming from some overlapping place. If you go to Knutepunkt, the Nordic LARP

"I hate to use the word legitimacy, but that's the word that feels right for it," says Cat. "It can hold its head up with any other medium. It is on their level. Obviously, the budgets are nowhere near. It's different... but in terms of the ideas that they're doing, in terms of the experiences they're delivering, and what they are addressing? Absolutely."

More about Cat's work at Pelegrane Press can be found on https:// site.pelgranepress.com.

KIENNA SHAW & LAUREN BRYANT-MONK

As a reader of *DIE*, you know that safety in role-playing games is important. For example, you shouldn't drag your group of players screaming into a hell dimension, at least not without everyone's enthusiastic consent. If Sol had had better safety tools, all this could have been avoided. Another theme of the 2010s is the increased awareness of these tools.

Safety tools are, to speak broadly, about finding ways to ensure everyone's having a good time at the table, and to facilitate difficult conversations. And it's worth stressing something key in the previous paragraph - we're talking *awareness* not *existence*.

"People have been developing safety tools for decades," says designer Kienna Shaw. The problem was that the information was often in small communities or defunct social media websites. "To learn about safety tools, you were asking people to do all of this online archaeology, and relying on them knowing people who knew people," says designer Lauren Bryant-Monk. This is no longer true. This information is now being curated and disseminated and *widely used*.

This is why I'm talking to Kienna and Lauren. They took it upon themselves to curate and compile the TTRPG Safety Toolset, giving each tool's original creators the credit and making it freely accessible to anyone who wanted it. In 2020, the industry

she followed, starting playing live. "I was living away from home for the first time. I was also going through a creative existential crisis," says Kienna. "I've always been very into writing, and performance, and I was in theatre, I was in dance, I was in creative writing all throughout my childhood. And then, I was now left unmoored, with that realisation of: 'What type of things can I actually bring to the table as a creator?' So, I was having a moment. And table-top role-playing games came in at a time where I was like, 'Oh, *that's* what I want to do. I want to be able to tell stories collaboratively.'"

Lauren had tried roleplaying earlier, as a twelve-year-old in a church group - which shows how far we are away from the days of satanic panic. It didn't click, but it stuck in the back of her mind. Years after, late in her Masters, she found a streaming game she liked, which led to everything else. "I actually went to my local comic book store, and I played in the Adventurers League," she said. "I was one of two or three women who went there every week, and then I found communities on the internet to play with."

They found each other in the Off The Table community. Lauren remembers seeing Kienna on a panel. "And I was like, 'Oh, she's Canadian, and she lives just an hour away from me. I should be her friend', says Lauren. And lo, they were. Both, despite

"We are coming into this time where it's no longer a taboo subject to look at."

gave it a prestigious Ennie award. "In some way, a symbolic win for all of that work that's been happening over the past few decades, of, like, hey, we are coming into this time where it's no longer a taboo subject to look at," says Kienna.

They're two creatives who've come into the field specifically in the period these *DIE* interviews have primarily covered - as in, 2010s. Kienna was in her first year of university and, introduced to gaming via a streamer

originally considering themselves solely players, found themselves merging into design. Kienna was inspired by a game jam, the *Emotional Mecha Jam* ("Make sad mech games," paraphrases Kienna.). When a snowstorm closed school the day before the jam ended, she took it as an order from the universe to create. Meanwhile, Lauren - a trained opera singer, and fundamentally informed by a collaborative approach to art - found herself writing a sad poem in the form of a game called *The Page*

I Didn't Write, based on the solo RPG *Quill*. She posted it, had people like it, made some money and realised that design 100% was an option.

And, along the way, they encountered safety tools.

Kienna met them watching *Off the Table*, with Mysty Vander using them. "This makes so much sense to have these tools to check in, and make sure we're navigating difficult content, and making sure everyone's still having fun," says Kienna. Lauren had a similar experience. She thought of how knowing about it would have impacted previous games. "I was thinking about all of the times when I've had lines crossed, often as the only young woman at the table, and not really having any way to express that I am uncomfortable in a way that felt socially appropriate," says Lauren. "At this point, I was playing in somebody's house, and so when you're alone in somebody's house, and somebody does something that you're not comfortable with, even if they don't mean it, even if they're your friends, it's still really hard to bring that out."

Kienna realised something - not only did many streamers not use these tools, many weren't even *aware* of them. She pulled together a quick reference guide and put it online. "I posted that, I went with my friends to a movie, I came back, and my notifications exploded because it got spread out," says Kienna, "and I realised, firstly, how many people didn't realise safety tools existed, and secondly, just how polarising it had been in the community at that time. I got a lot of harassment, and people being very abusive, because they're like, 'That's for babies. Just talk to people.' I'm like, 'No, that's not what this is.'" There was also the upside - general excitement about it, and people telling Kienna about all these *other* tools. She started making plans for an update.

Lauren contacted Kienna and suggested they do a panel about safety tools at a local con. The panel - Beyond The X-card - was meant to have a visual presentation, but that was dropped, so at the last minute they had to work out something else. Lauren suggested Kienna print out copies of her guide. Kienna mentioned she was updating it with more tools. Lauren noted she had a bunch *more* other links she'd gathered. They put

it all together, put it on a Google drive and handed out the bit.ly link at the panel. "That's how the Toolkit was born, was out of this necessity of something that we needed to give to people *right now*," says Laruen, "and then, it was really Kienna's forward thinking to be like, 'Let's turn this into something bigger, and something that we can keep adding to.'"

"We just wanted it to be easy, and we wanted it to be shareable for people who are new to this space, because it keeps growing, and the internet is ephemeral, people stop paying for hosting, and forums and websites, all of these kinds of things - they disappear," says Lauren, "and so, with both of our educational backgrounds, we're just trying our best to curate, and maintain, and conserve all of these really important pieces of gaming history." It's a fantastic, free, centralised and simple one-stop guide, and a great place to start thinking about this material.

X-card is arguably the most well-known tool. A card with an "X" on it is placed in the middle of the table. If anyone taps the X - or signals in a similar way - the element of the fiction that has just happened is excised, and the group steps back and takes another route. Clearly, this can be used to move away from seriously triggering material, but can also be used for things on unnecessary annoyances. Someone names a character after your ex's name, and you'd really rather not spend the next few weeks being reminded of them? X-card it. It's simply a no that the room respects, and does not question. In the *DIE* RPG, I describe it as having brakes on a car - and, on a personal level, I'm as suspicious of a game *without* something like the X-card as I am a car without breaks. As originally conceived of by John Stavropoulos, it's been widely adopted, and - like all mechanics in RPG - modified and expanded by others.

For example, there's Beau Jágr Sheldon's Script Change. Rather than a simple "no", script change used the metaphor of a video-recorder's controls to give people a way to quietly communicate more nuanced feelings. For example, "rewind" works a little akin to the X-card, while "fast forward" lets you be fine with the element, but you'd rather not actually linger on it. "Pause" leaves the fiction alone, but gives people a chance to take a break and talk about what's happening, before pressing "resume" to carry on.

You'll note that we're crediting all these tools to original creators. This isn't always easy, due to the aforementioned ephemeral nature of much RPG discussion. For example, they initially found that popular tool Lines and Veils is hard to source. "I think communities, and small communities like that, are really important, but it just makes things very, very difficult," says Lauren, "and so, from the one source we've been able to find for Lines and Veils, we know it's by Ron Edwards, but it's on a Reddit thread. That's the earliest discussion of Lines and Veils."

"I wish I could do this as a full-time job, honestly, because I wish I could just do all of that internet archaeology," says Lauren. "It's very important to me that we remember our past, and we take from the past, and preserve it so that people, maybe, aren't rediscovering old concepts, but they're building on old concepts to make things work for them today."

In Lines and Veils, players are all free to choose elements of fiction they either don't want in the game (a line - as in, a line one does not cross) or ones which they're happy to include, but don't want to linger on (veils - as in, pulling a veil over an event). For example, one of my standard veils is sexual content. I'm very happy for characters to shag, but I'm not going to sit and describe it with you. Not

"Let's turn this into something bigger ... that we can keep adding to..."

presently mentioned in the toolkit, groups have also used the concept of the palette - as in, a list of things the group are expressly interested in pursuing (as invented in Ben Robbin's excellent RPG, *Microscope*). These all interact, with the needs of safety taking priority - for example, if one player has a line in an element, while others chose it as a veil or even wanted it as part of the palette.

The palette also shows that safety tools aren't *just* about avoiding harm - they're about encouraging *communication*. The single tool I'd encourage any group to use, even those who are looking askance at all

by Beau Jágr Sheldon) where, rather than "rewinding", the player who has been triggered can choose to discuss it and then is given complete control over that content, and the direction that play will continue.

"A tool is only going to work for you if it fits your needs, and what you're aiming to do," says Kienna. "The reason why it's called the Toolkit is because it's like, 'Well, sometimes you might need a hammer, sometimes you might need a wrench, sometimes you might need a screw.' But I don't want to just give you a hammer and say, 'Go, fix all your problems with that.' I'm saying, 'Look at all

the safety tool. If we use a safety tool, especially one that happens mid-play, harm has been caused. How do we go back from that?"

Things are changing fast. The curatorship and gathering of the brilliant work of many people, and making it accessible, are some of those important steps to prevent the groundhog day of each generation having the same conversations. "It's no longer a fringe idea, and it's no longer relegated to specific spaces," says Kienna. "It's become a more mainstream thing and, because of that, now we're able to start pushing forward on those basic concepts of, 'Yes, safety at table, good.' Now, let's build on that. How do we do that? And taking in that huge variety of experiences, and people's perspectives on what safety at the table *is*, and being able to have more forward-facing, productive conversations about it, rather than just rehashing a 101 constantly, over and over again."

The TRPG Safety Toolkit can be found at http://bit.ly/ttrpgsafetytoolkit. More about Kienna's work can be found via kiennas.carrd.co. Lauren's website is at www.starvingsoubrette.com.

"Why does this happen? How can we avoid this happening in the future?"

of this, is Stars and Wishes, which Lu Quade developed from the previously existing Roses and Thorns. Here, at the end of a session, all players award stars and wishes. Stars are things in the game which you want to signal out for applause and appreciation - a player's choice, an attitude, a moment; just taking a second to say what you loved. Wishes are things you're hoping to see in future - specific elements of fiction, a question you'd like answered, whatever. Between them, it's a ritual that encourages camaraderie and cleanly tells people what you're looking for from the game... but it's also a safe way to express what about the game is *not* satisfying. Stating wishes is much better than screaming at your DM that you're bored of going down fucking dungeons.

But a key thing is that not all tools are universal. Tools have purposes. I use the X-card alongside Lines and Veils, because Lines and Veils - even anonymously - involves too much disclosure. In some cases, I don't want people to know about everything that upsets me, but *also* want a way to deal with something if it turns up. Equally, the X-card itself is upsetting to other players, who prefer to use something like The Luxton Technique (originated with the eponymous con-GM Luxton, written up by PH Lee and reposted

these incredible options that are out there, and you need to do the work to actually use them.'"

The use of these tools, like all parts of gaming technology, is an ongoing conversation. For example, now tools are more commonly known, some discussion has focused more on the *culture* around the tools. You can have all the tools on the table, but if someone feels unable to use them, that's also a problem.

"'Why does this happen? How can we avoid this happening in the future? Once we've played the X-card, how do we mitigate harm in that situation? And how do we let people know, especially marginalised people, that not only are you safe, but we will honour your choices in all of that?' And that's something that a tool can't do," says Lauren. "That's the work you've got to do as a person. But it's still a part of safety tools, because it's irresponsible to give somebody a tool and not teach them how to use it. That's how people get hurt. And so, that's where we've always wanted to go in the future - not just like, 'Here are a bunch of tools that you can use,' but, 'There should be more than one tool that you can use'; why you should be comfortable with many different approaches; and what happens when you use

MATTHEW MERCER

If you told my 1991 self that, in thirty years, millions would be watching people play role-playing games I'd presume that you were quoting from a *Cyberpunk 2020* sourcebook. It just seems desperately unlikely. To part of me, it still does.

I'd argue the explosion of RPGs-with-audiences is the single thing that's most pushed the form's popularization across the last decade. It evangelizes and it demystifies. DIE's editor Chrissy had seen me play RPGs around the house for years, and considered them alien. But podcast Harmontown's regular D&D game slot made her realise both what it was, why it could appeal, and that maybe she could try it. Across the last decade, I've found myself facilitating games for people who've never played before, but were rendered RPG-curious, either directly or indirectly, by places like *The Adventure Zone* or, relevantly, *Critical Role*.

The majority of these interviews have been about cult figures. Matthew Mercer, Critical Role's DM, has just shy of 750,000 followers. He's not a cult figure, except in the old rock and roll sense where someone could fill arenas but still not quite be in the mainstream. Critical Role is them playing in front of a huge streaming audience. They fundamentally invented Stadium D&D.

Like many good things, it's all by accident. Mercer was running a game for his voice-artist friends, and player Ashley Johnson told *Geek & Sundry*'s Felicia Day about it. Day suggested they should do it

personal. "We were worried that something that we loved would be tarnished by the negativity of the internet," says Matthew. They decided to give it a shot, figuring if it didn't work, they'd just retreat to brunch games around at Matthew's. Suffice to say, it didn't turn out like that. "It was reactionary. A lot of what we do is reactionary," says Matthew. "We're just trying to keep up with scenarios that present themselves, make the right choice, and then continue to scream directionless into the abyss." The striking image of *Critical Role* as an adventuring party being presented challenges by a GM and asked 'What do you do now?' comes to mind.

I've often filed role-playing in front of an audience as *D&D*-as-performance, but that's not how Matthew sees it. "We didn't set out to make RPGs as performance," said Matthew. "We were just letting people in." Early conversations with *Geek & Sundry* were about how they could blend it with other media and tweak it for the format - ideas they rejected. "If we're going to do this, we're not going to change anything," says Matthew. "You just put cameras on us. It's the only way this is going work, because at the base line, we play this game because we care about each other and we want to have fun. If we're having fun, hopefully the audience will have fun. That was our hope. And so, I think that's why a lot of people tune in."

I often describe RPG groups as bands. Despite growing up surrounded by musicians, Matthew's never played himself... but how Matthew speaks of

"We play ... because we care about each other and we want to have fun."

online, and Ashley brought the idea to the group. "Our first instinct," says Matthew, "was, 'This is weird. No.'"

That came from two reasons. One is that it just wouldn't work. *D&D* is a game which takes *hours* to play. In 2015, the idea that anyone would engage with video content longer than a minute or two seemed unlikely. The other reason was much more

Critical Role reminds me of bands a *lot*. There's one thing bands always say to interviewers: "We do what we like, and if anyone else likes it, it's a bonus." Journos mock it as stock answer... but as anyone who's been in a band knows, it's also a core creative truth. "I wanted to believe that as long as we stayed true to the joy we have at the table, that should be enough for people to want to engage," says Matthew.

I'm delighted that Matthew also sees unusual upsides to playing with an audience. "People tend to be a little more engaged when they're aware that there's an audience," says Matthew. "At any game table, people are going to be shooting the shit on the side, and checking their email, and telling little side stories, and that's totally fine and natural for a game table. What I do enjoy about being a livestream is it gives a reason for the players to be a little more in the moment all the time." It's an interesting aspect - by playing in front of an audience, a player group can be more present. *All* players are more present - including the DM.

"It's definitely made me take my world-building very seriously," says Matthew, "because it's one thing to be making a story for a handful of friends at a table, especially when you're having a few drinks. They're not going to hold anything against you for inconsistencies." It's also true for thinking about the world you're presenting. "I always built worlds to want to feel like it reflected the world around me that I wanted to see, and I'm thankful that I grew up in Los Angeles, which is a very multicultural part of the US," says Matthew. "It's not without its issues, but I was raised around many different people of many different backgrounds and perspectives. And even then, I have my own unseen biases baked into me through American culture, which is based on a very flawed system with systemic racism, and cultural biases that are baked in us, whether we want them to or not. So, as I learn and grow through these experiences, I want to ensure that my world-building reflects those lessons, and reflects wanting to make a space that's closer to the world that I would hope it to be and look forward to down the line."

This active consciousness is a long way from Matthew's entry into gaming. Like frankly all us gamers in a pre-internet age, he didn't have a clue. His mum brought home a bunch of *D&D* manuals from a yard sale. Only years down the line did he realise the purchase was prompted by his grandma on his dad's side. "She was the classic Southern Georgia grandma that lived in a cabin up in the Smoky Mountains," says Matthew, "but she loved Tolkien, she loved fantasy novels, and she briefly played *D&D* back in the day." She argued that at least Matthew would enjoy the

art. They were right. Matthew was a doodling, monster-obsessed child, and spent years poring over them... but not playing. "There was no way I could ever breach the subject really with anybody, or when I did, people had no idea what the hell I was talking about," says Matthew. "So, the books were very much just my little private reading for a long time."

This experience of folks not quite getting what an RPG was or could be is something that never really went away... at least, until recently.

"That was part of the reason that I wanted to do *Critical Role* in the first place," says Matthew, "because there were so many times in my life that that question came up in social circles and at events: 'So, how do you play a roleplaying game?'" Trying to talk through it was stressful, anxiety-inducing and incomplete. Now, it's much easier. Instead, he can point at any of the videos. "Just watch ten minutes of this and you'll figure out the gist," says Matthew.

It was only in his mid-teenage years that Matthew finally got invited to play. "My first games were, in hindsight, not great, but I was just happy to be there. The guys who invited me were seniors, and I was a freshman," says Matthew. "They were great guys, but it was less about telling a rich narrative, and more about being dumbasses." A custom Fighter class which let you be Ryu from *Street Fighter* and time-travel to go grab an In-N-Out burger speaks to the tone. Matthew loved it, but he had a nagging sensation. "I kept feeling like there was something more to it," says Matthew. "This could go deeper."

Eventually, when a Dungeon Master's power-tripping tendencies were too much, Matthew decided to start a splinter game to follow these instincts. It was tentative at first ("absurd") but he was getting closer to what he was looking for. "I began to really feel like DMing could be like being a director of a movie," say Matthew. "You set the

tone, you set the pace, you ratchet up tension and intrigue. You find elements of the players' choices and they affect the story. I instinctually I found my way of playing because that was what I wanted to experience. It's not necessarily the right way, because there is no right way to play the game, but that was more my style. And even then, for years, I was just playing in a vacuum because I didn't have any other experiences..."

In these times, there is a sense that unless you were an active con

> ## "By playing in front of an audience, a player group can be more present."

goer, we lived in all these pocket dimensions. Our groups all played what our groups played. Before the mid-2000s, Matthew was playing *D&D* and sporadically genre-mash-up *RIFTS*. Alongside, he got a day job - working in Quality Assurance in videogames, eventually becoming a producer. However, he was also burned out, and alienated by bad experiences. During a trip to Burning Man, he decided he needed to make a change. "I'd been doing a lot of community theatre at the time, bit parts in voiceover here and there," says Matthew, "and thinking, 'Maybe one day.'" After Burning Man, he decided that day had come. He had a little money saved, a willingness to live extremely cheaply and wanted to roll the dice. "I'd much rather try and fail than spend the rest of my life wondering, 'What if?' That would eat away at me." It led to a career... and now back to *D&D*. Ironically, those acting skills started in his desire to improve his dungeon-mastering. I'm also struck by his screenwriter-perfect character arc - Matthew joined the games industry, got burned out by game and left to do something else... and then he found a new way to express his love for games.

Matthew seems actively aware of the bizarre position he's in, and the responsibility inherent in it. If you're someone's introduction to the hobby, you're also their first role model. To a new generation of DMs, Matthew

Mercer is their Hendrix. I make the comparison and Matthew is as thrown as any grounded individual should be, but gets the point. "I've seen diatribes about the Mercer effect, and people talking about how *Critical Role* is the pornography of tabletop gaming, and that it's not realistic, meaning that it sets unrealistic expectations for the table," says Matthew, "and I'm like, 'Maybe? But it's just our table.'" I think again of the band metaphor - these are trained actors, in a tightly-knit family-esque group. You may be inspired by Creem to form a guitar band, but you're a fool if you think you start as Clapton. Plus it's not that simple anyway.

"I see stories out there of people who go in and have these expectations at a local game shop, and chide and shame people for not being as good as people in *Critical Role*," says Matthew, clearly horrified. "Whoever that is, you're a terrible player, and you need to learn how to 1) be respectful, and 2) understand that every table is

there, both large and small," says Matthew. "The indie tabletop game scene is thriving, and all it takes is a few questions on social media, or a few Google searches. On itch.io, you can find a lot of wonderful indie games that can fit broad scopes or niche narratives, and you'd be surprised, a lot of them are super cost-effective for your budget, and can really build some great experiences. So, don't feel like *D&D* is the only game experience out there for you, please. It specifically does a certain type of story well, and even one that we have to mess with on *Critical Role* to do what we want to, but it works for us."

No matter which *specific* game, you can see Matthew's desire to share the joy and power of games. Conversation turns to how games have allowed us to explore parts of ourselves, and how they've changed us. "While I was a ham around my family, when it came to social spaces, especially around ten, eleven, I was a little more introverted. I grew up with a stutter that I worked

them. I speak to him glowing having just finished their second campaign, and looking to the future, both for their streams and the worlds. He tries to at least jump into games to see what people are doing, support friends and especially one-shots but is aware that watching streaming games is an extremely time-consuming pastime. In some ways, the success can also be a cause for concern. "I'm a little worried about channels that make their entire thing about week-long streams. '24/7 streams, nothing but role-playing games around the clock!'" says Matthew. "That's pretty cool, but at a certain point, you're also cannibalising your own audience, because there's only so much time a community can engage with content." There's more than the stream. Last year, they launched the Critical Role Foundation, a charity initiative which partners with non-profits to raise money. Matthew has dabbled in game design since releasing his first self-confessed ramshackle home-brew class circa the *D&Diesel* with Vin Diesel ("which is still a very weird thing to say out loud"). Most recently, he helmed the team which wrote the *Explorer's Guide to Wildemount*, from *D&D* publisher Wizards of the Coast, which allows people to adventure in the lands charted by *Critical Role*. It's a lot. Yet at the same time, this is still clearly an intensely private thing for Matthew.

"I think it is an incredibly wonderful safe space ... to explore yourself..."

different and has its own energy. And once you allow yourself to find those differences and embrace those differences, you'll find that sometimes those tables are far better than a *Critical Role* table would be for you. There are many people who would hate to be at my table, who are very, very good gamers, but the way I run my game is not right, the style is not right for them. And conversely, there are many players out there that I would hate to have at my table."

Even the choice of the games they play is contentious, and there's explicit efforts to move the spotlight from the game they play, yet still stay true to what they do. When writing this, I'm aware that my tendency is to write "GM" (a more general term for whoever facilitates a game) and Matthew's is to say "DM" (a specific term from *Dungeons & Dragons*). "We play *D&D*, because that's what I grew up in, but there are so many other wonderful RPG systems out

through with speech therapy, and I just had a lot of challenges. Role-playing games allowed me a safe space to grow more comfortably," he says. "I have a lot of friends and people I've met through the years who used role-playing games as a space to figure out the person they want to be, whether that be from a morality standpoint, from a professional standpoint, from a compassionate standpoint, from a sexuality or gender standpoint. I've been more assertive through my games. I've learned to interject myself when I see somebody in public who's being preyed upon, whether it be seeing people arguing in the street, or even just trying to engage more with the human experience too. I think it is an incredibly wonderful safe space, with the right people, to explore and expand yourself in ways that you don't normally have the opportunity to do."

As *Critical Role* marches into the future, they're still reacting to what the DM that is the universe throws at

"Role-playing games have always been my solitude," says Matthew. "They've been my place where no matter if anybody cares about the things I do, me and my friends create something here that's personal and real and visceral that we all get to enjoy. So, for me, I could be destitute and in the worst job in the world, but as long as I have an outlet like role-playing games with the people I care about, that will keep me sane. At least that's the belief that I've had through a lot of my life."

He'll carry on doing what he likes, and if anyone else likes it, it's a bonus. And that's the weird magic of all of this: sometimes you find out that *millions do*.

For more about Critical Role go to critrole.com. He's on Twitter at @matthewmercer, Instagram at @matthewmercervo and Critical Role broadcasts (usually) on Thursdays on Twitch.

A LIFETIME AGO

There was a moment in my life where things were hard, leaving me with a deep feeling of inadequacy. I was physically and mentally frail, but I was also quite good at faking it. I was an art student dreading the moment someone would finally call me on my bluff and, quite frankly, the pressure was becoming too much.

This is when I met my role-playing group, engaging once a week in a fantasy world where I could forget myself and where 'faking it' was a truth in itself. It was like a lifeline, like a cocoon in which I learnt to function again, little by little.

It became my safe space for a couple of years.

I choose to think it stopped because I was finally ready to go and fight the whole world by myself. Through failures, heartbreaks, small wins and bigger ones. Through seven countries and countless new friendships. Some of them would last forever, some would be washed away by time.

It is kind of crazy to think that this frail thing I was became who I am now. And when I think about it, my roots are always in the memories of these moments when those people, with whom I am no longer in touch, and I were building a vibrant universe, in which I was an impossibly strong sorceress on a quest to become the strongest of her generation. She still lives in my heart and is still ready to fight for me when I can't.

This is dedicated to Oscar, Manu, Mehdi, Guillaume, Marc and Sebastien, wherever you are boys. And to my father, who gave me love for pop culture and pulp literature.

Stéphanie Hans
Toulouse, France

THREE YEARS IN FANTASY

I've talked a lot, as is my wont. Let's keep this one brief.

Thanks to Stephanie. You did it.

Thanks to Rian and Clayton. Rian: I've always wanted to work with you. It's been everything I hoped it would be. Clayton: we never seem to stop working with each other, and it gets better every time.

Thanks for everyone at Image. There's no publisher that lets a creator do what Image does. This is a book about infinite fantasy worlds, and I can't imagine there's one where a publisher would let us do a book like this.

Special thanks for our sensitivity consultants. We hit some material hard in the series, and needed to get perspective. Natalie Reed, Sally Couch and Ramsey Hassan were all fantastic, their contributions additive, in practice sharpening, honing.

Thanks to everyone who's played the RPG, especially the four players who I spent over a year running that first campaign with - Mink, Daniel, Saxey and C. Alice is thinking of you, always. The RPG ended up becoming an intrinsic part of *DIE* for me. I spent a lot of time trying to work out which was the tail and which was the dog before realising they're both methodology with which to observe *DIE*. You gain a truer understanding by using both - juxtaposing like a hologram. And thanks to Rook, Rowan & Decard, who've somehow decided that a writer who churns out sentences like the above is someone they want to work with to publish the game rules.

Thanks to you. The book asked a lot. There were times while writing I was wondering whether anyone would actually get it. To switch to my music metaphors, writing can feel like throwing yourself into a crowd from a stage, hoping people will catch you, knowing you could be about to crash onto the concrete and break your jaw. I always felt caught, in safe hands.

Thanks to Chrissy, always.

It's all for you.

Kieron Gillen
London, UK

FROM THE SAME CREATORS

WORK BY KIERON GILLEN AND STEPHANIE HANS:

The Wicked + The Divine #15
Collected in *The Wicked + The Divine* Volume 3

The Wicked + The Divine 1831 #1
Collected in *The Wicked + The Divine* Volume 8

Journey Into Mystery
Collected in two volumes, with Stephanie providing covers and interiors on the final issue

Angela: Asgard's Assassin
with Marguerite Bennett and Phil Jimenez

1602 Witch Hunter Angela
with Marguerite Bennett and more

FOR FURTHER INFORMATION PLEASE VISIT:

www.diecomic.com
For comic and RPG news, new issues and updates

#diecomic
The hashtag for whatever social media you use

ALSO FROM IMAGE COMICS:

The Wicked + The Divine
Volumes 1-9

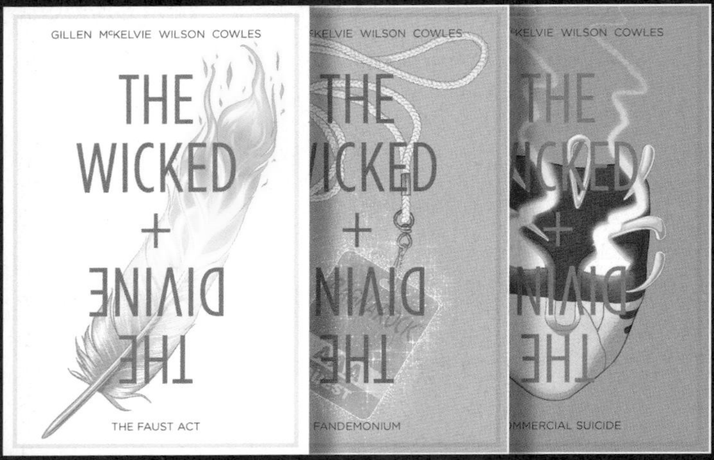
GILLEN McKELVIE WILSON COWLES
THE WICKED + THE DIVINE
THE FAUST ACT
FANDEMONIUM

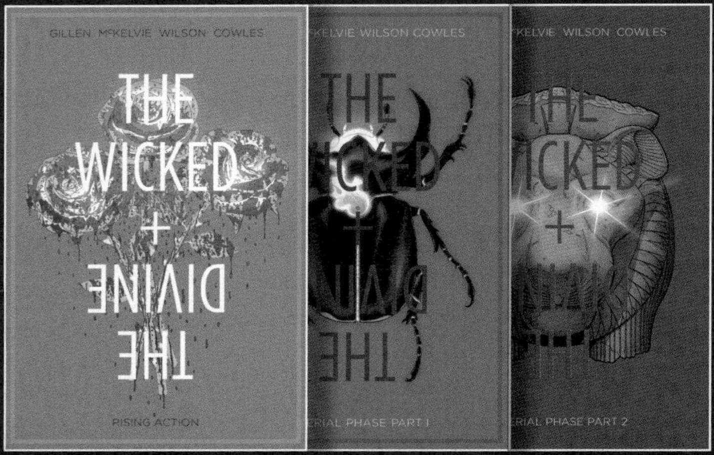
GILLEN McKELVIE WILSON COWLES
THE WICKED + THE DIVINE
RISING ACTION

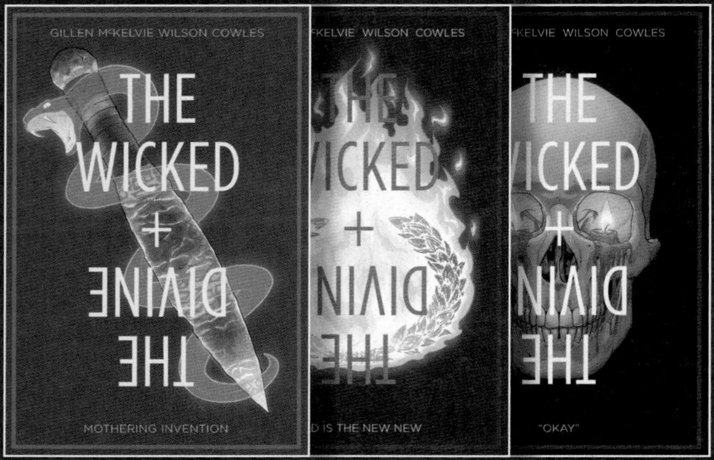
GILLEN McKELVIE WILSON COWLES
THE WICKED + THE DIVINE
MOTHERING INVENTION
"OKAY"

Phonogram
Volumes 1-3

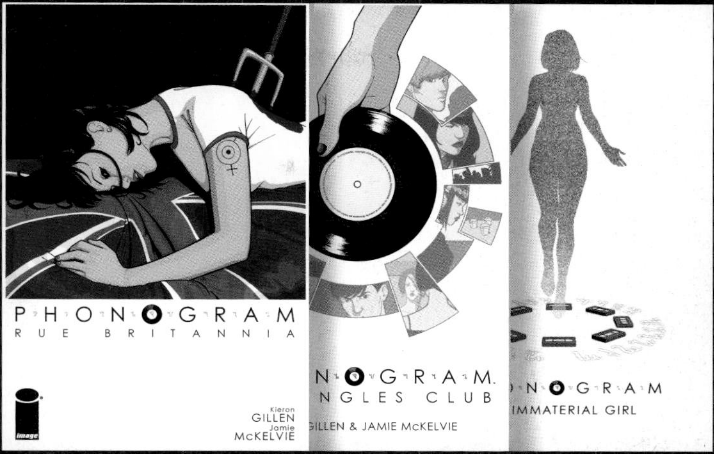
P H O N O G R A M
R U E B R I T A N N I A
Kieron
GILLEN
Jamie
McKELVIE
N O G R A M.
N G L E S C L U B
GILLEN & JAMIE McKELVIE
N O G R A M
IMMATERIAL GIRL

The Ludocrats
Three

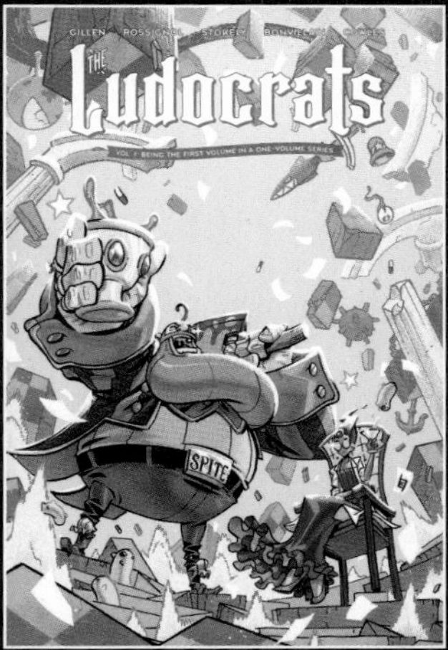
THE
Ludocrats
SPITE

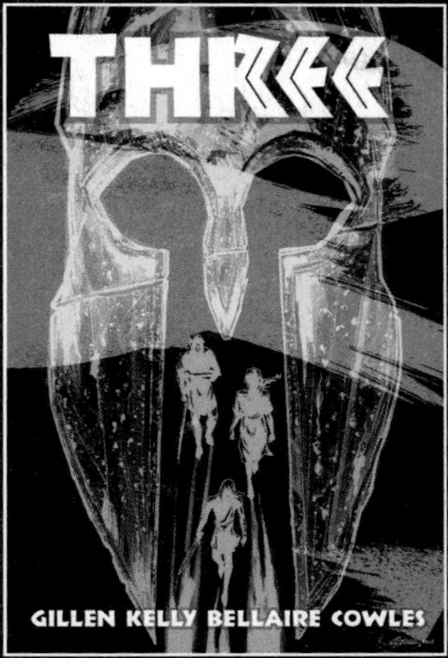
THREE
GILLEN KELLY BELLAIRE COWLES

FROM OTHER PUBLISHERS:

Once and Future
Volumes 1-3

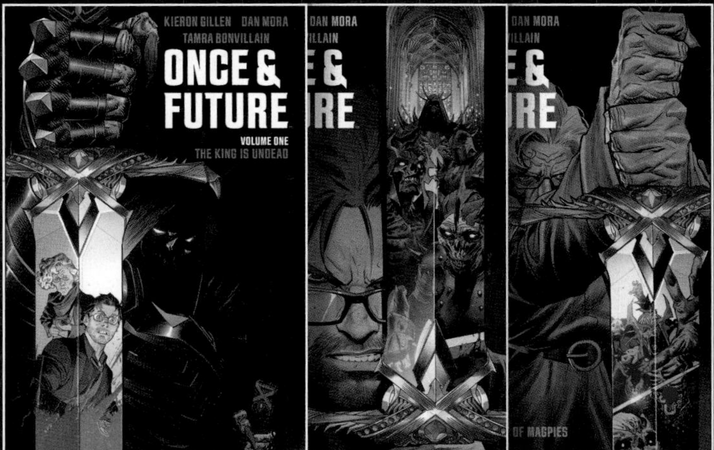
KIERON GILLEN DAN MORA
TAMRA BONVILLAIN
ONCE &
FUTURE
VOLUME ONE
THE KING IS UNDEAD
DAN MORA
ILLAIN
E &
RE
DAN MORA
ILLAIN
E &
RE
OF MAGPIES

TEAM BIOS

Kieron Gillen is a comic writer based in London, Britain. His previous work includes *The Wicked + The Divine, Once & Future* and *Young Avengers*. He mainly plays low intelligence barbarians or high charisma bards.

Photo: Mauricio de Souza

Stephanie Hans is a comic artist based in Toulouse, France. Her previous work includes issues of *The Wicked + The Divine, Journey Into Mystery* and *Batwoman*. She mainly plays clerics and wizards.

Clayton Cowles is an Eisner-award nominated letterer, based in Rochester, USA. His credits include everything. He has only played *D&D* once, and was a bard.